The Composer's 1

Skillful, his thumb dipped into the neckline of my gown and drew a treble clef along my throat. His mouth shifted and followed. His lips traced the arch of my neck.

When I felt his hands playing the ribbons of my corset, fingering the cording like pianoforte chords, I ran to the other side of the table and whispered, "I need to finish the biscuits."

"Georgie, I want your biscuits. I need them to be mine."

"The dough I've halved. It will make twelve. Is that enough?"

"There's never enough of you. I'm trying to say—"

"You should head back to the pianoforte."

"Why, Georgie? I was making music with *you*."

"This is a kitchen. The Duke of Torrance's enormous space with an oven and cabinetry on three walls—"

"The way you sound, the way you breathe, you're an instrument, a magnificent harp that my fingers must possess."

I eased to the wall with spices, my slippers stepping into the spilled flour he'd swept into a pile. "Look at these jars. He could have apothecaries train here."

"I hear you in my bed, singing my name as I love you. I want that. Don't run from us, Georgie."

Praise for the novels of Vanessa Riley

"Smart and witty . . . Vanessa Riley delivers the perfect historical read."
—Julia Quinn, #1 *New York Times* bestselling author

"Riley loads her expertly crafted romance with intrigue, droll banter, and steadily building passion. Readers will be hard-pressed to find a flaw in this big-hearted Regency romance." —*Publishers Weekly* STARRED REVIEW

"Mystery and simmering passion unite to keep you turning pages until the duke, lady and baby find their happy ever after." —NPR

"Bestselling author Vanessa Riley is known for her romantic Regency-era tales, and her latest is bursting with wit and charm." —*Woman's World*

"Vanessa Riley's *A Duke, the Lady, and a Baby* offers slow burn and ultimately satisfying romance between an heiress and a military hero." —Vulture

"Vanessa Riley has made a name for herself with her historical romances blooming with careful research that reflects a more accurate and diverse portrait of the Regency era." —*Entertainment Weekly*

"Hello, *Bridgerton* fans!" —*Library Journal*

"Riley is at her best when she lets her Gothic impulses out to play . . . [readers] will not want to miss this." —*The New York Times*

"Riveting from the first sentence to the last. Vanessa Riley's lyrical voice shimmers in this emotional, uplifting tour de force. One of the best historicals I've read in years." —*New York Times* bestselling author Kristan Higgins

"With strong heroines, swoonworthy heroes and deeply emotional stories, Vanessa Riley is a magnificent voice in historical romance—one not to be missed! *A Duke, the Lady and a Baby* is Vanessa at her finest." —*New York Times* bestselling author Sarah MacLean

"Everything you could ever want in a Regency and *more*! If you read only one duke book this year, make it this one!" —*New York Times* bestselling author Grace Burrowes

Also by Vanessa Riley

The Lady Worthing Mysteries

Murder in Westminster

Murder in Drury Lane

The Rogues & Remarkable Women Romances

A Duke, the Lady, and a Baby

An Earl, the Girl, and a Toddler

A Duke, the Spy, an Artist, and a Lie

Historical Fiction

Island Queen

Sister Mother Warrior

Queen of Exiles

A
GAMBLE
at
SUNSET
VANESSA RILEY

ZEBRA BOOKS
Kensington Publishing Corp.
www.kensingtonbooks.com

For Thomas White, Ruben Riley, Jr., Linda Riley, Brenda Riley,
and David Riley: Miss your smiles.

For everyone who forgets to live in every moment: Find your joy.
I'm betting on you.

PROLOGUE

Once upon a time a daughter of Gannibal, the Black Russian prince who was the godson of Peter the Great, had a maddening affair with a British diplomat, an heir to a ducal peerage.

Soon came a marriage,
a maverick son,
and a malevolent spirit that went against the young lovers.

Wed to the rivers of Saint Petersburg, she wouldn't leave. Overlooking the sneers of London, to the wealth he cleaved.

The marriage ended.

The couple separated forever and taught a son that love doesn't win.

Then the son became a man and found a love so true, but he gambled and lost.

His heart never recovered, and he vowed to reclaim every material thing that was meant to be his and more.

Wagering that time and distance and money made things change, the son discovered he was right, very right and alone.

Then a summons changes everything.

Can a bridge and a bet correct the past? It's a gamble a man of the line Gannibal will risk to win all that his soul has lost.

Chapter 1

Mark Sebastian, Son of the Marquess of Prahmn—The Wrong Side of Town

March 1, 1816
London, England

Never admit falling in love with a portrait.

Never talk of how the eyes of the painting followed me along the halls of Kenwood, or how the joy in her sun-kissed cheeks stayed on my mind.

Never utter a word of how a voiceless woman made of oils and canvas, not sugar and spice and other niceties, captivated my dreams.

Said aloud this would be the ravings of a madman, not an artist who hungered for beauty. I tried not to think of the painting or my foolish whispers said to her and rode a little faster to keep up with my so-called friendly companions.

"Will you be seeing her later, Sebastian?" Alexander Melton, the Earl of Livingston, hiccupped and wobbled in his saddle. "You can tell us."

"Leave the musician alone. We've had enough jokes at his expense. Artists are temperamental sorts, but that spurs their creativity." The Duke of Torrance was a new acquaintance that

Livingston and I met at a Farrington coaching inn. Before I could stop him, the earl gleefully told my story of being in love with the painted woman.

The duke, a tall man on a silver mare, looked confused for most of this. I wondered if foolish conversations differed greatly from crazy things said in Saint Petersburg. Half British, half Russian, he seemed distant or perhaps nervous.

"Will you be in town long, Your Grace?" I asked, hoping to change subjects.

"My current plans are up in the air. Once I get this first visit done, I will determine how long I reside in London."

He and Livingston began to discuss the perfect places to live.

My shame lifted and I secretly thought of living at Kenwood, being a music tutor and getting to see the painting every day.

"Sebastian? Sebastian?"

"Yes. Livingston." My cheeks burned. Then I relaxed, remembering the man couldn't read thoughts, only newspapers and science journals. "Did you say something?"

The earl leaned so far in his saddle I thought he'd fall onto his stupid head.

I wasn't so fortunate. Our new friend sped up and kept the fool upright.

"Thank you, Torrance." The earl grasped his reins a little tighter. "Sebastian, your mother sent you to Kenwood to ogle a painting. Now you're in love with Lady Elizabeth Finch-Hatton, a woman idealized on canvas in her youth who today is in her fifties and married. Prahmn will have a fit, but he might approve if you took her to bed for a prize."

"The Duke of Prahmn? Sounds scandalous." The duke's diction sounded crisp, very British, none of the nasally accent Livingston said a man born in Saint Petersburg should possess.

"My father? No scandals. He still has hopes that I turn to the church, the path of a third son. No, I was at Kenwood for renovations. Dry rot gave the new owners ideas. A large music room will be designed, but my mother offered my expertise." I sat up straighter on my mount. "I guess she finds me good at such things."

"Oh, Sebastian, you always sell yourself short. Your Grace, he's a musical genius. His name will be among the masters. No one knows more about the acoustics of a room than my friend. When he finishes his newest composition and wins the Harlbert's Prize everyone will know the name Lord Mark Sebastian."

I smiled as did the duke. Perhaps they'd both forget my enthusiasm for the painting of the Mansfield's nieces at Kenwood, Lady Elizabeth and her lively cousin.

Livingston reached over and slapped me on my shoulder. In prideful, drunken tones he said, "My friend is brilliant."

Fine. Maybe it was good the earl didn't Humpty-Dumpty on this cobblestone. Who else would sing my praises? One couldn't always rely on being your mother's favorite.

Nonetheless, this feeling of pride was short-lived as Livingston reared back and said, "Pity, a live female, one of flesh and blood and the proper age, frightens the sensibilities of our pianoforte master."

I fumed at him for being right. I was a master at the keys. The music in my head kept spinning and I remembered the portrait and the way the artist chose to paint her. The moment before she danced. Her smile and the way sunlight reflected from her satin gown would never leave my soul.

Music should be written for her.

Perhaps she was the muse to inspire my composition for the Harlbert competition. Then everyone, including Prahmn, would respect me.

We continued riding in silence, while a blustery wind blew at our backs. It was colder than it should be. Spring should be warm.

Soon we approached Blackfriars Bridge. The huge stone structure formed with high arches led travelers over the Thames. I thought we'd turn another way by now. The duke kept barreling forward. Working class, industrial, what could a duke want on that side of the river?

"Whoa, Torrance." Livingston cantered closer to him. "You said at the coaching inn you wanted us to assist you on a mission of life and death. You never mentioned crossing the river at sunset."

"Nearing sunset. There's plenty of time to go and come back." The duke offered him a withering gaze, one that could be given by Prahmn or any old man who'd been to war or battled great odds. Torrance had to be in his midthirties, ten more years than what I'd lived, about two less than Livingston. "For a man of science," the duke said, "you have strange superstitions."

"It rained on my wedding day." Livingston guffawed, and then sneered. "If I'd heeded and not gone through with it, I wouldn't have lost four years of my life."

My friend had a terrible marriage that ended when his wife abandoned him. "Well," I said, "perhaps if you hadn't run on so much and gossiped, you might've noticed the incompatibilities and fared better."

My barb made him shut his mouth, but my bitter words made my stomach sour. "Sorry, sir. That was uncalled for. No one knows what a gamble at love will bring."

"No offense taken, Sebastian." The earl looked sad, even wistful. "Damned woman. Would've been better off with a painting of her."

The duke glanced at Livingston. His mouth tightened to a dot. "Everything has challenges," he said, "and it's best to be selective. Give your heart too soon to someone unworthy, it's difficult to get it back."

"Thank you, Torrance. But, Sebastian, you can make amends by buying ale at the next stop because I'm not going over the bridge."

"If a little water frightens, you sirs will never survive a visit to my Saint Petersburg. Too many temporary bridges crossing plenty of rivers and streams. Here, you Londoners have it easy. Blackfriars looks permanent and sturdy. That good Portland stone should be sufficient."

"Torrance, the bridge is fine." I wove my horse between the men as if to keep the peace. "Let's all find a tavern and go on the duke's mission tomorrow."

Livingston swayed, pulling my scope from my saddlebag, the tube with lenses I used to bird-watch. "Oh, I see why you want to cross, Torrance. There's a woman walking over by the docks. I can take you to prettier ones on this side of the Thames. The price for the evening will be good."

We'd just met the duke and Livingston was trying to take him to a brothel. I grabbed the scope and, despite my better nature, took a glance at the object of the earl's attention. "You can be truly horrible. What kind of welcome is this for the duke? He's back from Russia, thinking of staying, and you're so drunk that—"

Can't breathe.

Can't think. Got to think.

Say a word, Mark. But nothing came out.

The two began talking or bickering. I cared not. I was grateful that their arguing might ignore my shyness, the dire feeling which sometimes stole my words.

Nonetheless, I returned the scope to my eye. I had to catch another glimpse of the woman on the other side of the river.

Was this twirling woman the same woman in the Kenwood portrait?

Patting my horse's mane, I couldn't settle or wait. I started toward the bridge.

"Can't hold your seat, Sebastian? Are you more sotted than me?"

I was, but not from beauty, not ale. "Just thinking of Kenwood again. Fine property. Nice music room. Made for twirling—I mean dancing."

"Thinking of the painting again? You need a real woman. Come with us, Torrance." Livingston sounded pained, almost normal. "Delay this dash across the bridge until tomorrow. It's too much of a gamble at sunset. That neighborhood—"

"Gambling? I don't do that anymore, but I'll reward whoever among my new friends makes it to the other side first."

"No, Your Grace, I might fall but Sebastian's always light in the pockets." Livingston leaned a little too much to the left and I reluctantly saved him.

"Torrance, he's too unsteady." I shoved the tube into my coat. "I need to make sure he gets home safely."

"What is that?"

"Your Grace, it's a pocket scope," Livingston said, slipping backward in his seat. "Young Sebastian uses it to identify birds—the ones in the sky and the beauties in petticoats strolling leisurely in the parks or gardens about London. The way his cheeks reddened, he's spotted one 'cross the river. What bird, sir?"

"A greenfinch, Livingston." I grinned a little, thinking of the woman walking on the other side of the Thames fluttering her arms in an emerald coat.

The duke sighed, then shook his head. "Perhaps, it would be better to do this alone."

Livingston nodded. "Goodbye! *Do svidaniya!*"

The earl started away from the bridge, wobbling the whole way. "I'd better accompany him. I wish—"

"I understand, Sebastian. If I settle in Mayfair, you must visit. I will be in need of a piano room, one grander than Kenwood's."

"You've been to the estate?"

"Several times. My father and Mansfield were friends. I too have stared at the same portrait."

The woman across the river—had the single Torrance found a match to the prettiest woman to pose for the artist?

Suddenly, I felt jealous.

"Go catch your friend. He looks as if he'll hit a house."

Torrance doffed his hat and started toward the bridge.

The leaning Livingston waved. "Watch the river, my tzar."

The earl had drooped to the side. He'd fall and hurt himself. Livingston was a fool, but my friend. I rode after the earl, wishing I'd made it to the other side of the Thames.

Chapter 2

GEORGINA WILCOX—RUN AWAY, RUN AWAY

I hated feeling helpless and voiceless.

My older sister wouldn't listen. She thought I couldn't handle death and sent me with the younger Wilcoxes to the kitchen to make sugared biscuits. I might be a good baker, but when did biscuits change anything?

My brother-in-law, Tavis, was still dying. He'd gambled badly and was now paying with his life. I folded my arms about me and thought about turning back. Instead, I spun around, a complete circle, and kept walking.

A man from the other side of the river barreled across Blackfriars Bridge like he chased cannonballs. I swirled to the left, moving closer to the side of the road that hugged the Thames.

The fellow on a beautiful silver horse didn't pass by. He stopped in front of me.

"Miss. Excuse me." His glare demanded my attention. I hated men expecting to have my time because my family chose to live on this side of the Thames, close to industry.

The road might as well be Wilcox Way, not Ground Street. Our house, offices, and warehouses were located down the lane.

"Miss, you must help me."

I gawked at him and his expensive charcoal-colored coat and hat.

Whenever I made coal deliveries with Mr. Thom, men like this, wealthy and important-looking souls, insisted upon speaking. In the next breath, they solicited for companionship.

Not today of all days. I couldn't be bothered and sidestepped.

The fellow maneuvered closer. "Did you hear me, miss? Is all well?"

"Yes. And I'm not a prostitute. Go away."

His jaw dropped.

He put a gloved hand to his thin mustache. "I suppose I'm glad you're not."

"Good." I spun and walked the other direction away from the man, away from death.

"Miss, you're a Wilcox? That sassy tongue can only be inherited through the blood."

"I'm a proud Wilcox woman." I stared but couldn't recall his face. "Who are you?"

"Jahleel Charles, the Duke of Torrance. Your sister sent for me. Lady Hampton said it was a matter of life and death."

Oh.

The letters Katherine and the doctors begrudgingly wrote succeeded. Tavis begged her to find the duke, his childhood best friend. "Go down the lane, Your Grace. The last house, that's our house for now . . ."

Sobs filled my throat. Why were the tears coming now? Hadn't I resolved that we'd lose everything? Oh, I hated that Katherine might be right about me not being able to control my emotions.

Remembering Mama's dignity, I raised my head and projected my voice. "The end of Ground Street. Please visit number twenty-two. Go now."

"Your voice is melodic." He put a finger to lips that were neither thick nor too thin. "Do you sing?"

"My family thinks I can carry a tune, but they are the only ones to ever hear me." I pointed again. "Katherine is waiting."

"I know she hates waiting, but I can't leave you. You're too upset."

"Sir, I walk . . . or run or spin when I'm upset."

"As in a reel?" The duke jumped down and held out his arm. "Then shall we have this walk?"

He bowed to me. "If your sister knew I'd left you in a state, she'd be vexed. We don't want Lady Hampton vexed. I remember it being a difficult thing to endure."

Shaking my head, I lowered his arm. "I don't need protecting, sir . . . Your Grace."

The man dug into his brass-buttoned greatcoat and offered me his handkerchief. "Perhaps I'm in need. Vexing can be hard to take. Come now. I also hate being late. Dance with me to the house."

His humor and compassionate tone made me relent. Feeling defeated, I wiped my eyes on his cloth, then started walking beside him.

Halfway to the house, he asked, "Which Wilcox sister are you? I'd heard there were three."

"Georgina Wilcox. There are four Wilcox women including Lady Hampton. She's the best of us."

He looked away, maybe toward the rippling Thames.

"You look flushed, Your Grace. Is walking too much?"

"*Nyet*. Memories, Miss Wilcox. Nothing dampens them. They are soaring like meteors, even when I crash to earth."

A poetic soul, and a bit dramatic. I supposed those words were for my benefit. "Sir. Maybe it's best we wait outside. It might be easier to listen for a servant to signal my brother-in-law has passed."

"That seems a shame to have come this far to be late." His tone was kind. "It is up to you. I will not leave you outside alone."

The man had traveled far to come at Tavis and Katherine's summons. Yet I wanted to admit to a stranger that all our family's problem stemmed from Tavis's dealings and Katherine allowing him to run everything amok.

The duke with large hazel eyes stared at me. Then he nodded. "Tavis Palmers, the viscount, and I were once close friends. Today we are not. I understand what you've said and haven't."

Before I could feign ignorance, or acknowledge a kinship with a stranger who too probably suffered at Tavis's negligent hands, a man on horseback appeared.

"Torrance," he called out, "I can join after all."

Before he could jump down, our man of all work, Mr. Thom, came from the stables wielding a pitchfork. "Be gone you, you creditor! Let the scarecrow come get 'em before you pounce."

Nothing was funny, but this made me laugh, maybe release a little of my frustration. "He has you like a rogue chicken, sir. So sorry." I turned to Mr. Thom. "Be easy. He's a friend of Lady Hampton's guest."

The duke waved this man closer. "He's no threat, Mr. Thom. I can vouch for him. This is Lord Mark Sebastian. I believe him harmless."

The fellow jostled his top hat, which exposed straight brownish-black hair. He opened his mouth to speak, but no words came out.

"You've dispatched Livingston to a ditch?" the duke asked.

His lordship's lips parted and again nothing came out.

Then he hiccupped.

I turned to the duke. "You brought a drunk friend with you. None of Tavis's friends are any good."

His Grace frowned and when he turned to his friend, the younger man whispered, "Gorgeous."

The fellow must be quite in his cups. Most, who weren't seeking courtesans, never talked about anything except my height, especially in comparison to my lovely sisters.

Me. I was tall at five foot nine inches. Yes, a tall Meg. At twenty-four, I'd describe myself as a tall wallflower. With my last birthday passing a month ago, I was beyond being a wallflower. I was a full-on matron. With no desire to be unhappily wed just to gain a new name, a Mrs. Somebody, or to give another fortune hunter access to the little Wilcox Coal money we had left, I refused all offers.

Charging myself with protecting us now, I folded my arms. "Your Grace, for my sister's sake, don't make a mockery of Lord Hampton's final moments. Perhaps you both should go."

"I've been summoned. But, Sebastian," the duke said, "while I appreciate the company, go back across the river. Find a close tavern—"

"There's one on this side. It's closer. You can wait for the duke there." I pointed, hoping to be rid of a fool that called me gorgeous.

The duke tossed him a coin. "Go sit at the tavern. Wait for me."

Mr. Thom, our man-of-all-work, waved a finger at the duke. "I like this one. He's free with his money."

"But . . ." The fellow hit at his chest. "Turban. Gorgeous."

His Grace came closer. "That painting at Kenwood. It wasn't Lady Elizabeth that captured your attention—was it, Sebastian?"

The fellow's cheeks brightened to a burning red color.

I stepped to the right. "That way, close to the lumberyard. If you hit water, you rode too far."

Tipping his hat, bowing his head, the young man trotted off.

Then I led the duke inside to await Tavis's death.

Chapter 3

MARK—WADE IN THE WATER

The smell of the Thames had never been good to me. I didn't visit it often but when I did, this rotten-egg smell awaited and set my nostril hairs aflame.

A few paces from the house on Ground Street, I straightened in my saddle. I no longer needed to play a drunken, speechless fool. Sobered by the woman's tears and her disappointment in my inarticulate conduct, I needed to be away.

But she was beautiful.

Such gorgeous dark eyes, and like Dido Belle's, the Mansfield cousin who had caught my heart; her sun-kissed face made me feel so warm. Styled in an emerald coat and silk turban, she was a modern version of Dido. This was a woman to know, a woman I could love.

Yet, the lady was a friend of the duke's. What good could he say of me?

I was a man without a fortune, with an inability to speak more than a word, a third done sonata. And Torrance already knew of my love for the Kenwood painting.

No, there was nothing to be done to recommend me, not unless I won the Harlbert's Prize.

Slacking the reins, I approached the swirling water. Rushing the banks, it looked turbulent. The air felt cold like an icy bath.

Whatever the Duke of Torrance had ridden into must be horrible. He looked as if he was about to be dunked in a river of fire.

Maybe I should've apologized and stayed.

Yet, exactly how was I to do that? I was a wordless buffoon whose love for an old portrait had me wishing for a stranger to be her.

Goodness. Yes, this woman was easy on my eyes and her voice could be an angel's.

My brother, Christopher, the navy man, wrote to me of his activities—his intense love affair with a woman he'd met in Bridgetown, Barbados. As much as he wanted to bring her to London, he wasn't as bold as his commander, Prince William, who escorted his Dorothy to Britain. My brother wouldn't dare, not with our father's famous prejudice against foreigners.

Let her be Catholic, or anything but Anglican, and the patron saint of hypocrisy—my father—would be indignant. A hint of color from anything but a summer tan would make him rage.

The cold wind blew. I'd be trapped here on this side of the stinking river because of my inability to assert myself, my lack of prospects, and loss of rational thoughts. Yet, I still wanted to know her and be worthy of her.

Winning the Harlbert's Prize would redeem me.

My friend Livingston went not to his brothel. He was safe from being seduced of his money and his own free will. I should be home working on my future.

The little man with a pitchfork accused me of being a creditor. Never been called that. I owed my mother everything, even my current living.

My father saw no use for me and my music. I was his spare's spare.

God forbid anything happened to my two brothers.

My mother's heart would be broken, and I'd have to turn into a lecherous, ignorant fool to please the father who couldn't be pleased.

Not me.

I'd rather go down, wade in the water, and drown myself in the foul Thames.

Chapter 4

GEORGINA—THE MOMENT NO ONE WANTED

I led the Duke of Torrance into our modest, yellow home—sunshine-colored paint, matching papered walls adorned every room. Not much else. Many possessions of my proud Wilcox family had been sold to keep creditors away.

The duke stopped at a sun-bleached spot. The window along the stairs had done its damage tattling about portraits that were missing.

Before he asked about it, I pointed him to our parlor to where a sofa and conversational chairs and a pianoforte congregated. "Your Grace, wait in here. I'll go see if Tavis is ready to see you."

"Please don't leave again." The duke sounded desperate.

Maybe I should've allowed his friend to stay. "I'm not going if you're not going."

"You have a sense of humor, Miss Wilcox. I like that."

Before I could curtsy and go check with Katherine and the doctors, I saw movement beneath the blanket thrown over our floral-patterned sofa. Then the dearest, angriest voice sounded. "Is he a bill collector? They come at all hours."

"Milaya, come out, please," the duke said. "I don't wish to be seen talking to furniture. It wouldn't be the first time my sanity's been questioned."

"My name is not Milaya. It's Lydia."

"Milaya means 'sweetheart.'" He took off his hat. "Please come."

"Tell him I'm not his little milaya either if he's come to take things."

I stooped near the blanket. "He's not a bill collector. Come out, Lydia."

Her little brown face poked out. The five-year-old glanced at him with her solid gray eyes and sniffly nose. "Then he's not here to buy the business? It's not for sale. It's Papa's. No sale."

"Fine," the duke said, "I won't procure it."

She came a little closer to him and tapped on his knee. "I said don't buy it. Leave it for Katherine. She loves it the most."

"You sure she'll still love it tomorrow, milaya? I hear it's a woman's right to change her mind." Until now the duke sounded reasonable and polite. These words held a tiny fiery barb.

Katherine might have to explain, but she'd stop confiding in us all when she married Tavis.

He set his hat on the sofa. "Why are you each worried that someone will buy Wilcox Coal?"

"Debt, silly. Our brother-in-law can't count so well. He spends more than he has. More than we have."

The little girl confessed all before I could reach her and clap my fingers over her mouth. Giving her the be-quiet eyes, I marched to her. "That's not polite to say, Lydia."

"But it's the truth. And since he mentioned our company, he must know."

Her wide eyes beamed when the duke nodded.

"I'm aware. I thought this might be a scheme to secure a sympathetic loan."

The gasp leaving my lips was true.

Shocked that he'd speak so freely, shocked that the outrageous request wouldn't be beyond Tavis, I stood still beside Lydia. Then I became bold. "But you still came?"

He looked to answer when his gaze turned to the stairs. "You sent for me, Lady Hampton."

The room suddenly felt hot.

Katherine didn't say a word, but she returned his greeting with a wordless expression that was part fury and something else.

I braced for her to rail at this stranger, this unknown friend of Tavis's. Like the sotted fellow who called me gorgeous, Katherine said a lot with her eyes but no words.

"Lady Hampton, I wish I could visit under different circumstances."

That's not what his countenance said. It had war painted on his pale cheeks.

I would step in and protect my sister, but she hadn't moved from her position on the stairs.

"Is he evil?" Lydia came to his shin, looking as if she would kick him. "Just tell me, Katherine."

"No, child," my sister said. "Let the Duke of Torrance see to his friend's dying wish. This way, sir."

With Lydia following closely, he walked to the base of the stairs. "I came because you asked, Lady Hampton."

My other sister, Scarlett, ran past Katherine and jumped around the duke.

Seeing she still had on the pair of men's slippers, black leather with a heel, from her last caper, I hoped the duke didn't think us all mad.

Yet, since he hadn't stopped looking at Katherine, I wasn't sure he noticed anything at all.

Scarlett tugged Lydia away and held her. "Is it true you bet a man a pound that you could scale Saint George's Chapel?"

"Yes, but I only made it halfway before slipping on a buttress and nearly falling to my death. It's not something I'm proud of."

"Because you nearly killed yourself." My tone sounded surprised, for men brag about stupid things.

"I was upset, Miss Wilcox, because I didn't win the bet. Then

I had to be fetched down by my father. It was awful. He said he taught me better . . . how to be a better climber. I don't gamble like that anymore."

"Nearly died. Pity you tempted fate." Katherine took a step. Her gray gown skirted the treads. She stopped one away from him and looked down on him. "You'd think grown men would know better."

"Anyone can be a fool or be fooled, Lady Hampton. Introduce me to this Wilcox. I've already had the pleasure of meeting Miss Wilcox and Miss Lydia Wilcox."

"That is Scarlett Wilcox. She's the third oldest Wilcox."

Hating her cold tone, I decided to help him. "The duke convinced me to end my run and return."

"Well, he's a smooth talker. Quite convincing, I'm sure." Katherine's tone would freeze the Thames.

"They're older than me," Lydia said as if it weren't obvious. "If he's good, let's get him one of Georgina's biscuits. They are good. So, he will stay."

"No," Katherine said. "He won't be here that long. I mean, he needs to go see Tavis now. Time is short."

He dropped his greatcoat. The brass buttons jingled when the wool hit the floor. The duke stretched out his hand to me. "Lead me."

Katherine looked as if she wanted to spit, but I led the duke up the stairs. The rest followed until we approached the bedchamber.

The door opened and Mr. Adam Carew, the brilliant physician who'd treated our family over the years, stepped out. "Your Grace, a pleasure to see you."

"You know the Duke of Torrance?" Katherine's brow rose. "I thought you stayed in Russia."

The prickly tone made Carew back up. "We went to Inverness Royal Academy, the Eton for mixed-race and West Indies boys."

"Then you went for more study and trained in medicine."

The duke shook his hand. "Carew, I intend to start science lectures again. I want you to come."

"Science lectures?" Scarlett started smiling.

Katherine's scowl deepened. "I thought you'd leave again after this."

The duke didn't look at Katherine or answer her. Instead, he focused on the physician. "Is the viscount's condition as bad as I've heard?"

"If you think I'm lying, Jahleel," Katherine said, her voice sounding hateful, more heated than I'd known, "you can leave."

And *Jahleel* was it now?

"What I meant, Lady Hampton, is that I know Mr. Carew is aware of numerous techniques. This diligent man from the colony of Trinidad combines the best of all sciences to treat patients."

"You are too kind, Your Grace. Lady Hampton asked me to visit for the same reasons."

"And she wanted an opinion other than the physician Tavis's family sent." I folded my arms and looked at the fellow who'd been at this house too many times, often with bad news.

"My conclusion is the same at this point. Lord Hampton will be gone within the hour."

Lydia started to cry. "Our Tavis gone now too."

Tears trickled down Scarlett's face. "He's a mixed bag, but he was ours. There's something in that."

"Remember his laughter," the duke said. His voice was small and kind and more human than Katherine's.

She continued to frown, especially when Lydia hugged the duke's leg.

My throat began to thicken.

No matter how much trouble Tavis had caused us, we did care for him. He made Katherine smile at the darkest point in her life.

"Things have seasons," I said. "I'll remember the good, never the bad."

"Scarlett, Georgina. Take Dr. Carew downstairs with Lydia for sweet biscuits and tea."

Carew patted Katherine's elbow. "Since there's not much to do here and the other physician is inside, I will accompany Miss Wilcox, Miss Scarlett, and Lydia Wilcox to the kitchen."

"I'll stay," I said. "I'll be with you, Katherine."

"No, Georgina, go show off your biscuits." She raised her hand as if to dismiss me. "You make the best ones with ginger and molasses."

Matchmaking? Tavis was dying and my older sister was trying to act like our mother, setting me up with the honorable physician. But Mama knew her girls and propriety, and she'd not try to *fix things* with a marriage on the day Tavis would die. "I'll stay. Scarlett and Lydia can reward our old friend."

Mr. Carew sighed and bent to the littlest Wilcox. "Yes, I saw you come into the world. I've sort of been part of the Wilcox family for a long time. I know when it's time to go and eat sweets."

"Don't talk about me being born. You're going to make me sound young in front of the duke. He smells nice. He's my new friend."

Scarlett took Lydia and led her away, asking Mr. Carew about recording facts about patients.

"Ma'am, you ask a lot of questions," the physician said with a soft accent that sounded of the ocean and drums.

My younger sister offered him a half smirk. "I'm just getting started, Mr. Carew. I need your thoughts on the system of trusses some men of science think can aid the backbone."

"Ma'am, I looked at your sketch. It's fantastical. Even if I thought it had a chance of working, Hampton's too weak. And I'll be overruled. The viscount's father has the physician they want inside treating him. That's not me."

His tone had turned to a hurricane, speaking of the prejudice we didn't want to mention in this house. Tavis's white family, led by his father, the Duke of Hampton, wanted a white doctor to administer care and perform the certification when the viscount expired. He refused Tavis's requests for money, which made our brother-in-law desperate. In the end, it was the color of silver, the color of money, which did him in.

Though his parents were so concerned about these color details, not a single one was here. Tavis's Blackamoor wife and sisters-in-law were the only family who loved the fool enough to be near in the man's hour of need.

Well, us, and the mysterious duke who kept gazing at Katherine.

She opened the door to the bedchamber.

"Sing something, Georgina," Katherine said when we all went inside. "Your voice is so pretty. Tavis may hear and feel better."

I began with a hum and then sang a melody of "Love Divine, All Loves Excelling," a hymn by Charles Wesley.

> *"Love divine, all loves excelling*
> *Joy of Heaven to Earth come down,*
> *Fix in us Thy humble dwelling . . ."*

Oh, did we need fixing.

Old Tavis too.

When I opened my eyes, Katherine had taken a seat in the chair beside her husband's bed. The once active joking man lay still in bandages and piles of blankets.

The doctor counted a pulse.

Poor Katherine took up Tavis's hand.

The duke, who looked more distressed, stood under the threshold muttering foreign words under his breath.

Chapter 5

JAHLEEL CHARLES, THE DUKE OF TORRANCE—THE BLASTED CONFESSION

The Hamptons' bedchamber smelled of mustard and sour tonics, a little like Jahleel's when he was last sick.

Looking at Katherine's thin frame, he decided she was too thin. Her back was to him, but it was elegant and straight. Wisps of ebony hair fell from her chignon, and he imagined the last time he saw her, coldly telling him to leave.

"Torrance? Is that you?" Tavis sounded tired, like he'd fought in a boxing match, a bout the man had lost.

Almost feeling tongue-twisted like Sebastian, Jahleel swallowed, then offered, "Rest, Lord Hampton. I'm here. As requested by you and Lady Hampton."

"Good." He closed his eyes. His panting eased.

An older man picked up the sick fellow's hand again. "Good. You finally made it. I believe he stayed with us to see you."

Katherine bristled. It was a slight jerking motion, but as always, Jahleel was attuned to every minute detail.

The physician glanced up at him. "So you are Russian?"

"English too."

Jahleel wagered that was not the question the physician, like most, wanted to ask. Most wanted to know if his mother was a Black Russian princess while examining Jahleel's features for signs of color.

If the curious doctor found yellow in his cheeks—that was jaundice from his last cold. He'd ridden all day, so there should be some brown. But in a year of little sun, Jahleel looked as pale as other peers who could attest to having two typical English parents.

"Mr. Carew said he knew you. Miss Scarlett Wilcox was insistent he'd be able to help." The physician's eyes were close together, hovering over a long, pointed nose. "She was right about Carew. He's treated many injuries from the wars and his home is in the islands. Those colonies are always in rebellion."

Steal enough people, deadly consequences will ensue.

With the Wilcox sisters of Jamaican descent, it made sense that they'd know others from the West Indies. In London, islanders stuck together.

Shaking his jowled cheeks side to side, the physician set down Tavis's wrist. "Lady Hampton, I'm sorry. He's barely with us."

Jahleel shut his lids. Those were the worst words. He said a prayer. When he looked at the bed again, he met Katherine's gaze.

Upturned eyes.

Flecks of gold on a blackened sea.

Then he saw them shimmering with water.

He drowned, and that empty space in his chest beat with some foreign drum.

And when her eyes hardened, and her frown deepened, he knew she still hated him, despised him for the lies the man in the bed told her.

Yet she chose to believe Tavis.

If she knew Jahleel like she said she did, then she would know he'd never abandon her.

So how dare she look fresh and beautiful and be poison to his soul.

"Jahleel," Tavis said. "Not a dream. You've come. I hoped you would. A moment alone with my friend."

"No." Katherine shook her head. "No, Tavis. We're in this together. I said I'd stay with you till the end."

"But I want you out. I must speak to the duke alone. It's my wish. My last request. Honor it."

She looked at the doctor.

He shrugged and said, "Five minutes, no more."

Then she gaped at Jahleel like this was his fault too.

Miss Wilcox took her arm. "Come on, sis. The duke won't let you miss the moment."

She stood and smoothed her prim dress. "Is that a promise, Your Grace?"

Katherine put up a dismissive hand and swung a man's watch from a chain about her neck. "I can tell time. All Wilcox women can."

The grieving wife headed toward to the door. "I'll be back in five minutes, not a second later. No need to depend on the Duke of Torrance for anything, Tavis."

Miss Wilcox made eyes at her sister as if to say she was being too harsh. All these antics would be over soon.

This goodbye would be done. Jahleel could leave with a clear conscience.

The door slammed and Jahleel was alone with his former friend.

"Get out of that bed and tell me what's the latest scheme. I won't judge you."

"Wish I could oblige. Not this time, Jahleel."

"Tavis. Can't you see what it's doing to Katherine? To all your sisters-in-law?"

Weak blue eyes glanced up. "I wish it was a jest. I can't believe—"

"What in God's name happened and why summon me?"

"A bet. Broke my back jumping a fence. Didn't win the fiver. Horse . . . put down."

Another stupid wager! "We're older, you fool. You have a wife who loves you. There's a family out there. They depend upon you."

"Couldn't resist a bet. Neither could you. That's why we're brothers, blood brothers."

"That sentiment was before the woman I loved ran off with you." Jahleel shook his head. "Just get better."

"Jahleel Charles. Finally the Duke of Torrance."

The last challenge had been rendered obsolete. His father's marriage to a Russian princess had been accepted as legal. The Court of Chancery had conferred everything to Jahleel, two years too late to afford the medical care that might've made a difference in his sister's short life.

His mother no longer cared to be the Dowager Torrance or to reside in London. Her cottage, a lovely pink dacha in Saint Petersburg, with easy access to the Neva River or Baltic Sea, gave her the peace she'd wanted.

Jahleel had fought too hard to be recognized and lost too much in the process to become a recluse in Russia. London would be his home now.

"Jahleel, you still there? My vision's going."

"If you want my forgiveness, fine. You have it. Try to get better for them. Physicians can be wrong. Let me get Kath—Lady Hampton. Maybe try a new treatment."

"No, not forgiven. Have to confess. Jahleel, I have to tell."

"No." He pounded back to the bed, inches from picking up the sick man and thrashing him. "Don't tell me how you loved Katherine all along and couldn't help—"

"I lied. I schemed. She turned to me in desperation, and I took advantage."

Jahleel blinked, looked at his own balling fist and prayed that the temptation to punch a dying man would pass. "Speak fast. Tell me this new lie."

"Truth." Tavis put a hand to his nightshirt, right over his heart. "Father cut me off. No money. You left."

"I left Saint Petersburg and Katherine to go take care of my father. That's what a dutiful son does."

"You made me swear not to tell anyone about your father's decline or the battle to invalidate your parent's marriage. Katherine . . . in trouble."

"What?" Jahleel clutched the bedpost to give his hands something to do. "What about Katherine? What kind of trouble?"

"You left . . . family way . . . cad."

"What?"

"Baby."

"I was to be a father? If I'd known I'd have given up my fight for ascension. I'd give up everything for her. You know how I loved her."

"Letter. I had Carew write this letter. Burn it once you read. Night table."

Jahleel stuffed the cut of foolscap into his pocket. "Where's my child? A girl or boy? Where?"

"Boy, but stillborn. You'd have made a great rich godfather."

Like he'd fallen off a horse, Jahleel dropped into the chair Katherine had abandoned. "No wonder she hates me."

"Yes. Yes, she does." Tavis coughed and smiled.

He cursed the dying man in Russian, offered some choice phrases in the Ethiopian dialect his mother had taught him.

Were five minutes up?

Jahleel could take no more revelations. "If you weren't looking like the devil, Tavis, we'd duel. I'd win and celebrate killing you."

"I'm evil. And worse. Her money's gone."

"The debts you ran up."

"Yes. House will go. Creditors. Don't know last time . . . paid Mr. Thom."

"How? How could you do this? I can't believe this. You had her and her money. You're losing them both."

"Letter. Read. Then you fix."

Couldn't feel his hands. Jahleel's palms vibrated like he'd have a spasm. "I can't fix this. You need to be in hell." He leapt up, again wanting to throttle Tavis. "You could've gotten word to me. You knew how I felt about Katherine. The strain of us ending, of her thinking I'd shamed her, that's what killed our baby."

"If I could take . . . back . . . I'd not've . . . bet. A fiver . . . too little to die."

"A fiver wouldn't do anything for the debts if Katherine has to sell her father's coal business. You horrible—"

"You fix."

Tavis coughed and wheezed, then finally settled.

With his hands pulsing to fight, Jahleel looked back at the door. He needed to escape and eased to the door. "You lied. You connived. You manipulated her—"

"Loved her. Don't forget that."

Was it a sin to kill a dying man? If he took the pillow and just held it on the fool's face, would anyone . . . ? Oh, Lord, what was he thinking? "Bye."

"Bet you can't win her back. And she won't believe the truth. She'll hate you more."

"I'm leaving. You've said your piece. This time you can't fix it."

Tavis's head fell back. "Damn. Tell . . . come back. Now."

Jahleel flung open the door and ushered everyone inside.

The weeping became loud.

"It's . . . all right," Tavis said. "I've mended ways . . . We'll keep our oath, the one said on our fathers' lives."

"But your father's still alive," Lydia said. "He refuses to come here because you married a Blackamoor woman."

The prejudice, the lies—it all made everything in Jahleel become fire.

"Metaphor, little sis. Jahleel. Bet . . . five pounds you can't love 'em like I . . ."

Tavis lay still.

The doctor moved to the bed and gripped the lying fool's wrist, then he put an ear to his chest. "Tavis Palmers, the Viscount Hampton, is now with the Lord."

No, he wasn't.

That blasted man was in Hades. Tavis was there now, lying to the devil, betting for spots with shade. Jahleel was sure of it.

Sitting by the bed, Katherine cried. Her sobbing sounded of pure pain. It was the most heart-wrenching thing he'd heard since his sister.

Jahleel drowned again. Katherine didn't have to look his way. Her powers had grown or he was still weak . . . still in love.

No.

When she finally looked at him, she said, "Thank you for coming."

Dismissed. The fire in her eyes was pure hatred. To talk of the secrets Tavis disclosed would seem opportunistic and cruel.

And what of Jahleel's feelings, the years he'd felt used and discarded by a callous harpy who claimed his soul in secret while seeking a respectable title in public? Did he not think until this very moment that Katherine was an opportunist or a thrill huntress, that she was anyone but a woman who loved as deeply as Jahleel?

He had to go, for he didn't know what to do with anything Tavis had disclosed. Before he could back away, the physician rubbed his fingers together, asking for an absent coin.

Oh . . . who knew what Tavis told him.

The duke nodded.

Poor Katherine and the girls couldn't be hounded by a doctor turned bill collector. "In the hall, sir. I'll take care of it."

Before he could follow the man, Georgina and Scarlett wedged into Jahleel's arms.

Then Lydia clamped again to his leg. He couldn't escape.

Yet holding them, helping them in this moment felt right.

Damn.

His reformed soul had accepted the wager. In that moment, Jahleel vowed with his Cossack heart to right things for Katherine and her sisters and to curse Tavis every day until the work was done.

Chapter 6

GEORGINA—A YEAR LATER, MAYHEM

March 7, 1817
London, England

I ran out of the house, leaving before my older sister stopped me with her mission of the day. With the coal business slowly recovering, Katherine seemed dedicated to it as if it were human, giving the baby more care than her late husband ever did.

Mr. Thom shook his fingers at me. "Where you going, Miss Georgina? Can't just run to Olympus like Hermes."

Frowning at him, I refused to be deterred. "Mr. Thom, I'm not running. I'm riding. Hand me the reins. You know where I'm off to."

The old man's face became serious. "He never misses a Friday. Go see what our duke is up to."

The Wilcox man-of-all-work had been with our family a long time. He was Papa's right-hand man. He and his sons drove our coal wagons until we were down to just two. He'd seen how the duke attending us had changed us for the better.

Scarlett bounced down the steps. "I have my medical books. I'm going to fix him. I know he's sick. He looked pale last week. He didn't feel up to taking a walk by the river with us like we always do. He loves rivers. Says his home in Saint Petersburg has many."

If an illness couldn't be fixed by soup or bedrest, a female's logic was ignored. But Scarlett was determined to right this. She wanted to be a physician, a woman doctor in the male profession.

From her herb garden in the backyard to her sneaking into science lectures, my sister wouldn't be deterred.

Before she could climb next to me in the gig—a beautiful two-wheeled carriage that my horse, Thunder, pulled—Katherine stood by Mr. Thom on the steps.

"Oh, boy," he said. "You got caught. Betcha a pound she's not letting you go."

Everyone stilled.

No one tossed out bets but Tavis.

My brother-in-law was gone, a year and a week. All of us, the duke included, took him to the cemetery. We offered prayers before His Grace returned us to Ground Street. Tavis's parents never came.

But the duke visited every week, every Friday morning until today.

"Get out of the gig. I'm sure Mr. Thom has to run errands, ladies."

"No errands. All done for today," he said, but then backed away, fleeing to the rear of the redbrick house as she glared at him. It was her mad face, like the one she offered us.

"Something is terribly wrong with the duke. I'm—"

"*We* are." Scarlett interrupted me. "This is an *us* project."

Katherine marched down the steps and stood in front of Thunder.

Seeing her scowl with her arms folded, foot tapping, reminded me of Mama. That woman could be severe when she was healthy . . . and angry.

"Katherine, you're not more than four years older than me, and at times you act like I need a guardian. Where's the fun-loving girl who'd always dared to take on the world?"

The frown that seemed permanently etched on her face grew larger. "You both need guardians to protect your reputations. With the coal company doing better, perhaps I should do what other guardians do and find you two husbands."

I looked at Scarlett.

She looked back at me. In unison, we said, "Katherine, you've become otherworldly."

"I'm serious. I've put off my duty long enough. And since you two don't pay attention to the business, I think it only right that you have your own households to manage. I will soon have enough for dowries for the two of you."

"Katherine." I shook my head. "I'm not marrying. And we're only doing better because of the duke. The man you hate has stepped in to help us."

Scarlett's cheeks turned colors like she held her breath. "You don't suppose she's the reason he hasn't come? Did you order him not to come back?"

"If it was that easy, don't you think I would've tried that?" Katherine huffed. "He's always here. I can't escape him."

Scarlett drummed her medical book. "The Duke of Torrance visits faithfully on Friday like he promised. He pays attention to Lydia, Georgina, and me. He's never offended by your low-toned barbs. He's a gentleman. And we think he's in trouble."

"Georgina, Scarlett, I mean it. Get out of the gig. Give me the reins."

"No, sister. Why don't you walk down to the coal office. Figure out how to save it without the clients the duke has sent."

Katherine's head dipped, and I felt sorry for how harsh my words sounded. But there was no changing my mind.

"What if I have to go to a client? You're taking our only carriage."

"This is a gig, Katherine. It's not our coal wagon or our coal dray. Wilcox Coal has those two conveyances to move people and coal. You only have to send someone to go get one. Mr. Thom, isn't that right?"

The little man had returned to rake the leaves falling from the cypress tree near the front of our town house. The March winds had shaken a few loose.

He looked away, still not wanting any part of our fight.

"Bye, Katherine." Scarlett sat back and waved.

"Both of you, out. You can't go to a man's house in the middle of the day unchaperoned. It's simply not done. The Duke of Torrance will not protect your reputation."

That didn't even seem true. This man had no reason to be of use to our family once his friend died. "If he cared nothing for us, we'd have never seen him again. Every week, for fifty-three weeks, he's been coming to our door. Something must be wrong."

"Katherine," Scarlett whined. "Go back into the house. Have your morning tea. Grouse about our mission of mercy if you must, but we're going to see the Duke of Torrance."

"Mr. Thom, help me tell them how wrong this is."

The poor man shook his head. "Not getting involved, Lady Hampton. I promised your father I would continue to make sure the grounds are good. Nothing else. Discipline is not me. Grounds good."

Mr. Thom had emigrated from Mama's beloved Port Royal, Jamaica. His English wasn't the best. But he was hardworking, and we could trust him. "But if I didn't have to rake or visit coal customers and I was a viscountess, I'd go see about the duke."

At that moment, Lydia ran from the house and jumped into the gig. "You should've *waked* me up. If you think for one moment I'm not going to check on him too, you've made mistakes."

"Haven't we all." Katherine covered her eyes. "All of this fuss over the Duke of Torrance?"

"Do we have another duke?" Lydia offered this advice with a grin, then a grimace. "We've waited long enough. He could be in trouble. We have to go see about him. He's my bestus friend."

Katherine's fists balled before she flattened her hands against her hips. "The Duke of Torrance is a wealthy man. He has a full staff and can manage on his own."

I'd try one last time to convince her, then I hoped she'd hop out of my way. This gig was going to Mayfair. "For over a year, the duke visits on Friday, every Friday, by ten a.m. He's the first visitor to call upon us. He takes us on walks by the Thames. He brings treats and he patiently samples the tweaks I've made to my Cornish Fairings."

"Well, obviously that's the problem. You've made him ill from those biscuits. Too much ginger."

Katherine's tone was full of sarcasm. She knew my biscuits were delicious. The experimentation was to find the proper icing sugar for them and then to try and make something the duke called kartoshka, made with leftover breads.

"Wait. You're saying my food did him in. Oh my goodness. Scarlett, look up stomach ailments. Katherine, move. We have to go."

"He's sensitive," Lydia said. "He can't be sick. If he dies, who will give us advice on spices or give us some from his homeland in Russia?"

Squinting at us, Katherine shook a finger. "You have been accepting gifts from him? I said no gifts."

I pointed back. "Move."

Then I felt silly and lowered my hands but kept the reins. "The duke has been wonderful to us. You're not the least bit concerned, Katherine, that he could be ill or injured? Why are you like this? Why can't we go see about him? Why can't we be the ones helping?"

"Oh, Georgie, you and your questions." She blew out a long breath. "Ladies, why must it be any of those troubles? He's a busy man. He could've found something better to do with his time."

"Kitty sounds very bitter." Lydia shook her head.

Our youngest was the only one who ever said out loud what everyone was thinking. "Kitty, we are wasting time," I said, mimicking the child's tone. "Go back in the house and figure out what new thing you need to do with Father's coal business—"

"*Our* business, girls. And, yes, we have new customers, but we're not out of trouble. Selling the business is still a possibility. There are loans to pay off, but for the first time in a long time, we're not bleeding money."

At this, I couldn't look at her. Katherine was good with numbers. She'd done all the accounting. Then she married and let Tavis manage the debits and credits on the ledger.

"The late Lord Hampton didn't seem that good at math." I pointed again to her. "Was he, Lady Hampton? Thank goodness the duke encouraged our creditors to give us more time."

Walking from the front of the gig, Katherine swung one leg in, and then the other. "Fine. You win. We'll look in on the duke, then we will head off to the offices. You girls need to start visiting the business to remind you of our legacy, or let me find you husbands."

I handed her the reins, and she started my horse trotting.

"But, Katherine, *you* didn't find a good one," Lydia said in a sweet and sincere, painfully truthful voice. "Why do you think you could get a good one for them?"

Wanting to laugh, I held it in. Katherine had gotten us underway, and I didn't need an upset sister changing her mind and stopping.

At the end of Ground Street, we turned left and headed for the bridge.

"He's unusual," my scowling sister said. "Be prepared for strange things in his household. I've known him longer than any of you. He's very strange. That won't change, no matter what he does or says. He won't change."

Katherine's tone sounded aggrieved, even irrational. Like she was convincing herself of something that wasn't true.

"You just like being mean to him," Lydia said. "He's our friend. He wouldn't abandon us. Even Scarlett wants to go, and she hates men. And Georgina runs from them."

Sadly, both things were true. I ran or walked away a lot. Scarlett, the little rebel woman of science, had also become His Grace's advocate.

"I don't hate all men. I just find them highly illogical. I don't have any idea why they are allowed to run the world."

"Just remember what I said." Katherine had us on Blackfriars Bridge. We'd soon cross the Thames and be in Mayfair in no time.

Shaking my head, I bit my lip and sat back, peeking at the ferries crossing underneath.

My prayers were that all was well with Torrance, that he wasn't sick and that we hadn't become a nuisance to him.

Nothing needed to change, except maybe Katherine's attitude.

I hated that she seemed so angry with our friend. If wishes had the power to become true, mine would be that my older sister would become easier on the Duke of Torrance.

We needed him, much more than he needed us.

Chapter 7

MARK—A PRESENT FROM A FRIEND

Sitting next to Livingston, in the rear of the bright green ballroom of Anya House, a few houses from my mother's Grosvenor Street townhome, her favorite of all of Prahmn's holdings, unnerved me. The crowded room was filled with gilt trim along the walls and seated men of science, even physicians from around the world, discussing important things like inherited diseases that sounded like the ailment that plagued our king.

"The Duke of Torrance has quite a gathering," I said to my friend. "I wonder where he is."

"A garish gathering, perhaps. But in a house this big, who knows." Livingston folded his arms as if he weren't impressed with the large estate with its multitude of rooms and gardens that had been pruned into a maze. "Sebastian, you are trying to avoid the answer to all your problems. You need a mistress."

That was his solution to everything. I was beginning to suspect that was why his wife abandoned him. I looked away, wondering how he could have a mind for science and be a lecher.

"Don't fret, my friend. I have arranged everything for you. I have picked out the perfect woman for you."

"Livingston, please stop. Listen to the cure-all from the next speaker."

He sat back in his chair. "Companionship is important. I'm

convinced that the right one will rid you of shyness and free your mind so you can finish your song."

It wasn't a song or a hymn. "Sir, I'm composing a sonata. Maybe if you weren't entertaining all the time, you'd know what I'm working on."

"And maybe if you had other activities, you'd be finished with this masterpiece. It's been a year."

Time was not my friend. Between finishing up the design at Kenwood, visiting Dido's painting, presenting ideas for Torrance's music room, and being summoned by my mother or Prahmn to meet potential heiresses that they felt worthy of marrying into the Sebastian line, I was consumed.

The minute I mentioned the Harlbert's Prize, Prahmn would talk of seminary. I was many things, but called to ministry was not one of them.

"And you're a gentleman. You shouldn't be working."

Oh. Livingston had continued to prattle about . . . well, probably about a mistress.

Men clapped and jerked forward.

"Sebastian, are you afraid of women?"

"No. I love beauty. Women can be the most beautiful of creatures, but I'm terrified of causing my partner misery. I see that daily with my parents. And then there are your experiences."

"You don't marry a mistress. The arrangement is temporary. Think of it as training for when you find the lady you wish to have your name."

I almost snorted. My friend could make sin sound elegant and purposeful. Oh, goodness, I sounded like a prude. Maybe I should think of the church. "Livingston, I must establish myself in music. That's my world. My creation has to be right. I can't be embroiled in foolish—"

"Then that is the problem: perfection. You don't have any fun. How can you expect to write a perfect song if you haven't lived?"

"I'm here, breathing. And it's a sonata."

"Yes, sonata. It's impossible to create a perfect work."

How could I explain the difference between right and perfect? I'd written dozens of stanzas, experimented with rhythm and varying timbres. None were what I sought. None would win the Harlbert's Prize.

And these hands were not idle. Four music rooms, including the one here, I had spent my time designing and been paid handsomely. But a gentleman couldn't speak of such things to my friend or Prahmn.

"Maybe you shouldn't be a composer, Sebastian."

My chest grew heavy.

No music.

No notes, sharps and flats, pouring out of my soul.

No hope of gaining Prahmn's respect.

"I'm pathetic. What am I without music?"

Livingston didn't say anything. Now he seemed to be paying attention to Mr. Carew.

No wonder when I asked the duke about the young woman on Ground Street, he kept changing the subject. Torrance must be protecting her from me. Such a shame, for her voice inhabited my dreams.

"Hey. Lift your head, man. You've not lost. You can do this. You can be a composer. Gain control. Mind over matter."

The clapping began again. This time, people stood.

When the din died down a little, Livingston said, "I said I have a solution. Did you hear me? Will you trust me?"

A tortured man hadn't a choice. "I surrender."

"Good. Sebastian, meet her in—"

Applause erupted. I pointed to my ear and shrugged.

Livingston waited for everything to settle. ". . . Garden. I see you suffering. This is the solution. You meet her there. As soon as you feel comfortable, reach for and kiss her. Actually, do it as soon as you can string a cohesive sentence together."

"What of her comfort? Am I to assume that she has feelings for me?"

"I've paid for her to be enthusiastic about you. For once, man, this is about you. Unless, you are . . . You've been with a woman, right?"

"Lower your voice. I don't need the science community to look back at me as if I am strange."

"Sebastian?"

"I'm not new. My brothers and I have been on excursions in the parts of town you frequent."

Livingston sat back. "Good. You've been deflowered. However, if that's not quite the truth, the courtesan I've picked especially for you will take care of that. Your creative stresses will be released. I cannot wait to hear about—"

"A gentleman does not talk about such things. Livingston, you are crude."

He chuckled. "I meant tell me about the composition you will finally finish. You don't have to mention anything about the woman or the pleasures you two enjoy. I want to know I was right. That sexual frustration or the fantasy you have with a painting is stopping your art."

Maybe my philandering friend was right. Nothing I'd done worked. "I'll have to keep designing music rooms to afford this mistress. You know I have a tendency to become attached to beauty."

Livingston chuckled, then clapped like the others who'd been listening to Carew's lecture. "You, my shy friend, will become a new man. And the Dowager Livingston's music room needs to be refreshed. I'll pay well, and my mother who loves music will enjoy the surprise."

I sank into the stiles of my chair feeling uneasy and unprincipled. Nonetheless, if allowing myself to be compromised by a courtesan led to a finished sonata and changed my dull existence, so be it.

Chapter 8

GEORGINA—A TZAR IN MAYFAIR

Twenty-one James Street was idyllically situated in Mayfair, near green parks and the gold coins of old money on Grosvenor Street. Windows on every level of its facade, the house had three visible stories and an attic. My mouth hung open as I took it all in, down to the thick, gold fencing that framed the pavement surrounding this residence.

I climbed out, tempted to stick my hands into my empty pockets, and I remembered the tipsy friend that first came with the duke. His Grace had mentioned him a few weeks ago. Something about him helping with music.

"Gorgeous." That's what he called me. I still remembered.

"Yes, it is," Lydia said and tugged on her gloves. "So, so pretty."

Katherine, who hadn't stepped out the carriage, pushed the child's bonnet higher on her sleek chignon. I waited for her to bring Lydia but my elder sister hadn't budged.

Scarlett shrugged, got out, dragging her heavy book.

I fingered a bit of worn gilt on the pages. "Where did you get that?"

"Never you mind, sis." She strutted away. The thing was large enough to tip her over.

But if it had what was needed to make our friend well . . . that is, if he was sick. I wasn't sure why that explanation stuck in my head more than others.

Four footmen in blue livery descended upon us like royal guards suspecting terrorists.

I threw up my hands. "We come in peace. We're here to see the duke, the Duke of Torrance."

Katherine handed the reins to one, then climbed out with Lydia. As if she was here of her own volition and wasn't carrying a squirming child, my sister looked calm. "His Grace will see us. Tell him Lady Hampton is here with the Wilcox sisters."

One fellow with smoky silver hair looked at the other, then clapped his hands. "Go inside, ladies. His Grace has given us strict orders to admit you, Lady Hampton, at any hour."

Her? I looked stunned.

Scarlett did too.

Holding Lydia's hand, a calm, almost regal Katherine marched up the three steps that led to the Duke of Torrance's double doors.

The silver-haired man stepped in front and bowed again. "Ladies, avoid the ballroom. The meeting has run long today."

What meeting?

Katherine smiled at me but not in a good way. She looked smug. "I see. His business was more important than you."

Lydia seemed thrilled, bouncing up the steps, grinning. "He expected us to come today." She rubbed her palms like they itched because the duke had thought of us.

The footman scowled, then returned to his dour tone. "That's been the orders for over a year. Since last—"

"Last March." Moving closer to Katherine, I whispered, "Oh, I see how we are included in his plans. The poor man has been hoping for us to come. And you've been too preoccupied or rude to return his courtesy."

She grabbed my arm as I almost spun into the grand hall. It was blue and white with gilt on the ceiling and on panels along the wall. "You're too young to know when a man has arranged circumstances to draw you in."

"Too young? I'm twenty-five, Katherine. You're only twenty-nine. You make yourself sound aged and the duke a demon."

"He's not a demon. He's worse. At least you can see the horns on Satan."

I dropped her hand. "Why do you hate him?"

Before she answered, Scarlett wandered to the grand staircase, causing Katherine to announce, "We need to stay together, dear sister."

Scarlett offered a pout. "The duke said that I could visit his library."

"I heard him. He said it's supposed to have maps." Lydia jumped about. "He said I could look too."

Katherine drew her hands together, clasping them tightly. "I thought we'd come to see if the duke was well, and then leave."

"We can do that *and* look at his maps." Lydia sighed with glee when the footman pointed up the gilded grand central staircase.

"On the upper landing. First door on the right, ladies. The Duke of Torrance is a little under the weather, but he is up and may be in the science meeting happening today. Anya House is very crowded and there are reporters, do be careful."

"Anya . . . Anya House?" For a moment, Katherine looked shaken. She stuttered. She never stuttered. "That's what the Duke of Torrance has named his residence?"

"Yes, ma'am, after his late sister." The footman turned back to Scarlett and Lydia, who'd already inched toward the stairs. "I'll try to make sure you're not disturbed. I know His Grace wouldn't like that." He bowed and pointed again to the wonderland awaiting upstairs. His debonair actions made the tails of his blue uniform sway as if a breeze flowed through the enormous hall.

Arm in arm, my younger sisters disappeared, bounding up the burgundy-carpeted treads. Well, our Lydia sort of dragged Scarlett. The words *science meeting* had Scarlett ready to engage. It was good to see our little Lydia with such energy. She'd had another bout of a spring cold. They usually took her strength.

"Sir, will they be safe up there?" Katherine looked concerned, very motherly. And with her half-mourning gray, very matronly. Reporters wouldn't recognize us as the daughters of the renowned Cesar P. Wilcox, one of the first Blackamoor men to make his own fortune in London. Papa's empire once included a second house, the wharf, and the brewery near Ground Street.

One of the reasons I loved walking or running down the lane was memories of him and his industry, when our name meant something.

"Yes, ma'am," a second servant said.

The footman snapped to attention as an older gentleman came to us. "The Wilcoxes. At last you've come. I'm Jonathan Steele, the duke's butler. He's moving slowly today because he's been a little under the weather. Knowing that you're here, he'll attend to you once he finishes dressing for the day."

"Mr. Steele," the silver-haired footman said, "I warned them about people drifting about the house."

"True," the butler said. "Reporters are always hunting for something, but His Grace needs the newspapers to spread the word about new discoveries. It's the only way to popularize research."

Steele sent the footmen back to their post, then turned to us. "You may wait in the study."

"No, sir." Katherine folded her arms and tried to appear at ease, but she, like me, had to be impressed with the fine blue paint and gilt-trimmed moldings. She continued, "We'll wait here."

"Very well." The butler walked a few feet and opened a door to the left. When he slipped inside, a rush of claps and noise ushered out. That had to be the ballroom.

Now it was just Katherine and me in the wide marble hall waiting for the duke. "See," I said, "he's been ill."

"Overslept from who knows what goes on here," she said.

"He's fine. His priorities took precedence over his coming to us. And lying about in bed?" Her cheeks flushed. "Wonder what crazy, debauched antics led to that."

Crazy and debauched? That didn't sound like the man I'd come to know. Granted, I didn't know what he did apart from his visits across the Thames, but his spirit was gentle. The man was always kind and listening to us. "A science meeting sounds important, Katherine. You make it sound selfish."

Her glare at me said that was exactly what she felt. "Georgina, we came. We will wait for a moment to see his face, and then leave."

"You sound so furious. The man has been nice to us. I asked you a question earlier. Sister, why do you hate the duke?"

A heated look flashed over her countenance. Her wide nostrils flared. Her black eyes reflected flames, glowing with the candles from the hall or maybe hell. "I don't hate him. I just don't like him."

Lie.

Didn't Katherine know that my gaze was her mirror? That these looking glasses saw into her soul and discovered bitterness? "Tell the truth. Why does he perplex you?"

"You're too young to understand, Georgina. That's why I'm here to protect you. You shouldn't be taken in by the Duke of Torrance of all people. Your head and heart need to see a trap for what it is. The duke's not worthy of your love."

Love him? My own sister didn't know me.

"Katherine . . . that's what you think?"

"There's no other explanation. It's easy to be taken in by someone so charismatic."

"To think I could be interested in the duke, a man who's been like the brother I'd hoped Tavis would be, but never ever was—you wound me."

"But it's obvious. You hang on his words. Your eyes lift when he enters our house. You've fallen in love with him. And he'll do nothing but hurt you. He'll never marry you."

"Katherine, you've gone too far. You think so little of me. And why on earth would I want to marry and be punished for the rest of my life, like you?"

"You didn't mean that. But the duke is horrible. Woe unto anyone who marries him." She drew her hand to her mouth. "Sorry—"

The Duke of Torrance was on the landing. Warm smile, light olive skin that looked more pale today. The energy and heat that radiated when his eyes met Katherine's was the same, or maybe it was stronger, for we'd . . . she'd come to him.

"Hello," the duke said. His motion was slow, but his face hadn't lifted from Katherine. "What's occurred?"

He hurried down using a cane. Immaculate in a jet tailcoat with silver-threaded buttonholes and velvet-looking indigo waistcoat, he seemed austere and commanding.

But his eyes, his gaze on my sister's burned. I wanted him to hate her words, hate the way she belittled his efforts, but that wasn't in his countenance. Why didn't he loathe the way she acted, as I did? Why must he seem to be understanding when she sought to make everyone around her feel insignificant? "I asked a question," he said. "What can I help with?"

"Tell him, Katherine. Tell him your lies. Make me feel even smaller than you do every day."

"Wait. Georgina. I didn't mean—"

I didn't stay to hear the rest.

I ran.

I ran down the hall past the open door of the ballroom, which was filled with men holding charts, hooting at another man with charts. Maybe they had life figured out.

I ran past a drawing room of paintings, portraits of men, including Blackamoor men, then I slowed in front of a watercolor showing women slaying an enslaver. It was cowardly to run, but I had no other power.

"Georgina, wait."

Speeding up, refusing to be coddled like the fool my sister believed me to be, I kept going until I was outside, knee-deep in the green gorse.

A wonderful garden surrounded me, lush bushes with roses and yellow flowers.

A little farther ahead was a tall maze. If I went inside it, I might be able to hide until I calmed. If she did follow, I hoped she'd not find my path. It was obvious we were on different ones.

After ten minutes of going about turns and twists of sculpted gorse, I was lost. All the corners and curves began to look the same. I didn't know how to get out, how to get back to the house or find a way to the mews.

Then I stopped moving.

I breathed fast like I couldn't fill my lungs.

Soon, I was convinced I wouldn't be found by Katherine . . . or anyone else.

I was alone, smelling pine and heather and something offering honey.

Mr. Thom was right. No matter how I tried I couldn't run to Mount Olympus. If only one could gain wings and fly away from an older sister's judgment.

Katherine was inside the grand house shaming me and the duke with her silly accusation. How could she? Why did she feel entitled to ruin my life? Mistakes or wins—they should be my choice.

Turning another corner, breathing in the cleansing pine, I decided I'd make kartoshka, one of the duke's favorite desserts from Saint Petersburg. That would make up for Katherine's nonsense.

Showing him extraordinary kindness might teach her a lesson.

Clearly, I was more upset than even I wanted to believe if I could stand in this beautiful place and plot revenge.

Humming a hymn, I settled. I needed to go home. The duke was well. We were still welcomed, wanted friends in his world.

On my next turn in the maze, I stumbled onto a bench. Plopping down, with arms folded, I figured this was as good a place as any to rest. I sang aloud, a hymn of peace.

"Such a pretty voice."

Loaded with books and papers, a gentleman came from the other direction.

"Oh, hello," I said.

He didn't respond. His lips shut and he stared.

"We've met before," I said. "You came to Ground Street with the duke."

He nodded but didn't say anything.

His staring at me continued. Then it seemed he dropped his papers and books.

"Let me help you." I moved to the pages littered in the grass. Some looked like notes. Others were sheets of music.

The man didn't move.

Then the wind shifted the papers.

"Are you going to help me, sir? I'm not here to merely help you."

Groaning, he pitched his head up and down, but still no words.

Perhaps he had a problem with his speech. Mr. Carew had told us about some of the patients and conditions he treated. I was sure this would be something he'd know how to help with or show me how best to communicate with this person.

Finding someone with true difficulties took some of the steam from my heated teapot. I touched his arm, catching his sleeve by the buttons. "Be at ease, sir. I do not mind helping at all."

He stilled. His gaze went to my hand.

I stopped moving. Being used to having Tavis around, I'd forgotten that some chose not to associate with us. No matter how much my father had accomplished, my brown skin touching his darker coat might be an offense.

This gentleman in fine wool coat dyed deep blue noticed. He put his palm on my hand before I fluttered away. "Don't go."

"I did not mean to be so forward, sir."

"You're helping me, miss."

He'd spoken at last. His voice was pleasant, midrange. He might even be able to carry a note, if he sang. "Well, let's work together, sir, to help you."

"Help me. Right."

Hopping around like rabbits, we stepped on pages and chased others.

I grabbed the last. "I think we've done it."

He set his pile on the bench, carefully weighting the loose papers with his books.

Then he clapped. "Thank you for this dance."

Was that what he called this? The gentleman had a sense of humor. I offered him a curtsy. "Anytime you wish for a partner to stand up in a garden reel, find me."

"You are easy to behold."

This fellow came closer. Nice smile, nice dark, dark blue eyes. We were the same height. I didn't feel too tall or too short, for the first time in a long time.

"You must think I'm silly. A grown man tripping over his tongue because a beautiful woman stands before him."

His cheeks burned red. Mine began to heat. "Being shy can cause difficulties. And we haven't met in a while . . . Lord Mark Sebastian."

"You remembered." His face was scarlet. "How kind when I know your life has changed greatly since last year. Is that why when I asked Torrance of you, he distracted me? He didn't wish for me to intrude."

This man asked of me? I felt my chest warm. The more he gaped, the more I became fire beneath my emerald coat.

And he was right.

Our circumstances had changed because of the duke's influence, but Katherine's hatred of him could cost us everything.

"You . . . you don't have to answer. My friend Livingston said

you'd meet me in the garden." He took a big breath. "I can't believe I'm talking to you. Can't believe I managed more than a
word."

Not sure who Livingston was. As long as it wasn't Katherine
looking for me, I was indifferent. I glanced at Lord Mark Sebastian. "Last time we met you said barely anything."

"Nothing but 'gorgeous.'" He rubbed at his neck, then stood
up straight. "Yes, you are, more than ever. It's wrong for us to talk
like this. To meet under my friend's influence."

What was he talking about? What friend?

If I questioned him, he'd probably become silent again. Nonsense words were better than none.

Nonetheless, I hated guessing what people thought. Katherine always made me figure things out. Her secrecy, all the hidden
thoughts, caused problems.

He began to fix his crooked cravat. "I'm not sure what my
friend has said to you, but I'm painfully shy. I'm not a libertine or
a monk. I've had my share of broken hearts. My current circumstances don't lend to suitability. Most women prefer a man of
more means or a title in his own right. I'm a composer. Well, I've
chosen to be one."

When he got to talking, he did run on, but at least his gaze was
upon me, and only me. That rarely happened if another Wilcox
like Scarlett were around.

"You haven't much experience, Miss Wilcox?"

"Not with mazes. I've never been in one. I sort of lost my way.
Do you know where the mews—"

"Oh, must you go now? This was just to meet." He whipped a
hand through his brownish-black straight hair. "When shall I see
you again?"

"You wish to see me again?"

Wiping his hands on a wilted handkerchief, he kept staring.
"Yes. Yes, most definitely."

He said this without hesitation. I liked that.

"Miss Wilcox." A long breath escaped his lips. "I'm at your disposal, but I don't think I can . . . we can't do what my friend said."

His cryptic words sounded very odd, and Lord help me, I became Lydia, curious as to what he meant and willing to go very far to oblige a needed laugh. "I can't help you unless you're clear. Tell me what you've been instructed."

His cheeks burned, far past garnet. They'd soon darken to the color of my favorite gloves, berry. He came close to me. "The gentleman said a professional woman would meet me in the garden. The woman, a courtesan, would draw out my creativity like a muse . . . Forgive me, I'm very nervous."

This fool thought I was a courtesan. This was an insult.

I blinked and readied to slap him, but the fellow seemed like he was about to faint. "What did your friend tell you to do when we met in the garden?"

"Something about kissing quickly to ward off my nerves. Livingston said you'd give me confidence. He claims that you will free my creativity. But that won't happen. I'm far too nervous."

"Am I not what you expected, sir?"

"Mark, Mark Sebastian. You're one of the most beautiful creatures I've ever beheld. There's a painting at Kenwood. I'm in love . . . I'm rambling again. All I know is you should never be a courtesan. You're an angel with a heavenly voice and face. Don't do something for money that will destroy who you are."

Oddly, his fight to save me was dear. It had been a long time since anyone cared enough to make a fool of themselves for me or one of my sisters. I decided being mistaken for a courtesan wasn't as bad as a man thinking me too good to be sullied.

He came closer and put my hands delicately in his. "Yet, if one must buy your attention, I've no doubts that a moment with you is priceless and that I'll wish to see you again and again. One time, one temptation, wouldn't be enough."

Oh.

Didn't know what to say. But with Katherine coming my way, gawking, how could I resist embarrassing her?

"Well, sir. Your luck has changed. As this is my first moment in this new profession, I'm offering samples."

I took his cravat in my fingers and towed the willing gentleman into a kiss.

Chapter 9

MARK—SOME KIND OF TROUBLE

Heaven.

Evergreen bushes sprouting yellow and white buds surrounded me . . . us in the garden of Eden, otherwise known as 21 James Street, the Duke of Torrance's in-town residence.

The full lips of a woman, delicious and smooth, enticed my soul.

She was a bird, a lovely greenfinch, with a song that began to free notes in my mind.

I was lucky.

A goddess had come down to me. I had to protect her, covet her as I had Dido and all the other treasures in my life.

Miss Wilcox couldn't be a courtesan. I couldn't share her.

I, Mark Sebastian, had known passion. I'd been foolishly in like, not love.

This was different.

Her kiss fired my flesh to flames and burned to ashes the walls blocking my creativity. All my nerves and worries were made to hum. The composition in my head—I could feel it getting unstuck as I felt her curves molding to me, submitting. And so was the stanza.

My pulse metered the rhythm, faster and faster.

This kiss, this waist in my arms melted the impasse. The first quarter notes—I saw them and could add them to my sheet music.

I heard the next notes in my ear. *Dadum. Dadee.*

Miss Wilcox could be my muse.

How could I keep her from becoming a courtesan?

My jealous, zealous nature refused to think of her being anyone else's inspiration.

Despite the noise about us, I deepened the kiss.

And she let me.

Perhaps this woman was inspired too.

One kiss wouldn't do, not for me, not ever, not from a goddess.

Hands wrapping about her hips, drawing her closer.

"*Vot eto pizdets!*"

Russian? Didn't know what the words meant, but the tone sounded of death.

Deserved, undeserved—I kissed the courtesan goodbye, savoring the softest mouth ever, trying to hear in her passion the final notes.

A scream—another woman's.

The goddess leapt away when a cane hooked my shoulder.

Yanking hard about my arm, it drew me from paradise.

"No, don't kill him!" she said. "My doing."

"Sebastian!" The Duke of Torrance shook his fist. More Russian spewed and when I looked at the courtesan with her curly hair free of her turban, his courtesan . . .

Wham. The duke whacked me across my head.

He drew back for another strike. I blocked his advance. "It's not . . . well, it's mostly not what you think."

"You're seducing Lady Hampton's sister in my garden."

"Well, that's right, but she kissed me first. Then I . . . kept going. But she's become a courtesan. Livingston sent me . . ."

The duke looked to hit me again, but the goddess and the angry sister held him back.

"Can't you be trusted in my home, Sebastian?" His Grace shook his cane at me. "Miss Wilcox is no courtesan. She's my guest. This is her first time to Anya House and you debauched her. Lady Hampton will not let her visit again, nor any of her sisters."

"That's correct," the angry one said. "Is this how all your friends act?"

Torrance wasn't looking at me or even saying these words for my detriment. His audience was the woman beside him.

She dropped his arm, then embraced the goddess. "Did he hurt you? Georgina, are you all right?"

The goddess touched her mouth. "Yes. Fine."

The smile those lips elicited from my soul made the duke whack me again.

Chapter 10

MARK—OUT OF THE PAN AND RUNNING

In the Duke of Torrance's garnet-red study, I stood silently, trying to figure how I would explain my new wife—the courtesan, not-a-courtesan—to my father. I'd kissed or been kissed by an innocent-not-so-innocent goddess in front of His Grace and the angry sister who I now knew as the fiery Dowager Viscountess Hampton.

"I can't believe this," she said, pacing back and forth. "Georgina, did you not consider the consequences? Your reputation—"

"It's intact, unless more gossip has been spread, like about me and the duke."

The viscountess's eyes grew big.

Neither woman said another word.

The goddess sat in a chair near the big windows behind the desk that overlooked that enchanted maze. She seemed angrier at the sister than me.

The dowager continued to pace.

Funny thing.

I'd had an image in my head of widows being old. They were stately or persnickety, but decidedly ancient.

Though persnickety, Lady Hampton, like the goddess, was

young. She couldn't be more than a few years older than Georgina Wilcox. Their expressive eyes were similar, dark and bold.

She turned to me like she finally remembered I'd followed the two into the study. "Sir, how do you intend to fix things with my sister?"

Fix?

Fixing would be an apology or a wedding or a duel. I wanted none of those options. I'd love to celebrate no longer being tongue-tied. The oft utter-less organ found another use. Instead of struggling for words, it savored Georgina's kiss.

"Well, sir? What—"

"Katherine," Georgina interrupted. "No one saw us, just you and His Grace. Unless you intend to tell everyone and accuse us of something worse than a simple offering of affection, I think we should all forget what happened."

Practical and heartbreaking, how could this lovely greenfinch in the emerald coat sing that we should forget hope or magic?

I didn't want to be forgettable.

I didn't want the Dido I imagined or the actual Georgina to say that I was.

The duke entered and leaned at the threshold with his dented cane. "Great. Everyone is still alive and no more kissing has occurred?"

Was it wrong to long for more affection and wish to live? I shook my head. "Torrance, can we get on with this inquisition?" I made my voice deep and even annoyed. "I wish to make amends and not draw additional thrashing."

The duke didn't move. He seemed tired, even pained. "This wasn't something I expected. A scandal here, never. Anya House is to be pristine. A place for welcoming knowledge."

"You still hate to be surprised?" Lady Hampton's scowl left me and found the duke. "You like gambling upon expected behaviors."

"I don't like to misjudge people, Lady Hampton. Taking

chances upon a soul that can wound me or those I care for are mistakes I don't make easily." He lifted the staff again. "I struck you, Sebastian, to get your attention, not to kill you."

Could have fooled me.

Fingering my brow for a bump or bruise, I found none. "I suppose I should be grateful for your benevolence."

"Sir, please take a seat. The inquisition, as you put it, will begin after I get confirmation from my butler that no one saw the commotion. I'm a bit under the weather and gathered my strength to make a brief appearance to conclude today's meeting when I encountered the viscountess and the fleeing Miss Wilcox. You do like to run?"

"I do, Your Grace. And I told you, Katherine, that the duke was ill. I'm glad you've not abandoned us." The young woman shot an angry countenance at her sister, but Georgina hadn't looked at me much.

I wished she had.

"Abandon the Wilcoxes?" His Grace straightened, glaring at Lady Hampton. "How could you think such? There are no others I'd like to show my Anya House and the beloved music room this interloper has designed."

"How can you jest, Your Grace?" Lady Hampton started toward the duke, then stopped. "My sister's life is held in the balance awaiting confirmation from this mad Russian court, and you are concerned about music."

"Music." I adjusted my jaw and continued, fighting my anxieties every moment. "Music is important."

"Did she say 'mad Russian,' Sebastian?"

"Yes, Your Grace."

"How quickly you forget, Lady Hampton. Mad British too. I'm both. My home is both. My future, including the future Duchess of Torrance, will accept both. Now settle in and wait. You do know what waiting means?"

His tone sounded angered but the look he offered her—part hurt, part misunderstood, part duel at dawn, a touch of desire—

was pure confusion. But I understood it. I lived with such angst in regard to the fairer sex.

Lady Hampton rolled her eyes and fled, quickening her pace away from the duke, crossing the wide golden-yellow tapestry to peer out the windows.

The exposed glass showed men leaving Anya House. The maze and all routes to the stables overflowed.

Someone had to have seen me and Georgina.

"I can't believe this," Lady Hampton said. The long sleeves of her plain gray gown billowed with each of her steps. Like the goddess, she was trim, just slightly less voluptuous than the woman who compromised me—and I had compromised right back—in the garden.

"We've been so careful." Lady Hampton's voice was low. "Our mother, on her dying bed, told us to guard our virtue. I thought we all understood. Ruin can happen so quickly. How could you, Georgina?"

Georgina the goddess—I liked the sound of that and the way she glowed; sitting on the yellow sofa made her brown skin look more tanned like Dido's. The oversized cushions made her tall height seem dainty, someone to protect.

Then I realized *I* wanted to protect her.

"The kiss meant nothing, Katherine. I was impulsive. Your Grace, I am to blame, not the gentleman."

Didn't like thinking my kiss was nothing.

Deep breath, fool. I needed out of my troubles, not to add to them. Nonetheless, it was good that she'd admitted her part. A lesser woman might've lied.

Still, this honesty stung. The kiss still stirred my blood and it was thirty minutes ago.

Yet, I forgave her and became immobile, watching the goddess flick a falling lock of tightly coiled curls from her face. Tears shimmered on her cheek.

The strain made her cry. The notion of marrying me might've too.

Her sister came to her and swooped the thick jet lock of her curly hair back into the tight chignon. Did it feel as silky as it looked? The goddess's skin was.

Shaking my head, clearing my thoughts of her . . . sort of. How did one forget a perfect dream? "I . . . ah . . . I want to say I'll do whatever is necessary to protect . . . the young lady."

The duke rolled his eyes.

Lady Hampton's grimace deepened.

But the goddess smiled, and I felt lighter.

Mr. Steele knocked, then entered the study. The Scottish man was someone Torrance had met in his extensive travels. The duke bragged about him all the time.

The blank face—his ash-blond hair neatly parted, the crisply pressed, orderly mantle he wore—gave nothing away.

My heart pounded.

He whispered something to his employer, then left.

Torrance's expression didn't change.

My pulse raced. Blood and those humors Carew lectured upon sloshed in my veins.

Wasn't sure if I was found to be guiltier, but I had a feeling the risk-taking duke would use it to his advantage.

"Well?" Lady Hampton asked. "Does Georgina escape with her reputation? A woman can't live things down as easily as a man. She'll be damaged, while the gentleman just moves on . . . to a peerage."

The duke started a slow walk to his desk. "Let me sit. I want to be comfortable when I say what must be said."

My stomach crumbled, then folded. I gulped my last morsel of free single air.

Someone saw.

I'd ruined a lady.

The duke moved along his wall of books and stopped at a sideboard full of bottles. He mixed something from two or three vials, and then added a yellowish distilled liqueur.

Georgina bolted to him. "You're in pain. Have you eaten anything?"

"I'm fine, my dear, but do stand away, lest your sister again accuse me of making you fall in love with me."

What? Had there been a first time?

Who was this girl . . . the one I was to make Lady Sebastian?

I rubbed my temples. I was losing my mind, succumbing to the Russian-English madness. "End my . . . our misery, Torrance. Tell us what the butler said."

The goddess frowned. It was too late to rephrase my complaint . . . our fate.

With his last steps, the duke looked more discomfited. Was it sickness or an injury he suffered?

Lady Hampton came near and he straightened. She poked him in his chest. "You caused this. You need to fix it."

He grabbed her hand and kissed it, making a big sensual show, even sniffing her wrist.

Lady Hampton pulled away, wiping wet lip prints from her hand. "No more joking."

"Then no poking." Torrance sat on his desk, moved the marble chessboard and ivory carved soldiers out of his way, and turned toward her. "And how is this my fault?"

"Your house. Your friend."

"But your sister and your antics that made her run and act tempestuously. It seems, even with the high walls of my maze, privacy was breached. Mr. Steele said a few intended to cut through the garden to get to the mews—reporters included. Chatter about the kiss stirred."

Georgina stood up again. "I knew there was a way out somewhere in the garden. Where's the mews? To the left of the maze? I still want to leave."

"No, sister. No one can go until the duke fixes this. He'll conjure something up from his dark heart. It will be a trick or joke or lousy wager, but it will work. Jahleel gets what he wants."

She'd used his given name. And it sounded more than a casual reference. It was heated and torrid, sounding toxic like poison.

The way his thick brows fluttered as his gaze and half smile settled upon her seemed to indicate the duke caught the slight or endearment too.

Torrance drummed the smooth desk surface, causing a few of my papers to flutter. "Lady Hampton, you almost impress me. Surely, it was your idea for your sister to compromise the son of a marquess. Anything to gain a title. That's so disappointing."

"I did no such thing, Your Grace."

He eased into the leather chair. "But, *dorogaya*, my lady, choosing an impoverished noble is very much your handiwork."

Lady Hampton's eyes softened at whatever the Russian word Torrance said, but the rest of the sentence about me being poor made her gasp. She rose and pointed her finger in his face. "Your year of redemption isn't enough. Your entitled attitude—"

"Ah, pointing again, *dorogaya*." This time he nipped her index finger with his teeth.

She drew away. Panting, looking wild-eyed and crazed. "Are you trying to compromise me too?"

"If you're not going to play by the rules, I feel no need to have restraint."

After taking several large breaths, I decided to try to say . . . something. "This arguing . . . solves nothing."

Everyone looked at me as if these were the only words I'd ever spoken. My face heated, but I had to continue. "You're not well, Torrance, and you're not acting like yourself. You wouldn't deliberately vex Lady Hampton when I am in the wrong. I am."

Almost smirking, proud of having uttered a complete sensical sentence, I stood up straighter. "I'm wrong."

Nodding, the duke went around his grand desk, pushed at a chess piece, and sank into his chair. "You're right about being wrong. And I don't believe anyone is rational right now. Nonetheless, I do have a plan to fix everything."

Lady Hampton, who now had her hands locked behind her

back, gaped at him. "Tell us. Please let it be anything other than Georgina being forced into a marriage of strangers."

"Poor strangers on both sides. With the way my departed friend, Lord Hampton, worked the Wilcox fortunes, you can't afford anyone else draining your finances."

"Now wait a minute, Torrance." I was ready to poke him in his pointy wide nose. "I'll be no burden to my wife. I need more time to finish my sonata. I'll earn my way as a composer."

He waved me away. "I've seen your work. It's good. Your skills on the pianoforte are superb. I've no doubts of you succeeding, but your compromise is now. The problem is now. She must marry now."

The goddess gasped. "No. Marriage wasn't my intent. Your Grace, I don't know him. He doesn't know me. Scandal is better. I don't want an unhappy marriage."

Those expressive eyes said everything she hadn't, that she'd seen the suffering of a battling couple. I had too, and I also wanted none of those memories to become mine.

Thoughts of my mother and the sacrifices she'd made to be a proper marchioness and maintain dignity for her sons weighed on me, smothering my lungs as though one of the duke's heavy bookcases had fallen on me.

I gazed at Georgina and again became wordless. There was no way out of this but marriage. "As a gentleman, I must insist—"

"Noble. Noble." Torrance threaded his hands together. "Here's my plan. You and Miss Wilcox will pretend to be engaged. You will spend a proper amount of time together to keep up the pretense. Teach her a song to sing."

"A pretend engagement," Lady Hampton said. "And a song? She never exhibits in public. She gets too frightened. How does anything you said help?"

"Katherine. Stop speaking about my faults like they are a disease. And I'm right here. I can open my mouth."

"That's what got you in trouble. You kissed a stranger."

"Is it better to do so with someone you love?" The duke

hummed something that chased Lady Hampton to the grand window behind his desk.

He turned to Miss Wilcox. "Seems like you don't have a problem exhibiting in public with Sebastian. That will come in handy at an event I will throw."

"Can't we just go away quietly and pretend this day didn't happen? Your Grace, I don't want to marry Lord Mark Sebastian."

"Let's hope no reporter writes about what they saw. They always make things sound so much worse. But the odds are great that they did. Juicy gossip will make better headlines than any progress in my science meeting."

"I can withstand gossip," Georgina said, but her gaze lowered from everyone to the fretwork carvings of the desk.

"It's one thing to be rash, but to be vilified by gossip in print is abominable," the duke said in grim tones. "It can become unbearable being written about in the paper, day after day. This type of disgrace can last a lifetime. My mother still refuses to come to London because of what she's seen."

This was the first time he'd said anything of the princess in a long time. Livingston mentioned something of her and the difficult battle Torrance had claiming his peerage.

"A pretend engagement," he continued, "keeps Miss Wilcox as a respectable young lady who let her overjoyed fiancé have a first kiss. The public nature of the ball I will throw will find a new suitor, one so taken with you, he'll convince you to end your engagement. There's nothing like a woman's commitment to one young man to attract others. Right, Lady Hampton? It's not uncommon for a heart to be swayed. When love is new or unequally shared, theft is easy. That gossip is bearable—a change of heart, as opposed to the gossip of loose morals or a calculated attempt to entrap a man with a title."

The viscountess's countenance turned a deeper shade of rust. The duke's words seared like a fatty beefsteak over an open flame. We all could be tied to a pit with fire licking and hissing at us as we burned. "Scandal . . . hurt more than pretend."

Georgina looked to the door as if she wanted to flee. "Your Grace, are you saying that a public pretense will let people see his lordship and I as a couple?"

"And as not well-matched. Miss Wilcox, they'll think that you momentarily fancied your music teacher and will believe you when you beg off. Sebastian is known for music and bird-watching. You will have to exhibit at least once or twice to attract positive attention. And suitors will need a chance to see you. Singing will do that."

"Exhibiting in public?" She shook her head. "For once my sister is right. I'd be terrible singing for suitors."

"Yes. No." I cleared my throat. "Your voice is lovely. I've taught friends of my mother's. Music is always on my mind. Everyone will expect my partner to follow suit."

I moved closer to Georgina and pointed to my temple. "Music gets stuck in here. Often, I'm desperate for it to come out. But I'm also desperate to fix this. Torrance's crazy plan will work. I heard you sing. You will dazzle people. The rightness of our pairing will be apparent. Then you will break with me because of a new suitor or an exasperation at my wanting you to perform. Brilliant, Torrance."

"No." Lady Hampton frowned. "This is too risky. Why not beg off now? There's no need for such an elaborate ruse. If they must marry, they should do so now and quietly."

Georgina looked at me like I'd match wits with the angry Lady Hampton.

What could I say? As a gentleman, I couldn't agree to not marry. "You have the power, Miss Wilcox. It's in your hands as I was before. I'll do what you wish."

She bit her lip, then said, "I don't think—"

"Quiet." Her sister covered the goddess's mouth with a shaking palm. Then she lowered it. "Our mother went to great lengths to keep us respectable. You know that. I've done . . . you have too. This must work or everything is ruined."

"No, Katherine. The past has nothing to do with now."

The duke stood and sat at the front of his desk. "Miss Wilcox, what Lady Hampton isn't saying well, is that begging off now will let the ton believe the worst, that Sebastian never had any intention of marrying you. The reporters will ruin your name, damaging you and your younger sisters' prospects. What the papermen love is to stain Blackamoor women for wanting too much or gaining advantageous marriages or possessing things the ton doesn't think they deserve."

"No," Georgina said. "I don't—"

Lady Hampton groaned. "The papers will think you're a doxy."

"Or a courtesan." The word flowed from my lips before I could stop it. "I made the same error in the garden."

The viscountess looked as if she would vomit. The duke closed his eyes and mumbled in Russian.

The goddess in question ran from the room.

Chapter 11

GEORGINA—ESCAPE INTO THE GARDEN AGAIN

Trying not to slip on the polished floors of Anya House, I rushed past Scarlett and Lydia. They were on the stairs but didn't stop their chatter. Me fleeing was a common occurrence.

"Miss, please wait."

The gentleman chased after me.

In the garden, I was close to the maze's entrance, but I stopped. I still didn't know the way to the mews.

"Please. Miss Wilcox. Can we imagine that I caught you? And we do have an audience."

Turning, I could see the window to the duke's study. Katherine's face was pressed against the glass. Then the duke closed the curtains.

"I suppose that means His Grace trusts you to convince me to return."

Lord Mark Sebastian traipsed in front of me. "I don't care about their antics. It's ours—"

"Our antics? Don't you mean mine? I've gotten us into this predicament."

When I glanced at the gentleman to witness his agreement, I saw nothing but smiles. "What is this, sir? Why are you not angry?"

"Because I can talk, actually say words with you. I struggle with expressing clear thoughts with someone so beautiful."

He seemed sincere. "I'm happy that you can be entertained, but our futures are ruined because of my impetuous nature." I crossed my arms. I needed to leave Anya House . . . London . . . be anywhere but here. "Can you point me to the mews?"

"You can't go. We have to work this out."

"I don't want to be a bother. And I don't want someone to feign liking me, even for a moment."

He stepped closer to me. "I kissed you back because I wanted to do so. I enjoyed every moment. If I must pretend to be your fiancé, I'll do it with pride."

I shielded my eyes from the bright sun, which made me squint at him. "I've made such a muddle of things."

"Because you wanted to kiss me. Could I at least be humored? Did you find me irresistible?"

With a shrug I started to laugh. "It was to make my sister angry."

"Well, you succeeded. And as a man who battles to be articulate around the fairer sex, your laughter does nothing for my confidence."

One glance at the duke's window, I saw the curtains move. "They aren't giving us privacy." I groaned and walked to the opening of the maze. "Be a dear and tell me how to get to the mews."

"Can't tell you, Miss Wilcox, not till we know what our plan is. We are in this together."

"Why, sir? Can you tell me that?"

He rubbed at his throat and his breathing became heavier. Then he settled and stared at my face. "Scandals are difficult. My father, the Marquis of Prahmn, he's taken great pleasure in embarrassing people he's had difficulties with or whom he judges as not being worthy. I've seen how their pain is exploited. Once the newspapers are alerted to the slightest innuendo, your good name will be ruined. I saw two young ladies on the stairs. I'm assuming those are your sisters."

"They are Wilcoxes. Scarlett and Lydia Wilcox."

His hand fluttered near mine, but then fell away to his side. "They will pay, you know. My mother's sisters . . . I don't want your sisters to pay for what we've done."

Magnanimous, he was. But this was purely my fault. Sticking my palms into the pockets of my emerald coat, I needed to own the truth alone. "You shall be fine. Why lie about being engaged?"

"We don't have a choice, Miss Wilcox."

"There's always a choice."

He looked away to a white-and-blue bird that sat at the top of the high shrub wall. It screeched something awful. "The magpie has an odd song and terrible reputation, but they are gentle."

"You do love birds. That's not a lie, Lord Mark Sebastian."

"No, Miss Wilcox. And though I made a terrible mistake of assuming you were something . . . someone else, I want you to know that I am sincere. I am gentle. I will not have you hurt in this."

"But you won't be hurt. Men always get away with everything."

"Who will take my music seriously if my personal life is terrible?"

"Lord Byron is scandalous. His poems are adored."

"Miss Wilcox, there's a difference between being a dashing rebel and a laughingstock. I will be a buffoon. And you will be ruined. We can't have that."

This man, this stranger who held me and kissed me back with passion and abandon, wanted my trust. I wasn't sure why, other than maybe he was the rarest of souls, one with a strong sense of decency.

"Believe it or not, Miss Wilcox, I don't want your name in the rubbish papers or any gossip's mouth."

"I don't know you."

"You knew me enough to kiss me." He reached again as if to touch my coat sleeve. "That was a small joke." Standing tall, he lifted his chin. "I'm Mark Sebastian, the son of the Marquess of Prahmn. I'm a composer. I want to write of love and throwing caution to the wind. Our moment in the garden was the closest I've ever come to being bold."

"I'm Georgina Wilcox. I bake a little. I like music. I sing too. Are you any good at creating songs?"

"Very good. Well, sort of good. But lately, I can't concentrate." He tapped his temple again. "My next sonata is lodged in here. I can see it, the beginning notes on paper. There's a crescendo. Then nothing. Livingston says I'm too tense. He says my muse is blocked."

"Muse," I sighed. "Is that a scientific thing? Is it an appendage or something?"

He nodded. "Every creator must have one. I chose mine to be you."

"Sir, if you expect me to be the courtesan your friend wanted, I am not her."

His head dipped. I could see his lips moving.

"Are you praying, sir? Prayer does help."

"No. Yes, it does. And maybe I should be praying for you to agree. I'm not Byron. I don't dare walk on the wild streets. My friend Livingston had to procure a courtesan because I couldn't . . . This isn't helping. Honesty is overrated, but it's all I have."

I reached for him, his coat sleeve of fine blue wool. "Honesty is the best start."

His fingers covered mine. It was an easy touch, a light hold. "Can I pretend to have fallen head over heels for the mysterious Miss Wilcox? Can I for once walk into a dinner and know I have a partner without someone politely looking around for another person with wealthier pockets?"

Looking up to the magpie, who'd suddenly gone silent, as if it too waited for me to gain courage and agree, I decided to try.

"You sound desperate. Our situation is desperate. Maybe a lie is right? No. That can't be."

"Then let's make this as true as possible." He cleared his throat. "Can I be daring and protect you? Can I dance on the edge of scandal and know that my reputation can only increase? This union serves me well."

"You sound envious of Byron. You want to be Lord Byron? He's a scoundrel."

"I want his freedom. And for the first time in a long time, I saw more of my song in my head when I kissed you. So if a little courtship can get you away from scandal, enhance my reputation, and provide the notes to complete my sonata, it will be worth it. I will be truly heartbroken when you break off with me at whatever event the duke has planned."

"What if we do this and you remain unable to compose?"

"I'm positive that a live muse, one talking with me, is what I need. But we could kiss again and test my theory."

"You make me laugh, Lord Mark Sebastian. I trust that the passion to protect me will remain. I'm not to be in more danger with you."

His face tensed. The blue eyes clouded like a winter day. "Of course."

"I need to think on this. Let us go back to the duke's study."

He didn't offer to take my hand, but he walked at my side.

Stepping into the duke's study, the calm I'd regained shattered under Katherine's withering glare.

Chapter 12

MARK—BACK INTO THE FIRE WITH MUSIC

We held our breath in unison and reentered the duke's study.

Her sister and the duke talked low but their odd bickering continued.

As his gaze took notice of us, the duke said, "You should be impressed, Lady Hampton. Sebastian possesses a lovely courtesy honorific. His connections are impeccable. That's all that matters to you."

"Can you be serious for at least a full moment?"

"I have a watch and a schedule, Lady Hampton, pick the time. Oh, look, the young lovers have returned."

The duke stood with vigor next to the frowning viscountess. "Miss Wilcox, have you decided in Sebastian's favor or have you fallen for me again? Must I best a new suitor once more with my cane?"

I offered him a smirk. "If I wasn't in the wrong and didn't respect my elders, I'm sure I could have given you a better fight."

"Stop it," the goddess said, "Your Grace, your lordship. I'm glad you didn't hurt him or break that cane. It looks like an antique."

"It is. Belonged to my grandfather."

Truly? The cane didn't seem Scottish or Russian. It must be something his father's father acquired on his travels. Livingston mentioned something about him coming from a line of explorers. The faces carved into the cane looked African.

Sort of an odd thing to have in a room of Blackamoor women. I hated to think of the liberal duke possessing a relic of colonization or worse.

Torrance picked it up and hooked it under his arm. "Did you two have a nice chat?"

I thought so, but the lady who'd decide was quiet.

"Miss Wilcox, you haven't kissed him again in the garden and changed your mind? If you have, I think that clears me of your sister's charge that I'm your favorite."

Lady Hampton groused. "Heaven help the next woman who'll be sentenced to your love. But do continue telling us your plan. Tell us your gamble."

"My plan? You mean my way of helping your family and Sebastian out of scandal." He offered a hearty chortle, then made a softer expression at Georgina. "Lovely Miss Wilcox. I need to hear your thoughts. Though I begrudgingly think highly of Lady Hampton, I need your voice. I only want the best for you."

The goddess wasn't saying anything. She and Lady Hampton were glancing at each other on opposite sides of the massive desk as if it were some sort of ritual or they were commanding the opposing forces of his chest set.

The duke's gaze swiveled between them, casting each a fretful look. "Well, Sebastian, looks as if you've dodged this entrapment."

"Um. Ah, she didn't." My throat began closing up again, but I couldn't be silent. This was for her and me. "We . . . I thought we'd decided to try."

The goddess had become a statue, motionless and speechless. And I blithered. "Guess I'll never be daring."

Torrance shrugged. "I'm at a loss. And I should've bet the viscountess something very interesting to prove her sister wasn't in love with me. But I don't gamble anymore."

"Sure you don't." Lady Hampton turned her fury back to the duke. "You and betting. I'm sick of all wagers."

"You're sick of losing, Lady Hampton. Your late husband probably made more faulty ones than anyone alive. What made him so desperate? I wonder what kind of married life your husband had? Did the *joy* of loving you add to his short life?"

The viscountess, maybe for the first time, seemed stunned, rendered breathless by this barb. Her cheeks went from fiery red to ash.

"Stop it," Georgina said. "Lord Hampton is gone. He'd be so disappointed to know his dearest friend and my sister—his beloved, tireless widow—couldn't get along. Your Grace, you don't know all that my sister has done for him or our family. You've known us a year. I've watched her for years doing whatever was necessary for us. Please stop."

"It's all a jest, Miss Wilcox. I admire Lady Hampton. I truly do. She's a survivor. Nothing is wrong with that." The duke turned back to Lady Hampton as if to see if she agreed.

It was the viscountess's turn to be wordless, standing statuelike with big black eyes looking close to breaking into tears. Then she blinked, and what seemed soft became stone. "No need to take up for me, Georgina. I don't care for the duke at all. I don't want him in our lives. He's bothersome. Bothersome. And—"

"And manipulative. That's usually one of your complaints."

"Stop it. I wanted to see how long you two could go without bickering. Not even one minute." Georgina's voice rose. "It should be possible. But you two like conflict. You're both forgetting our present concerns. The duke's not well and I compromised Lord Mark Sebastian—"

"I obliged, ma'am," I said and admired her more. The way she spoke held such life and strength.

"Thank you, sir . . . for adding that."

"Lady Hampton," the duke said, "those two strangers seem to get along after a kiss. Perhaps we should do the same and make up. On the lips, or on the forehead like a good little girl?"

The viscountess slunk back.

And the duke laughed. "I'm guessing you care nothing for strangers or me."

"I know my sister. If his lordship is your friend, he's not a good match for Georgina."

"I agree with this, Lady Hampton," the duke said, "and if I had my druthers, I'd find someone who'd be perfect and wealthy enough to help with the mounting debts."

"You know how dire our finances are?" The older sister looked shaken.

The goddess became angrier. "Of course he does, I told him. Why do you think we've been given more time?"

"Georgina. You told him and he acted? And you, Your Grace, you both have kept this secret?"

"Wilcoxes are good at keeping secrets, Katherine. I suppose a duke is too. Yes, I told him, sister. We needed help. And he asks every time he visits on how to be of use. The Duke of Torrance comes to us every week. He pays attention to Scarlett and Lydia."

"And he pays attention to you." Lady Hampton's voice quavered like that magpie, a jealous magpie.

"Yes, Katherine, because he cares. We chat about my fears, my interests. We take calm walks by the river, and he'll not leave until he tries my biscuits."

The biscuits were actual biscuits—I convinced myself of that. I kept reminding myself that she kissed me, not the kindly duke who could buy her and her family everything.

Lady Hampton went to her sister and grasped her shoulders

like she'd shake her from her coat, but instead she hugged her. "You're scared for us? I didn't know. Why didn't you come to me?"

"You don't listen, Katherine. Sometimes it's easier to speak to the duke."

Torrance sat back in his chair. Did a wince come along with his growing smile? "I try to be of service. The girls have grown on me. I want them happy and protected, just as I promised Lord Hampton, my dear old friend."

With a swipe at her eyes, the viscountess let go of her sister. Lady Hampton looked ill.

The duke ran a hand through his curly, sleek hair. "Shall we call a truce for the sake of the family we both love, Lady Hampton? May we begin an alliance?"

"Between us, Your Grace? I doubt it would last."

This back-and-forth was spinning out of control. It was my symphony. I had to conduct all the warring instruments and amplify the lead violin. I needed to act with courage, to take control. Grasping Georgina's hand, I dropped to my knee. "Miss Georgina Wilcox, will you fake-betroth me?"

She blushed again. Her cheeks became very bronzed on her sunny brown face.

The duke's hazel eyes squinted at me, at her. Then he winced aloud and said, "Good. That seems to have worked out."

The viscountess leaned over him, then she turned to the window to stare again at the beautiful maze. "What's wrong with you anyway? You were unsteady in the music room."

"The doctor said an earache, I believe. You know Mr. Carew. He's now my personal physician."

Why did it seem as if Lady Hampton's fingers on the windowsill were looking for the latch to open the glass and leap to freedom? The goddess wasn't the only runner in the Wilcox Family.

"If we'd known you were busy or ill, we'd not have come and these events wouldn't have happened."

"Again blaming me, ma'am. You'd think we were married."

She gasped, and he sort of grinned. "Well, Lady Hampton, all in all, your concern might be the first kind thought you've shared with me."

"It's polite to ask."

Torrance closed his eyes for a moment. "Good to know we're not beyond politeness."

"Excuse me," I said, with my leg starting to cramp. "I hate to interrupt, but I'm still kneeling. Miss Wilcox, and maybe all of you need to accept my faux proposal."

The goddess drew me up and kept my hands. "Yes, I accept. These two will have to do their best to get along."

"Thank you, Miss Wilcox." I wanted to lean in and kiss her but stopped. The duke still had his cane handy, though I wondered if he had the strength to wield it again. He looked to be seriously pained.

"I suggest Miss Wilcox move in as my ward." The duke stretched his palm along the desk. "That will make this faux courtship easier."

"No. No. No." The older sister's tone became pitchy. "No splitting up. And here with your friends and meetings, you'll have her completely ruined."

The duke's hand on his cane tightened. "Lady Hampton, a guardian who fails her charges should be dismissed. It was your wrong claims that caused this."

Lady Hampton opened her mouth, but nothing was uttered. She stepped away, far away, and sank onto the sofa.

The careful duke winced and lowered his chin. I didn't think he intended to offer a barb so sharp that it not only shredded her anger but her pride too.

Torrance sat back, twiddling his thumbs. "I'll have a few small dinner parties to introduce the couple. That's a good way to begin."

"I'm not ready for any party," Georgiana said. "Can we be less public?"

"Less public? It has to be public. He has to show you off to the world. Sebastian," he said, "how do you suggest getting her comfortable?"

"Torrance, what if for the next few weeks Miss Wilcox meets me here for music lessons? I can raise her confidence."

The duke pouted a little. "How does that help?"

The goddess made large eyes at me—a feat of wonderment in jet and gold.

Though I felt myself becoming flustered, I rushed to spit out my idea. "With her as my pupil and 'fiancée,' people would assume that our acquaintance came naturally through our lessons. Held here, they would be respectable. And let's say she'll exhibit, not at any dinner but at your ball."

"Brilliant," Torrance said. "Georgina Wilcox will garner attention. A connection to me will be a benefit. And if Lady Hampton can improve Wilcox Coal in enough time, she'll have money for a dowry. That will be another inducement for a proper gentleman to make an offer and free you, Sebastian."

The goddess looked hopeful, and her eyes lent me energy.

Lady Hampton nodded. "Then Georgina can break with Lord Mark Sebastian because of her new options. A woman who sings well and has the acquaintance of a duke will be noticed. The penniless third son of a marquess won't stand a chance, and everyone will understand her decision."

"Yes, because everyone thinks like you." The duke's tone sounded more heated. Then he smiled or remembered that he should be smiling. "Perhaps I will add something to a dowry. That will take the pressure from Lady Hampton fixing the family business."

"No. We have enough debts." The viscountess waved at him like he was an errant puppy, not a man being overly generous. "No, Your Grace."

"When have I listened to you, especially when you are wrong?

I can give money to whom I wish. If my sister Anya lived, I would dote on her. I will dote on Miss Wilcox, and Miss Scarlett Wilcox, and Lydia Wilcox too. They are as dear to me as anything."

"Thank you, Your Grace," Georgina said. "I trust you."

"Then, it's settled," the duke said. "The pretend engagement between Sebastian and Miss Wilcox has begun. My ball will be after Easter. It will be the first of the season. After forty days of Lent, everyone will come out for decadence. You'll have her ready, Sebastian. I'll make sure Mr. Steele knows that you two will have exclusive use of the music room."

"And we'll brace for what the papers will say," Lady Hampton said. "Hopefully, there will be no gossip at all."

"Let's pray for no scandal." The duke stuck out his hand. "The Assyrian king Shalmaneser III in the ninth century pressed flesh, clasped palms with a Babylonian ruler to seal an alliance. He had the image carved in stone. Let's put our hands together. Come now, you first, Lady Hampton."

"No inappropriate Russian example?"

"None today, dorogaya, my friend."

Georgiana and I shook his hand. The wide-eyed viscountess too. Then the duke looked at the goddess, my faux fiancée. "And you led them all to come see about me. I will never overlook kindness."

"Are you implying that I can't be kind?" Lady Hampton crossed her arms and Torrance said something in Russian that made her roll her eyes.

As those two descended into a new spiral of polite bickers, Georgina smiled at me.

My pulse fluttered.

No longer hesitating, I touched her hand. "It's our Shalmaneser agreement too."

Then notes came to my head. *Da dadum* . . .

"Quick." Taking her with me, I returned to the duke's desk. "Quick, man, a pen."

"No contract or oaths are needed for a false engagement. I trust you."

"The notes." I could see the next stanza clearly. "Please."

His Grace whipped open his drawer and searched through papers until he drew out his inkwell and a dull quill. "Here."

Lady Hampton came near. "What's he doing?"

"Finishing a sonata," Georgina said. She understood and didn't let go of my hand until I put down the pen.

Chapter 13

GEORGINA—HIDING IN PLAIN SIGHT

The drive back to 22 Ground Street was quiet.

Katherine said nothing.

My other two sisters were quiet too.

I wasn't sure what they knew, but everyone understood that when Katherine was angry, silence was best.

With our mother always sick before her passing, she'd become like our mother—disciplinarian, counselor, cook. Our father also relied upon her as if she were the oldest son.

I glanced at her. With the veins on the sides of her neck bulging, my older sister would explode at any minute.

Passing the wharf, the warehouses, the brewery, I wondered if anyone would speak first.

No one.

The gig stopped and we all filed out. Katherine lagged behind, close to Mr. Thom and the carriage.

On the steps of our house, Scarlett raised a hand as if she sat with our tutor. Whatever it was she wanted to say, she swallowed it and started to open the door to the house.

Lydia bolted from her side and stepped in front of Katherine. "Why do you have to ruin everything, Katherine? The duke said he wouldn't be stopping by for a while. It's not fair. It's not."

I bent down to her and held her. Her frustrated little body

shook. Worse. She felt warm. Her fever from last night had returned.

"Lydia," I said as I released her, "we will be going over to Anya House for the next couple of weeks. We'll see him. We'll see plenty of the duke. I'm sure if you are nice to Katherine, she'll make sure you always get to come."

"Good. 'Cause he's my friend." She pointed a finger at Katherine. "Don't take him from us."

The eldest Wilcox had tears in her eyes. "You want to see him that badly?"

"Yes. He's my friend, my *bestus* friend. I love him. He pays attention to me better than Tavis, even Papa. Today, he showed me his special book of maps. He said I could pick any place and be a princess where I wanted." Lydia started to cry. "Anywhere. No one says that to us."

Katherine scooped her up. "I'm sorry. I won't take him from you. I understand. I understand."

The little girl hugged her neck. "He's mine. I need you all to understand. The duke's mine."

When Katherine set her down, the child twirled round and round. Her cream hem bobbed beneath her coat. "A princess. I can be a princess now. That's better than anything."

"You can't love him. He's a grown man."

"*Nooooo!*" Lydia threw up her hands and ran inside.

Scarlett held the door for her but stayed on the steps, looking at me and Katherine. "Lydia is special to us. She loves the duke. We should keep him in our lives for her benefit alone."

Katherine didn't move or speak a word.

She looked hollow, empty.

Lydia was special to us all, but very special to Katherine. When the child was born, our little Lydia almost died. Her twin was stillborn.

Katherine and Mama sometimes acted as if Lydia had borrowed time.

The current Wilcox crisis wasn't about health. It was about

me. "Sis. I know you're disappointed, but I think the duke's plan will work."

"Yes. Everything he does is better. He's made my Lydia love him more."

Katherine was almost never weak. She was solid and strong. Only death and dealings with her marriage to Tavis made her cry.

Right now, her face had become the Thames.

I wanted to close my eyes and run in the house. I couldn't, but I didn't know what else to do.

"I'm sorry," she said. "I'm sorry I'm not good enough. That nothing I've done is good enough. I was a disappointment to Mama. I let Papa down, now I can't protect you."

She turned and started walking, then running toward the Thames.

Mr. Thom pointed at me. "Go after her. Doesn't matter what happened today. You broke her. Go fix her."

He didn't need to say that. I knew what I had to do. I waved Scarlett back to the house, and then started running. "Katherine, wait."

My sister kept going. Soon, we both were at the banks.

The sun had begun to set. It glowed over the waves.

The timberyard building and the shipping warehouse were along the Thames.

The river.

Rough and turning.

Loud with ferryboats and commerce.

Side by side, my sister and I watched things move.

But we stayed still and silent.

The wharf Papa used to own was nearby. The brewery too. Tavis sold them all for gambling debts.

And we did nothing to stop him.

"Why did you kiss him, Georgina? You know how Mama stressed our reputations. You saw how I failed. My carrying on shamed the family. I put so much strain on her weak shoulders. No wonder she died a year after Lydia was born."

"She lived long enough for you to wed. That's something. But Mama was always in pain. She kept getting sick. You didn't kill her. She wanted you happy. She consented to you marrying Tavis and made Papa come around."

Katherine swiped at a tear. "You know our father didn't want 'no broke White man with a title' taking advantage of the hard work his Black hands had done. But that's exactly what I did."

"But Mama thought Tavis was what you wanted. You loved him, and his title made us respectable."

"Respectable to whom, Georgina? Tavis's debts robbed our family of dowries and the marriage opportunities for you girls that his title was supposed to bring. We are less secure because of him . . . because of me."

Her head dipped and she rubbed her wrist against her wet cheeks. "The duke has brought us new clients, but how long do you think he will keep the creditors at bay? We may still have to sell Wilcox Coal to pay off my husband's debt and get dowries for you and the girls."

"Don't do that for me. Maybe the duke's plan will work, and some wonderful person will find me at the ball and not require a bribe to marry me."

"You want to be the coal Cinderella? Or as the duke would say, *Vasilisa*, the heroine of a Russian folktale about a disadvantaged girl who survives and wins."

"I don't look at us as disadvantaged. We're having hard times. Everyone has hard times. Katherine, you know a lot of Russian for a man you can't stand."

She left me and went a little closer to the water's edge as if she chased the sun. "Go back inside. I've lost to the Duke of Torrance. He knows what's best."

"It's not like that," I said. "It's—"

"What is it, then? Another scandal that would break Mama's heart? I need to fix this and make up for all of Papa's sacrifices. I will sell the business I love if that will make you girls acceptable brides for the uptight people across the river."

"I don't want uptight. I don't even know if I want marriage. But you are not in competition with the duke. He wants to help. He's been helping."

Her chuckles sounded bitter. "Then you aren't paying attention. The duke wants me humiliated."

"Why, Katherine? The man has been nothing but nice to us. I asked him to help. He's offered money, but I knew you'd never take it. So, he's gotten us clients. That's his way of doing something."

"Behind my back. All the whispering and walks you two did with Scarlett and Lydia was to tell him how badly we needed his help to be saved." She dropped to the ground and drew arms about her knees. "No one is loyal."

"Loyal to what? Katherine, if you haven't noticed, we're destitute. Lydia might be learning math, but Scarlett and I can add and subtract quite well. Your husband stole money from the coal company. He put loans on our house. That's why we tried to sell everything up to the moment he died. That's why so many things that Mama decorated the halls of our house with are gone."

"Tavis gambled all the time. He wouldn't stop. I couldn't get him to. I tried."

"And you covered up his sins. You did everything for him and financially hurt us."

Katherine put her face to her knees and wept harder. This desperate sound, it always came with a death. Maybe all the lies and secrets had finally been crucified.

Moving to her, I dropped to the ground. A night like this seven years ago, Katherine came home from her great adventure changed. We sat at this river, I put my arms about her. I repeated what I said then. "You're good. Kitty, you're good. A lady should try to leap for the moon and be allowed to fall and fail. But we are Wilcox women. We're proud on this side of the Thames, as proud as the fashionable people on the other side."

"I was a good wife. He saved me when I felt low and worthless."

"And you loved Tavis? You loved him always?"

She didn't answer. I guessed some secrets would never die.

"Well, you were proud he made you his viscountess, but you never forgot you're a Wilcox. A proud Wilcox. You ran the business when Papa got sickly. If we hadn't let Tavis run it, it would still be thriving."

"But I did. I ruined us again."

"We helped. When Papa died, you felt it right to defer to Tavis. No one objected. In two years, Tavis ran a hundred-thousand-pound empire into the ground."

A boat moaned somewhere close. It stirred the waters like flowing tears.

Katherine sobbed and so did I.

We'd lost so much. A new scandal could take away our last bit of dignity. This time it would be the death of Wilcox Coal. "No one will do business with laughingstocks or a company run by Blackamoor women if they feel their sons are endangered of being ensnared by a Wilcox sister."

Her arms tightened about me. "Don't cry, Georgina. The duke is right. Everything will work. You'll see."

She swiped at her face. This version of Katherine, her being open, telling me what she thought, couldn't go away until I asked the question that had burned until the day Tavis died. "Why did you let your husband control Wilcox Coal? You said he'd be good for business. You talked us into it. Why take such risks for a man you didn't love?"

My sister pulled away. "How dare you? I loved Tavis. It might not have been the things you read in novels or the fantasies that made you kiss a stranger, but it was love. It wasn't loud or crazy. It was calm. It was what I needed."

"Needed after what? What happened on your grand adventure? You came back pregnant. What—"

"To the grave, Georgie. I can't speak of it." She started to breathe heavily.

I wrapped my arms about her again. "Keep your secrets, Katherine. I'm sorry that I've almost ruined us or that I reminded you of the worst time in your life. If Lord Mark Sebastian was another type of man, he could've hurt me. I realize how foolish I was."

"You need to think. A gentleman won't keep you safe because of a kiss."

Honestly, safe wasn't my first thought.

Shocking my sister was all I'd had in my head, but the second kiss with him was different. The way his hands felt on my back, the way he touched my hips wasn't safe at all.

"You're impulsive, Georgina. And your folly will affect Scarlett. She's twenty. She might want to marry. No one will want a Wilcox if we are a scandalized family."

"I was impulsive. But, Katherine, we have to see the duke's plan through."

She nodded. "I'll sell the business if I must. I need to give you and Scarlett your inheritance. If I can get the business very profitable, I'll be able to pay Tavis's debts—"

"He's gone. He can't keep making us poor."

Katherine gulped air, that sulphury smell of industry. "I must get dowries and husbands for you and Scarlett. I'll not let the Duke of Torrance spend his money on us, not anymore."

To tell Katherine that she didn't know what I or our sister wanted would make this woman weep again. She'd cried too much. "Let's focus on my faux engagement."

"If no one writes about us, Georgie, we might be all right. No scandal. Then we won't need the duke."

"Well, Lydia has set her hopes on marrying him. In twenty years, if he's still single, I doubt he'll require a dowry."

I said this as a joke. The man clearly loved Lydia, all of us, like sisters, but the flicker in Katherine's eyes spoke of hate, like an angry bear wanting to tear at someone taunting her cub.

Then her jaw eased. "I know the Duke of Torrance waits for no one."

She wiggled free and stood with her hands in the pockets of her coat. "We need to go see what you'll wear for your lessons. The duke will make it a showy affair."

She straightened my shoulders, pushing at the seams of my pelisse. "Perhaps Mama has something in a trunk."

Katherine headed back.

My sister was still trying to hold on to a pretense. She wanted our family to be something it wasn't.

Yet with the folly I'd brought to the Wilcoxes, I couldn't dissuade her. I had no choice but to follow our leader and hope for the best.

Chapter 14

GEORGINA—SISTER IN THE HOUSE

When we walked back to the house, the horse and gig had been put away. The street was vacant.

Katherine stopped in front of our steps. Her gaze, like mine, went to the lit parlor window. I could imagine the Christmas celebrations when we all were here, healthy and thriving. That little room around the pianoforte would be where we gathered.

"Such good memories."

"We'll have them again, Georgina. I'm going to get us out of this problem. It's my fault. I see that now. Maybe it took the Duke of Torrance's interference to show me."

"Katherine, we're a family," I said, but then she interrupted.

"Yes. We'll do it together. I will save this house. And if we're going to try and save Wilcox Coal, to keep it, we need to try now. Can you help? Are you willing to help?"

Brow raised, I nodded. "Of course, I am. But what are we going to do differently?"

"I don't know. Maybe I can get a loan. Something that would be easier to pay back than every club and gaming hell in town."

The vulnerable woman by the water had disappeared. The warrior, ready for battle, stood at my side.

I felt lost. I wanted the human Katherine, the one I could talk to. The one who could be weak and comfortable in her shoes and made me feel fine that I wasn't perfect.

"Are we going to be completely honest, Katherine? Wilcox women typically don't lie, but we sure don't say all the truth."

Katherine shook her head. "They need to believe the engagement is true. One wrong word, or look, could reignite gossip."

"What about telling Scarlett and Lydia that we're still facing the possibility of losing the business or even the house?"

"No, Georgina."

Shrugging, I started for the door.

"Georgie, please. What's done is done. I can't shame Tavis. He's gone and I want him to rest in peace. But from this day forward, I will be more open. Let's start tonight."

"But you said—"

"I changed my mind. Tell them you are engaged to Lord Mark Sebastian, but the engagement won't last. The not lasting is the truth."

My sister was right. We surely needed a new Wilcox tradition. "Fine."

Deciding that some progress was better than none, we pressed inside and yanked off our coats and went to our sisters in the parlor.

Scarlett pointed to seats. "It's come to my attention that you two have some explaining to do. What has happened? The silence is weird even for us."

Standing up tall, I took a deep breath. The air was scented with roses. The parlor always smelled like this, like Mama's cologne water spilled on the rug. Perhaps Lydia found a vial and dipped in it to avoid a bath.

"I'm engaged," I said.

"To who?" Scarlett sank into a chair and started clapping. "The Duke of Torrance?"

I wrung my hands, and then just said the words. "No. Lord Mark Sebastian, a friend of the duke's, proposed today."

"On a first meeting?" Scarlett slipped all the way to the floor. "Wait a minute. The last time someone married someone we didn't know, we got Tavis. Nope. Turn him down."

Well, that went a little better than expected.

Lydia jumped up and down. "My sister is engaged and not to the duke. He's still free. I can still marry him."

Scarlett propped her hand under her chin. "Um, Georgina and the duke would be more expected."

"Tell our sister why that would be more expected." Katherine clapped, rallying this foolish notion. "See, Georgie. I wasn't alone in thinking you loved him."

Scarlett wriggled her nose. "No. She doesn't. But at least we know the duke. And he'd make a good brother. He's been a good brother."

Lydia danced, but then became winded. "If I can't marry him, he'd make an excellent brother. He's so good to us. And nothing but good things have happened since the duke has come into our lives."

No lying to my sisters.

No hiding.

Just the truth. That was a motto I needed to put into action. "The engagement was a mistake. I did something pretty stupid. As soon as it looks like the chances of a scandal are gone, the engagement will be over."

"Stupid's not love." Lydia's eyes sparkled. "Perhaps you got a prince. Then you can be a princess too."

"No, Lydia. He's not a prince. He's a nice man, but he and I will break off this engagement. I believe we'll find that we are not compatible."

Our littlest girl's hands froze. "Then why agree? That seems wasteful and can hurt people."

The child was very smart. There were so many ways to hurt a decent fellow as well as our family.

Nodding, I almost wished I could tell her something that didn't sound so foolish, but the truth was just that. "Then let's be careful when we spend time with him. I'll need you to tell me what you truly think of him."

"Careful?" Scarlett glared at me. "This is horrid. Women

shouldn't have to act like this. We should be able to be ourselves, not fretting to have a husband or keep a pristine reputation. Men don't do that. They carry on and sin all the time."

"But men made the world. Or, they run it." Katherine laid her head back. "I hate this too. But we have to go through with this for our sister's sake, for all of us. Mama made us promise not to court scandal. She made me promise to keep you all safe."

"But she was wrong too," said Scarlett. "With Papa's health failing, she thought Tavis was our answer. He wasn't." Scarlett's voice was harsh but her words were true.

Katherine sat up straight and leveled her shoulders. "You are right. And now we have to know that we, Wilcoxes, are the answer. The four of us working together can do anything. Georgina will get to know this man who proposed. If she changes her mind, I know the way in which she conducts this public courtship will be respectful. Her reputation will remain pristine."

Lydia, smelling like a sweet spring rose, tugged on my sleeve. "Are you happy with this? I mean, I am. He's not the duke, but is this good?"

"Lord Mark Sebastian is very nice. He loves music. I'll get lessons."

"Why?" Lydia asked. "You play very well. Mama made you have lessons. All three of you had 'em."

"Well, I'm sure if she learns anything new, she'll show us." Katherine ushered Lydia to her side. "We will teach you."

"But his instruction is not for pianoforte lessons. He's supposed to teach me to sing in public. I have to sing at the duke's ball. He's holding one after Easter."

"Oh, no." Lydia wrinkled her nose. "You don't ever do that. Lots of luck to you."

"This is wrong." Scarlett bounced to her feet. "So we are just supposed to get to know a potential new brother, but you don't think the engagement will work. Well, I don't mind not getting one if the last is any indication of the quality of men of the world."

She covered her mouth, but her sentiment was shared.

Katherine shrank again, sinking into the blush-pink floral tapestry of the couch. "We'll have to spend more time with the duke at James Street. I suppose that will make things better."

Lydia looked at Scarlett. She ran to her and the two danced.

"I may have been hasty. Take as long as you like in this engagement. It might not be such a bad idea," Scarlett said. "The books in Anya House are stupendous. And downstairs there are meetings. I love science meetings."

With Katherine glancing at her, Scarlett turned away to the pianoforte. "I mean I heard they are great."

My newfound pact for honesty wouldn't include telling on Scarlett. Instead of going to the market, she sometimes dressed in disguises to attend medical seminars or lectures at the Royal Society.

I'd keep her secret. There'd been enough intrigue tonight. "At the duke's house, we have to behave. That includes me."

"If you say so." Scarlett cast the comment over her shoulder as she walked to the little girl, and then dragged the excited Lydia from the room. "Bath time for you. You need to be fresh as a daisy. We'll be visiting the Duke of Torrance at Mayfair soon."

"Can't I have a bath then? Not now. I smell good."

"Now."

"Wait," Katherine said. "Let me do it. Let me spend time with my Lydia. I want to make you look like a princess tonight. You're so special. And so loved by us all as you are."

The little girl came and leapt into Katherine's arms.

"Hey, you feel a little warm, Lydia."

"I don't want to be achy. And I don't want a bath."

Hugging her like she'd disappear, Katherine carried her out of the parlor.

When their footsteps could no longer be heard, Scarlett sat beside me. "So you're going to sing in public."

"Yep."

"And you will have a public courtship because this man is titled?"

"Yes. I mean no. The duke believes that it's best to court in the open, 'cause . . . I have to tell you the truth. I kissed a man to spite Katherine and was caught. A reporter might even have seen us."

"You kissed a stranger? Wow. Oh, my. So bold."

"But now Lord Mark Sebastian and I have to act as if we've secretly courted and are now being open. It will go better when I beg off."

Scarlett paced a little, then stopped. "Because you may have been caught by a reporter you have to pretend to have been in a longer courtship?"

"A woman who kisses a man she hasn't met before is a fool. The man who deals with her only wants a harlot. Who would believe I kissed an unknown man and that was all it was? I'll be ruined. My ruining will ruin you and Lydia."

"The duke thinks this will work?"

"He suggests we court publicly. He also thinks if I do well, exhibit very well, the attention will bring new suitors. Then, it will be more understandable that I begged off."

"Are you going to consider someone else? Do you want to marry?"

It was a possibility. Begging off to nothing might be difficult, but I wasn't Katherine. I'd not settle in marriage. I needed to be inspired. "Scarlett, let me survive performing without looking foolish. I'll see what happens."

"Georgina, you made a mistake. It takes a strong woman to say she changed her mind."

"I wish it was that simple. I've given my word. I must follow this path. You are fearless, Scarlett. But I'm not you. And his lordship wants this faux engagement to help his music."

"That seems odd. You sure he doesn't have other plans?"

I shook my head. "The duke pretty much insisted that Lord Mark Sebastian comply. Scarlett, I need your support. Our sister hates being around the duke. We need him if this is to work."

"Tavis must have told Katherine awful things about the duke, and she believed it. I don't want to talk ill of the dead, but he had to have lied. He lied a lot. He probably lied a lot about the duke."

Something broke up that friendship. The Duke of Torrance's commitment to us, the women our brother-in-law left behind, seemed strong. "How could the two men have been close friends? We knew nothing of the duke until Tavis was dying."

"I can't believe the duke ruined their association. He seems too serious and the man has science meetings. He can't be bad." Scarlett put her hands to my face. "Maybe as we help with this public courtship, we can discover something to help Katherine see the Duke of Torrance is not a horrid man."

It would take a great deal of work to change our eldest sister's mind.

As Scarlett walked in circles, then a figure eight about the chairs, I listened to Katherine's voice telling Lydia she'd have a bath in the morning. "She'll probably gentle her to sleep."

"Katherine does that in Mama's old rocking chair." Scarlett stopped pacing and went to the pianoforte that sat in the corner. "She'll hold her forever."

Scarlett began to play. We kept the simple instrument tuned. I was glad Katherine never sold it.

The notes meshed together and offered a very slow rendition of "Robin Adair." "The engagement, was it the duke's suggestion?"

I lifted from the sturdy Chippendale chair. "Yes. How did you know?"

My sister started to chuckle. "Anything that would draw attention to you would never be a suggestion from Katherine."

"Wait. No. What are you saying? Katherine doesn't want me to have attention? You make her sound narcissistic."

"No. No. No, Katherine is the most humble woman in our acquaintance. But something's happened to her, probably more than we know. She doesn't want any of us to have attention. It's as if the shame she felt long ago stays with her, with all of us."

"How do we hide in London when we're so different from most? We cross over the river, we stand out."

"We stand out everywhere. We were once well-to-do. A cultured, loving family with two parents who built a fine house. We inherited our father's successful businesses. Women were running them just fine. Now it's all a memory."

The music changed. The tune was slower. It made the keys mourn.

"Katherine's unrecognizable now from the sister we had growing up," I said. "We have to help her. She's become a bitter widow. She's bitter and hurt, but she talked to me, just a little bit, before we came in."

"Perhaps we should say something to the duke. He might be able to do something."

"Katherine will hate us if we involve him. We'll have to figure things out." I leaned over and kissed Scarlett's brow. "I trust you and we're smart. Like Papa said, we can build anything."

"In science, the seed is destroyed to germinate a plant. Things have to be broken down to make something new. Can we truly survive Katherine, or any of us, being destroyed?"

I stood near the pianoforte. "Let's try. Scarlett, I didn't like the way the duke looked today. He's young, in his thirties. As long as nothing is seriously wrong, Lydia's nonsensical plan of marrying him in twenty years might work."

This was London. Old, wealthy men married young women all the time. I just hoped someone would get really smart and make the duke fall in love, truly in love.

"He's a good-hearted man," Scarlett said and made a run along the keys. "He's very kind to Lydia. Men typically don't have time for children."

Bumping her with my hip, I sat beside her. "Duet time. Come, let's speed up this tune."

We played "Robin Adair" faster and faster, until we were both laughing hard. Smoke should have been coming out of the pianoforte for all the pounding of the keys.

With a dramatic flourish, Scarlett finished our piece. "Well, if your fiancé ever heard you play, he'd truly love you."

"Why?"

"Georgie, he's a musician. They adore music and you might've missed how he paid attention to you from the moment you walked into the garden."

"You saw?"

"Yes, I might've come down and gone exploring. And then there are a few academic papers I borrowed. Men are so untidy. They left them after the meeting let out."

Oh, no. We were liars and thieves. "Just be careful with whatever you have. We'll put it back with my first lesson. Monday."

"Good, I have two days to read them all."

Leaving her to study . . . and plot, I headed to the kitchen to bake. I wished I was as smart as Scarlett. Today had proved me to be an impulsive version of Katherine.

I needed to do better and figure how to survive singing in public as the new fiancée of Lord Mark Sebastian. For everyone's sake, I needed to be bolder and brave and inspired by music and truth.

Chapter 15

MARK—WHAT HAD HAPPENED

I climbed into the carriage of the Earl of Livingston after a Sunday morning with my mother. I escorted her to church at Saint George's, and then retired to a wonderful brunch at Prahmn's in-town home, a lovely house on Grosvenor Street, not too far from the duke's Anya House.

"You always look a little miserable when you come from your mother's. Did she foist upon you more marriage candidates? Doesn't she know a man in his twenties is not to be tied down? Marriage is overrated."

"Livingston," I said, losing the will to talk, "Mother was the same as always. Over toast and her favorite jam and biscuits, I was told of the many women she and her war council of friends thought would make a proper wife."

My mother did seem extra animated or even fretful. Had the gossipmongers begun saying they'd seen her youngest son attempt to ruin a woman at Anya House down the road?

"Yes, Livingston. She wants me to have a proper wife. That means a woman of certain breeding with a large dowry."

"A third son's lot. It's not like your elder brothers will share their fortunes."

Gerald was heir to all of Prahmn's assets. Christopher came back from his naval career at sea and did as Lady Prahmn wanted and married one of her handpicked, wealthy, proper women.

"I'm just glad you offered me a way of escape, Livingston. Lady Prahmn can be a bit much to take. I'm not partial to her innate belief that she's always right."

"Mothers are women too."

Though the earl was the kind of friend who'd risk his soul to rescue you or lend aid, he wasn't the type to be reasonable when it came to women or marriage.

Turning down busy streets, I half listened to my friend talking about his current research. He seemed animated, discussing something about inoculations and blood. Something excited him about Carew's presentation at Anya House.

"Yes, they put blood from one dog to another through a duck's quill. A duck's quill. Both lived. The physician didn't exaggerate. And having too much blood didn't kill the pup."

"What about the duck?"

"No. The dogs. Blood is a necessity for life. We need to learn more."

"To be sure." That was my common response to one of Livingston's monologues.

He glanced at me over his spectacles. "You're not paying attention."

"'Course I am . . . sort of. There's a lot on my mind."

Livingston knocked my shoulder. "Sebastian, I know your mind is elsewhere. You're not humming. You have no paper or quill."

"Perhaps they are all being used for experiments—the paper, quills, my head."

"Sebastian."

"Please, go on. I'll try to stop dwelling on Brooks's rib roast. Hopefully, they'll have the claret we had last week. It will be a delicious combination."

My friend began talking or, more so, lecturing again.

Windblown brown hair bobbing as he recounted more of his research, the earl seemed very pleased. If he were a layman, not a peer, he'd be a renowned physician.

"Sebastian, are you in there? You don't look right. Let me guess. The mad Duke of Torrance forced you into some scheme after I left. What did he bet you?"

Torrance betting? "What are you talking about?"

"It was a long time ago, but he has a history of outlandish betting. I've been waiting for when he'd start again. What did he get you to do?"

Livingston was a man who loved to research and gossip. Would he keep the false nature of my engagement to himself for me, his dearest friend?

I thought not.

So, I'd offer him a bit of the truth. "Well, I've been convinced to show the woman I have an understanding with, my secret fiancée, how to exhibit with confidence. She can sing."

I'd heard her hum. It was good. I'd learn if Miss Wilcox could truly perform tomorrow.

"Secret fiancée? I'd heard that you'd had a little fun recently, but fiancée? An engagement? Please say you are joking."

I should've known he'd heard of the commotion at Torrance's. "It's true. You're one of the first officially to know. My secret entanglement will be made public at the duke's ball. Unless it's already in the gossip columns."

My friend's mouth opened. "You're serious. Have you lost your mind?"

"Yes, and I've committed myself to teaching my fiancée to exhibit with confidence. It will be a test for her. My life will be exhibiting. The wife of a composer should understand."

Livingston looked distraught. He clung to the edge of his seat, his nails digging into the tufting. I suppose he waited for me to burst into chuckles and say this was a lie.

I couldn't admit that to him. The truth would be all over London by tomorrow noon.

"My hope, sir, is that she takes to it. I want her to be happy as my bride. But I must prepare myself if she can't and breaks with me."

"Looking for the worst already?" Livingston shook his head. "He got to you. The duke and some woman got to you. I cannot believe this."

"Who? Who got what?"

"Women. You can't trust them." His face turned beetroot red. He sputtered like he'd been shoved off a cliff. "You've fallen prey to a pretty vixen. And Torrance has helped. I can sense it."

"Sir, you seem to be falling ill, perhaps we should not dine tonight."

"Not ill. Horrified. I'm horrified for you. Don't you know what marriage will do to you?"

Squinting at Livingston, I folded my arms, readying to raise a shield against his onslaught. "You're visibly repulsed, and yet I've not told you who or how or why?"

The earl sank on the seat, pouting like an angry child. "A woman of marriageable age sunk her hooks into my friend and made him come up to scratch. All this time, I thought you were dedicated to music. You've been courting a woman. She's the reason you haven't finished your composition."

"Calm down, Livingston. You're coming unglued. Talk again about your research. We won't say another word—"

"You had to have compromised someone. I know you, Sebastian. You haven't had time for anything."

This was true, but I had to make this course of action seem logical. "Well, when we talked about me meeting a courtesan in the garden, I had . . . I had already happened upon a woman with Torrance. We met again in his garden. Your talk of a courtesan and gardens made me relax and talk with her. I proposed before I knew it."

"You idiot. You weren't listening." His fist rose up as if he'd punch through the carriage roof. "I said you'd meet Madame Zula in a few weeks in Covent Garden, not any garden. I can't believe I'm to blame."

If Livingston was going to take my half-told story and put the blame on himself, then so be it. Perhaps that would keep the man from gossiping about it.

My friend took a big breath. "Tell me you're trying to find a way out."

There was a way if the duke's plan worked. But announcing the full truth to the earl would make it fail. My friend wasn't the malicious sort, but him being this agitated was as good as calling up the papers and announcing the scandal in gory detail.

Having become so jaded by his own miserable marriage, Livingston couldn't help but say or do the wrong thing in pursuit of rescuing a friend from the altar.

Like my music, I arranged the facts in my head, then stroked the key and exhibited. "I knew she was what I wanted instantly. I'll marry this girl. My life is changed for the better."

There. That sounded right. It possessed enough zeal and contrition and passion that Livingston seemed moved.

He nodded as if he'd analyzed every word. "You're actually in love. You wish to marry."

"I do. And I will unless she changes her mind. So, please don't ruin this for me. Say nothing."

My friend was plotting. His hatred of marriage might be something to aid me, stirring up other candidates to sway my intended. "Who's this woman? Maybe there's a scandal I can uncover and force her to release you."

No. No. That's not what I wanted. "Wait, Livingston. I don't want to call off this marriage. If the young lady changes her mind about me, so be it. But no dredging anything up on her or her family. I'll never speak to you again. I'm committed. Miss Wilcox is . . . is a goddess."

"Wilcox . . . Would that be a sister of Lady Hampton?"

Oh, dear. Of course the man would know. "Yes, the sister of my intended, Lady Hampton, is a nice woman, but a little prickly. She tried to talk her sister out of marrying me. I assume she's only looking out for her sister's welfare."

"You've become engaged to one of the Wilcox sisters? The daughters of the coal king."

What? Coal king? As in a lot of coal or a fortune in coal or ruling a country with coal? "I suppose. Georgina Wilcox is probably one of the prettiest women I've seen in a long time. Of course you've heard of them. You make it your business to know about pretty women and gossip."

"It's not gossip. It's insurance. Someone has to protect the men from marriage-minded mamas or viscountesses who are trying to ensnare unsuspecting men for their daughters or their sister."

"It wasn't like that at all. Lady Hampton is horrified. She will work to change her sister's mind. She thinks I'm a fortune hunter."

"Perhaps those Sundays with your mother have indoctrinated you. You've become the fortune hunter Lady Prahmn expects."

That was a dismal thought.

I hoped Georgina or Lady Hampton didn't think that of me.

"Well, I'm glad we are both friends of the duke. Torrance is very protective of the Wilcox family. He can attest to my character."

At this, Livingston chuckled.

I've seen this man laugh at a lot of things, but this was a maniacal, evil laugh.

"What is it, sir? Why does Torrance trying to protect the young woman make you sound unhinged?"

"Do you know the duke's history? You don't, do you?"

"Tell me." I sighed and steeled my stomach. "Tell me what you know."

"Torrance fought to gain his title. The decision in the Court of Chancery was very close. The opposition to him claiming his due was intense. Many hated his parentage."

"Why? He's half Russian, half British. Our kings are Hanovers. Many in the ton have Germanic or Prussian roots. Why be bothered by Russians?"

"It's not the Russian blood that caused the problem. It's his Blackamoor roots. He's half that as well."

Livingston didn't stutter. And I remembered the cane. Torrance had said it was his grandfather's. It was African. One I'd assumed he acquired from other people, not belonging to his ancestors.

"I know it's hard to tell, but he has them. Ghanaian or Ethiopian, I think. Torrance's line can be traced to the Black prince of Tzar Peter's court."

"I didn't know."

"Well, you only met him a year ago. It's not something that comes up in simple conversations. It seems not to matter to you. You chose Miss Wilcox. But color or, more so, race matters to some."

My gut tightened. My friend, I thought from all his research, was enlightened. And I had seen Beethoven perform with George Bridgetower, the Blackamoor violinist championed by the Prince Regent. And I worshipped the compositions of Chevalier de Saint-Georges, whose talent rivaled Mozart's. I'd come to understand that music arose from the soul. It had nothing to do with skin pigment.

"Do you have a problem with Torrance having his title, Livingston? Will you object to my wife and not bow to a daughter of the coal king?"

He tugged at his wilting cravat, retying it. "I've watched the dissection of human flesh. Everyone looks the same underneath. Shed blood is red from all bodies. I've no problem with Torrance. Or your prospective bride. I hate the institution of marriage. I wouldn't wish it on any man."

My stomach eased. I wanted to believe my friends all thought the same. Yet, I knew my father, and probably the heir, wouldn't be so liberal. The spare with his past affairs might be, but Christopher was married and back in London.

"Sebastian, if I were of the marrying sort who needed funds, the wealthy trade class would be where I searched. The Wilcoxes are prime targets. But I have money and will never wed again."

Except for mistaking a gentle lady for a courtesan, I believed I was a reasonable judge of character. "Thank you, Livingston. It's reassuring to know my friendships are good."

"Thank me when I get you out of this entanglement."

"Well, if the lady has her head swayed by someone in a better position, I think it would only be fair to step aside. Thankfully, you'll not marry. I don't want to lose dear Miss Wilcox to you, Livingston."

There.

My tone sounded merry, musical. I hoped it started Livingston thinking about eligible bachelors who might show enough interest that a young woman could plausibly renege on my proposal.

But with his vigilant stance against marriage, I doubted he'd encourage others to try to court Miss Wilcox.

Twisting his hands, I saw the cogs in his head turning. If not trying to name potential suitors, what could he be thinking?

I sat forward. "Tell me the gossip on Torrance or the Wilcoxes that you must be holding back. You seem to be plotting."

"Nothing on Torrance or the Wilcoxes, I'll have to ask around—"

"Please don't. I don't want this engagement to get the wrong attention."

"I don't have to do a thing. Once you speak to your father, he'll cause a stir."

"He doesn't pay attention to me."

"The man will now. He'll take this engagement personally."

"What does Prahmn have to do with anything? My father will be cross that I, ah, um . . . arrived upon this decision without including him. But we've never seen eye to eye on much."

Livingston blew out a long evil laugh. "You won't have a meeting of the minds on this. Your father tried to influence the Court of Chancery to prevent Torrance's accession. He didn't want a peer who was Russian or Blackamoor."

My father did a lot of ugly things. This, I didn't think him capable of.

But I didn't have a reason to suspect Livingston of lying.

"I wonder, Sebastian, if Torrance supported this alliance to make the marquess madder than an angry bull."

That was a good way to describe my father, mad and bullish. "Prahmn's away on holiday. This should be concluded before he returns."

"What? No. No eloping!"

Couldn't tell Livingston the plan was to gain more suitors for Miss Wilcox so that she could gracefully beg off at Easter. "I suppose. But our wedding will be after I've secured my spot in the Harlbert's Prize for Music. Once the plans for the Royal Academy of Music are created, like the Royal Society, I will have a position. All Harlbert's Prize winners will be considered."

"You aspire to a profession? I suppose that's one droll way of earning an income."

Livingston was a first son and the heir. He could pursue whatever he wanted. He had the income of his lands to afford his leisure and his research, particularly in the area of disease. It was a noble cause for him. His father died from smallpox.

Nonetheless, my friend was bitter from his wife's abandonment. She ran off to Scotland to gain a divorce. The action, the gossip, left him broken, changed.

"My friend, I have to afford my new wife. I don't want coal money. The Marquess of Prahmn will definitely cut off my funds."

"The Wilcox woman, this secret romance, is the cause of not finishing your entry." He groaned. "She's been a distraction. You have to agree. You've been struggling. I arranged Madame Zula for nothing."

"You give my apologies to the madame. And now that I've secured Miss Wilcox's affection, I can concentrate. My submission has to be a brand-new piece, one never played for the public. It has to be perfect. Every time I get close, the notes go away."

"Well, you're too high-strung. You need to relax. A gentle-woman isn't the answer. That's why I arranged for you to meet Madame Zula at *Covent Garden*. You'd have had your pick of *her* flowers, instead of finding one in Torrance's garden."

Livingston sat back and drew his hands to his head like he'd been seized with a headache. "You actually want to marry Miss Wilcox? Where have I gone wrong? Should've gotten you to Zula last year."

We were silent until the carriage stopped at 60 St. James's Street. Brooks's.

As I started to step out, Livingston stopped me. "Let's get to the betting book. I bet you a guinea that you'll falter and won't marry the Wilcox chick."

Why would I take a bet I hoped to lose? "I'm not going to wager on my future happiness. Now, come on. Let's go in. Still buying dinner?"

"Yes, I'm buying dinner. And I'm floating you a guinea for this wager. We're going to find that famous book and write this bet in it. That way when I win, I'm not emptying your pockets."

"If that will get you to not mention this anymore, then fine."

As we entered the establishment, the Duke of Torrance was leaving.

I nodded.

He did too. "See you tomorrow for my friend's first exhibition lesson."

With a doff of his dark hat, he walked to the other side of St. James's Street and boarded his carriage.

He didn't have the cane.

The man looked better too.

My friend knocked my elbow. "Wonder if he already put a bet in Brooks's book?"

Chuckling, Livingston went inside.

And I sort of stood there, my mind filling with questions. Were Miss Wilcox and I pawns in a bigger game, one of the duke's making? Did he take advantage of this scandal to even a score with my father?

Livingston popped back out. "Oh, come on, music man. Tell me about this latest piece over a fine dinner. We'll fret about bets and weddings later."

"Right." I followed my friend into Brooks's, wondering if all this faux engagement was a gamble for a duke with secrets.

Chapter 16

GEORGINA—A FIRST LESSON

The music room in Anya House should be a place of miracles. The gilded trim, the walls bearing the magical color of rose always stole my breath. It was the same hue reflected in the Thames when the sun set. I felt I should cover my head in reverence as one did entering church, but I let my freshly washed curls be free.

Pulled up high with an onyx ribbon, the tight curls fanned out like a crown.

Lord Mark Sebastian stared at me for a long moment. Then he danced his fingers along the pianoforte's keys. "Miss Wilcox, let's try the hymn again."

Did he not like what he saw?

Was I unkempt or had he never seen a woman be free?

Waiting for his rhythm to settle, I no longer refrained from twirling. My gold-and-yellow dress, we'd found at the bottom of Mama's trunk. The gathers about my natural waist dated the skirting but enhanced my figure and made the gown ready for movement.

"I can't concentrate if you keep spinning. It's also difficult for you to sing, Miss Georgina."

"Almost on a simple first-name basis."

"Well, ah . . . I . . . Miss Wil—"

"Georgina. Sir, you can be familiar. We are pretending to be a couple enraptured. Servants and guests stopping by for science meetings can poke their heads in or slow-walk past and see me twirling to your music. We are on display."

He fingered a few more keys. "I need you closer, here by the pianoforte concentrating. Your voice is quite lovely, surprisingly so."

My mouth formed the words *thank you*, but my tongue refused to say it. Instead, the part of me that wanted to run, that wanted to escape scrutiny, went for an argument. "Why? Why does my voice surprise you? Courtesans can sing. Women who love the sun can too."

He looked up, but his hands never missed a note.

"It's surprising because you actually have the passion to carry a tune. You could be proficient with practice. You definitely must learn to breathe and sing."

"An unexpected answer. An honest one."

"Would I—" His hands made a run on the keys. "Would I be anything else?"

"I don't know, Lord Mark Sebastian. Could you be?"

"I could be Mark. I mean I am Mark. I need you to count and breathe."

"And be familiar?"

He closed his eyes. "You're beautiful. I'm attracted. I need you to sing."

His words rushed out, so honest and free of guile.

Yet, this made me self-conscious. I forced air slowly across my lips. "Fine. I will practice, even if you find my voice surprising."

This time he stopped. His piercing gaze cut into me. "Uncles, parents, and paramours gush about a young woman's prospects. They are often wrong and are being generous to solicit my help or to attract my attention. Seems a third son with connections is still a worthy alliance."

"Thank you, I think."

His brow rose. He must find my sentiment odd, but I didn't want to hear how my voice was "good for a woman with my background." I didn't care to know how his stumbling upon me, thinking me a courtesan was refreshing.

"You seem annoyed, Miss Wilcox."

"And you seem too easy with this arrangement."

"Why should I not be? You sing well when you focus. I get to play upon this extraordinary instrument and listen to how the room I designed captures echoes and elongates notes. Since Torrance is not your uncle or any relation, and he's not come to see us practice, I suspect he's not a paramour. This is not some game we are playing for his benefit."

"We *are* playing a game. We're trying to survive a few lessons and hope to hear no gossip."

"It's early, Miss Wilcox."

"I choose to believe we've not been discovered. I'm not ruined. You are free. Then I don't have to sing at a ball."

To celebrate, I spun and watched the brocade fabric of my skirt billow. "You should concentrate on the joy of being out of these circumstances too."

He bit his lip, then settled again playing the pianoforte. "I don't claim to understand women and what mortifies you or gives you pause or makes you dance. But you're a beauty, Miss Wilcox, and you can sing. You're not taking this lesson seriously. It makes me mad to see talent being wasted."

I stopped mid-twirl, walked back, and laid my palm flat on the waxed surface of the musical instrument. "I bake too. Does that make me a baker?"

"Wouldn't know, ma'am. I haven't had your biscuits. The duke has."

He sounded jealous, and it made me laugh. "His Grace is like a brother to me. You needn't be jealous. You're my fake fiancé. I will not cheat on your sentiments, but if you have a better attitude, I might bake for you."

When I chuckled this time, he did too. "I'm sorry, Miss Wilcox."

"Georgina."

"Georgina, I'm very deliberate when it comes to music, everything about it. And . . ."

"And what, Lord Mark Sebastian?"

"It's Mark, the composer who can't finish his sonata. I had it and now the notes have stopped again."

"I'm sorry, Mark. But that's no reason to grouse. And grousing doesn't bode well for our ruse. Remember, we are pretending to be a couple intended for matrimony."

"How far do we take this, Miss Wilcox? My mother has sent a note requesting to see me. If she's heard of my secret alliance, she'll want to meet you prior to the duke's ball. Would you like to meet her? Are you willing to take this ruse to that extent?"

Looking at his earnest face, charismatic blue eyes, I did wonder what his parents looked like. What traits of theirs did he have? From whom did he get his dimples?

"Georgina? I have a friend who complains I don't listen. I think I understand now."

"I heard you, but I don't know what to say. What if I meet her and like her? Won't I feel awful begging off. And what if she doesn't like me? Well, then there will be hard feelings. I don't think we should create more hate for the world. What say you?"

A puzzled look shadowed his face.

"Well, my lord, you might not know what I mean. Or maybe I've asked too many questions. Forgive me."

His mouth opened then closed, but no words came out.

"Please, start playing again. I'm ready."

He did but this time it was a song I did not know—something slow and haunting. "Your singing is good."

"From a waste to good? What do I owe the change in your assessment?"

He lifted one hand and tapped his temple. "You're purposely trying to distract me. Is something wrong? Or is this the reason you don't exhibit, no one has the patience to play for you?"

"Very simple, my lord. Fear. Crowds looking at me make feel very chilly. You can't sing cold." I listened to how he played, the command he had on the pianoforte. "And you have no fear of the public?"

"I have fears. I fear beauty being spoiled, of not creating beautiful work."

I offered him a smile. "Those are greater fears than I've known. How do you withstand?"

He flipped through sheets of music. "At least I summon courage. Talent isn't a torture."

"You're neither a torment nor a torture, Mark."

"That is good. For kissing you is the thing that creates fantasies. I'd not want you to regret that moment or any moment I perform for you."

Closing my eyes, willing my cheeks not to become fire, I turned about the room. The hymn Mark played was by some man named Pleyel. "This composer wrote songs of worship and vanity."

"Sort of the same thing, Georgina. I suppose some worship an intelligent woman. Others think it vanity."

"Did you just call me vain?"

"No. Helen Maria Williams wrote the words you half-heartedly sing. She is to blame for exposing you."

He laughed and smiled at me and loosened his cravat. "You are a wonder. So bold with your questions, but timid when you sing. I'm sure practice could change things."

Perhaps the frustrations he'd shown at me, at himself, even the smidgeon of jealousy of the duke, were the things that kept him from writing his music.

He tapped his finger. "Enough of a rest. On the third count, let's begin."

Trying to get that breathing thing right, I sang.

> *"While Thee I seek, protecting Pow'r,*
> *Be my vain wishes stilled,*
> *And may this consecrated hour*
> *With better hopes be filled."*

"What is the hour, sir? We've been at this a while."

"Barely two hours. But that was better, Georgina."

Going to the window, I looked at the empty street. The sun poured through the glass.

"We'll take a break in a moment." My teacher's voice pulled me back to him, not outside this house and running to see where the lane led. Never did learn where to find the shortcut to the mews.

"Perhaps we should try another stanza," he said in a louder voice, then yanked a watch from his blue waistcoat. "Actually, let's keep going. We have another hour before our time ends."

That sounded sad.

We were not very far into this piece, and I knew no more about my teacher or what he longed to compose.

"I will miss this music room tonight. It's very feminine compared to His Grace's study. And it's very different from my house."

"How so? Doesn't everyone have Russian tapestries? Torrance had very specific requirements. He wanted it designed for a woman's pleasure. I think it might be a tribute to his sister or something for his future duchess."

"Then, I think he must add more paintings like the watercolors behind you." I came back to the pianoforte. "Do you have sisters, Lord Mark Sebastian?"

"Afraid not. I met Miss Scarlett and Lydia Wilcox. They seem full of life."

That was a beautiful way to describe the two, or even our house on the other side of the Thames, full of stomping and arguments and slammed doors.

"Yet, having seen the concerns and worries that gentlewomen have, I'm not sure I'd like to see a sister having to put up with these rules only to be coerced by my parents into a match that may make sense on paper but not her heart."

"If she were truly in love, that wouldn't make a difference to your parents."

He looked away, concentrating on the ivory keys. "Silence. I guess that is an answer." I bit my lip for a moment. "When they find out about our faux alliance, will they be angry with you?"

"Yes, but this ruse will be done by the time my father returns from holiday. If my mother knows, I doubt if she will say anything."

"If your father, the Marquess of Prahmn, does find out about your escape from my clutches, what will happen?"

"I'll have to sit through a few lectures and threats of being cut off. Life will go on. And then my mother will have a new list of vetted candidates awaiting me at the next ball."

That sounded wretched. Yet, the gentleman was so matter-of-fact, removed from it. "You don't mind being a rebel, even a fake one?"

He lifted his hands and dropped them to his hips, exposing more of the check-patterned waistcoat that swaddled a muscular physique. "I suppose I don't. But don't credit me with false bravery. I'm cavalier because I know this is temporary. The separation from truth and make-believe helps me."

This made me laugh.

"But such negative talk, Georgina? 'Clutches' sounds criminal and you shy away when I call you gorgeous. Why?"

Now it was my turn to be quiet. I shrugged.

His gaze stayed on my face. My cheeks felt warm, felt stroked by an invisible touch.

"*Da dum. Da da dum.*" Mark flew from the seat to the nearby table. He ripped the cork from the inkwell with his teeth, then began furiously writing. "Yes. Yes. Yes."

The pleasure in his voice scared me. Then I realized he'd written another stanza in his piece.

I stayed quiet, hoping that whatever anointing he'd gained stayed with him, set in his soul to give him all the music he desired.

Ten minutes passed.

His quill stilled.

When his eyes closed, I knew it was gone. The inspiration or the notion had departed.

"Sorry, my lord."

He scooped up the cork, which had fallen by his boot. He closed the bottle and put down the quill. "Nothing to be sorry for. I have another piece of it."

"What are you working on? Why are you so perplexed? You're more angered over this than your parents' lectures."

Mark turned to me. "You wouldn't understand."

I stepped closer and examined the page, even humming what I saw written. "Try. This is lovely."

"You read sheet music? Of course you would, Torrance only knows exceptional women." He turned back to the pages and put his hands to his head like he wanted to smash his skull. "This will be my entry to the Harlbert's Prize if I can finish. It's a once-a-year competition. If I win, it will be the beginning of my career."

"A career for a gentleman?"

"Yes, some of us aren't wealthy or wanting a wife that's an heiress. I wish to be a recognized, celebrated composer."

"That sounds vain. A new piece that will dazzle the committee will make you renowned? How odd, to need a prize to say you're good when you already are."

He packed up his papers, then went back to the pianoforte. "I freely admit not understanding women, but I think you need to understand men a bit more. Just because I say a thing, doesn't make it so. Prahmn will never just take my word."

"No, I quite understand. You need a group of men to tell your father."

Lord Mark closed the instrument just as Katherine stepped inside. "Are you ready? We really need to get back to . . . Lydia. Am I interrupting something?"

"Lady Hampton." My music teacher bowed, took his papers

and went to the door. "No. I've just asked Miss Wilcox to study a little more before our next session."

"You do the same. We meet here tomorrow?"

"No. Wednesday. I have an appointment tomorrow."

"Where will my fiancé be off to?"

His gaze marked me with heat, like it was impertinent to ask. But this was me crossing that line of make-believe and caring. I did care. I wanted Mark to achieve his goals.

"Bird-watching in Hyde Park. I'm hunting for the rarest of flying creatures. The habit relaxes me. My current selection of a muse is temporal and testy."

He left and Katherine gave me a look that was a cross between *Well done* and *What have you done?*

I took her by the arm, looking forward to our drive back to Ground Street. Perhaps she'd educate me a little more on men and their need to be accepted by everyone except those who care about their dreams.

Chapter 17

GEORGINA—PRETTY GOSSIP GIRL

Wednesday's lesson started in classic Wilcox fashion: chaos. We, the daughters of the coal king, lay claim to Anya House. The running and jumping of the moat—the steps began immediately.

With Lydia feeling better and Scarlett not disappearing for one of her missives—escaping to the Royal Society or reading a stolen science paper—the full Wilcox clan came to visit.

I watched from the music room as Scarlett interrogated the duke about some sort of advancement in heart research, and Lydia literally danced about the man, telling the duke of the latest story I read to her. I'd picked up a used copy of *Pride and Prejudice*, published by T. Egerton.

The author's name was unknown, but at least the attribution was more than the words "By a Lady." This time it read "By the Author of *Sense and Sensibility*."

One glance at my music teacher thumbing through his sheet music made me feel a little more sympathetic to his creative plight. *Pride and Prejudice* was on its second printing but the author couldn't put his or her name to the work. Celebrated, thousands of copies in print, and the credit was given to an anonymous person.

For Lord Mark Sebastian, the thing he labored upon, put all his hopes in, this sonata would be his first published work. He was brave enough to want his name on it. Yet, so driven to make it perfect, he might never finish.

"Stop running, Lydia." Katherine's voice echoed down the hall. Dressed in more gray, varying between shades of dingy silver and dull pewter, she moped behind the duke. She seemed forlorn and even forgotten.

The younger Wilcoxes delighted in the duke and all the opulence his Anya House offered. It made me understand Katherine's feelings and even my teacher's of not being enough.

"Georgina, please come away from the threshold. We need to begin. Are you ready?"

"I am." I crossed the big room and stood at the pianoforte. "I told Mr. Thom about you."

His brow wrinkled. "Excuse me?"

"He's my family's man-of-all-work. Mr. Thom is a good man. He hopes you are one too."

Mark put down his papers and offered me his full gaze. "You cannot attest to this? I mean, my willingness to play along with our false relationship should say something."

"It does. You are kind, but you could also be bored. You might find this a great amusement."

His brow wrinkled. "Oh, I see."

"I mean, you've told no one, right? You're waiting for the ball for the big revelation."

Now his smile returned. "I shared our false love with my closest acquaintance. He completely disapproves and is trying to save me from ruin."

My eyes popped or exploded or both. "What? He doesn't want you with the likes of me?"

"It's not you, per se. Livingston hates the thought of marriage. He thinks it's an abomination."

Mark stretched his fingers, then settled his palms on the oak bench where he sat. "If you wish for me or my friends to not want this faux arrangement, say so. Don't cozy around. You question whether I see you. Yes, I do. You're a beautiful woman. One of the prettiest of my acquaintance, Blackamoor or White, poor or rich."

When worked up, this man said exactly what he felt. He held nothing back. I liked that. Offering him my widest, brightest gaze, I said, "Thank you."

"Why thank me for saying the truth? Even though our arrangement is a fabrication, there's tension between us—it's almost like you and I forget that part, that we are playing a game."

"Does that mean you don't mean what you've said?"

"No. I mean, yes. I mean . . ." His lips snapped close. His eyes followed for a moment. Then he whispered, "I meant exactly what I said. I like you. I think you're gorgeous. So don't assume something to be negative. I don't do well under pressure."

He peered at me fully, like it was the first time seeing me. "You say I want men to approve of me. That is true. I want you to as well."

His blue eyes captured mine, and I felt that breathing would be a problem whether I sung or not. I clutched at the buttons of my pelisse. I hadn't taken it off yet, so I could run outside in the cooler weather. Didn't think I could will myself away.

"Sir, I don't mean to cause strain. I have questions. I ask them all the time of friends and family. Perhaps, in this room, I feel safe enough to ask you."

"Georgina, I want you to be able to ask anything."

"Then it is settled. Outside the music room, let there be decorum and scripted behaviors. Not in here. Within these walls, let there be magic."

His hand moved along the keys. Then Mark rushed to a side table. I ran and uncorked his bottle of ink as he readied his quill. "*Da da dum. Da da dum. Dum.*"

His fingers glided about his paper, making quarter and half notes as easily as they did on the pianoforte.

Mark wrote and wrote. Then he stopped, seized me about the waist, and waltzed me to his hum. "*Da da dum. Da da dum. Dum.*"

Then he stopped, bowed, and backed away. "A thousand pardons." His face reddened. "But you did say in here there's freedom. I paid attention to that part. Actually to all you say."

"You're celebrating. Did you finish your sonata?"

He sank onto his seat at the pianoforte. His hands moved quickly across the keys and I heard the tune of "Robin Adair," a bit of Handel, and something wondrous with lots of chords. His pace slowed. The music lowered to a whisper.

"No. But I'm closer. I'll have it. And I think that you, you are to blame."

"For the distraction?"

"No, for the little shifting of my world that's letting the music seep out. I, for one, will never regret you kissing me. I think I will have a song birthed from it."

"Pregnant from a kiss. That's dangerous."

"It happens, I've heard."

"If you say so, your lordship."

His lip curled. "You're doing it again, being bothered by my compliment."

"Doesn't seem to bother you to do the complimenting. I do appreciate it. It's better than being insulted."

"I can't believe you hear insults."

"Not all the time." Moving to the nearby portrait, I stared at the new collection the duke had installed. These faces looked like politicians or prime ministers. "I try to avoid the noise. But walk the wrong street. Go to a market unfamiliar with my family. Read a newspaper or gossip pages when something political happens in the colonies or in Parliament around abolition, and you see slights. It's hard sometimes to miss them."

"I'm sorry."

"When you say I'm pretty out loud with no caveats or regrets, your words are easy to hear. I hear all of what you say."

We shared a glance again. Then he looked away and began searching through his papers. He seemed to have an infinite supply of pages with notes. His handwriting was very good.

"Found it. Georgina, let's work on your progress." He played the Pleyel hymn.

"While Thee I seek, protecting Pow'r,
Be my vain wishes stilled,
And may this consecrated hour
With better hopes be filled."

When I started the second stanza, he stopped.

"What, my lord? Did I get the words wrong?"

"That's not it. You do well for a line or two. When it's time to raise your pitch and hit the high notes, you lose your confidence. Then you gasp."

"My lungs failed me again. I'm trying my best."

His fingers moved across the keys seamlessly as he looked toward the window. When he looked my way, the notes changed, not smooth, not even. It felt a little chaotic.

Then I was trapped in chaos, waiting for something familiar to touch me, to grab me and settle me in place.

"Pretend it's a question. Deep breath to draw it to you, then push. Push it away. Let's try again." The music ramped up but I couldn't get past the first line. "Miss Wilcox?"

"My voice falters. Exhibiting is difficult when people look at me."

"I'm looking at you, Georgina."

"You are and it doesn't feel as if I've done something wrong."

He breathed in and out, the same rhythm he played. "It's you and I in here. There's no shopkeeper. Neither Mr. Steele nor any of Torrance's staff have interrupted."

"Steele is a nice fellow."

"Am I a nice fellow?"

He was. My height, and a little stocky but with muscles, which I was sure powered his arms as he played, I thought him quite fine and enjoyed the way his deep dark eyes became a little bluer when he made magic with the keys. "Maybe too nice, my lord."

His lips curled. "I've never known my nature to be a problem to anyone other than you, Georgina."

"But you say you've never met anyone like me."

His chuckles sounded merry, but then he stopped. A serious expression consumed his face. "What happened to the bold woman who kissed a stranger in the garden?"

"What do you mean? I'm standing right here."

He shook his head, played a few more chords before stilling his fingers. "No. You're timid. You're singing how you expect me to want to hear the music. There's no freedom in your tone. It is very closeted. The slightest bit of distraction causes you to muffle your words, then your breathing gets ragged. You're not singing with everything you can."

"But I'm in tune. I'm singing the words. I honestly don't understand."

The duke came into the parlor. "What's going on? Not arguing in here too."

"No, Your Grace." I bowed. "My tutor is trying to explain movement or singing. I don't know."

Torrance lifted my chin. "The bits I hear are good."

"The bits over Lydia's shrieks." I shook my head. "I don't know."

The duke tugged on his emerald waistcoat and clapped his hands. "I don't hear any music, but I don't see any kissing. That must mean serious things are happening here."

"Things are going, Your Grace," I said. "Lord Mark is trying, but I'm still too nervous to sing with freedom."

"She's good, Torrance, but she'll never gain the interest of the entire ballroom if she can only sing a few lines without becoming nervous."

"Perhaps there needs to be other beautiful things to distract Miss Wilcox. You solve problems by running. Dancing is a different kind of movement." The duke came to me with his hand extended. "Sebastian, play a good waltz. I wish to dance with the prettiest woman in the room."

Being the only woman, I assumed he meant me. "I just talked with my music teacher about too many compliments."

"Nonsense. There's never enough." To my teacher, he said, "Play something livelier."

I looked at Lord Mark. He seemed a little uncomfortable, but then began to play "Robin Adair."

The duke had my hand and twirled me slowly around, following the perimeter of the room. All the people in those new paintings watched us. I felt giddy.

"Imagine, Miss Wilcox, you're in a lovely gown of emerald satin."

"No, a warm rose. Like this room."

"Nyet, you must stand out. Different from this. You'll be a vision. A Vasilisa come to my ball."

"Ah, your Cinderella."

"Yes, you must be in something bold. Something with lots of lace. Imagine all eyes on you."

My heart drummed. "Like the horrid people along the wall glaring at me?"

The duke stopped, then nodded. "These paintings are not right. I must do something else." He turned to our musician. "Faster, sir. Faster."

His steps quickened and I kept up. "You must be feeling better, Your Grace."

"I am. But sickness is a part of life. I'm glad when it doesn't last."

Images of Mama, her lameness, touched my mind. Even Lydia's illnesses. She'd had a fever a few days ago. I stopped dancing.

"What's the matter, Miss Wilcox?"

"Just thinking of the past, Your Grace. We've lost a lot. Death has visited too often."

He took my hand again. "We must not let it win. You fight every day to get out of bed and live in the light. That's what my mother believes. I do too."

A sadness I hadn't heard or seen was in his eyes. Before I could ask him what made him glum, the duke whipped me away, spinning me around the room.

I followed his lead and soon our waltz caught the rhythm. "We're chasing the music, Your Grace."

"Chase it. Sing it. Win it."

Was it right to sing out loud while in the duke's arms? Mmm. No. I hummed the melody instead, but the Duke sang in my stead.

"What was't I wish'd to see?
What wish'd to hear?
Where's all the joy and mirth,
Made this town a heaven on earth?
Oh! they're all fled with thee."

Full circles, dizzying turns, he stopped, and then led dizzy me to the pianoforte. "Now practice the song. You know the words. I've been listening to the practices."

"Robin Adair" was a fun song, but Pleyel's hymn was sober.

With a glance to the duke, then my tutor, I closed my eyes and went for it.

"When gladness wings my favored hour,
Thy love my thoughts shall fill;
Resigned when storms of sorrow lower,
My soul shall meet Thy will."

When I was done, I felt sick. But the duke clapped.

Lord Mark had a grin. He approved.

"It is something, sir," the duke said, "to see a woman find her place in the world as simply as in a song."

My tutor stopped and closed the pianoforte. "You're proficient. You're talented, Miss Wilcox, but the duke won't be able to dance with you when you exhibit."

His tone was tight, almost touchy.

"No, he won't." Katherine entered the music room. "If he did before your performance, His Grace would be singling you out. That won't bode well. The gossip is out that there's a secret engagement involving my sister and an unidentified gentleman, a peer. Everyone will assume it's you, Your Grace. That's not our plan."

My sister had a newspaper in her hand. She laid it out on top of the pianoforte. "Someone saw you two at Anya House. They must know the secret lover is the musical Lord Mark Sebastian."

In black and white, a cartoon portrayed a skinny fellow leaning on top of a pianoforte kissing a large Blackamoor woman. The Gilroy cartoon made a cruel joke of both characters, but especially the one who was made out to be me. She was abnormally twice the size in comparison to the fellow. The figure seemed old, ugly, matronly—a terrible wallflower, a horrid tall Meg.

Yet, the very worst thing was the comment bubble above saying *Massa is cute.*

"They spared no trope in this foolishness," the duke said. "Lady Hampton is correct. The caption, *Miss Coal finds a peer*, is particularly telling."

After another look at the horribleness, I questioned if it was us—Lord Mark and myself—or someone trying to tarnish everyone at Anya House. "Very odd. We were in the garden. Yet, the artist put us in here. Look—the exact number of paintings on this wall are the same as in here." I counted again, noting the five picture frames in the cartoon matching the five watercolor landscapes hanging behind the pianoforte. "This is this room."

Mark picked up the paper. He paled and looked up at me. "This is terrible."

My heart pounded. "This is a warning to you, my lord. The cartoonist withheld your name, this time."

"They want him scared away," Mr. Steele said. In his arms were several copies of the same *Morning Post* newspaper. "Lord Mark Sebastian, it's pure intimidation. We had so many reporters here the day of the science meeting. I should've been more on guard."

"This is a home, Steele. Not a fortress." The duke retrieved the paper, balling it in his hand. "My residence is meant to be welcoming. It's a place for science to progress. Cures for the illnesses no one speaks of can be discussed here."

"There was a slight mention of the meeting next to this scandalous illustration."

"It's not enough. More will suffer." The duke's fisted hand trembled. His face filled with the frown of a man caught in fresh mourning. "Sorry, my dorogaya, my Anya."

My sister, maybe for the first time ever, glanced at him with compassion. "There will be more time, Your Grace. More days for good works." Her voice was low and unusually warm. "Everything, including medicines, takes time."

The duke turned from her to his man. "Steele, our people, our sources couldn't stop this?"

"No, sir. No matter what I offered, they refused. I have good knowledge that all the Town's rags will have similar images, but they will probably reprint this one. The artist, the terrible Gilroy, is popular."

The butler used some choice foreign-sounding words, but I could tell they were curses by his harsh, grumbling tone. Then I knew that dorogaya was an endearment.

"I'm horrified," Katherine said. "Miss Coal . . . They might as well have said Wilcox. Everyone will know it to be us."

"We must fight this, madam," Mr. Steele said. "Many fear interracial and even interfaith marriages. These two have become another target in the bigger fight against abolition."

"Practice is done for today." The duke ripped the paper in two. "As much as it pains me to say, Lady Hampton is right.

Mr. Steele too. This faux romance must become bigger and more public. Joy must defeat the darkness."

"More public? No, Your Grace." My throat closed up a little. I wanted to pound the top of the pianoforte in protest, but Mark must've known.

He put his hand along mine, his finger stroking my thumb. Then he slyly drew back as if he were merely aligning his papers. "Torrance, what do we do?"

"You'll still be able to beg off at my ball, Miss Wilcox," the duke said. "But I insist that your heads are up and that you and Sebastian be proud of your courtship, no matter how false it is. None of the Wilcoxes are made for the shadows. You will not be condemned because of a fool's cartoon. Nor can Anya House."

My feet felt cold thinking about being out in London as a couple, for the world to see and mock. "I don't know, Your Grace."

"Only a fool hides a diamond in the dark. Only a fool abandons a gem in the dark because he's too afraid of it being seen in the light."

With the newspaper pieces crumpled into a tight ball, he handed them to Steele. "Burn this. Then get my largest carriage available tomorrow. We must do an open walk. Lady Hampton, you and I shall chaperone the couple at a park."

My sister looked terrified. "Are you sure we shouldn't stop?"

The duke took her hand, then released it as quickly. "It's bigger than us. It's a fight worth having. One I wish I'd fought years ago. We can never run scared. It never works."

I nodded. "You're right. We must lift our heads."

My music teacher looked oddly pleased.

"Are you committed, Sebastian?" the duke asked. "I understand—"

"Of course," Mark said, his voice sounding deeper and very strong as he gathered his things. "I want to fight too. I look forward to Hyde Park tomorrow. Good evening, Your Grace, Lady Hampton, and my lovely faux fiancée, Miss Wilcox. I'll be proud to take a walk with you."

"Maybe show me some of your special birds, sir."

"Yes, and we should dance a few times at the ball, now that Torrance has shown me you are proficient in that as well. Your Grace, I'll handle her waltzes from now on. She's my betrothed."

"Of course, the faux suitor takes precedence."

Mark's smile and bursting dimples shone for me. And I suspected he was happy—happy to help and happy to claim all my dances, taking them away from the duke.

Chapter 18

MARK—SUMMONED BY THE MATRIARCH

Upon returning to my residence, I found a note from dear Mama shoved under my door. My mother didn't deliver it. She wouldn't come to my bachelor's lodgings on Jermyn Street. She was not a writer, and my father dissuaded her from the idea of having a scribe like a few fashionable ladies had.

Yet this note, on Prahmn's blue stationery, was written in her hand.

I'd been summoned, summoned by the Marchioness of Prahmn. Running a hand through my hair, I centered in front of my mirror. Not too disheveled. I should go now.

Delaying a visit to my mother was not a good idea. My father was still on holiday. This would be the best time if I wanted to avoid arguments.

The Marchioness of Prahmn never argued. She never raised her tone, she merely offered a look that wounded you in the heart.

Setting my papers on my desk, I looked at the music I'd written today. Miss Wilcox *was* my muse. There was no denying my reaction to her, her turns of phrase, the openness of those magical eyes—she healed the blockage in my mind. A few more lessons and the sonata would be done.

Walking out of my lodgings, I headed on Jermyn Street to the mews. Collecting my horse, I rode to 75 Grosvenor Street and arrived just before sunset. Mayfair addresses—white houses, red-brick manors, limestone and Portland cement, palatial residences like Anya House—filled this expensive part of London, reaching heights to bask in the pinkish rays that the inhabitants probably assumed they owned.

It would be very dark by the time I left. I doubted I'd stay the night. Tossing the reins to a groom, I said, "I'll not be here long."

The fellow nodded and I headed into the house.

Like the Duke of Torrance's Anya House, there was plenty of marble and gilding. Yet, this hall was decorated with statues, copies from the Italian Renaissance.

Prahmn wouldn't pay for an original, but he'd not let anyone know differently.

I marched past the footman and was intercepted by the butler, Mr. Reginald Chancey. "Lord Mark, I had not expected you until tomorrow."

I held up my mother's letter. "I decided to act early on the invitation."

Chancey had been with the family since before I was born, a wise, cheery man with serious brown eyes that matched his deeply sable skin. "You'll find her in her parlor. She had asked for no visitors until tomorrow."

The fellow seemed insistent, but I couldn't wait. Waiting made things worse. Waving the note again, I headed deeper into the house. I didn't stop until I happened upon Mama's parlor.

Sprinting ahead of me, Chancey announced my presence, shook his graying, balding head at me, then headed out, probably returning soon with a service of tea and an ear ready to listen.

When I entered, I found my mother, eyes covered, lying prostrate on her favorite chaise with an arm bent over her brow.

Blossoms of the floral silk covering the chair that wasn't blocked by her slender body bloomed. It made her seem as if she lay in a garden. The heavy scent of lavender lit the room. I went to the dying fire and poked at coals, then I tossed on new ones from a shiny brass bucket by the spit.

I wondered if this fuel was from the weekly delivery and if it was from Wilcox Coal.

"Mama, are you well?"

"Miserable," she said, before rising like a phoenix. "You came early."

She waved at me to come kiss her hands, drawing me deeper into her special place, a parlor complete with a harp that no one played, in front of a bookcase brimming with rare editions that no one cared to read.

Lacy mobcap on her strawberry-blond head and wrapped in swaths of satin and silk robes, she looked like the very elegant woman I'd always known. "Sit, Mark. We need to talk."

"That's what your note said. Will Father join us too?"

"Prahmn is still . . . still on holiday." She choked out the words but stopped short of saying what was readily known. Father had gone away with another new mistress to Scotland or somewhere abroad.

Deciding whether to take a seat in the Klismos chair by the fireplace or the hard Chippendale closer to the chaise, I decided instead to stand in this very yellow room and take the tongue-lashing like a man. "You requested to see me. I'm here, let the punishment begin."

"Mark, you're very dramatic." She sort of giggled, probably trying to ease me into a false sense of hope. "I think you get that from me. So you're forgiven for interrupting."

Chancey returned with a tray of cups, a silver teapot, and a bottle of Father's best brandy, Calvados, an apple brandy from Normandy. "This is for the both of you."

The butler had seen millions of scandals in the Sebastian line, and nearly all of the Sebastian men had courted folly. My brothers were no paragons, my father no saint. I'm not sure where that put me on the scale of things.

"Sebastians are better at hiding things than you, Lord Mark."

Chancey's tone sounded like I had disgraced my ancestors. "I will be near with the medicine, ma'am." He bowed and left us.

Mother made herself tea and poured more than a jigger's worth of brandy in her cup. "Mark, it seems that you had a little bit of an interesting week last week."

I chose the Chippendale and took a cup of the chamomile sans the brandy. "It was interesting. I made a lot of progress on my sonata. I think I will be able to submit this year to the Harlbert's Prize."

"Um. Mmm. Oh, this is hot." She looked at me and batted her sea-blue eyes. "I was talking about your newest friend. What do you have to say?"

There were a lot of things I wanted to say, or question, but my mother wouldn't listen. Like my friend Livingston, she listened to gossip. Of the particulars of my life, unless it had to do with my or my brothers' choices of a bride, she heard nothing.

"Mark, I asked about your new friend. I should know about who you spend your time with."

"Truly? You wish to know? You want to know about the people whose music rooms I designed? What about the pupils I've garnered? What about the committeemen who will hear the sonata I'm working—"

Her expression, drawn cheeks frowning while sipping on brandy and tea, said *No, no music.* "Mark, I gave you music to help you be expressive. You lost your words so often."

"How could they be heard over Prahmn screaming at you?"

Her lips disappeared, then she took a long swallow from her cup. When she and Prahmn fought, his odious temper silenced me and her.

Thank goodness he was not here. As much I thought I could now handle his critique, my tongue, as it did at the worst times, would betray me.

"Tell me, Mark. It's your mama. Humor me. You always do."

A joke? That's what I was?

"I once tried to tell you of my enthusiasm for a painting. You laughed as I wrongheadedly bared my soul. Why should I expect differently?"

This had been my life. I was a spare's spare. I would probably only be useful to the Sebastian line if that transfusion thing Livingston was working on came to pass.

"Mark, is it true you are engaged to one of the Wilcox girls?"

"How do you know anything about that family?"

"I know enough, Mark. They supply the coal to the house."

"So you're upset that I'm rumored to be in a relationship with a tradesman's daughter?"

"Are you?"

"You know how rumors go. Where did you get such nonsense?"

"The papers. There's a sketch that looks a lot like you on a pianoforte."

"Am I the only man in London who can play an instrument?"

She slurped more from her bone china cup. "You've been very different, Mark."

"Different? It's been a week since I last saw you. We sat at the dining room table where you went through a list of suitable candidates. I remember half were industrious daughters of wealthy men of trade. Why are you letting this cartoon upset you? And if it were true, why would my choice be different from yours?"

"Your choice made the paper. That's what's different. If your father were here, he would have a conniption. The upset would be grand."

"What do I do that *doesn't* cause him to be disagreeable?" I shot up, turning to the books. The gilded pages I fingered were tattered and smelled of tart aged ink. "I am not in a scandal. That doesn't even look like me in the *Post*."

"Ha. So, you do know what I'm talking about."

"I read the paper. It's a scandalous sketch. Gilroy always looks to cause an upset."

She seemed to accept this, sipping less liberally on her doctored tea. Then she rose up and pointed at me. "The Dowager

Livingston said that's you in the *Post*, you and your scandalous love."

Livingston.

My friend, the paranoid fool, told his mother. The network of mothers in Mayfair stretched far. They went to work and contacted the Marchioness of Prahmn. I knew it was a risk telling Livingston. But it also made the faux relationship more believable. If my close friend knew of it, the illusion of a connection between myself and Miss Wilcox seemed truer. I breathed a little easier knowing our scheme had begun to work.

"There's a young woman I care for."

"A strumpet."

"She is not that. I don't want her to suffer for being free enough to dance to my music. I wish she were always about to twirl. Mama, I want her to be wildly herself."

Yet, as I looked, my mother's face turned redder and redder. She feared my association with Miss Wilcox.

"My heart breaks for you, having such pitiful and small-minded beliefs." I stepped toward the door. "I need to go, Mother."

"Mark, wait. I love you. I want you to be happy. But you know your father will refuse to support your marriage to anyone he doesn't approve. I won't be able to save you this time. I won't be able to help at all."

My mother did her best for me.

Though she never stood up to my father directly, she aided my moving out and having my lodgings far from here. She insisted that I had the best lessons even when Prahmn balked. I lost count of the music room designs I'd influenced because of her bragging of my skills.

And she never laughed when I told her I wanted to be a composer.

Those might seem like small concessions. But they were huge in the house of Prahmn. "Goodbye, Mama. I'll see you Sunday. We can pretend this conversation never happened."

"Mark, don't go without answering. Are you engaged to the Wilcox woman?"

"Her name is Georgina Wilcox. And she is the finest person I know. Mama, I'm not asking you for anything. I know your position. But know that if I marry, it will be someone I love and respect. I'm interested in Miss Wilcox. What I feel was not public, but it has now become public. These papers put her in danger. I won't stand for that."

She flopped onto the chaise, draping her silken hands across her face. "Oh, what will become of you? Of me? My heart—"

"Mama. Listen. I know you can hear me. I'll never put you in a position of choosing between me or my father. I know where your priorities align. I won't ask you to help again. Go back to the war council and complain of your hardheaded son."

"You make jokes, but can't you see the little things I've done? And trust me. I know marriage is difficult. You must understand that such a union will require a lot of support. A marriage to Miss Wilcox will require your father's blessing. You won't have it."

"Does it matter? Prahmn's away with his latest . . . friend. Not exactly a paragon of strength or virtue. And you haven't had much success making him do what's right by agreeing with him."

She popped up and came very close to giving me a well-deserved slap.

"Sorry, Mama. Prahmn is your choice, one you made for your family, your sisters, not your heart. I'll choose my happiness. I cannot speak to what Miss Wilcox will or will not do. We will have to see. None of this requires your approval or my father's."

Mama paced, then flopped again onto the chaise. "What of your obligations to your family, Mark? Our public names—"

"You have the heir and a second. They're following the paths you want. As I've always known, I'm inconsequential to the plan. You've all made that very clear. So I respectfully decline taking your advice. I'm following my heart. I know not where it will lead, but it's going to be exciting."

"What are the coal woman's aspirations? She obviously wants a title like her sister. None of us will ever call her Lady Mark Sebastian. She will be snubbed, cut direct at every turn. Are you ready for that? Are you ready to be cut away from us?"

Georgina's words about some people not being kind when she shopped in places where they didn't know her family struck me to my core. It burned like acid deep in my chest when I realized "some people" were my family. "I suppose I'll have to get used to being in places where no one knows the Sebastians. That means I'm going to have to learn not to care."

"Not care about your family? Mark. Family is everything. You can't walk away from it. And what of the Harlbert's Prize committeemen? You think that they will think differently from Prahmn? You believe they will award a prize to a man of the ton who chose a coal wife?"

My music meant everything, but my honor was my soul. "Of all the slights I'd ever endured from my father, this one from your lips has to be the worst. Mama, if you think for one moment I'd turn away from love because of dark-hearted fools or my mother's hatred of Miss Wilcox's beautiful brown eyes and skin, then you don't know me."

I left her speechless, blinking, and rushed out to the landing.

When I trudged down the stairs to the grand hall, she called out to me. "Mark, I'm just trying to look out for your best interests."

Standing in the shadow of the warrior Augustus of Prima Porta, she called out, "Mark, you didn't agree. You always agree."

"If I ever did, it was because I wasn't listening. Mama, I did hear your words this time. I've heard them with my whole heart. I respectfully disagree."

Walking out of the house, I heard her run back to her parlor, her tragic chaise, and the brandy she used to comfort herself.

The butler was on the portico directing the groom to get my horse. Chancey gave me a nod. "Standing on your own is hard, my lord. But it's the first act of walking in your own power. Have a good evening, sir."

Reciprocating with a dip of my chin, I went to the drive and mounted my horse, then started back to my lodgings. I needed to finish the sonata. My father wasn't going to take my refusal very well. They were divided on many things, but concerning whom I would marry, the marquess and marchioness were in agreement.

I needed my own income.

More than anything, I needed to succeed without their help. This desire wasn't about Georgina or the Wilcoxes. This had been building for a long time. I must find my power and stand tall.

No woman wanted a man who couldn't be independent. No composer who wanted to set the world on fire could lack a backbone. Seeing Georgina and this ruse through was a sort of training process. I had to succeed and claim a future that I made with my own hands.

Chapter 19

GEORGINA—A RIDE IN THE PUBLIC

Covering for my sister Scarlett's sudden disappearance—she'd had Mr. Thom drive her to some lecture—I insisted we take Lydia with us to our first public appearance in Hyde Park.

We wouldn't have to pay for someone to watch her, and Katherine and I could keep our eyes on her.

Last night was a bad one for the little girl as she sweated and coughed until the sun began to rise. Her fever broke this morning.

By noon, she was sore but determined to go see her duke. Who could stop the recovered ball of energy?

Our little Lydia seemed overjoyed to see him, hugging his legs like he'd disappear. In this grand carriage, she sat between the duke and Katherine and wore a blue bonnet on her sleek dark hair, nestled in a thick coat to keep her warm. The spring chill commanded the morning.

The little girl looked so happy and leaned on him. He didn't seem to mind. The man rallied in her attention, or was it because the connection annoyed Katherine?

"Smile, Lady Hampton," the duke said. "You seem uncomfortable, as if you've been forced into my carriage."

"It's an open landau, Your Grace. Everyone can see."

"That's the point, dorogaya. That tawdry artist Gilroy has been in my home and chosen to make a mockery of an adorable couple. A potential love like this shouldn't be denigrated. It must be celebrated."

Adorable? A tall Meg and a shy, stocky composer? Maybe. I wanted to say *fake couple*, but I understood his point.

Lydia climbed onto his lap. "There's Lord Mark."

The little girl waved. Her antics placed her all over the duke, knocking off his hat, exposing his curled, onyx hair.

"Lydia, get off him." I tried to coax her to be calm, but she wrapped her arms about his neck. "You don't mind, do you?"

"Nyet, my lovely dear." His arms enfolded about her and he chuckled. "Ah. Happy . . . warm, little one. Are you well?"

"Oh, yes, My Grace. Mine." She shot a petulant pout to me, and then Katherine. "All better now that I'm with you."

He made her settle, like a doting big brother. "No map adventure in my library, my little one, if you don't mind Miss Wilcox or Lady Hampton. And we must have our map time, my newest dorogaya . . . mine."

Katherine's cheeks darkened, and I was confident that "dorogaya" wasn't an insult but something loving like "sweetheart." Had the duke been openly praising my sister all this time?

"Princess hour. Princess hour." Lydia winced as she rubbed her hands together. "I'll be good."

Katherine glanced the other way. Suddenly, the Serpentine, the big lake in the park, was of more interest.

My gaze swiveled back to my approaching music teacher. Strong steps in dusty boots, loose cravat, carrying a satchel surely brimming with organized papers, he walked with zeal, even pride, to come to us, a carriage full of people of color.

As he came closer, I saw his handsome face, his focused dark blue eyes, which appeared intense and lovely, and the laugh lines that led to big dimples. If I were vain and armed with this newly discovered appreciation of a casual, confident man of the arts, I think I could agree with the label *adorable fake couple*.

Lord Mark tipped his hat, then climbed into the carriage and sat next to me. "Fine morning."

Lydia doffed the duke's hat. He laughed and signaled for his driver to begin.

My music teacher drew from his bag a gold tube and held it close to his wide chest as if it were his treasured sheet music. "I've brought my trusty pocket scope to hopefully see some birds. How are you, Miss Wilcox?"

"Fine," Lydia and I said at the same time.

"Ah, Miss Lydia Wilcox. I meant to address your sister, but I'm glad you are well."

"Yes. No more coughing. I'm feeling fine."

"Little one, you have been sick?" The duke held the child up like he could spot that she'd had a cold.

"Just a little, but nothing out of the ordinary for the spring, Your Grace," Katherine said. "Sniffles and a fever."

The duke squinted at her. His brow creased as he settled the child next to him. After touching her forehead, he made sure her crooked bonnet was secure. "A cold head can get you sicker, little one. You're feeling a little hot now."

Lydia put her head against his shoulder.

His gaze at Katherine hardened. My heart sank as I thought, *Great, another man repulsed by a sick child.*

"She's a little warm, Lady Hampton." His tone sounded stiff, even more accusatory. "Perhaps we should've deferred."

My sister looked panicked, but said, "She's fine. She refused to miss today."

"All the beautiful flowers can make for scratchy throats," Lydia said. "But I'm not sick anymore. No missing this. I didn't wanna not see you."

"She does get sick often in the spring, Your Grace." I added this to try to make the duke look easier, but little Lydia was sick often throughout the year. I always thought of Mama when the child didn't feel well. I bet Katherine did too. "But she was dancing this morning, like always when she comes to see you."

He put his arm about Lydia and again kissed her brow. "I'm glad you are here too. I would make the world stop for you."

The happiness bubbling in the child's eyes brought tears to mine. Katherine's too.

"And I have so much I want to tell you. I drew the map. And . . . there was something else . . ." Lydia shivered. "I'll remember."

"Well, you will tell me later." The duke took off his scarf and wound it about her shoulders. Then he put a finger to his lips motioning to Lydia to let me and Lord Mark chat.

My music teacher seemed distracted, gazing toward the plane trees with his scope to his eyes. In Hyde Park, so many of the trees stood tall with the bark flaking off like camouflage.

"If you are not going to pay attention to Miss Wilcox, Sebastian," the duke said, "we could've postponed."

"Bird-watching with my faux fiancée will be my pleasure, Torrance."

The duke tapped his lips. "The last time you had that pocket scope, you were telling me of birds and the music room at Kenwood."

Mark's mouth opened and shut. No words came out, but he shook his head.

He gave a loud sigh. "Being here where things are true, not painted, Torrance, is why I prefer Hyde Park than a stuffy estate."

"No inside." Lydia coughed and said it again. "We wanted to go for a drive with the duke today."

"Settle, sweetie," Katherine said. "You're always a little irritable when you don't feel well."

Lydia pushed my sister's hand away and clung to the duke's arm. "I'm fine. I'll be good."

One would think Katherine beat her by the way she shivered and protested.

"You're with me, my sweet." The duke imitated Katherine's voice. "And that means you'll be good."

"Yes. Yes."

He turned to Lord Mark and me. "Why don't you two take a

walk, then come back. Then you can talk. We can chaperone from here and meet you at the Serpentine."

Katherine shot heated glances at me, but when my music teacher grasped my hand, I couldn't see anything but the path called Rotten Row.

Bright yellow daffodils led us to another arbor of plane trees. These had more peeling bark that exposed the tender, lighter skin underneath.

"Do you think, Lord Mark, that these trees shed secrets to cast them away or do they expose them to the world?"

"And good afternoon to you too, Miss Wilcox. I see we start immediately with your questions."

"Well, you know me. And I don't know how long you'll stay?"

His brow furrowed.

"Use your scope. Look at the stares."

The man didn't take my hint to look at the passersby who glared or those who casually peered our way. He motioned for me to follow him down the path.

I did and tried to focus on nothing but the flowers and the towering planes.

When ten minutes or so passed with no talking, I stopped. "The trees seem brave, sir. Braver than you and I."

He worked his jaw, like it had become stiff. "Trees don't speak. They could be petrified."

"Still braver. We're walking side by side, not touching. Their leaves touch. They share the lane, and we merely travel along it with a wide gap between us. I'd say they are braver."

He gaped at me. It felt as if this was the first time he'd allowed himself to do so for more than a glance. Did he approve of my straw bonnet with rose-colored trim, my pale blue gown with a matching ribbon in my hem? Mama's trunk and Scarlett's talent for sewing made this outfit stylish and well fitted to my curves.

"Nothing wrong with a little quiet, Georgina. You get to hear the birds and how the wind talks to the branches."

Mark moved a little closer, and then began walking.

Deeper in this section of Hyde Park, with no viewing eyes, he stopped again. "How are you this morning? I had to pretend I didn't see the vile cartoon at the coffeehouse I visited this morning."

"Oh. My sister Scarlett said the Gilroy cartoon was littered on a bench at the Royal Society."

"How did she go there? I thought it was just for men. Maybe I misheard something Livingston, my science friend, has said."

He folded his arms. "Miss Scarlett Wilcox does seem to get out a great deal. And for a younger sister, that's impressive."

Oh. Oh. I'd said too much. "Um. She visited someone or something. But she was mortified for you and your family as well as ours, and she let us all know."

"What did she say?"

"Oh, nothing too important. Something along the lines that this was a defeat for women all over the world. I heard words such as *misogynistic* and *farce* and why would I have to be portrayed as a freed slave."

Looking at it again, with the Blackamoor women saying "Massa," I realized this was worse. Oh, goodness. "Gilroy drew me as an enslaved woman with her slaver."

My limbs froze. The stories my father told me of the time before—when he had been enslaved, before earning money for his freedom—washed over me. Wanting to vomit, I shivered and looked away.

Mark took my hand. He wrapped it about his forearm. "Steady yourself."

He was well muscled in his dark emerald coat. "Sounds as if she gave you a truthful mouthful."

"Scarlett is very matter-of-fact. She doesn't temper her opinion. If she could be a man of science, well woman of science, she'd be one. And as far as her critique of Gilroy's horrid drawing, I can't fault her logic."

"Umm. Neither can I." He led me off the path and into a

grove of trees, then released me. With a finger to his lips, he took his treasured tube and looked through it.

Without a word, he drew my chin to the direction he'd spied, then put his viewing barrel to my eye. "Look up," he whispered. "Do you see it?"

I did. A cute little creature, a bird with a yellow breast and bright blue feathers on his head. "So pretty."

"You are. And it is. He looks a little thin. He'll fatten up from the insects buzzing around all the flowers in the park."

Reaching for the scope, his sleeve cut across my bosom. Though the touch was brief, my breath seized. I didn't realize how close we were watching birds.

I had no complaints and looked at him describing his favorite habit.

"Look at the yellow feathers upon her breast . . . stomach . . . the bird's stomach."

My laughter made him relax, and he seemed unbothered that we stood so close, that there was no beginning or ending to our shadows. If anyone saw, there would be no doubts now. We were together, and that niggling feeling that Lord Mark was only pretending to be comfortable with me, a girl of a lower station, from the other side of the Thames, went away.

"Mark? What do you call the little fellow?"

"A tit."

Blinking, I backed away. "Excuse me?"

"Not a teat. Not you, yours. Hmmm. The tit. It's the bird. Oh, my goodness, never noticed. Well, I did notice." He wiped at his mouth, then pointed. "It's a yellow-and-green tit. That's what it's called."

His brows rose. "I'd never call you tit or any kind of saucy woman."

When I started to giggle, he released his breath.

"Sort of a tit for tat, my lord. I know you'd not be disrespectful. You're a gentleman."

"I am, but I do sometimes wonder what it would be like to be a rake or rakish. Dashing as Lord Byron—I wonder if that would make the notes flow."

"You, a rake?" I shook my head. "No, not you."

His face darkened, then he heaved a little sigh and turned his face to the sky. "Perhaps that's why you kissed me. I radiate safe and boring."

Did the sentiment of being kind hurt his feelings? He *was* kind. I *did* feel safe with him. "Then I'm the same, for I'm enjoying this walk."

"I'd like to think, if we'd met under different circumstances, that we'd be friends."

"We are friends now. Well, that's what I feel." I adjusted my bonnet and spun to the right. Didn't fully catch him saying the same.

"You are a puzzle, Georgina. One I enjoy figuring out. Yes, we're friends. And I like when you're bold, when you're funny, and when you are shy around everyone but me."

"I'm not shy around my sisters or the duke. Little Lydia definitely wouldn't call me that."

He lightly put his fingers to my chin, turning my gaze to his, then tilting my head. Mark slipped the scope into my hand again. "Take another look before he flies away, and then we'll continue our walk."

The little fellow squawked, and then flew away. I handed him back the scope. "I see why you love bird-watching."

Part genius, part recluse, part nature lover, and from the kiss I was desperate to remember—a lover's lover. Mark held out his arm and escorted me among the tattling plane trees, showing me more birds. His attentive gaze and our shared laugh almost made me forget about the couples we met along the way, walking or in carriages, who stopped and stared.

Chapter 20

MARK—BUMPING INTO BIRDIES

The retrieved pocket scope in my palm felt heavy but not as weighty or as frigid as the stares I received accompanying Miss Wilcox into Hyde Park's brush. Her questions, her gentle laugh made me forget the annoyances and absorb the beauty of the grounds. This London treasure was green and—unlike last year, the coldest in a century—lush with flowers. Azaleas and bluebells put pops of pink and blue everywhere.

The abundant nectar called to the birds and this bird-watcher. My usual secondary habit, of viewing the season's fairest maidens strolling with their mamas or newest suitors, was something I abandoned. Why stray with a goddess on my arm, no matter how safe or boring she thought I was.

She sighed with pleasure as I showed her another red-chested robin.

Was it odd to enjoy the sounds she made? She was an instrument, like a beautiful harp, but one meant not only to be admired but listened to, sought out, and loved.

It wasn't the first time notions of deeper feelings for Georgina Wilcox crossed my mind, my heart. It was why I didn't appease my mother. Even if this was a false romance, the time I spent admiring Georgina was true.

Something about being my own man made me want a woman

who understood what that meant. The complexity and precarious nature of my position could only be sympathetic to someone who in her own way had taken a stance, rebelled, and now lived with the consequences.

"Lord Mark, I've always loved the outdoors. I walk along the Thames. The duke has come with me too."

Oh. Torrance. Helpful Torrance. "What is it you both like about walking near the Thames? The smell of sulfur. The crowd of boats."

"We . . . well, I like to listen to the water."

"Listen? Not watch it and the waves? How does the song of the water compare to a tit's or a robin's?"

"Let me think," she said. In deep thought, probably searching for the right words, she hummed, but I only noticed how shapely her silhouette looked when she crossed her arms—nicely curved, thick hips meant for a full embrace.

"The Thames moans. Sometimes it swishes, lapping at the shore. It sounds lonely, like these birds. The tit and the robin are looking for their mate. The river sounds as if it mourns the loss of love."

"That's depressing, Georgina. And hauntingly beautiful."

She offered me a glimpse of a smile, then quickly turned away. "What is it?"

Drawing her hand to her face, she whispered, "They're looking at us. I hate the angry glares."

Swiveling, peering through trees, I saw a couple, a middle-aged woman and gentleman in a military-style hat, standing at the bend in the lane gawking. I was tempted to take my scope and identify these two, but to know the names would make it worse.

While many saw Georgina and me and didn't seem to care, other couples had stared.

Some slowed and pointed at us, others backed away as if we were a plague.

The anger I felt at my mother's warning doubled in my heart.

"Don't grimace, my lord. Ignore. The angry couple went another direction."

I'd like to think my scornful gaze wore them down, that I'd protect Georgina from physical harm, name-calling, or any other slights the two had cooked up.

Yet, I knew the truth.

Cowards hated confrontation.

And unless they were without a reason to run, they'd still be on this path awaiting their moment to ruin mine.

My companion's voice, her sweet tones drew me from my fury. "Please, Mark. Don't let them antagonize you. Ignore them. Just another curious set of eyes wondering if we were the ones in the cartoon. I think we are too handsome a pair for that."

Her soft, matter-of-fact tone, her lyrical chuckles, cut like glass. This shouldn't be a way to live, awaiting random acts of unkindness and having to excuse the ones that intrude upon your peace.

I couldn't say anything. I was too stunned at how easily she accepted the slights.

One simple, grunted *fine* had to replace the off-color sentiments I wished to utter.

But I peered at the serene beauty at my side, one who looked unbothered and refreshing in a pinkish-color-trimmed bonnet that shaded her olive skin, skin shimmering like luminous pearls.

"The bird, my lord. Are you stopping to show me another bird?"

"Yes, but let's go this way, deeper into the hedges."

The gorse was sculpted, pared back, allowing a line of daffodils to make a solid yellow streak. It was a golden trail, something to follow, something to make my mind focus on nature and the most natural thing in the world, a wonderful woman.

"Tell me what you'll do when you win the Harlbert's Prize. Will you crow about it like a magnificent magpie?"

"Perhaps. There are quite a few people I would want to know."

"Like who?"

"My father would be an obvious candidate." The man didn't appreciate art and possessed no true love of music. Why else would he allow such hideous copies of Roman statues in the Grosvenor house? "Yes, I'd love to see his face admitting he was wrong."

"Just, Lord . . ."

"Lord Prahmn. And add my mother and her war council. I suppose it's wrong for me to want some understanding from them."

"If it's not something they can truly give, will you be fine with that? My sister had to accept that Lord Hampton lost his family when they married."

"Doesn't sound like much of a family, Georgina."

Looking over my shoulder, I saw the gawkers had cleared. The path was again ready for our leisurely stroll. I led Georgina and refused to let an inch of sunlight separate us.

"I'm sorry if I ask too impertinent of questions. I've sent you running deeper into your thoughts."

"Running. Yes, Miss Wilcox. Yes, to being lost in my head, but no. No, to your question not being worthy of an answer. I suppose I'd want my brothers to know. My elder brother, Gerald, likes music. He adores Haydn. He's the only one to encourage me. To be fair, the second oldest, Christopher, he'd already sailed to war before I showed any true talent."

"All brothers. Sisters are all I have. I would've liked to have a brother." Her eyes held a sense of sadness.

"But weren't you close to Lord Hampton? I'd been given that impression when we first met."

"I liked him. He had a great sense of humor. My sister's husband was good-natured, but he troubled Katherine. I think she . . . we thought he'd open up his world to us. That his influence would grow Wilcox Coal. It did the opposite, and he put a great deal of pressure upon her—"

"To change in some fashion or to ignore the stares."

Georgina glanced at me and nodded. Though tall, we were the same height, mouth to mouth.

"If I said I'm sorry, I guess that would sound patronizing."

"Still feels good to hear. Makes me feel less otherworldly too. But let's not acknowledge them or give credence to their questions."

"The questioner wants to ignore questions?"

"Yes, Mark, for they want to know why is she here, why does she smile and look so confident? Where is her shame? Doesn't she know she's breaking a rule?"

Georgina stooped and picked a white bud from the gorse and twirled it in her fingers. "Or worse—"

"There can't be anything worse than what you've said."

Casting the flower back to earth, she sighed. "Some want gratitude. Where's the gratitude? Why doesn't she humble herself every moment she enters a forbidden room? Doesn't she know we've allowed her to exist? I guess it's my privilege to be allowed to live."

Her heavy lashes sparkled. They were damp.

The prettiest flower in Hyde Park had sprouted tears like morning dew.

Stopping under the heavy bough of a chestnut tree, I retrieved a handkerchief and softly mopped her eyes.

"There's nothing to say," she remarked, "but sorry."

"You haven't done this."

"Haven't I? I've entangled you. I have good breeding, but manners and thoughtfulness aren't the same. I should've thought things through. The angry faces could be people who would be Wilcox Coal clients or men on the Halbert's Prize committee. My impulsiveness could ruin all our futures. This cure for my reputation could do the same thing." Georgina stared into my eyes. "I'm sorry I got you into this."

She regretted our kiss.

I didn't.

This goddess took the cloth from my fingers. For a few

moments of pleasure, the pressure of her fingertips was against mine.

It would be wrong to kiss her now, to take her in my arms and taste those plump lips once more. Then I heard notes.

They were as clear as the birds' tweets. *Da da dum.*

But I'd have to remember them. I'd rather stay here, watch the sunshine reflect on the flecks of gold in Georgina's wet irises and contemplate how to kiss her.

She waved her hands and pushed air toward her face. "I'm making something into more than what it is. I'm well. Let's think of it as a joke, my lord. The sketch in the paper is someone's poor joke."

"Remarkable to take the insults and twist them into something milder."

"Of course." She finished wiping her eyes. "People who care nothing for me can't be a part of my thoughts. That's control. I don't wish them to have that."

"Then why are you nervous when you sing?"

"Because singing for the river or close friends is a joy. Singing out loud to strangers is for them. I give a performance, and I'm expected to take their judgment. I have to wait for their approval."

I'd assumed Georgina shy, like me. This was so much more.

Last night, I left my mother's thinking I was my own man, that nothing could harm me.

One look at how self-conscious my world made Georgina, how she had to close her eyes to sing the lyrics out loud, I hurt for her.

"I envy you, Mark. You're a gifted artist. And you have the courage to accept an audience's praise and their condemnation. You have to be very confident to do that. That's a gift."

"You are gifted. It's my job to build your confidence to exhibit."

Holding out my arm to her, I wanted her to seize it, to hold on to me like she knew I'd protect her. I would, no matter the cost.

When another staring couple passed us, Georgina walked at my side with more sunshine between us.

I gulped and had to accept that she didn't believe in me—not for her safety, not to defend her dreams.

If I failed at music, I could grovel and still be welcomed back into the Sebastian fold. I was a peer's son, a lord. And with promises to conform, maybe even go for the church, all would be forgiven.

But what of Miss Wilcox?

The Wilcoxes had money problems with their coal business. I doubted if their finances could sustain a prolonged scandal. Clients like my mother and her network could make things difficult.

Watching people watching us, I knew I'd survive the newspapers and the gawkers, but not the goddess. She and the Wilcoxes would be devoured by those who fed on gossip.

Chapter 21

GEORGINA—THE CIRCULAR SERPENTINE, OR WAS THAT SERPENTS?

Walking with Mark, I concentrated on the grounds we explored. Hyde Park was a playground for avid bird-watchers. My delightful guide started showing me many things when the crowds lessened.

"There are quite a few mating calls." His cheeks became pink. "Lots of different nuanced ways to profess their love."

I'd never seen a man blush. Papa didn't, but it was hard to surprise him.

Tavis didn't. Though his schemes shocked us. "You know the differences."

"It's music." He took his scope out and craned his neck to the tops of the trees.

The air smelled of rich lavender.

I bent and picked a white daffodil offering scents of spice and vanilla. "I haven't baked in a week. I haven't made biscuits."

He turned his gold tube to me. "I'd love to have your biscuits. I mean they look so . . . good."

Standing up straight, I cast the petals away. "Has the duke been bragging about them?"

Mark's face scrunched. "No. Yes. I can see for myself that they have to be good."

Rolling the scope between his fingers, he became silent again. "Georgina is a very formal name. We should return to Torrance and Lady Hampton faux-closer. I want to give you some sort of endearment."

"Georgie. We call my sister Kitty when we want her attention. I assume you want mine."

"Very much so . . . Georgie."

My smile broadened at how easily he said Georgie. We walked around the bend. The large lake called the Serpentine was ahead.

More daffodils, a mix of yellow and white ones, led the way.

Hyde Park in bloom was a haven of tall trees—more aged plane trees and sweet chestnut.

"I see Torrance found some shade."

The carriage wasn't too far away on the other side of the lake. Lydia must be in the duke's lap. Katherine was on the other side, almost as far from him as possible. "They don't seem to be feuding, but I wish that they could become friends."

"Looks can be deceiving, but I think the lady despises Torrance."

"Mark, has the duke spoken of why they feud? Why is the Duke of Torrance dismissive of my sister, his best friend's widow?"

"I was going to ask you why Lady Hampton hates the duke. I know the only reason he visited Lord Hampton at all was because your sister asked him to. I suspect their connection, the duke and the dowager, precedes the friendship with your brother-in-law."

That made sense, didn't it? Was the duke somehow a part of Katherine's great adventure?

And if he was, wouldn't I or Scarlett know?

A fast-sounding gallop came from behind.

Mark took my hand, led me to the tall grasses to the left of the path.

A man charging closer stood in his stirrups yelling, "Sebastian!"

"Company, Mark," I said, and he smiled back.

The fellow on horseback ripped the hat from his head and waved it like a flag to surrender. He slowed his mount, a dapple-gray mare, inches before crashing into Mark. "Sebastian, you foolish man. Renege, man. Don't set a wedding date."

"Livingston, you're a cad. He's always joking," Mark said, holding tightly to my hand, keeping me from running. "This is Miss Wilcox. I told you of her."

"Pleasure to meet you, miss." The Livingston fellow turned all his attention on Mark. "So you're just taking part in the peacock parade? No deeper alliances? Both of you shall escape with your lives unencumbered?"

"Lord Mark, is he all right? He seems pretty bothered. Suggest your friend go get refreshment or merely stare at us like the others."

"I'll recover instantly, miss, if you tell me you've decided against my friend. Marriage is such an unhealthy business. It ruins the best relationships. Just fool around. Be free."

Mark started to laugh. It sounded uncomfortable, a bit unhinged, like the rider. "Such a kidder. Miss Georgina Wilcox, this is Alexander Melton, the Earl of Livingston."

Scarlett had mentioned Livingston several times. Hard to believe this excitable fellow hoping for a faux break in my false relationship was the same brilliant man my sister admired.

"The great researcher. I've heard great things about you, sir."

Like I'd spoken in another language or something fanciful, Mark squinted at me but then shrugged.

Livingston cast questioning eyes upon me too. His mouth held a sardonic line. "I wish I knew more of you. Our mutual friend Sebastian here has not said very much about you at all."

My hand tightened about his lordship's arm and I turned to him, playing up our fake romance. "This has been a secret. Our dearest relations knew nothing. I'm terribly sorry that we've been unable to share. That may soon change."

"Yes." Mark patted my fingers. "Now that Lady Prahmn knows, courtesy of your mother, the Dowager Countess Livingston, everyone will learn of our good news."

"No," the earl said. "That was supposed to dissuade you."

I'd seen people become red but never this shade of purple, lest they were no longer meant for this world. The earl turned darker and grayer than a grape.

"I thought you were my friend," Mark said.

"Sebastian, I am. It slipped out, and then I felt obligated to explain—"

"To the mother you rarely see. The one trying to find you a new countess to marry and secure grandchildren and an heir."

"She'll do nothing of the sort to me. Marriage is an evil business. You both should avoid it like the plague."

Mark fondled my fingers. "The heart knows what it wants."

The earl groaned. "The heart also pumps blood coursing with disease all throughout the body. I don't think a heart which can't tell the difference between good blood and bad blood should be trusted."

"Lord Livingston, sir, I can see why he said little about me. You're not very encouraging, though my sister, Miss Scarlett Wilcox, has read a paper of yours recently. She found it intriguing. I can't believe I've met the author."

The earl looked happy for a moment, then his smile dropped and he made his horse back up. "Oh, this woman is good. She'll go for the kill straightaway. She finds a weakness—"

"Like your vanity, sir." Mark's laughter grew, but his heated gaze remained on me.

"Oh, she's very good. Lady Hampton has probably taught all

the sisters how to ensnare peers. Get out while you still can, Sebastian. Marriage is dangerous. It's dangerous for the both of you. Keep your friendship. Have fun, then flee."

As I brought my hand higher on his arm, Mark gave me another warm look.

I couldn't figure out where he focused—on my broad pointy nose, my large eyes, or the lips that wouldn't mind a third kiss, one as indecent as our second.

"Livingston, you run along," Mark said. "Tell your mother you've seen us, and you did your duty to try to break this relationship."

"I'm not done yet. Sebastian, Miss Wilcox, ending this will be for the good, for you both. Trust me. Marriage is horrible."

"I guess we'll know if she formally accepts my hand at Torrance's ball."

Mark's words sounded true.

My unpredictable heart stopped, then beat again in a floppy, foolish beat.

Was this pretend?

Weren't we still in make-believe?

Frowning like he'd eaten bitter, bitter lemons, the earl rode off.

Mark picked me up and swung me around before setting my feet on low clouds, or the ground. Couldn't tell where my slippers were or if his words were true.

Did he love me? Was it possible?

And how did I feel about him?

"Well done, Georgie. That will give Livingston a special tale to tell his mother. We're the season's young lovers."

It was pretend.

All for show.

My heart slammed against my chest, and then crawled to a mournful rhythm.

"Georgie, something wrong? Did I hurt you picking you up? I must say I lost my head."

"Gravel. There's rocky gravel under my shoes. Let's go to the duke's carriage."

"Yes. Well done." Mark offered his arm. "Let me steady you."

I took his help, for that was all he offered. Nothing more.

"You two look guilty." The duke shook his head. "Well, one does. The other looks angry. Succumbing to the heat, Miss Wilcox? It's surprisingly warm today."

Mark helped me inside, then settled in beside me, looking very pleased. More of his keeping up our act, I supposed.

Why was my disappointment growing? Hyde Park had been magical.

Until it wasn't.

And I couldn't run from the truth. I was a fool falling for a joke, one I'd created.

The duke gazed at me as he shifted poor Lydia in his arms.

The child had wrinkled his burgundy waistcoat, but he didn't seem to care.

"Shall we," he said, smiling at Lydia, "take a final spin about the park?"

I answered no at the same time Mark said yes.

"Again. Please. Again." Lydia's voice sounded tired. She yawned and snuggled closer to the humored duke, hugging him about his neck.

Though Katherine rolled her eyes, the duke seemed to love it.

But Lydia's little brown face seemed redder. Was it too much sunshine? It was a brilliant day.

"Katherine, Lydia doesn't look so well."

"She's . . . fine. Not fine." My sister stretched and put her wrist to the little one's brow. "Oh, no. You're very warm."

"I said so," the duke stated. His tone was curt.

My sister ignored him and focused on Lydia. "Are you feeling poorly?"

"Another ride. Again. Then we stop and rest."

Irritable. She sounded miserable. And when she became extremely ill, it always began with a recurring fever.

"Are you achy, Lydia?" I leaned forward and touched her sweaty hand. "She was good this morning, unless you didn't tell us. Lydia."

When she tried to hide her aches, she fidgeted or wanted to be held in your arms, just like the duke did now.

He wrenched off his gloves and put his finger to her temples. "My goodness, you're very hot, my friend."

"Just a little. Go again. I'll be better."

She winced when Katherine tried to make her sit up.

Then she started to cry.

Mark looked so concerned. "Torrance, let me get her some help. Maybe some water."

The duke glanced at Katherine. "I don't know what to do. Lady Hampton—"

"Of course, you wouldn't." My sister tried to take Lydia, but the child refused.

She wrapped her arms tighter about the duke and began sobbing. "I want the duke."

"It's fine. Your friend's here." He knocked off her bonnet and fanned her brow.

"I don't want to marry you anymore, Your Grace. Marry Georgina or Scarlett or even Katherine. Then you can be my brother. I don't want to lose you from my life. You care so much. You'll make me better 'cause you love me."

It was heartbreaking to hear the poor child's logic of what would cure her.

She began to groan. The pain she must've been hiding made her little body shake.

Mark stood. "Livingston was just here. He's as good as a physician. He'll know what to do."

The duke, with a click of his fingers, had the carriage moving. I caught Mark's arm and kept him from falling out.

Katherine clasped her hands together; her gray gloves made her pose look severe, dour. "Where are we going? What are you doing?"

"Honoring Lydia Wilcox's request." The duke rocked her like she was a babe.

Lydia had given up her dream of being his duchess for something that could be attained now. She wanted the duke as a brother.

I wasn't marrying the duke.

I knew Katherine hated him.

Scarlett. What did she want?

"I'm going to make you better. I'm not letting you leave me until you are." The duke kissed Lydia's forehead.

"Take us home, Your Grace." Katherine looked scared, very scared.

"No, to James Street. We're not far. I have a doctor who can get there quickly."

"Your Grace," I said, "Lydia gets colds very easily. She refused to miss this drive. We didn't know she was ill again."

"'Again'? Ask Sebastian. I always have doctors and researchers at Anya House. It would be no trouble to get her the best help possible."

Katherine shook her head, but she didn't say no again. The duke had the means to give Lydia the best.

"Lady Hampton, you could return with the young lovers for an afternoon drive. We can't forget our current mission. Then, when you all return, a simple dinner will await. It will be simple. We are in Lent."

"I'm not leaving her. I'll—"

"When you return, I suppose you'll see that I do know what to do for my Lydia."

"Your Grace, you don't need to do—"

"Nyet!"

Talk about changing colors. The duke was beyond red. I wasn't sure dragons had such a color.

"Lady Hampton," he said, in a slightly calmer tone, "I've waited for you to ask for my assistance. To tell me what to do to make things right, but you're too stubborn to allow me to be a bigger benefit to Georgina, and now you'll risk Lydia's health to spite me."

"Jahleel, please. I wouldn't."

I wanted to say something, but this fight wasn't their typical one. It was deeper and darker, the glimpses, the looks between them, worse than anything I'd ever seen.

And Katherine looked scared.

With a huff, she sat up straight. "I'm sorry, Your Grace," she said with her teeth gritted like a snarling mama bear. "Now give me Lydia."

"Nyet."

"This is none of your business."

"Lydia has made it my business. Lady Hampton, I haven't made a bet in six years. How much do you want to wager that I have the power to make sure Lydia Wilcox is protected and remains in my care until she's healthy and able to walk from my house?"

"You wouldn't go against my wishes." Her voice wobbled. "You—"

"Lady Hampton, you claim I'm heartless and manipulative because of a faulty notion of the past. You don't know the man I've become or what I am capable of. My wishes come first. I will make Lydia well."

This man, who'd been friendly and nurturing and even fun, had the money and influence to do whatever he wanted. The Duke of Torrance's world was different from mine, and even Mark's. The duke had power, true power. He'd use it.

The determined man signaled again to his driver to hurry. The very showy landau would soon be at Anya House. He'd given us no choice.

Mark squeezed my hand.

I hadn't noticed, not until we'd almost arrived, that he still held it.

Sort of needed his comfort, even if it was for show.

Something very wrong had changed in this carriage ride.

And Katherine, our leader, sat alone, looking deathly disturbed.

Chapter 22

GEORGINA—THE WAITING

Standing on the landing of the second floor of Anya House, I viewed a wonderland. From the soft blue walls to the long thick rug running the length of the corridor, the upper level, though as big as downstairs, was warmer, more intimate.

Nonetheless, I felt encamped in a hospital, something cold and dark. For three days we'd stayed here waiting for Lydia's fever to break, for her pain to lessen.

Though the duke welcomed my sisters and me as guests, he'd changed. The jovial man was gone. This version was serious, conferring with the league of doctors who he charged with caring for Lydia.

I believe I even heard various languages talking about our girl like she'd died.

The last doctor, Mama's last doctor, was in with her now. Mr. Carew was diligent. If Lydia had the constitution of our mother . . . the illness that tormented Mama, he'd surely know what to do.

Scarlett came up the steps carrying a cup of tea. "For you, sis."

Didn't want tea, just answers. I set it on the table in the corridor. Then I grabbed Scarlett and held her, held her like I'd do Lydia if she ran out the door, like I'd do Katherine if she moved from the child's bedside.

"Georgina. We have to have faith. His Grace has brought an

entire group of physicians to care for our little girl. She will be well."

"I don't know, Scarlett. You didn't see the duke. He's furious. It's like he's blaming himself for Lydia being ill. Then he blames Katherine for not noticing how sick she was. They are both so furious and yet so scared."

She rubbed my back, hitting the tension that led to my neck. "We know how hard Kitty is on herself. But the duke, it's like he's fighting for Lydia, like he thinks—"

"That she might die like his sister."

Scarlett nodded. "I hear bits and pieces, but Anya Charles, the duke's little sister, died about Lydia's age. And it sounds like she had these pains and fevers just like Lydia."

My hand flew to my mouth and covered my lips.

My sister nodded again. "He's fighting for Anya, what he would've done if he had secured his title and money without delay. The poor man thinks he could've saved her."

Scarlett was the smartest person in any room. "Tell me what you believe."

"The symptoms, the fever spells and pains—Lydia has what Mama had and probably Anya."

"The mysterious illness that keeps coming back until they die."

"And Mr. Carew believes this too." Her voice became low. "There's no cure-all."

I looked at Scarlett, meshing the images of Mama suffering and the memories of the evil sickness that made a vibrant woman stay in bed for weeks and months at a time. The thing laudanum and Papa's prayers could barely fight. The lost hope that made some wish for a gentle passing as much as healing. "Mama at least had a whole life. Lydia's is just beginning."

Scarlett's thumbs were on my cheeks, swiping at my tears. "Drink the tea. She's getting the best care. We must—"

The door to Lydia's bedchamber opened. Mr. Carew came out with the duke. "Torrance, I have seen reduced symptoms with a careful phlebotomy. It reduces viscosity. There is a belief that too much blood is the cause of the pain."

"She's so small." The duke shook his head. "Maybe more ice cold towels to swaddle the child to address the fever."

"Torrance, it might help. I'm not sure."

"Willow." Scarlett's voice had a high pitch. She was either on to something or was about to cry. "Willow bark tea might help the fever, Your Grace, Mr. Carew."

"Ah, the scientific little Miss Wilcox." The physician's brownish-black eyes lifted behind his spectacles. "You've been reading. That's dangerous for a woman, especially a young lady fresh out of leading strings."

She glared at him like the tiger I knew Scarlett to be. "Mr. Edward Stone did research on willow. In his papers, he noted the bark helped reduce fevers. Willow is similar to Peruvian bark, which helped in cases of malaria."

The duke nodded. "Let's try the young woman of science's suggestion before anything. Carew, you're an advocate of blood letting, your phlebotomy, but I want the pain and fever gone first."

"Phlebotomy, Your Grace," Scarlett said, "will reduce the amount of blood in the body. That can change the viscosity and allow the blood to flow better."

Mr. Carew's lips had been pursed like he was about to be dismissive, but as soon as Scarlett mentioned viscosity his eyes grew big. "Yes, lower the viscosity. That may break the fever permanently. It should reduce her pain."

The duke glanced at my beaming sister. "What would you do? I trust your advice."

"Torrance. She's a woman who's read papers. Some very good papers. I know Scarlett Wilcox is extremely smart, but I've cared for little Lydia since she was born and Mrs. Wilcox before that. I'm a physician of twelve—"

"I agree with Mr. Carew's assessment," Scarlett said. "But it should be a small letting. And let's first try willow bark tea to give her a bit more strength to endure the procedure better."

The duke took Scarlett's hand and kissed it. "Do it, Carew, as the young woman of science has prescribed. Miss Georgina, Miss Scarlett, keep Lady Hampton calm as the physician does what's necessary. She's fought everyone whose opinion differed from Anglican prayers, cold towels, laudanum, and her waiting approach. We need to try something different."

"That's all we've had, Your Grace." I looked at him half in defense of Katherine and in defense of our situation. "We haven't been able to afford much else, and our pride has kept us from bothering Mr. Carew."

The physician turned his frown upon me. "Never think of compensation when a life is in the balance. Too many suffer. Too many of *us* suffer because medicine and physicians are the luxury of the wealthy. That needs to change. I need to change it. Good health is a human's right."

My sister bowed, then came and took my hand. "Thank you both for listening," she said. "And I agree, Mr. Carew. That's why I read scientific papers. Someone has to advocate for women."

Carew's handsome face eased. He tugged on his waistcoat, a lovely, patterned thing of black and scarlet threads. "That's why the Wilcoxes are my favorites. You know how to kick a mule gently."

I agreed but needed to give these men a harder kick. "You both know what this is? Mr. Carew, you've always known. Tell us."

The man from Trinidad with the pleasant accent nodded. "It's an ancient illness. I've seen studies that it affected the Africans under their warm sun. The folktales say that a mutation by the gods to make Black bodies less susceptible to malaria now brings this blood disease to Black bodies no longer on the continent."

Standing in this grand hall of this grand house, we all knew none of us had a choice of why our ancestors *left*. The papers mocked trafficking and enslavement. This illness was another punishment upon our flesh.

"My grandfather, Gannibal, made the best use of his forced transport, befriending Tzar Peter." The duke swallowed hard. "Paths, like time, can be so different. And the thing about the gods, they can be fickle."

"Yes, Torrance. I suppose some sacrifice wasn't enough, and now this sickness can affect anyone." Mr. Carew clapped his hands. "We have a plan. Let's get to it. There's willow bark with the kitchen spices?"

"Of course. As well as ginger for you, Miss Georgina, if you feel like a distraction."

As the physician went down the stairs, music filtered up.

"Or you have other distractions." The duke hummed a few notes of the marching tune. "Sebastian has returned?"

"No, Your Grace," I said. "He never left."

The duke nodded. "Good man, Sebastian, but I suppose the new portrait in the music room has kept him entertained."

New portrait? I hadn't noticed, but I'd barely left this spot outside Lydia's door.

"Ladies, help Mr. Carew do his best. If Lady Hampton needs to be carried out, I'll handle that myself."

He stopped mid-step, halfway down, and turned back to us. "Well, she might be a bit of a tiger. I'll get Sebastian and Steele. The three of us can drag her out so Carew can work."

Shirtsleeves rolled up, waistcoat open, the duke, who looked like he'd already been wrestling in the streets, went down the rest of the stairs. His humor had returned, but he was still spoiling for a fight.

Scarlett opened the bedroom door and I saw a sight I hated—Katherine sitting next to a sickbed, holding a deathly ill person's hand.

Chapter 23

GEORGINA—DID HE JUST PROPOSE?

I watched the duke pace outside Lydia's bedchamber. The heavy door painted light blue with picture-frame molding separated us from the bed where the sick little girl lay. The willow bark tea lessened her fever, but it hadn't broken. Bloodletting would be done within the hour.

Our Lydia seemed to be hovering between lucidity and pain, life and death. And there was nothing I nor my sisters could do.

Scarlett, who I sent to get a few hours of sleep, felt so guilty. It was she who had convinced the duke to try the willow. Was the delay of Carew's procedure worth the slight improvement?

"Your Grace, perhaps you should try to get a little sleep. We don't need you relapsing with your spring cold."

"Thank you, Miss Wilcox. It's good to count on someone to look after my health. It's good to have someone concerned for another."

"Well, I am grateful for you. You've proven we Wilcoxes can count upon you."

The duke looked up with bushy, unkempt eyebrows. "Your sister Katherine was right. I didn't know what to do. But I'll be damned if I don't try everything. My Anya, my little sister, suffered. I didn't have the means to be of aid. Up until now, I have had everything but a reason to be generous. Your family gives me a reason."

"Katherine will fight you. She can't help it. But my sister must see you're doing the best for Lydia."

"Your sister doesn't trust me. I know. I made a promise to Anya . . . Lydia. I will fix all the problems."

"How do you intend to do that? Be a part of her life forever? If Mr. Carew is right, there is no cure. This struggle will continue, and as good as you are to us, our season ends after your ball."

Music filtered in the air.

It was soft, delicate to my ears.

Another one of Pleyel's hymns.

"I suppose I'd need a reason more than friendship to be connected to the Wilcoxes. Something permanent and legal. I think I know how to solve this *connection* problem and your scandal."

"What, Your Grace?" I stretched. We were in dire need of levity or a miracle. He might have one. "Tell me."

"Well, from what I see, Miss Wilcox, you're spoken for. Pity, you'd make a hell of a duchess. Unless you aren't?"

What did he just say? "Not your duchess?" I looked at him with amusement. "And you know it. Why are you trying to make me laugh?"

"True. It is a joke, but maybe it shouldn't be."

"Say what, Your Grace?" I forced my bulging eyes back into my skull. "You're kidding?"

"Forgive me for thinking aloud, but you are reasonable."

"Reasonable? Not beautiful or charismatic or smitten with unimaginable love. *No thank you* to this line of thinking."

"There are plenty of reasons to marry other than love. A wife who's a friend, and a friendship that cements familial bonds is something to consider. In sickness and health, a partnership . . . a partner who will look after one another, making sure they are protected and their wishes are carried out is important."

"In sickness and in health is an important vow. Shouldn't there be more to marriage?"

"When you realize you can't have what you want, you must take what you deserve. I need peace. Making a tranquil life is something one can claim. Maybe it's something we can claim."

My heart pounded.

He was serious.

Had Katherine been right? Had she noticed a connection between the duke and me, other than friendship? Noooo. He was like a brother, a good one. "What are you saying? Be clear."

The duke rolled his insignia ring about his finger. "There's too much mourning in Sebastian's song. Too much in my house and my heart. Sometimes you have to ask yourself, why keep fighting? Why war for the hope of love when friendship might be better? It definitely adds more tranquility to a life that's been spent alone."

The hymn Mark played was exactly that, mournful and low as an air of defeat wrapped around the duke's words. For the first time, I looked at an influential man of riches, born to a station so much higher than mine, and saw nothing but sadness.

"Your Grace, I know you aren't asking me to marry you."

He said nothing and moved to the rail overlooking the first floor. The gold thread in his waistcoat glittered like the ones in the rug.

I glanced at the marble tiles below. Up here, they were puzzle pieces. The picture they formed was complete and orderly, not out of place or confused like my spirit.

This marriage offer from a duke would make my mother proud. So much good could be done for my family if I said yes.

Slight squeaks made me notice that the duke had changed from boots to slippers, low ones. They looked comfortable. The man needed comforting. Every time he stepped into Lydia's sickroom, Katherine's scowl ripped him to pieces.

My sister's disapproval tormented him, but marriage to me wasn't to be a means of avenging her disregard. I'd not be comfort to a man I didn't love. "Your Grace—"

"Yes, Miss Wilcox." He stooped and picked up a bit of lint from the carpet threads.

I froze, thinking he'd knelt to propose.

When he bounded up, I breathed again. "Very nice rug, Your Grace. I like the one you've laid for Lydia. She likes to leap out of bed. It will be good for her feet."

"I hope after Carew's procedure she will be up soon, Miss Wilcox. She's too young to suffer."

I glanced away from his mourning spirit and examined the beautiful tapestry below my slippers. It was nice and thick, gold and cream. It seemed perfect for toes, while on the lower floors, the glorious tile and marble said formal shoes and full court dresses. This was the duke's life, a public side and a hidden personal one. My heart went out to a man who had everything and nothing.

"*You're* too young to suffer, Your Grace. Do not let my sister's opinion, which had to have been formed by Tavis, make you think less of yourself. It sounds so stupid telling a duke that he shouldn't settle, that he's worthy to be loved."

With his humanity shining in his hazel eyes, he glanced at me. "Lord Mark is a fool if he lets you go."

"I wasn't. We're not—"

"I talked to Sebastian. He could've left at any time. He went away last night merely to pack a portmanteau of clothes. He should be working on his new composition for the Harlbert's Prize, but he stays for you."

I crossed my arms, covering the bodice of my wrinkled brown gown. "He hasn't said this to me."

"Words shouldn't matter so much, not with clear actions."

Mark stayed for me. It touched my heart, but this was wrong. "I should tell him to work—"

"Tell him that you love him. That he's too young to suffer, thinking he's a failure because he's not a winning composer. You told me not to settle. I tell you to look and see what I see. Do not forsake love. You might not have a chance to reclaim it."

"This is all pretend, Your Grace. Remember your plan. I think it's succeeding. Plenty of people saw us in Hyde Park. I like Lord Mark a lot, but once the ball is over, the scandal will be over."

"Over, truly?" He put the lint in a pocket and stretched like the world was weighing on his shoulders. "Steele has picked up more gossip sheets. They've run tattle pieces or the foul cartoon on the scandal."

"Oh. It's been so many days since the incident in the garden. It should go away."

"Becoming a duchess would make everything go away. It would also keep all the Wilcoxes in my life. That's the peace I can attain. I would be happy. I could make you happy too."

It was an honor to have an offer from the Duke of Torrance. A marriage would secure everything but my heart's happiness.

"The only reason to refuse, Miss Wilcox, would be to admit your heart is taken."

"We've caused so much trouble being on this side of the river. It will be best for the Wilcoxes to go back across the Thames and find ways to keep Wilcox Coal afloat. Then a friend wouldn't have to feel obligated to take care of us. We shouldn't be your or Lord Mark's concern."

"Who should be concerned? When you told me of the debts, it was not new information. I'd discovered every loan Lord Hampton took out. I even sent wages to Mr. Thom."

"We are so indebted to you." There was no way to pay him back. Mere friendship wasn't enough. "I don't know what to say."

When I lifted my chin, I witnessed anger roiling in his eyes. "Lord Hampton and I were friends a long time. I knew exactly who he was. The secrets he took to the grave are grievous, but that's who Tavis Palmers was. His debts are not yours to pay. You make decisions for yourself."

Nonetheless, accepting the duke's proposal would be payment, payment in full.

"A marriage of convenience is the obvious choice. Your Grace, I should say yes, but what happens if I say no?"

His lips thinned for a moment, and I took the time to look at his handsome face, the thin mustache that curled about his dimples, the wavy hair that needed brushing like his brows. He was tall and fit and towered over me in a way that made me feel secure.

"We can't go back to how we were a year ago, Georgina."

He used my given name. His slight accent made it sound like *Yorvina*. It was pretty and delicate. That's not me. "Would that be bad to go back, Your Grace? We walked as strangers by the Thames, then as friends."

"I listened to the difficulties you shared. Our friendship is peaceful. You are beauty and grace."

"You make a compelling argument, Your Grace, but won't I be a shadow of what you truly want?"

For the first time his gaze broke.

He shoved his hands behind his back and turned. "A shadow can demand I leave your lives. I don't want to fight her or feel like a stranger anymore."

It made sense.

All of it.

Somehow Katherine came between the two friends, who both loved her. When she returned home from her great adventure changed, broken, who had her heart? Which man had thrown it away?

I wanted to know, but Wilcoxes kept secrets too.

This one was Katherine's, the secrets as well as the duke's heart.

I put a palm to his sleeve and turned him to me. "You're the kindest man. I am forever your friend. And as your friend, I'm going to pretend this conversation did not happen. That my mother who worshiped titles is not tossing about demanding that I become the Duchess of Torrance."

"How does one forget a logical conclusion? Lady Hampton believed it possible for us to have an attachment. Why shouldn't we marry? I need to belong. I want you all to belong to me."

My anger at Katherine pushed me down the rebel's path, but I couldn't do this to her. "I don't know what to say. My family needs a champion, but I thought it would be one of us girls."

"Then I will say the answer. Nyet. I must renege and be a heel. Family obligations have doomed many girls." He threaded his fingers together. "You can't marry someone in love with another. You and Lord Mark Sebastian have an understanding even if you can't acknowledge it."

"And you have one with Katherine."

My wait for him to acknowledge my words was for naught. The duke gripped my hand and kissed it. "The composer's no fool. He must see the jewel you are. He's blinded by his belief that he has to win a prize to be successful. Having a full heart and a house of love are the greatest successes."

It was my turn to not acknowledge what the duke said.

My heart could be wrong. Yet, I hoped he was right, that Mark did love me as I loved him.

"He has the talent to win the Harlbert's Prize, Your Grace. I'm not going to talk him out of his desire."

"Maybe he needs someone to tell him the truth. Maybe that someone is a bold young woman who kissed a stranger in a garden and rejected a duke."

"If Lord Mark and I share something of meaning, it can wait until he finishes. He can—"

"Nyet. The newspapers are creating folly. Until they have a new scandal, they'll repeat their lies and make you and Sebastian laughingstocks. So let a man decide what's important. Don't take away his choices. He'll hate that more."

The duke's pacing began again.

I decided to give him some. "That little girl loves you. We all do. And I must tell you, Lydia had decided to marry you before she gave you to one of us. Don't take the child's suggestions so literally. Or, if you can't change things with Katherine, wait twenty or more years, Lydia will accept you."

Deep, baritone chuckles—the duke laughed with his whole

chest. "You, Georgina, are a treasure. But rest assured, I do not plan to be alone for the next twenty years. I'll claim a duchess."

He didn't say anything about love or loving again. That was tragic.

"Why haven't you tried to win her again?"

His chin dipped. "Reasons. Far too many of them."

With his slippers, he smoothed a wrinkle in the rug. "This is a rya. My mother weaves them on large looms. She also creates tapestries for the walls. The rya keeps the home warm. I find the polished floors very cold."

"In the absence of love, you have a rya? What is stopping you, Your Grace, from telling my sister that you've never stopped loving her?"

Head craning to the ceiling, he stretched his arms wide. "When you find art, you have to hold on to it. But the artist has to want you to claim it. She wants nothing to be mine."

"Is that what happened, Your Grace? You couldn't hold on to Katherine, and Tavis stole her away?"

The door to the bedroom opened. Mr. Carew came out. I saw a picture of him in my mind—Mama's last doctor, and then him leaving Tavis that final time.

And I prayed this wasn't another of those moments. "Mr. Carew, please."

"Miss Wilcox, Lydia is resting easier. We shall try the bloodletting. Where's Miss Scarlett? She should be here."

"Changed your mind on leading strings, Carew?"

He flashed a smile of perfectly white teeth. "A learned man can learn. And Miss Scarlett Wilcox should witness the results which she also advocated."

"I'll go get her." I turned in the direction of the bedchamber Mr. Steele had assigned us. "Then I will run . . . and make some biscuits."

"His Grace's kitchen could save lives from his spice wall alone." Carew's voice traveled down the corridor.

I wanted to ask him about his favorite treat, the kartoshka. "Your Grace—"

But he was already half inside. I watched him slip behind Katherine. She'd barely moved from her spot at the side of Lydia's bed.

Like a pendulum swinging, the heavy door closed.

Nothing could be heard, not even arguing.

That feeling of helplessness surrounded me like a heavy shawl, the sobering pianoforte's music playing in the atmosphere.

"This is going to work," Mr. Carew said. "Hurry your sister." He went back inside.

I ran to Scarlett's room, wishing for favor and time.

Yet neither waited for anything, not deadlines or patience or passion, or even love.

Chapter 24

MARK—LET THE MUSIC PLAY

I put my hands on the keys, closed my eyes.

The piece should be there.

It wasn't.

Dido's stare had taken it away.

In the middle of the chaos with the ill little girl, the duke had done some decorating. He'd arranged to have the portrait of the Mansfield cousins on display for his ball.

Her poise and pose, readying to dance, reminded me of the many days I stared at her. Why this painting? Why now when I hadn't thought of her since Georgina and I had been practicing?

Obsession over a painting was ridiculous.

Yet it was here at Torrance's request to torture me.

Putting my fingers to the keys, I began to play my melody. And I tried hard to ignore the portrait, a set of mere brushstrokes on a canvas of a woman gone from the earth.

Why wonder about her thoughts as she stood before the artist?

How many hours had I labored over the song Dido must've had in her head the moment she twirled from her cousin?

I started playing again from the beginning of my composition, getting the beat right, the nice three-quarter measure. This piece was intricate and swift and right in its crescendo.

Then nothing. It was gone again.

Was this Dido's doing or my fears for Georgina? The horror on her face when Torrance took the unresponsive Lydia upstairs chilled the marrow in my bones.

I wanted to be upstairs comforting Georgina, waiting with her for news. Lady Katherine didn't want the duke there. She definitely didn't want me there either.

Fingering a key, I started playing Pleyel's Hymn 143. I swept my hands across the ivory and played it by heart.

When I closed my eyes, I saw my Georgie. She was my future, but how could I reach for her without a new song?

Humming, masculine and deep, sounded in the hall. Torrance stepped inside.

I lifted from the bench. "Any news?"

"No, but Mr. Carew is trying a new tactic. We have more waiting."

Rubbing his chin, he looked at me. "You seemed disturbed. Has Steele shown you more gossip rags?"

"No. I just feel helpless." I sat back down and began playing the hymn.

Torrance came fully inside. His cravat was gone, as was mine. The fastidious burgundy waistcoat that I'd admired days ago was wrinkled and open, hanging about his drooping shoulders.

He went to the portrait of Dido and Elizabeth. Standing in front of it, he touched the gilded frame as if Mr. Steele had hung it improperly.

"What happens if you do not finish your piece for the competition? It's weeks away. Right after my ball."

"Your Grace, I will finish. I have no choice."

"There's always a choice." He walked over and put his hands on the pianoforte. "This tune is dull but good."

"It's not mine. It's Pleyel. It's meant to be sung. When Miss Wilcox sings and I play, it will be divine."

"Do you have another plan, sir? The scandalmongers are still brewing. Since we've not done any more public events, Miss Wilcox's reputation might be too damaged to save with merely a good performance. We can't let her or the Wilcoxes be more de-famed."

"I don't have any plan. The one we are doing now is yours, Torrance."

"I see. I thought as much. That's why I asked Georgina Wilcox to marry me."

My ears popped.

The music died.

I couldn't feel my fingers. I took a breath. Then another.

After a moment, I slapped myself to awaken, to make words happen. "Then, congratulations."

The duke smirked. "That's how you react to the woman you love marrying someone else. You did better with the painting."

I coughed and filled my empty chest with air. "How am I sup-posed to act?"

"You could ask how your supposed friend would marry the woman you love."

I looked at Torrance and wanted to hit him. I wanted to drive my fist through his big nose. But what could I say to a woman who deserved everything, that I could give nothing? "I think the words would be congratulations. She'll make an excellent duchess. Give her her heart's desire."

"What of your heart's desire? Or are you still in love with what's not there?"

I lifted from the pianoforte again. "Is this a test of some sort? Is that why you brought the Kenwood portrait here?"

"Well, I like the portrait. But I need to know if you'll forever engage in fantasy as opposed to the true world where a man goes after and protects what is his."

Torrance talked in platitudes while a hole consumed my gut. "Did she say yes?"

He went to the side and straightened a portrait that hung be-hind the pianoforte. "Your father will think Miss Wilcox is after a title, even a courtesy one at that, if you were to propose."

"She doesn't care about that."

"Prahmn will say she's after money."

I went around the pianoforte and stood within punching distance. "That's not Georgie."

"Georgie? Oh, Sebastian, you've become quite familiar with my friend."

"You know her, Torrance. If she said yes to you, then it's because she actually loves you."

Torrance smiled as he blocked my fist. I'd aimed for his nose. "Miss Wilcox basically said nyet. She refused to accept my title and money. She's a special woman."

I think I started breathing again. "How can that be? She knows I could never give her the things that you could."

"I don't believe she asked for the things I could buy. She's concerned about a composer finishing his sonata."

"Georgie said that? Georgina Wilcox would wait for me?"

He tweaked the frame again, leveling it. Then, the duke stepped back and admired his handiwork. "This Wilcox woman is idealistic. And she already said you were a great man whether you finished the sonata or not."

He led me to Dido. "This beautiful woman, who does favor Georgina, was an asset to Lord Mansfield. I like to think that his love for his niece made him work to legally eradicate enslavement. He did what he could for her, but he couldn't change the world fast enough for her."

"What are you saying, Torrance?"

"I brought Dido to give you a choice: a fantasy where a woman will wait forever for you to act like her champion, or the real woman who needs a champion now. What will you choose, Sebastian?"

"My future is determined by the Harlbert's Prize. I should have my piece finished in time for the competition. Established as a composer, I can have the music and Miss Wilcox too . . . if she'll wait for me."

"Like the gods, women can be fickle. I mean, a lady who doesn't wish to be a duchess might not gamble her future on a man who thinks he has an infinite amount of time to write the perfect song."

"Just a few more weeks, Torrance."

"So you will be done. And at my ball, you will propose. That will end the scandal. The newspapers can say no more."

"I have to win or score very well. Then, it will prove we have a future."

"Funny, I sort of think she believes you have one now."

Shoulders slumping, I tracked back to the pianoforte. "I don't want to disappoint her."

"So, you're willing to risk losing her to someone else? All because you think you'll be a different man if you win a prize."

"It's an award my mother and Prahmn will recognize. You know the challenges Miss Wilcox and I will face. I'll need my parents' blessing. I have to make sure that any bride is protected—a Blackamoor wife, even more so. And children. How will they be received if my parents refuse to accept my wife, my children, and my profession?"

"Their opinions won't matter to a house built on love."

"It always matters. It matters if I can't afford a home. Being poor doesn't make the best plan."

I began to play.

Torrance hummed. "This is lovely, but it's taken. Haydn's *The Seasons* is popular. So do not enter it in the Harlbert's Prize. Perhaps you should share your composition with Miss Wilcox, let her be more than a muse. Let her be your partner. She's three-dimensional with life and vigor. She can help."

"No, Torrance. This is my work. It has to be mine, done on my own."

The duke clapped. "Hear, hear! Dido has heard you. But she's not offering applause. Fickle, I say." Torrance chuckled and fingered one of the brass buttons along his waistcoat. "Painted flesh is limited but, like a true woman, she will not be moved by promises."

"You know that's not what I mean or what I'm doing."

"I find making those separations problematic. And the future should be planned by two."

Humming, the duke turned and headed toward the entrance. "To be young and so impassioned about the future, thinking there will always be another chance for magic—that's folly."

His tone was cryptic. The duke wasn't a subtle fellow.

When he greeted Georgina in the hall with the physician, Mr. Carew, a man with a thriving practice and a similar background to hers, and who'd known the Wilcox family a long time, I think I understood.

My stomach knotted.

My keystrokes became harder, firing with passion and jealousy. I looked at Dido, joyful Dido who'd been painted the moment before she ran. With the options Georgina Wilcox had before her, I was the most unlikely direction for her to turn.

Chapter 25

MARK—KITCHEN CONVERSATIONS

For twenty minutes or more, I played the pianoforte for my audience of Dido and Elizabeth, pounding the keys until my fingers throbbed. I added not one note to my composition.

Torrance's speech had done what I supposed he'd set out to do: made me a jealous fool. Stepping away from my lifeless audience, I walked out of the music room and headed to the kitchen.

Hearing Georgie's laughter come from the back of the house, I prepared to see a cozy sight.

But I wasn't ready.

Two people—she in his arms—chuckling, with flour scattered on them like snow and along the wide cedar planks of the floor. Holding to an upper shelf, Georgina hung there as Mr. Carew supported her.

"My lord," she said in a voice that sounded surprised and winded, "Mr. Carew and I have had a bit of a disaster."

Like orange flames in the hearth, I burned. I was in a fake relationship, but I no longer felt as if we had a faux commitment, but something true. Shouldn't my pretend lover be faithful to me, not enjoying a moment with Carew?

Getting my mind to clear of wishing to haul Carew away from my fake fiancée, I cleared my throat. "Can I assist?"

His ashy-brown hands, or powder-doused ones, were about her waist. He lowered my goddess to the floor.

"Lord Mark," she said, giggling as the fellow picked up her fallen ladder. "Mr. Carew, you have been too helpful."

The two laughed again.

"Quite a disaster," I said. "Let me help you clean up."

Humored, wiping his hands on a cloth that lay on the table, Mr. Carew turned back to Georgie. "I think Lord Mark Sebastian can assist you. I can take this willow bark tea to my patient."

"Is Lydia Wilcox better, Mr. Carew?"

He nodded and smiled. His spectacles were dusted. "Yes, she is. The letting broke the fever. This tea will keep it away."

"Mr. Carew is being too modest. He's saved little Lydia's life." She handed him the teacup. "We are forever grateful."

"My pleasure," he said, gazing at her too long, probably noticing how the chocolate gown swathed her hips. The white strings of the apron cinching her waist left nothing to be imagined and led me to that lone memory of embracing Georgie in the garden.

"Get some rest, Miss Wilcox." Carew nodded to me and left with the steaming mug.

Georgina dusted her palms against her apron. "Are you serious about helping?"

"Command me, Miss Wilcox. Tell me how to assist."

She went into the larder and brought back a broom. "Do you know how to sweep? Men of the ton rarely know how one of these works." Her chuckles persisted.

"I'm serious. I'd like to help. I need something different to do or think about other than Pleyel."

Glancing at me, her warm eyes fluttering over my countenance, she handed me the broom, then moved away, hurrying like she'd done something wrong. Georgina went to a bowl on the other side of the table and began pounding spices in a mortar and pestle.

This thing—I'd seen Chancey use one. I pushed the broom at the floor and tried to gather the excess flour into a pile. The broom left streaks. Wasn't sure I was helping. But I did hit at dust stuck to the ladder.

"I'm glad I didn't knock over the jars. The duke has many herbal medicines—chamomile for skin irritations, milk thistle for the liver, and valerian for calm. Mr. Carew was telling me what each herb did."

"In the morning, if there's no change with Miss Lydia, I'll suggest to Torrance to bring Livingston. Lord Livingston's brilliant mind must be consulted."

"I think . . ." Georgia glared at me. "I believe Mr. Carew, with Scarlett's help, is providing the best care. I'm not sure your shrieking friend would be helpful."

"Merely a suggestion." I hoped my voice didn't sound tight . . . or jealous. "I want the best for your sister."

"Mark," she said in even, slightly annoyed tones, "I'm sure your friend is intelligent, but so is Mr. Carew. My sister Scarlett is impressed with the credentials of both men. I trust her. She'd be a physician if it were possible for a woman."

"To be sure."

"Yes, sir. Despite what the *Post* or *Globe* or some inhabitants of Mayfair may say, some Blackamoors aspire to book learning."

I'd made her mad. I was wrong and I knew it. "My slight jealousy of Carew and admiration of my friend may have made my tone sound odd—"

"Oddly condescending. Yes."

She cracked an egg. It wasn't a gentle tap.

Fool that I was, I'd had a similar conversation with Livingston. Then, it was I who was suspicious of his views. In one instance, I'd exposed something terrible in me. Ignorance.

"I've known of learned Blackamoor musicians, men of great talent who composed scores of work. I envy that freedom. I didn't give the same understanding of such excellence to men and sisters who follow science. I apologize."

My answer seemed to satisfy her. She frowned less, and the second egg wasn't massacred. She cracked it and dropped a perfect yellow yolk into the bowl.

Yet, I wasn't satisfied. I didn't want to think some form of prejudice resided in my heart. "Georgie, in my ignorance, I hadn't heard of many Blackamoor men being allowed to study medicine. I know of doctors who sew up wounds or yank a tooth, but not learned professionals, never a physician. Carew lectured at one of the duke's meetings, but I didn't pay attention. I tried to write my sonata while listening to Livingston tell me he hired a courtesan."

"The fact that doctors are looked down upon as hacks but the word *physician* sounds grand is another invention of the ton. A person in pain needs help. They don't care if relief comes from a gentleman or not. And I think it takes a lot of skill to pull the right tooth. Where do you suppose those of us not in Mayfair would get medical aid?"

Walking around the table, I wanted to kiss her hand and beg forgiveness. She needed to see that I could own my faults.

"Georgie, we've talked about a cartoon that depicts the worst when races mix. We need to be able to talk of the politeness that sweeps around tolerated prejudice. I didn't know. I'm sorry. I only want the best for your sister."

"And the best can't come from Mr. Carew?"

"It could. It has. He could have the deepest understanding." I lightly tapped my fingers along a knot in the table-board but dug more deeply into my blindness. "Georgie, I'm trying to say that I automatically assumed the most intelligent souls would be like Livingston. That's wrong. But please don't hate my friend. He's a gentleman with an income. He's been scorned badly by marriage. That doesn't make him evil. He's human, flesh and blood."

"Why are you telling me this? You could keep your views a secret. That's what others would do. I know many saw the Gilroy cartoon and laughed."

"Actually, Livingston and my mother were horrified. They hate scandal."

She beat the ingredients in her bowl like it owed her money or had said something foul about one of her sisters. "If it wasn't you in the paper, they would laugh at what fool had been entangled by a daughter of the coal king."

"Yes. They would."

Georgie struck her dough, which smelled of ginger. "You should go compose your sonata."

My tongue began to tighten, and I felt my words being twisted into knots, but I had to tell her everything. "I must be completely honest with you. I wish . . . wish to come to you with all of me. My thoughts. My flaws. My hardships. My joys. You need to know that somewhere in my head I harbor these thoughts. I need you to challenge me, help me grow."

"You are grown, Mark Sebastian, Lord Mark Sebastian. I cannot control your thoughts. Nor do I want to be that guiding voice in your life."

"But you already are, Georgie. You have become important to me. And my jealousy—"

"What?"

"Yes, jealousy and sense of entitlement. I mean, you're my false fiancée. I take pride in that. I don't want a handsome man within a foot of you. You need a spice, come to me. I'll be spicy."

Her eyes sparkled like diamonds. She gaped at me. "It takes a big man to admit his weakness and when he's wrong."

I took the spoon from her hand. "I'm a big man, and you've become my weakness."

Dipping close to her lips, lips I'd dreamed about every moment since our last kiss, I took Georgina Wilcox, my Georgie in my arms, and put my mouth to hers. A jealous fool could become a learned man if it meant having this, a passion birthed from deep down, reaching all the way to the music woven in my soul.

Chapter 26

GEORGINA—COOKING UP THE TRUTH

Mark had me in his arms, kissing me while I had my hands full of flour.

"Forgive me," he said.

I might've gotten out a yes, before his lips found mine again.

Sweet like honey and cardamom, Mark's passion was better than I'd remembered. His hands encircled my waist, my hips, nestled me nearer.

Suddenly, I wished to be closer, close enough that I could reach into his mind and free his song.

Any anger I had at his tone left with his true apology.

But this, seeking me, wanting me, hungering for me in the kitchen, heated through any resistance I retained.

Skillful, his thumb dipped into the neckline of my gown and drew a treble clef along my throat. His mouth shifted and followed. His lips traced the arch of my neck.

When I felt his hands playing the ribbons of my corset, fingering the cording like pianoforte chords, I ran to the other side of the table and whispered, "I need to finish the biscuits."

"Georgie, I want your biscuits. I need them to be mine."

"The dough I've halved. It will make twelve. Is that enough?"

"There's never enough of you. I'm trying to say—"

"You should head back to the pianoforte."

"Why, Georgie? I was making music with *you*."

"This is a kitchen. The Duke of Torrance's enormous space with an oven and cabinetry on three walls—"

"The way you sound, the way you breathe, you're an instrument, a magnificent harp that my fingers must possess."

I eased to the wall with spices, my slippers stepping into the spilled flour he'd swept into a pile. "Look at these jars. He could have apothecaries train here."

"I hear you in my bed, singing my name as I love you. I want that. Don't run from us, Georgie."

His words silenced my ramble. Mark said he wished to love me.

He came closer. "Please don't run because I am not going to run. I have no more notes. Where they should be is your laugh or the sound of you saying my name. Even how you ask questions spins in my mind every waking minute and more when I drift to sleep."

Mark took me again in his arms and he held me. With brow against mine, he said, "Georgie, will you be my world. You are my every obsession, true and lovely. I need you to be mine."

This time when he kissed me, I melted against him. His arms held me safely and securely. His mouth sculpted mine, guiding my response, showing me how to relax and breathe.

He was passion and fire.

And I loved him.

A noise in the hall made me push him away. "We can't keep doing this. His Grace's housekeeper and butler both acquiesced to my using the kitchen. If I'm caught—"

"In the throes of passion with your fiancé, would that be wrong?"

Climbing up the short ladder, I wiped up the last of the spilled flour from the wall of jars. "It's a game, remember."

"That kiss was no game. My confession is true."

"None of this can be true. It's what we agreed."

"We can un-agree."

"Mark, that's not a word."

He came to the ladder and put his hands out to steady it. "What if we turned our false secret courtship into a true one? Come down, Georgie."

It was safer up here. I couldn't be weak and make a mistake that would ruin me and my sisters.

"Then I will wait for you to come down, Sweet Georgie."

My music teacher stayed at the bottom of the ladder with arms stretched wide to teach me about love or being in love.

Yet, I already knew.

I saw what it did to Katherine, and I felt the ruining of the duke by the loss of love.

Though I was sure I did love Mark and I knew I liked the way it felt to be kissed by him, I wasn't going to be left devastated by love. I wasn't a gambler. I couldn't risk the misery of a broken heart.

"Please come down." His hand was on my ankle, by the lace of my chemise. His finger heated through my stockings.

I jumped from the ladder.

He took my hand and steadied me. "Why are you frightened by me, Georgie?"

"I'm not frightened by you but by what this means. Mark, what are you asking me?"

"You're a gentlewoman. I am a gentleman. Let's be engaged. Let's love."

"And then what, Mark?"

"Be happy?"

"That's not an answer." I climbed back on the ladder. "We should try some of these spices. I'm looking for the right thing to add to my biscuits."

Before he could respond, I handed him one. The label was in Russian. "Wonder what *spetsiya* is?"

Mark took the jar and popped open the top. "Shall we?"

He whipped a finger in and I did too. At the same time, like we were performing a ritual, we stuck the samplings into our mouths.

And began coughing.

"Pepper. Strong pepper," I said when I could swallow without tasting fire.

"Let's stick to the containers in English." He cleared his throat. "There must be a pump and water in the larder. Let's find it."

We went to the closet-sized room and began to roam about in the dark.

Mark was behind me. Then his arms were about me.

He spun me and kissed me with his fiery mouth.

With hands at my hips, I found him rushing, lifting my hem, touching my bodice, making me feel like liquid, like a rolling boil, like I'd soon be nothing but steam.

I didn't want a moment or a memory in the dark. "No. No. Mark."

He backed into the light.

I smoothed my bodice of wrinkles and picked up my apron, which had fallen. I wanted to wear it like a shawl to cover the swells of my bosom that his hands had lovingly caressed.

My cheeks had to be flame for I wanted more of his touch. It might be wonderful to be free like vapor.

"Georgie, marry me." He took out a handkerchief and wiped at his brow. His waistcoat had wrinkled, his shirt too. "I've not wanted a woman so much, not like this. You're in my head."

"Am I crowding out the notes?"

"Yes. No. Of course not." He stuck his hand in his straight dark brown, almost black hair. "Everything is a torment. If I could have you, have your love, I might be free."

"But then, what would I be? A wife? A mistress of a third son? I have no fortune. I don't think the Marchioness of Prahmn would be pleased with such a bride."

"She'll come around. She always has."

"And your father? Will he come around?"

He rubbed his brow. "He . . . they don't matter. This is about us."

"I saw my brother-in-law be rejected. It was painful for Tavis. Do you want to go live across the river and use your scope to view Mayfair, the world where you used to belong?"

He put his hands to my shoulders. "Georgie, you're getting ahead of yourself."

"I'm not running right now. But I'm heading to the truth. You've said you want my love, that you want to marry me. Shall I be the excuse for no sonata? No Harlbert's Prize?"

"What?" Mark pulled away. "Georgie?"

"I know your parents will blame me for ruining you. But will you blame me too?"

"Georgie, no. How can I convince you?"

"Every naysayer will claim I distracted your genius. Your very smart friend Livingston will state I'm the cause of your misery. He'll crow that I stole the notes to your music. That my problems or concerns overshadowed yours."

"No, Georgie, he'll claim I'm in love with you because I loved the painting of Dido."

"What? Is this a fetish? You love a painting of a Black woman and now you care for me?"

"Yes. No. Livingston is wrong. Georgie, I wouldn't do that. You're not a painting and I'd never blame you for my failings or every time I wasn't good enough."

"I can't take that chance. Make-believe is safer. That's the world where Lord Mark and Miss Wilcox live happily ever after. Not 1817, Mayfair."

His cheeks became red; he was speechless.

My heart was safe in my chest. I went back to the dough I'd been making. "I've let the eggs sit too long. I hope that doesn't make my biscuits flat. The duke loves my biscuits."

Mark folded his arms. "You've had a chance to rethink the

duke's offer. You're looking to be the mistress of this place, the Duchess of Torrance. The duke told me bits of your conversation."

"Nonsense. His Grace is a friend." I watched thunderclouds cover Mark's face. He didn't believe me, or that a woman would turn down two gentlemen to maintain her peace.

"Is money important to you, Georgie? In a husband, is that a consideration?"

"One of many. Does he have to be as wealthy as the Duke of Torrance? No. But he must have some prospects. Children have to be provided for. And look at you."

"Yes, I'm quite aware of my circumstances."

"My brother-in-law was cut off from his family. He relied on my sister's money. Men look for means as well. His habits almost bankrupted us. If a man can't stand on his own, no matter what he inherits, he's not much use to a wife."

Mark put his hands in his tailcoat pockets. "Well, I suppose that rules my name off your list. I will inherit nothing. I have very little."

"It should've been off the list when you thought I'd marry the duke. Or when, for a moment, you thought Mr. Carew had my eye. You hurriedly wanted to make love to me, merely to claim me. We've exchanged no vows, or done anything to make the moment mean something other than my ruin."

"Is this what you think of me? Georgie, I profess to thinking myself in love. I'm not that experienced with women. Most of you terrify me, but don't doubt what I feel. You are music."

"How do you wish me to be your music when you have doubts? You alone have my kisses and you question my fidelity to our false alliance. Shouldn't I have doubts about you saying anything to bed me?"

"It's a larder. No bed. Just standing up, holding you, centering you in pleasure, worshiping your body . . ." He covered his mouth. "A thousand pardons. I shouldn't say—"

"At least you've said aloud you want me, but that's not enough."

"Georgie, if I tell someone I want to marry them and they don't believe me, then we have a problem. Perhaps we are of two different worlds."

"We are. And it's nice to cross the river, but you have to choose where to live. We can wait until you win a prize to go forward with our life. Anything before will have Livingston and everyone else saying I was your ruin."

"I *am* ruined, Georgie. I can't stop thinking of you. It's too late to turn away because I am in love with you."

I moved farther from him. "No. Don't say any more. I won't be swayed to a bed or wall."

"There isn't a wall between us except the ones you are building to keep us apart. Why are you twisting my words? You know I struggle with them. I don't want to offend you. I want to love you."

I started stirring the stiff dough. All the flour was wasted. If I put this on the table, it would stick. None of these biscuits would be any good. Mark and I wouldn't be any good, not when the passion died.

"Georgie, I know you feel what's between us. Our struggle is in vain. We should be together."

"I don't want struggle, Mark. I don't want to work so hard at being in love. That's what the ton wants for couples like us— troubles, humiliation, strife. That's what Gilroy's cartoon captured, two fools exhibiting about a pianoforte, being lovey-dovey, while the world plots their doom." I shook my head, then went to the waste bin and dumped the dough.

I turned and took a long look at the man I loved, dark hair and eyes, and knew what I felt wasn't enough. "At the duke's ball, I sing. You play. Then we end our secret affair as we had planned. We stop now, no one is hurt. We can go on as friends. No one's future is changed."

He wiped at his mouth and headed toward the door. "I gave my word. I'll continue our charade. Maybe this heartache will clear enough space for the notes to flow."

"I want you to win, Mark. But I need to win too."

With a bow, my music teacher left.

When I no longer heard his footsteps, I ran to the larder, pitched my biscuit bowl into the sink and cried.

Chapter 27

MARK—LESSONS IN LIFE

Once Torrance gave me word that Lydia Wilcox had opened her eyes and had even gotten out of bed, I knew that the child would live. Relieved, I packed up my books, told Dido I was hers again, then took my portmanteau and left Anya House.

The stars were out.

I couldn't see them while hiding in the music room.

Staying in there, even when Georgina passed with the most fragrant biscuits I'd ever smelled, was difficult. My stomach wanted to betray me. Blast it, I wanted to return to her and understand what I'd done wrong.

I had to have fouled things up somehow. If she wanted me to win, why did I feel like a loser?

No one wanted to struggle. I couldn't control what my parents thought, or the ton.

But why should that matter?

My mother was my champion. Surely, she could help me sway Prahmn.

Not wanting to wake the grooms who worked in the mews, I walked toward Grosvenor Street. I'd return in the morning for my horse.

I counted the lights on in the houses I passed. Most were dark. One might be having a late dinner party. I heard the music of dancing and imagined people whirling to the tune. Yet the picture of a resolute woman saying she wanted the fake relationship over something true made me ache.

Other than the Carew business and the duke stuff, what had I done wrong? With each of these crimes, I could attest to being a fool. Then there was the stupidest thing: admitting to loving Georgie. I'd never told a woman that before.

Was that so wrong, to admit what was so right?

Maybe I didn't have the answers for what tomorrow would bring, not the ones she wanted.

But I was honest about my heart.

I wanted Georgina Wilcox.

I loved Georgie Wilcox.

I wished to marry Georgie.

A half hour of walking brought me through the cool night to 75 Grosvenor Street, the house of Prahmn, and perhaps the realization that Georgie didn't want to marry me or anyone.

She ran initially from the false alliance, and now that things were true, she ran from us too.

Slipping into the house through the service entry, I found it quiet. But Chancey, the light sleeper, caught me. He shook his head and admonished me to be quiet.

There were questions I wanted to ask him, but the diligent man didn't need a fool keeping him up asking the meaning of life.

He gave me a candle to keep from tripping over the stairs and waking the house.

Standing in the quiet hall, I listened to nothing.

No music.

No servants scampering about.

My mother was probably the only one home, and she'd be upstairs in her bedchamber, asleep to the troubles of the world, or at least the dilemmas facing her younger son.

Up the curving stairs, I went straight to the music room. Like my mother's parlor, it had beautiful windows, lovely sheers that shimmered and reflected the starlight. It was too late to begin playing, but I sat at the pianoforte. I tugged out my papers from my stack and looked at the notes I'd written. *Da da dum.*

The glimpses of the melody that unfurled when I held Georgina, now I saw them all. The fear of rejection by the Harlbert's Prize committee had been dislodged by something more immediate and true: Georgie's rejection of starting a life with me.

The pressure I'd placed on my creativity gave way to my ego. My heart being destroyed because my offer to be a loving husband, an honorable mate, was rejected was a crushing blow.

A song could be fashioned by this loss.

A life together should be a lasting choice.

Candlelight flickered at the door. My mother stood there in a gorgeous pink robe and paper curlers peeking out of her matching mobcap.

"Mark? That is you."

"Yes, Mama, I was in the neighborhood."

"At three o'clock in the morning? You were at some wretched neighbor's dinner party and they didn't invite me? How rude." She chuckled. "You all right?"

"Yes. Quite fine." I, the liar, opened the pianoforte and stared at the keys. From my portmanteau, I took out my bottle of ink and quill.

Papering the melody I heard in my head became easy. This new sonata was full and sweeping. It was everything, and it came from deep inside me.

When I finally looked up, I saw my mother still standing there, holding the candle, gawking.

"Mama, is something wrong?"

"No. I like watching you create, but I thought you were your father. When his little adventures go wrong, I find him here sulking, looking for someone to listen to his troubles, remind him that he's not an old fool."

Is that what she called my father's affairs, *adventures*? How could she be so forgiving for such open betrayal?

He was an old fool and my mother still cared for him. I gazed at her and wanted to ask why.

But that was their marriage.

It was not the type of union I ever aspired to. I wondered if that was what Georgie thought I was asking.

"Mama, you can go on to bed. I'm just going to sit here and work on my sonata. I think it's going to be good."

"They say heartache is the best teacher."

Well, then I should be a genius by morning.

She came inside the room and sat in the small chair by the window. Putting down her candle, she pulled her hands together. The Prahmn family jewel, a lovely ruby ring, glimmered on her finger next to a simple silver band, something her father gave her.

"Was it worth the ruby, Mama? Father's a fool to keep hurting you."

"You get numb to it. I've actually become a very strong woman. Yes, it takes a great deal of strength to walk into a room where half the people are gossiping about you and the father of your children. You have to learn to look serene, knowing there are women in your midst who take pleasure in your downfall."

"Mama, if I asked someone to marry me, is that what she thinks I'm asking? Is it possible she believes marriage is a misery?"

For a moment, my mother looked very serious, more serious than I'd ever seen. She leaned back in the chair, touching her finger to her nose. She said, "Marriage can be wonderful. There are some memories which are the greatest joys in my life. I shared them with your father. Others I've shared with my children."

She looked down at her ring. "Prahmn and I were not a love match, not on his part. I was wealthy, a little too carried away by his ardor, and a little too naïve about life. My father had a special license curried by the archbishop. We married. My family's reputation remained spotless. I have a title and an often-empty bed."

I'd never heard her say this so plainly, why she'd married my father. "I'm sorry, Mama."

"Both people have to want the unity. There's no comfort in being a wife who doesn't have her husband's favor. There's no comfort for a husband who's lost his wife's respect."

I banged the keys by accident. "What does it mean to lose respect if you keep forgiving him?"

She rubbed her arms as if a breeze fell upon her. "Can mean a lot of things. It means not caring about what's important to him. Making sure he sees how his latest mistress snubs him. Encouraging the son who wishes to shape up to pursue his heart and the woman who has his."

"What?"

"The Dowager Livingston sent her son to see me directly. He told me you've stayed at Anya House waiting for Miss Wilcox's sister to recover. Your father barely waited for me to be out of labor."

"Well, Livingston doesn't have the latest gossip. She's rejected me."

"Oh. If there's a way to recover her, try. Remember what brought you together."

Couldn't believe my mother's words, but I heard them. Then I heard more of my song. *Dada dada. Dada da dum.*

I dipped my pen in the ink and began to write. Furiously, I filled the page.

When I finished the last stanza, my mother was asleep. She'd stayed the entire time, listening to me hum and write my notes.

The work wasn't finished, but I had a good foundation. In life, in love, in creating this sonata, I had that. Things weren't easy. I fought for every note, but I had them. No one could take them away.

Georgina Wilcox, my stubborn Georgie, was worth fighting for. But I had to win the goal I put in place.

Getting this sonata done, establishing my career, would show her I could be counted upon. Winning the Harlbert's Prize would show her I was my own man.

Yet, I wasn't.

I sat in my mama's house, writing at her piano.

Shaking my head, I corked my ink.

An independent composer was worthy of a woman like Georgie Wilcox. I had to become him. Sacrifices now would pay off in the end. And we still had our faux relationship to keep me in her sphere and close to her heart.

Chapter 28

GEORGINA—BACK TO NORMAL NEVER

Life had settled back to normal on Ground Street. We all sat around the breakfast table eating fresh scones that I baked with the fruits and fresh cream the duke had sent.

Two weeks had passed since we all left Anya House, two weeks since we last saw the duke or Mark.

Lydia was joyful and bouncy and healthy, humming and stuffing her cheeks with bits of bread and cream. "Love this. Can we go see the duke?"

Scarlett looked at me. I glanced at Katherine as she whispered, *Never.*

Lydia's eyes became big. "I thought one of you would marry him by now. I gave him up for you."

Scarlett, who I confirmed hadn't been asked, stood up. She wore men's slippers under her long skirt. That meant she had breeches underneath and would be heading to the Royal Society or one of the duke's meetings. "I'm going to the market," she said. "Shall I bring anything back?"

I wanted to say *no new trouble* but that would be hard for Scarlett.

"Just be home before sunset," Katherine said. "We need to

discuss the offer I have on the table. I've found a buyer for Wilcox Coal."

"What?" I shook my head. "You were supposed to get a loan. Not sell."

"No banker wants to extend credit. It's a fair offer. We can pay off Tavis's debts. The house would be unencumbered. I could invest the rest to support us and offer dowries—"

"For Lydia. That's how long it will take to earn something sizable." Scarlett went to the door. "I don't want to run the business, but if you think it's best, then do it. I want to be free of everything Tavis touched."

She ran out the door. Katherine looked as if she'd been kicked in the face.

Lydia went to her and hugged her neck. "Tavis was funny. I wished he liked you more. He might've taken better care of us."

The little girl took another nip of her scone and dashed upstairs.

Katherine folded her arms and rocked in the chair. "Come on, Georgina. Tell me how terrible this is for you, how terrible Tavis was, or how terrible I am."

I lifted from my chair, went to my sister, and kissed her brow. "There's nothing any one of us can say to you that you haven't already said to yourself. You know what you did, you know what Tavis did. None of that is your fault. You were married, you didn't have a choice. Marriage takes it all away."

She reached out and grabbed my hand. "I did have a choice. Wilcox Coal was ours, not mine, and I gave Tavis full control, trying to prove to him that I loved him. That he had my respect. Then he proved over and over that he wasn't worth any of it—the love or the respect. I will never forgive myself. For what could've happened with Lydia, I'm just happy Mr. Carew has promised to always be available to us."

Katherine rarely admitted that she made a mistake. I didn't know what to say or do with that. I looked at her and wondered if this was defeat talking. There had to be a way to save everything.

Then I knew there was a way. "Katherine, have you thought about asking the duke for help? I'm sure he would give us a loan. I know he'd do it on good terms. Then, we could truly make a new start."

She folded her arms. "He's still here. The food on the table. The rug that he sent to Lydia."

"Katherine, she likes the rug. It's warm and cozy for her feet. He even got her to promise to keep her socks on when walking over the carpet. The duke will do anything to make sure she doesn't get sick again."

She covered her eyes with her hand. The only thing stopping my sister from seeing the good the man did was her pride.

Katherine rubbed her temples. "I can't ask." She groaned and shook her head, and then stopped. "We just have to get through the ball in a few weeks and remain respectable. I don't have to make a decision on selling until then. If I can find a way to stomach asking, I'll do it for you girls because you deserve me trying everything. Asking a favor of Torrance would be everything."

With a *good day*, I left the table and headed to the parlor. My debut singing with Mark still had to happen. I still had to pretend to choose a new suitor to break off with him or something. That part of the plan was fuzzy.

Nonetheless, the *Post* had a new Gilroy cartoon, a party with abolitionists and more comically drawn mixed couples. The scandal hadn't died.

Fingers in position like Mama taught us, I began to play and sing my hymn.

Our little pianoforte didn't sound as strong as the duke's, but it was a lot safer than practicing with Mark.

The urge to send Mr. Thom with a note to apologize. With Mark, I'd found a new way of running away from pain. All I had to do was dredge up every potential problem and all his and my flaws and that was enough. I made Mark as bad as Tavis. I even sounded like Katherine in doing so.

At least I had run from heartbreak.

Mark wasn't Tavis, but I couldn't take the risk. We Wilcoxes had been through enough.

After leaving Scarlett and Lydia at home to do chores, my sister dragged me to Wilcox Coal. It was Friday. The Duke of Torrance had sent word that he'd visit at the house today.

I had a feeling Katherine purposely left to avoid seeing him. I wanted to see the duke and make sure that it was meetings keeping him busy these past two weeks, the two weeks since we left Anya House.

Didn't want him to be sick.

After Lydia, being ill had a whole new terror associated with it.

Katherine was a good sister, a good person. But like our father, she was loath to apologize. She needed to say those words to the duke. He'd been sweet to us and continued to be. If she asked, he'd definitely give her a loan to keep Wilcox Coal and be rid of the creditors.

Mr. Thom came in from the last run of the day. "Got a new coal customer." His tone was bubbly, but his hands and face bore black dust. "Another one of the duke's neighbors wants us."

"Excellent," I said.

"Soon, ladies, we'll have all of James Street. Next, his entire neighborhood."

He doffed his jet hat to me, and then Katherine. "Your papa would be very proud. You're growing this business again. Girls can do better at the runnin' and the mathin'."

After wiping his hands clean, he took off his fine red coat that matched the color of our company's painted wood sign and left.

The door rattled shut and it was just me and Katherine again.

"Don't start saying what I know you're thinking."

I brought my fingers to my chest. "Me? What could I know?"

She balled her hands, and then dropped into the chair behind our father's old desk.

For a few minutes, I could see him there with his quill in one hand and ledger book in the other.

"Since you don't want to talk about the obvious, why did you bring me down here?"

Katherine glanced at me. "I'd love for you to get inspired by these walls. I'd love for you to love this place like I love it, like our father loved it. That's why he sent me away to finishing school to learn accounting."

"I admire the business. It puts a roof over our heads. It once employed a lot of folks on this side of the Thames. But it's not what I want to do with my life, Katherine." And from what I remembered, Katherine being sent away for schooling didn't add to her happiness.

Her great adventure, which caused Tavis and the duke to fall in love with her, she never talked about. Maybe today was the day.

I moved about the creaking wood floors and went to the other desk on the other side of the room, a smaller desk. One where Katherine had often sat as Papa worked.

"Kitty, this place is you. Being in business was your dream. What happened the summer of your great adventure? When did you meet the Duke of Torrance?"

My sister winced like I'd poked her. "I don't feel like talking about the past."

I tapped the desk. "Then I'm going back to the house. I'll get Lydia to ask him for a loan."

"He wasn't a duke yet. I didn't know that he'd be one. He was plain ole Jahleel Charles, but there has never been anything plain about him."

Spinning around, I couldn't believe my ears. "Keep talking, Kitty."

Her mouth opened wide. Then she snapped her lips closed.

I waited but she started looking at ledger books.

"You tried, Kitty. Try again tomorrow."

When my fingers clasped the doorlatch, she said, "Don't go back. He's bringing Lord Mark Sebastian with him."

My feet froze. "What?"

"The duke's note said he would bring Lord Mark with him. I didn't think you wanted to see the composer. So I brought you here to—"

"To run?"

She looked away, then reared back in the chair, putting her short boots along the desk's blotter. "Papa would have made things easier for you. He would tell Lord Mark to stick to the plan and not confuse you. Since our father's not here, I have to step in and help."

"So instead of teaching me to stand up for myself, you want me to hide. Somehow, that doesn't sound like you or Papa."

While we both fumed, the door opened. Mr. Thom returned and ushered in the duke and Mark. "See, they are both here, your lordship, your dukeship."

Our man-of-all-work made an exaggerated bow, then strutted from the office.

"So this is the famed Wilcox Coal office," the duke said. He again had the cane with the African-looking carvings. Though he looked fit and healthy, I wondered if he'd been sick. Yet, I'd ask about that another time when my hands weren't sweaty.

Mark presented himself to me. "Shall we take a walk, Miss Wilcox? I'd like you to show me your favorite spots to walk along this side of the river. That will give Torrance and Lady Hampton a chance to clear the air between them."

Not wanting to be rude, not ready to admit that I'd missed him, I agreed. "Yes, that will give the duke and my sister a chance to talk about Wilcox Coal and other important things."

I gave Katherine the evil eye or my pushy one. This was our opportunity to save Wilcox Coal. All she had to do was overcome her pride and ask the duke for a loan.

Mark held out his arm to me and we proceeded out the office, leaving two grimacing individuals to battle.

Chapter 29

GEORGINA—A WAGER FOR MY LIFE

The Thames, in the afternoon, was a cluttered sight. Barges taking people and goods from shore to shore competed with ships darting down the river to head out to sea.

The noise of it sounded like life, busy and full. Yet Mark and I, both full of life and no sickness, were quiet as squirrels scurrying along the banks.

"Umm, you look well, Miss Wilcox . . . Georgina."

With a nod, I pointed him to the spot between the tavern and the lumberyard. "You can have a better view here. It might inspire you."

"Georgina, you never worry about being here amongst the industry?"

"I grew up on Ground Street. Everyone knows everyone else. Nothing but good honest people live and work here."

"Oh, I see."

"I wish you did, Lord Mark. There are a lot of misconceptions about this side of the river."

He stopped, gently tugging on my arm until I moved my hand from my pocket to his palm. "Can I say I'm sorry? Can I say I've missed you?"

"You can say all of that. Whether you mean it or not, that's up to you to decide."

"No, it's you who must change my circumstances. I offended

you. I only showed my desire for you. I had no plan to truly offer about how we'd live, how I'd earn a living. I was not being fair. I took many things for granted."

He looked contrite. The way he held my hand, so softly with his thumb rubbing against mine, I knew everything. That he truly wanted my forgiveness, and me.

"You are forgiven. Anyone can be overcome in the moment. My biscuits are quite delicious."

"But I still haven't had one." He laughed, and I did too. Then we walked a little deeper between the properties to get to the shore.

"It looks the same here. I don't think the sides matter." He took a long breath of the sulphury air. "The duke's ball is coming up. I want to show you favor. I want everybody to see that you have my attention. I don't want to fake break apart. I want to ask for your hand, properly."

I squinted at him, trying to figure out how to tell him I hadn't changed my mind. "How does my not begging off dispel the rumors about us, about that kiss? You had to have seen Gilroy's latest horrible cartoon."

"I did, but it's a reprint of one of his earlier horrible pieces. There have been rumors about us, couples of different races, always. The politics that are happening make those against such unions crazed. We can't let them stop us."

"I don't want to be an example for the world. My sister suffered because of her husband. All of us have. I can't."

"If you didn't love me, then I'd understand. But I think you do. We're not playing anymore. Or at least, I'm not playing anymore. I want—"

I put a finger to his lips. I didn't need for him to say that he wanted me to be his wife or that we'd have a happily-ever-after or that we could build a family and a life together. "Here are my conditions to consider. You tell me if they've been met."

"Conditions, Georgie? This is a negotiation?"

"Conditions." I started to walk back to the office.

"Wait. Tell me what they are."

Folding my arms about me, I said, "Have you informed your parents?"

"My mother knows. Prahmn is on holiday."

"Do you have their blessing?"

"My mother's."

"Do you have their assurances that your powerful father will not use his influence against us or my family?"

His handsome face looked down to the river. The Thames had no answers, not for this.

"Have you finished your sonata? Have you entered that great competition?"

"No. But I'm so close, closer than I've ever been. The committee will love it. You will love it."

"Close is not good enough. You need to finish. You need to be established. You need to be so advanced that if Prahmn changed his mind, he couldn't hurt you."

"My father wouldn't hurt me. The gossip of his cruelty would hurt him. He'll not do anything to open the Sebastians to scandal."

These answers offered no comfort. "Have you ever finished a sonata?"

"Yes, but always after the deadline. Then I play in public at one of my mother's parties or Prahmn's Winter Ball."

"Then use one of those. They must be good if you intended it for the Harlbert's Prize."

"They've been played in public. That disqualifies any work I've already written. Why are you so resistant to this notion of us being committed? I think we can find a way to be happy."

"It won't work. I don't want to be made the villain because you didn't get the things that you want."

"Then I know what I must do."

"We can remain friends?"

"No. I must finish the sonata by the time of the duke's ball. You shall see me submit it. Then, Georgie, you need to be prepared to be public about our engagement."

"At the duke's ball, we are supposed to end this false relationship. I'm supposed to let you go because of new interests."

"We can do that. We can even do it publicly. But the very next day, I will cross the river and be on the street where you live, asking to start anew."

Mark claimed my hand again and led me down Ground Street. He seemed cheered, while I was less assured.

At least I listened to him, and I think he heard me. If he couldn't finish the sonata by the duke's ball, Mark would walk away from us. I wouldn't have to be the villain.

When we returned to the office of Wilcox Coal, I heard a lot of shouting—angry Russian, frustrated, feminine English.

When I opened the door, I saw the duke seated on top of Papa's desk and my sister walking back and forth in front of him, listing numerous faults that I didn't think were his.

Had Katherine mixed up Tavis and the duke?

Mark coughed, trying to get their attention.

The duke acknowledged us with a glance, but then he went back to antagonizing my sister. "Look, here come witnesses to hear for themselves how you put pride over everything."

"You egotistical fool. I don't need you. None of us need you."

"That's why the Wilcoxes, a once proud Blackamoor family, are crumbling. It's clear, Lady Hampton, that you'll not do what's in the best interest of yourself or your sisters, particularly the sweet child Lydia. I've made a promise to her, as solemnly as I would to Anya. It's why I've acquired all of Lord Hampton's debts. Everything that would take away Wilcox Coal or your house on Ground Street is now under my control."

Katherine sputtered, her face grew darker and fiery. "No one asked you to do this. You're always overstepping your bounds."

"What am I to do, Katherine? Am I to let you starve in the streets while I dine well in Mayfair? Am I to let your father's legacy come to nothing because of the fool you married? Nyet, that's your job to destroy everything."

She turned away. Her eyes were glassy.

The duke wasn't wrong about Tavis and the damage to our family, but he wasn't right in making it Katherine's fault. I stepped forward, holding my breath to enter the fray. "The only reason she married Lord Hampton was to restore her honor and to use his connections to help Wilcox Coal."

Katherine's countenance faltered. "Georgina, go. Lord Mark, take her home. I can finish this and get rid of His Grace."

"Yes, get rid of those who help, and hold on to the memory of the fool who put you in a position of weakness."

"Don't call him that. Have some respect. Lord Hampton was there for me when I needed someone. His friendship never abandoned me. No one else can claim that."

For the first time since Mark and I entered, the duke glanced down, seemingly unsure, even sorrowful. He fingered the highest carving on his cane, the head of a lion. "Tavis always had good timing, not good luck or good judgment, though."

This made Katherine gasp. "Are you saying I wasn't worthy to marry?"

He raised his gaze, gawking as if that was the stupidest statement ever uttered. "Tavis knew how to find me. He should've sent for me. I would've come back for you."

"The world doesn't work on your schedule, Jahleel."

"Is there a reason why you couldn't wait for me to return? Tell me a reason, a truthful reason. I need to hear it from you."

My sister swiped at her eyes, like she wasn't minutes from sobbing. "I couldn't wait to marry Tavis. He loved me. He was there when I needed to be supported, not abandoned for May-fair."

"Tell me, Katherine. Look at me and tell me why, when you had my support, my love. Why couldn't you wait?"

The room felt like Hades. The gaze between them was so intense that the walls of Wilcox Coal should be on fire. Then it hit me in my gut—every moment, every stolen glance that danced between them, was their past love, all the ruining secrets of my sister's grand adventure.

"Jahleel, you know nothing about love or commitment. You left. You took your path. I chose mine. Nothing else." She looked at me. "Nothing can be changed. It is done. Over."

"Torrance." Mark pointed to the door. "Let's leave. When a lady demands we go, we must."

The fierce lift of the duke's chin, the flicking of his hand dismissed Mark like he was a child or a servant. "I need an answer. I must hear if I have misjudged Katherine. I need a reason for all of the pain."

Mark backed up and whispered to me, "Perhaps you and I should leave and let them finish this. They need to finish this."

"You were right the first time, Lord Mark. Take the duke and go."

"Kitty, calm down. Think of what we discussed. Save us from our present troubles, not win an old fight from the past."

"Miss Wilcox, you are right. Sebastian too." The duke rubbed his palm against his weathered cane. "This needs to be finished right now in a language that Tavis taught his wife: a bet."

Katherine dug in our father's desk and found a handkerchief. "I thought you didn't bet anymore. Another lie?"

"Oh, Katherine, how droll. I gave up gambling for Lent six years ago. Today, it's warranted. A simple bet. Winner takes all."

Mark tugged my sleeve and edged closer to the door.

Even though this was grown fools' business, business Tavis had set in place, I couldn't leave Katherine. "Please stop this, both of you."

"Georgina, stay," Katherine said. "For a bet to be honored, it must have a witness."

"You hate gambling, sister. This is crazy. Never bet more than we can afford. The duke can buy everything."

"I need him to know I can't be bought. My opinion of him will never change. Jahleel, show everyone your true colors."

"Never make a wager when you're angry," I said. "You two are matches and kerosene."

"What about Wilcox Coal? That would be a better . . ." Mark bit his lip. "Shutting up now."

I left him and stood close enough to touch my sister, to let her collapse against me and let out that sob she'd stubbornly refused to shed. "Kitty, no. This is ridiculous. Your Grace, I beg you to forgive my sister and I pray that you be on your way."

Katherine turned to me and shook her head. "Not this time. He's proposed a wager that will rid him from my life. I'll take it."

"And there you have it, Miss Wilcox. My dear Katherine is entering the betting stage, slipping into the sickness that dragged Tavis down. A better man would save her from herself. I'm not a better man. I'm a determined one."

"Miracle. He admits to not being a god."

He scoffed, said something in Russian that added more red to her bronze face. "If she wins, all the debt instruments I've paid in full will be given to the Wilcoxes. All these bills will be liquidated. You will owe nothing. Your house and Wilcox Coal will be unencumbered."

Mark drew my way. His blue eyes widened and he whispered, "The bet will crush her."

No. The duke was a good person. "What is it you get if you win?" I covered my mouth, but I had to know if anger had turned my kind friend into the devil.

"Not much, Miss Wilcox . . . Katherine, my dear Lady Hampton, will marry me. And you and all your sisters, especially Lydia, will be wards under my protection at Anya House."

"Torrance, you're betting for a wife and family." Mark bit his lip, but his laughter wouldn't stop. "You want to wed a woman who hates you, to have a full house. Have more science meetings, man. Don't subject yourself to torture. We should've brought Livingston. He'd set you straight."

For someone who'd just tried to convince me to marry him, this was the wrong thing to say. "My sister isn't a torture."

"I can speak for myself, Georgina." Katherine took a long cleansing breath. "I am fully capable of telling these two to go to the devil."

"The *d'yavol* can take his due now," the duke said. "I can simply force bankruptcy of your business and foreclose on the house. Is that what you want, Katherine? That's what others were plotting to do. The bank, the creditors have been smiling in your face and laughing at Gilroy's cartoons."

She gritted her teeth at him but didn't answer.

He shrugged, slipped around her and sat in Papa's chair. "This is comfortable. Sebastian, remind me when I sell off the assets to keep this chair. It will go in my bedchamber."

Mark was speechless and useless.

I shook Katherine. "End this. Apologize. Don't let him take what's left of Papa's legacy or you might as well have let Tavis destroy us."

"My fault." Her breathing became rough. "I need this bet. Give me the rest of the terms."

"While Miss Wilcox and Sebastian were away, you berated me about not knowing your sisters or you. That's what you claimed. I think I do. I know I do. The bankers don't want you to use the sale of Wilcox Coal for dowries. That's what you told them. You've obviously thought you could find them husbands."

"The bankers . . . did you send them?"

"No. But I've made it my business to know yours. I will give your sisters dowries and find each of them a good and proper husband. I can do this for Georgina and Scarlett before you can."

"That's a stupid bet," she said, and I agreed.

"Stupid maybe, but I should do something to honor Tavis. This bet will break no one's back."

"Katherine, apologize. No betting. This is crazy." I grabbed her hands like she'd fallen down a dark well.

Yet, the way her black eyes raged, I didn't think there was any turning back or finding the light.

"Jahleel, I don't want to marry. Not you or anyone. But I'll be your mistress for a season."

"Mistress? Not a wife. A true mistress? Are you serious, Katherine? What about scandal? What about Mama?"

"I'm a widow. Society doesn't notice us much. Many peers make mistresses of us, and no one cares." She stood up tall, like she awaited punishment. "Avoiding scandal, trying to do what's best is why we are in this horrid position. Yes. A mistress, sharing a bed. Pretending to care, making you more crazed for the memory of a girl you once loved . . . Yes, Jahleel, but only for a season."

He rubbed his chin. "I counted on a lifetime. My lifetime. If you and the girls spend two nights a week at Anya House starting now until the next season ends, yes."

That would be a year of shuffling across the river. A year and three months if he won.

The duke stuck out his hand.

Katherine almost took it but stopped. "Lord Mark doesn't count. Their playacting relationship ends, no more between them. So, he doesn't count in this bet."

"That would mean you're asking the duke to find me someone else, someone not Lord Mark." My stomach hurt. I didn't want to marry, but I truly didn't want to marry someone who wasn't Mark.

"Yes, but you told me yourself you're not ready to marry. So, Lord Mark Sebastian is not the one. The duke will have to find you someone else. Or, he can give up now and say I won."

"Nyet! Never. Sebastian counts on neither side." He rose

from the chair and clasped her hand and shook it, then kissed it. "It will be a pleasure to have a proper mistress again."

Katherine took her hand from him and slapped him, but he caught her hand and held it to his face. "Gentle. Gentle. I like my women to be easy."

He released her and moved to the door. "Let me know which days. The games begin this week. Lady Hampton, prepare to *win*."

"Torrance, don't you mean you want her to lose?" Mark followed him. "I mean, I want you to lose and not find Miss Wilcox a mate."

"For Lady Hampton to truly win is to gain the security and joy that comes with my protection, whether that be for a season or forever will be up to the betting gods. Come along, Sebastian. Let's let the ladies lock up my coal company."

"It's not yours, Jahleel." Katherine sneered at him like she wanted to slap him again.

His light olive skin still bore a red print along his jaw.

"It's still ours," I said. "It's still Wilcox Coal."

"And I know my sisters!" Katherine's voice was loud. "You won't find them a match."

"*Do svidaniya*, ladies."

The two left, and I turned to Katherine. Her emotions were so volatile, she shook. She wept.

I embraced her. Rocking her in my arms, I whispered, "What have you done?"

Chapter 30

MARK—EARLY WORMS OF MAYFAIR

As soon as the morning turned to a decent hour, I was on the steps of the Duke of Torrance's Anya House. For the past three days, the man refused to talk of anything but some process to find Georgina a perfect match.

Perhaps today, a cooler head would prevail.

Mr. Steele greeted me in the hall. "Lord Mark. I didn't think you'd come today. You were already excluded from the competition. Pity. I thought you and Miss Wilcox were a good match."

If only my future bride thought the same. "Where is Torrance?"

After a footman took my hat and gloves, Steele led me to the dining room.

"His Grace is enjoying his breakfast. He has a good hearty appetite. Please don't upset him."

"What? Everything about this insane wager is upsetting."

Steele offered me a patient smile. "Do you expect him to back down, to be a better man? Why? Why shouldn't he do what he wishes and get what he wants? Any other man would act the same, why not the Duke of Torrance?"

Two wrongs, a thousand wrongs, made nothing right. "It's a ridiculous wager. Miss Wilcox deserves better."

"Are you saying better for her or better for you?"

"Steele, I'm talking principle."

"Principles almost denied Torrance everything. If he wishes to act like the rest of the ton, doing what he thinks is best for pleasure or amusement or self-interest, so be it. Let him break eggs instead of walking on their shells."

The butler knocked, announced me, and then let me in. Then he whispered, "Privilege looks different in darker hands."

I stopped mid-step and wondered if my confusion was in fact that. Torrance had always been good-natured, extravagant, never cruel. It was unnerving to think of him acting like my father, uncaring about anyone but himself.

Regardless, I barged inside. "Torrance, we have to—"

Another surprise sat across the duke's grand table. Livingston. Goodness, no. This couldn't be the duke's pick. "Torrance, we need to speak. I assume you've calmed from earlier this week and can discuss things rationally."

I pushed into the dining room the size of Mother Russia, where the duke sat at the head of a mahogany Chippendale table. He wore a long, fluid robe that had seed pearls lining the opening. It was artsy and bold, different from the immaculate waistcoats and trousers Torrance typically wore. He studied me as he forked at potatoes.

"Sebastian, I'm surprised you've come. Determined to join us? Sit."

"You didn't say medieval dress for breakfast."

"Didn't invite you, Sebastian. But sit."

The duke waved me to the table set with immaculate china and glass goblets.

"Sebastian, are you here to provide intelligence on Miss Wilcox? Share her likes and dislikes? That information would be useful."

Useful to pick a man who wasn't me. The duke had to be otherworldly if he thought I'd offer any nugget for another to woo the most beautiful girl in the world.

"I don't believe I know Miss Wilcox well enough to offer that opinion. I will help where I can." There, that sounded good and vague.

"Have some breakfast, Sebastian. There's a wide selection."

The table was filled with every imaginable type of roll and croissant and muffin. The egg dish looked savory and delectable, but so did the plate of potatoes. Potatoes that smelled like chocolate. "What is that?"

"Kartoshka, my favorite dessert. Miss Wilcox intends to make them for me. It is sponge cake crumbled and molded with cream and dipped in chocolate. Her biscuits are fine. I suppose her kartoshka will be amazing."

Although having never had Georgie's biscuits—I was sure that's what he spoke of—I didn't have an appetite. "Not hungry, Your Grace. I came to talk about this bet and the conditions and see if there's a way to convince you not to go through with this."

"You want me to lose?" He glared at me over his goblet. Then, he again pointed to a chair. "I'm curious as to why. I thought it was in both our best interests that Georgina Wilcox is given her heart's desire."

"Well, yes, but having you select whom she's to marry doesn't seem wise."

"I'm of the opinion that a woman, given the proper amount of information, can make a rational decision."

Livingston chuckled, his laugh cold and sober. "Torrance has a number of very interesting ideas that he's going to test. I'll help to make this scientific."

"Are you one of the candidates, Livingston? I thought you were against marriage."

"Heavens, no." He stabbed at a piece of beef and put it into his mouth. Then he grabbed two kartoshkas. Taking his time, chewing everything slowly, he delayed before delivering his full answer.

"I'm very much against ever marrying again. My support of

Torrance's experiment does not change that. However, I'd love a scientific approach on the matter. Understanding how the female mind makes this type of selection will be important for me. Then I can always avoid their traps."

Why were they both like this?

About to turn and leave, I was struck by the similarities between the earl and the duke. Both surely had had women break their souls. The loss of love or a relationship had turned them into sour beings.

Would that be me if Georgina married someone else?

"A logical process," Livingston said. "I will help Torrance select the perfect candidate for Miss Wilcox. Logically, she shouldn't be able to say no. He'll surely win his wager."

"Sebastian, our friend understands winning is important. But as I was explaining to Livingston, this must be a big scientific test. Can logical beings, like ourselves, influence emotional women into saying yes to an ideal candidate?"

"Does that mean you both are invested in finding the right husband for Georgina Wilcox? You don't care if Miss Wilcox is happy as long as you win the wager?"

"I do care," Torrance said, "but I must win this bet. We all should be happy with the right husband being selected and me winning."

Livingston nodded and cleared his plate. "This shall be fun."

Frustrated that I couldn't get through to either man, I flopped into the chair. It took everything in me not to bash their heads together. This flawed experiment could hurt Georgina. Whether she would be mine or not, that woman deserved to be happy.

Livingston stood, dusted his fingers of cocoa, then pushed in his chair. "I've spread the word at my club—"

"Oh, no. More gamblers."

"Sebastian, let the earl finish."

Livingston clasped the lapels of his dark blue jacket and proceeded to strut. "As I was saying . . . men at my club and some from the Royal Society have been invited. We should have a good crowd this afternoon. Excuse me, gentlemen, I'm going to prepare—"

"My study," the duke said. "It's big enough but not too big. Perfect for the games or more so the parade of suitors to begin."

Parade? Were these two going to make men show off in front of Miss Wilcox?

"The study it is, Torrance." With a nod, Livingston left the dining room.

Almost raising my hands in prayer to beg the duke, I groaned. "This isn't right."

"Rest assured, I truly have Miss Wilcox's interests in mind. I'll not let anything untoward happen to her. I only win if she believes my candidate is the best husband. We both know she refuses to marry just anyone. She's not easily swayed. She'll not choose a person who won't make her happy."

"And what of Lady Hampton's interests? Is your hate of her clouding your judgment?"

The smile on Torrance's face evaporated, like water in a hot pot, sizzling to become steam. "The woman is my concern. She has free will to decide what's best. She can even back out of this bet if she'll come to me reasonably and apologize. But such a wise act is beneath her. She'd rather rot in hell than admit she's wrong."

"And you wish to be married to that? A bitter woman will destroy you."

"No. Suffering doesn't matter. She'll act accordingly. And I'll know that all the sisters will be provided for. They are gentlewomen. I can assure they will be married well and protected. That makes everything right."

"What's the great sin you are trying to fix, that you don't care about your own happiness?"

The duke looked over his goblet. "You ask a lot of questions like a certain miss. I think you need to finish a sonata so that you can see about your own future. Do it quickly and gain another chance with Miss Wilcox."

"But that doesn't help you, Torrance."

"As I said, I want each of the sisters happy. I think she truly cares for you, but you both have no future together if you're not a successful composer. That's what you've told us all."

I had, hadn't I?

He sipped and seemed to gaze at the remaining kartoshkas. "Remember, if you can win her, my wager is a draw. Scarlett's potential matrimony will be the deciding match. I have a whole year to learn and nudge her in the right direction."

"And you still get a full house of Wilcoxes. I joked about this other day, but it's true. It's not Lady Hampton you want. Well, not alone. It's the whole family."

The duke downed whatever was in his goblet and slammed it on the table. "I made a mistake a long time ago. I'm setting right what I would've had: a warmer, closer relationship with them. Those girls, especially Lydia, would've always been welcome here. And I could've seen to her medical care from the beginning. To have her not suffer like my sister is worth the punishment of a shrewish woman."

His logic was flawed, but his concern for the Wilcoxes was unimpeachable. I envied his self-control, this man who cared more for these ladies than his personal happiness. Steele was right. Power looked different in the duke's hands.

Rising, Torrance dropped his napkin into his chair. "You'll just have to trust me, Sebastian. I shall go dress. The candidates should be arriving soon."

He walked to the door. "Sebastian, stay. I think I'll find your opinion on the men as fascinating as Livingston's. It may be more valid, more emotional, because you know Miss Wilcox. Our friend will be clinical. That won't make the best assessment."

What was clinical about actually loving someone?

Everything ached all over again, as if Georgie herself had just rejected me once more. I wished I could be clinical or as cold and removed as Livingston and wish Miss Wilcox well in choosing a mate.

I could do none of that, not with Georgina Wilcox choosing anyone to marry who wasn't me.

Chapter 31

GEORGINA—ALMOST HOME

At the grand dining room table, I sat in my chair listening to the violinist the duke had hired to serenade us through dinner.

The beat was lively, quarter time, I think. I shuffled my slippers under the long white table skirt.

Going to Anya House had become part of our routine, a steadying force for the Wilcox girls. On Tuesdays and Wednesdays, we stayed and dined and laughed.

Well, Lydia and Scarlett laughed.

Sometimes I'd slip in my solidarity with Katherine and let out a chuckle at the performers His Grace had provided to give us entertainment.

Acrobats entered with juggling balls and whipping flames as they paraded around his dining room table.

"Everyone enjoy." The duke held up his glass of berry-colored claret. Scarlett and I had matching goblets. Katherine and Lydia had water, with no chance of it becoming wine. That was fine. They both needed other miracles—a restoration of a bitter heart and a permanent healing of a currently healthy little body.

Lydia stood and clapped. "Again, again."

The child was in heaven.

Even Katherine's stoic face seemed to crack a smile.

The jugglers headed out after we offered them our rapturous applause.

The violinists stayed, playing a joyful tune.

Waving his finger to the rhythm, the duke asked, "Are you all pleased?"

Was he joking? The man entertained as if the room was stacked with all the highbrow of the ton.

"It was good, Your Grace," I said. "But you needn't go to such expense or trouble."

"Why not? If I know you deserve to be indulged, shouldn't I give you that?"

Affectionate Lydia leapt into his lap, hugging his neck. "You're the bestus. Thank you for such a good time. I look forward to these days forever."

"Time for a bath and bed, Lydia," Katherine said. "You finished dinner hours ago."

Lydia offered her a terrible pout. "Too much excitement. The duke does everything so nice."

"True. But, little one, Lady Hampton is only doing what she thinks is best for you. Plenty of rest will keep you strong."

"No, she's not. If she wanted what was best, she'd figure out how to be here all the time."

The face he offered Katherine, all of us, wasn't a gloat but a countenance of radiant joy. I'd never seen him so happy. He'd found a way to claim that peace he'd been searching for.

The man loved having us here. We weren't a nuisance.

My heart agreed with Lydia. The duke was the bestus.

This felt more like home than across the river. Every time we returned, 22 Ground Street seemed sad, empty.

"But I still smell good." Lydia's voice was soft and whiny.

"Yes, you do," the duke said with a chuckle, "but you obey Lady Hampton, and there may be a surprise on the bed table."

Her little brown face glowed. "What, Your Grace?"

"Your own bottle of cologne water. I think it's lilies."

The child's eyes grew large. She jumped down and headed straight to the personal maid he'd hired for her.

He'd hired one for each of us. When we were younger and Papa's business was growing, we had a lady to do the cooking and another for the wash. We'd also had a lady's maid that we shared.

One glance at my older sister and I could feel the weight of condemnation falling upon her shoulders. Her posture slouched. Her eyes followed Lydia, holding hands with the kind woman in a blue-checked blouse and billowy white apron leading our Lydia out of the room.

Wanted to utter that our change of circumstance wasn't her fault.

In truth, it was.

Now I was a doxy in the public papers and my sister, rather than be the Duchess of Torrance, would be a territorial fluttering tit in private, wearing gray mourning feathers for the entirety of her season as the duke's mistress.

"The dressmakers will be here tomorrow," the duke said. "They need a last fitting before finishing your gowns."

"Your Grace." Katherine sat back. She seemed to lack the strength to roll her eyes. "You've given the girls enough."

"Bollocks. Never enough."

He clapped his hands and the musicians played louder. "Now we dance. I must see if we—"

Mark came into the room. "Your Grace, Lady Hampton, Miss Wilcox, Miss Scarlett Wilcox."

He made a grand bow. "Sounds as if the ball has already begun."

"If that were the case, there would be dancing." The duke passed me and Katherine and presented himself to Scarlett. "Madame Science, at my balls, everyone dances. I know Miss Georgina can. I suspect Lady Hampton was dazzling on the arm of the viscount—"

"No." Katherine sipped at her goblet. Her tone was sharp,

ringing like shattered glass. Then she lowered her voice. "No balls as Lady Hampton. Never had the opportunity."

Both Mark and the duke glanced at her, then away, as though they'd stumbled upon her private grief.

But it wasn't private.

It was shared by all of us. Her choices had made us reclusive.

My love for my sister was without measure but our blind devotion to her had led us here.

Then my rash actions made things worse.

But now I could fix all. "I understand, Katherine. Finally, I do. I can sacrifice too."

Her gaze cut to me. A well of anger and fear covered those familiar eyes. "Don't. Don't do anything rash."

"Rash should be my second name." I lifted from my chair.

"Lord Mark," Katherine said in a panicked voice, "will you dance with Georgina?"

Reddened cheeks, he looked hesitant.

"At least a Wilcox asked this time before entangling you," the duke said as he offered his hand to Scarlett. "Dance, sir. Wilcox women are the finest ladies in London. Then go to Dido for consolation. She will remain with us until after the ball."

The painting in his music room would console him? Before I could ask what the duke meant, the musicians changed from playing a reel to something regal.

Mark had my hand.

As Katherine watched, the four of us performed the minuet, then switched to the cotillion.

The formidable footwork tangled up my genius sister. Scarlett wobbled, forgot when to turn, but the masterful duke made her actions seem more fluid, less stiff.

Mark was superb. As easy on the pianoforte's keys, it seemed my music teacher could float us about the room and bring me with him to the clouds.

"Have you finished your submission?"

"I, ahh. No. Been distracted, helping the duke interview can-didates."

"A new position for his science meetings? A research patronage?"

"No, candidates for you, for the silly bet he has with Lady Hampton."

I knew the duke was doing something. He wasn't the type of man to let anything go. Yet, to conduct interviews without me being present sounded very heavy-handed.

"Talking about me and my desires must bore you. That's stopping your muse."

"My muse is you. I'm glad no one is coming up to snuff. The sooner the duke realizes that none of these men are for you, the sooner he'll end this farce."

What was the farce? That my future husband could be chosen based on interviews? That there was someone in London for me? Or that I couldn't find happiness unless it was with Mark?

"Don't you think it ridiculous what Torrance is doing?" he asked. "You should tell him and end this."

End the bet and end the fantasy we lived on Tuesdays and Wednesdays?

Take away the care and attention Lydia received?

And Scarlett?

When I spied her, she seemed to be keeping up with the duke. The girl who'd rather be reading was laughing and remembering the footwork Mama had taught.

Scarlett was twenty, the age to be presented. Had Katherine and Tavis's marriage not been ostracized, our younger sister might have invitations all about town. Her world could be so expanded beyond the books where her imagination lived.

"Georgie, are you all right?"

"Just remembering something Mama said about . . . dancing. Mark, if you've made no progress, how will you make the deadline?"

He twirled me away. When I returned for the next part of the dance, he said, "I have time. If not this year, then next."

"But what will you do for a whole year?"

"My mother will have me design music rooms for some of her friends. She's good at finding things like that for me."

He wasn't to be his own man this year, not if he depended upon his mother's favor. He was the doting version of Tavis, a kinder, no-gambling version.

"You stopped, Georgie. Have I tired you?"

"No . . . my lord. Not at all."

But actually, truthfully, I was fatigued, fatigued at thinking I could wait for Mark to show me that I could put my faith in him.

"Georgie. You will be lovely at the ball. It will be a shame that you must break our secret engagement."

"Yes. A shame."

"Pick no one. Neither will win the bet if you do not choose."

The answer was obvious. I needed to do what Katherine had been unable to do, marry the right man. "Time waits for no man. Let's switch partners."

Mark looked hurt, but he handed me off to dance with the man with a plan.

The Duke of Torrance was an excellent partner. Light on his feet and mine. As he always did, he gently turned me about the room.

The breath I held burned my lungs when I finally released it. "I accept."

"Accept what? That the rhythm is too slow, my dear?"

"No, Your Grace. I will comply with whatever, or whoever, you choose. I know that you only have my welfare, my family in mind."

"Always my utmost concern."

Mark tried to bump into our path.

As if he had a set of eyes in the back of his head, the duke turned a different way. "Excellent, you will not—"

"But I want to be a part of the process. Let Scarlett and me sit in on your next examination session."

"The parade of men." He stopped dancing. Then, as if the

notion hadn't occurred to him before, he clapped. "Excellent. That will add to the process. You will complete this logical investigation. Brilliant."

He swung me around, not quite like a rag doll, maybe a congratulatory puppet.

Though Katherine and Mark looked on with glum faces, I knew this to be the best for me. A proper dignified marriage out of the shadows would restore the Wilcoxes to the glory our parents meant for us to claim.

And my dear friend would keep his fantasy family, his found peace, for at least a year.

Chapter 32

MARK—BANGING OUT THE TUNE

Staying the night at the duke's house didn't make sense, but I did. I was clearheaded, not inebriated. I could get in my gig and be off to my lodgings. Or I could walk beneath the stars to my mother's.

Instead, it was me and Dido and the beautiful, lonely pianoforte.

My fingers hammered across the keys of the pianoforte.

Seeing the duke and Georgie dancing together incensed my blood. I'm not sure what happened. I thought her knowing I had more time to work on this composition would mean something. Her concerns that we might be rushing would be eliminated.

But somehow my news pushed her into the duke's arms and made her a willful participant in his bet.

One brief touch during our minuet, one smell of roses in her hair as we switched places in the cotillion, raced my pulse. I had nothing, not a farthing, not a complete song, only an undeniable dream of her.

I loved her.

At this hour, close to midnight, she was upstairs slipping into bed.

And all I wanted was for her to be here by my side or for me to be by hers.

How did I bungle this so badly?

Playing the piano again, I let my mind and fingers work the tension out of my soul.

Clapping.

When I looked up, I saw the duke standing in the doorway with his arms extended. Nightshirt and slippers, sporting his fancy pearly robe, he offered a full-bodied applause.

"I'm probably waking everyone up or keeping everyone up."

"Little Lydia is asleep. Lady Hampton left to do some paperwork for Mr. Thom. The other sisters are doing whatever young women do before retiring."

"Well, I apologize."

"Never, Sebastian. A master at work is a thing of beauty. To hear such passion in this song is amazing."

"Mozart is a wonder."

"Mozart played by a maestro with all the emotions—anger and loss and hunger—is a gift to the world."

He stepped to the Kenwood portrait. "I keep thinking of the resemblance between Georgina Wilcox and Dido. I see why you were instantly taken by her."

"It wasn't instant. I'd asked about Miss Wilcox for over a year before I found her in your garden."

His back was to me, with his arms folded behind. "You knew where she lived. You could've tried to visit. I did not know where Katherine was, not until she'd married Tavis Palmers."

"Are you going to tell me what happened? Why you abandoned a woman you obviously loved, or why you proposed to her sister?"

"Nyet and nyet. But I will say I will never again wait or have the woman I love wait for me to build or do. I will act. Time is a gift we cannot manage."

I jumped up with my fists extended. "I want her to be happy. And I want to beat senseless any man she chooses who is not me."

"You're funny, Sebastian. We both know I'd break you. But I am not the person you should be mad at. She hasn't chosen me but the idea that a man will want her hand and have his life in order so that they can build a new world together."

"Georgina Wilcox is too smart to allow you and a bunch of men to pick her husband."

Torrance chuckled. "You had a spring flower in your hands, the bud opening at your touch, and thought you could delay watering it until autumn. When a rose is in full bloom, it will not wait. It will be in someone's hair or buttonhole."

The man was right.

I was a fool. "These weeks they've been coming here, when Miss Wilcox was resistant to marriage, I stopped pushing so hard. I wanted to give her time, but she may have been testing my resolve."

"The logic of a woman is something I will never fully understand, except that Scarlett—she frightens me with her intensity. But I've learned two things. Honesty in both your desires and fears is important. And a woman must never doubt your feelings for her. If she does, that's ground for someone else to harvest."

I sank to the bench. "I doubted her and myself. Now she'll be someone else's wife."

I began to play. This time it was the tune stuck in my head.

Torrance hummed, but all I heard was Georgie's voice from our practice earlier today.

"She will partake in the parade of suitors that starts tomorrow and has agreed to marry whom I choose for her. As her guardian in the matter, I'll not pick a volatile choice. Nor will I be swayed by a man who's unsure."

The duke strolled to the door, his long white robe fluttering like an angel's. "Stick with your music, Sebastian, and Dido. She will wait an eternity to be admired."

My fingers shrank away from the keys.

Nothing Torrance said was untrue. My love deserved the world—something kind and free, where she ran or twirled for pure pleasure, never fear.

A better man would leave things to the duke and let Georgie enjoy her choices.

Good thing that wasn't me.

Chapter 33

GEORGINA—PARADE OF MEN

The duke's red study was filled with men. I sat off to the right of his desk in the corner with Scarlett. She'd taken out a quill to score candidates.

"Such a collection, all here for you," she said.

Wasn't sure they were here for me or the food or the circus-like atmosphere. Tall and short, big-boned and skinny, Black, Brown, and White—all God's children were in my sight, hunting for a wife.

This was the duke's science meeting gone wild.

Country-looking fellow, red from working in the sun, decked in his church-best—onyx tailcoat and black glossed boots—stood off to the side eating my biscuits, the batch I'd made this morning.

"He owns a large farm beyond London," Scarlett said.

"I guess wealth was the price of admission."

She nodded and shuffled through her notes. I stared at all my suitors.

Dandies with ideas on chemistry appeared in bright-colored regalia—waistcoats of stripes, strawberry reds, and silky starched shirt collars.

I wondered whose physiques were true or cinched with a girdle. Mr. Thom said they did that over here. He'd seen all manner of things on his coal routes.

Katherine couldn't stomach this process. She drove a coal route today. Mr. Thom needed assistance with our growing business. I think my sister still hoped to pay the duke back. Miracles happened, but I doubted Wilcox Coal could gain enough income before the ball.

"Georgina, I think that's Lord Fellows. Second son, man of science. I see him at the lectures held by ministers of the Royal Society."

Ah. The peers would come.

The second and third sons of the impoverished ton—well, they looked that way with high-set noses and the air of wishing to be set apart.

The only member of Tavis's family who came to visit was a distant cousin in line to inherit Tavis's title. The gentleman, with his perfectly starched cravat and tasteful dark waistcoat that said *notice me but stay back*, offered polite conversation and then quickly left.

Oh, goodness. He was here, sitting in the rear near the grand bookcase with one of my Cornish Fairings in his greedy hands.

"The duke must've promised a very large dowry to get such a show." Scarlett's voice stung. The good feelings I tried to hold on to slipped away.

With one of my new sleek slippers, I stepped on my own foot. Clad in the silver satin slippers and a dress of light rose lace and silk, I might not look the part of someone important, but I was. I, Georgina Wilcox, mattered and that care-for-nothing family of Tavis's needed to be gone.

"What are you doing, Georgie?"

"Waving to Mr. Steele."

The duke's man came to me. When I had his ear, I whispered, "I need you to rid the room of refuse."

He looked confused, then I pointed to the new Lord Hampton. "Take the waste out. Toss the new viscount to the street or drop him in a coal chute. And make sure he has no more biscuits."

His brow wrinkled, then Mr. Steele nodded, his face filling with a wonderful, malevolent grin.

With a clap of his hands, groomsmen appeared and hauled the affronted man out of the study.

The Wilcoxes had enviable connections. Joy and pride swept through me . . . until I saw Mark and his friend entering the room.

I settled into the corner, behind the duke's desk, looking longingly out the window at the maze. "Scarlett, perhaps we should take a walk. Get some air. It's very sunny today."

She rolled her eyes. "Don't you move. You will not run. You're worthy of being sought after. You're a prize, even if the man you regard can't see that. Now let the scientific process select a proper candidate."

With her quill extended, she tapped my nose. "You can still reject the winner at the duke's ball. For once, you have control."

Yes. I did.

Instead of running, I sat up straight. "Let the games begin. Make sure you carry the one to get the right answer."

My sister smiled and I did too. It felt good to have her here. "I'll be with you every step, Georgie. So, let's get this process right."

For a moment, she gripped my elbow, then she slipped into her investigative posture, quill threaded through her fingers, papers in her lap covering her robin-blue skirt.

Finished with refuse duty, Mr. Steele returned with the duke. Immaculately dressed, easy in his stride, His Grace glanced at us and his diverse selection of candidates, then took his seat at the desk. "Ladies. Gentlemen. I'm so glad you could join us. For the past few weeks, many of you have submitted yourselves to interviews to be recommended to the heiress Miss Georgina Wilcox."

Welp. That meant the duke had put up a lot of money on my behalf.

Scarlett poked me with her elbow. "The Earl of Livingston is here."

Why? I thought he was against marriage.

"Don't frown, Georgina. Someone will think you are dismissing them."

I was. Mark's friend was garbage. "He's surly."

"Surly? He's brilliant. I watched him lecture. Very detailed studies. He's been helping the duke with the selection process."

"No wonder this has been abominable. I doubt he could tell a good match if it were his boots."

"Stop." She smothered a giggle. "We must seem serious, sober in our thoughts. We can gossip with Katherine later."

The ache in my heart for my elder sister's blessing stung anew. She'd never give it. I felt more understanding for Mark wanting the same from his family. He looked at me, then disappeared.

I thought he'd left Anya House but a glance out the window exposed him.

The way my heart fluttered exposed me.

His tortured piano playing had gone on long into the night. Part of me wanted to go to him then and try to make him understand why my marrying someone else was best.

A man would not understand. They could marry late. They'd never be looked down upon for being childless. They'd be slightly chided for having children out of wedlock.

London called single women like me a tall Meg, a spinster. Mark was young and his bachelorhood was celebrated. In twenty years, he too could marry Lydia and no one would think anything was wrong. Men had time to dither.

Not fair.

Yet when had it been for women—women like me?

Mark waved, curling his fingers as if to ask me to join him.

That would be scandalous to go and meet him where our troubles began.

Then I snapped to attention.

The duke began asking questions of the candidates.

Scarlett noted scores on the paper.

And I listened intently to each answer. One of these men could be the one I'd been waiting for, someone available now, ready to support the Wilcox family and my desires. My future husband deserved my undivided attention, not the lover I let walk away.

Chapter 34

MARK—HILARIOUSLY HAUGHTY HAUTE TON MINUS HIM

Scooping up the last chocolaty kartoshka, I listened to Scarlett Wilcox's line of questions. They were pretty good. She'd eliminated a lot of candidates.

"So you're saying that if your wife wanted you to not go to the races and bet on ponies, you will do that, Mr. Armstrong?" Scarlett asked the gentleman at the far end. He bred prize mares for the Prince Regent that he'd run at the Bibury races. I believed he had an interest at several racing tracks.

The man puffed his cheeks like a chipmunk and said, "Well, there are many considerations. But if my wife were so inclined, and this would lead to her happiness, it would definitely be something to think about."

Georgina turned to her sister. "I think that's a no."

The Earl of Livingston, who was also sitting near, tried to hold in a snorted laugh and failed miserably.

The duke crossed his arms and leaned back like he'd fallen asleep.

Would Torrance admit this was an abject failure?

I cleared my throat. "Perhaps we should take a break. The gardens are lovely."

"Excellent suggestion, Sebastian. Gentlemen, please go to the

dining room. There are more treats, but the ginger Cornish Fairings made by Miss Wilcox are gone."

Blast it. Was I ever going to have this woman's biscuits?

His Grace probably offered the enticements as a way to remind the gentlemen of Georgie's domestic skills.

It wasn't a *her* problem.

It was a *them* issue.

This was a room filled with lackluster performers who'd
openly lie to try to gain her dowry.

Before the meeting, Mr. Steele and the housekeeper came
and cleared the sideboard of Torrance's strange liqueurs and
elixirs and filled the space with pastries and scones and choice
meats. They were all but gone. The men feasted and missed the
obvious dessert, Georgie Wilcox.

It was an impulse to wave at her, to get the running lady to
come to me. But she stayed safely inside, away from more scandal and me, a man whose future was in flux.

Livingston walked over and offered a glass of champagne.
"Oh, this is going swimmingly well. We've weeded out candidates of quick tempers and the gamblers."

"Honestly, sir, this is a disaster. The ones remaining are better
liars."

"O, ye of little faith. Trust me. Trust the process." He rubbed
his hands together like an evil minion. "The only woman to
tempt my friend to think of renouncing his bachelorhood will
soon be taken. That's a celebration."

"Maybe I'm the old-fashioned one, but love should be
enough, for her and me."

Livingston laughed so hard, I thought he'd faint. "No, Sebastian. What does love have to do with it? Or anything? For a
woman, a marriage is security and trust. For a man, it's trust, a
warm bed, and a partner to reach the hard-to-reach places. None
of it is worth more than your freedom."

"Freedom to buy courtesans and spend your time gossiping
with your mother? Yes, you've surely done a great deal with yours."

He took a ginger-smelling biscuit hidden in a napkin and ate it in front of me. "Well, if you had married her, you would need to ensure she sent me a basket of these Cornish Fairings regularly. The woman is gifted."

"I'm in pain, and you torment me with her biscuits."

His face darkened. The levity in his brown eyes disappeared. "My wife did the best thing by leaving. If you can't be happy that there are good choices for Miss Wilcox, perhaps you should consider walking out the door and going back to the safe, distant music room."

"What, you want me to go to Dido too?"

"What? Dido Belle, the Kenwood painting, is here?"

"Yes, Torrance arranged for it."

"You twat, Sebastian. You're in love with a painting and transferred your lusts to a real woman. You made Miss Wilcox a fetish. Go to your music. Stay away from her."

"No. No. Not a fetish. I know the difference between paint and flesh. I love her flesh. I mean, I want . . . I want Georgina Wilcox." I put my palm on his sleeve. "Calm down, sir. Help me find a way to win her. I'll gamble everything for her."

He closed his eyes for a moment. "You can't do this to Miss Wilcox. You can't make love to her and allow her to make life-altering decisions when all you're experiencing is some Pygmalion transfer emotions. It's not to be borne."

My mouth hung open. I was speechless, truly without words.

A gentleman bumped me, offered his apology, and walked with his friend to the sideboard. One I recognized as the man who bred ponies for the races.

"She's a little brighter than I expected, but I thought she'd be fairer," he said. "Maybe that's only the girls sent up from the plantations in the Caribbean."

"Yeah," the friend said. "This one's just from across the river."

They chuckled amongst themselves.

I looked at Livingston.

We exchanged no words but each of us grabbed a man by the shoulders and hauled them out of the study.

"What's the meaning of this?" The big fellow who'd made the river comment adjusted his tailcoat. "We have not been dismissed from the competition."

I pointed to the door. "You failed the test. Both of you must leave."

"Don't make a scene," Livingston said. "Just leave."

"Let's take this outside." The one who made the plantation comment chortled.

As soon as the four of us were outside and the footman had closed the doors, the horseman put up his fists. "Let's settle this quickly, I have a prize pony to win."

I wrenched him up by his lousy tied cravat.

Livingston grabbed the other, and my friend, the man of science, gave him a chop perfectly centered in his back.

Before the buffoons could regain their balance, we threw them onto their buttocks and watched them bang down the steps of Anya House.

The fools cursed and shook fists but spent more time complaining of shock.

"Does your helping toss out men mean you are done with this, Livingston?"

"In science, you must eliminate the outliers. This was manual ejection of bad data. Those fools needed to be excluded from Torrance's experiment."

Mr. Steele came outside and tossed hats and gloves at the fools. "As the duke would say, do svidaniya. Goodbye!"

He closed the doors, then disappeared. The man asked no questions, as if it were an everyday thing to expel visitors by force.

Stretching, Livingston said, "If a woman must marry, it should be to someone good. Someone who'll be kind and respectful."

"My sentiments exactly. That's why I must stop—"

"No, Sebastian, you won't. I wish no ill will to Miss Wilcox, but there are a lot more fools like those two in this world. You haven't the means to protect a wife, any wife. A woman who has a background and life that's different from yours needs more. You're a good man, Sebastian. You'll stand up to strangers but not your family. Prahmn will be worse than the folks we just kicked out. He can hurt you and the Wilcoxes."

I couldn't move or respond.

That saying about a broken clock being right twice a day was correct.

Livingston said the truth aloud to my face.

And I was ashamed.

The vaulted prize I needed to become established, I'd pushed my entry to next year. It must feel so arbitrary to Georgina. The delay meant I'd need my family's support.

How cruel that must sound to her, to think her husband might be dependent on the whims of people who could turn her—us—away.

No woman should be made to endure any abuse for the sake of love. Yet that was how I'd been telling Georgie our lives would be.

I wasn't as good as the horrid pony owner, a man who could provide for a wife. That boorish man could offer a woman security.

The notion to be a better man and step aside started to burn, scorched my fingertips. Yet when I stepped into the duke's hell, his red study with the parade of men roaming like Hades's Cerberus, I felt sick.

I glanced at Georgie. I wanted to touch her. I wanted to sear a memory between the two of us that would be lasting.

But moments ended.

Memories faded.

I shrank into the corner, hoping all the science came to the conclusion that none of these candidates would work. I needed one more chance, just a little more time, but the hourglass for Georgie's and my future had drained of sand.

* * *

After another round of questioning and further shrinking of the candidate pool, I retook my position in the back next to Livingston, waiting for Torrance and the Wilcox sisters to return.

I believed they'd gone to the maze. The Wilcox women floating on his arms were stylish and graceful. The goddess, my goddess, had the perfect skin, lovely and warm. Unlike my sainted Dido, her chignon was free. The prettiest, tightest curls were pulled high.

The doors to the study opened.

The duke led the ladies back inside and helped them to sit beside his desk.

Torrance turned to the younger. "Miss Scarlett. It's your turn again to ask the remaining gentlemen. We should pick candidates with whom you'd want your sister to get more acquainted."

Wait. Did my ears deceive me? Was Torrance backing down?

Miracle. I could sing Georgie's hymn.

The younger Wilcox looked pensive, making marks with her quill. "Since the science isn't working, let's start at behavior, social behavior."

The duke's face blanked, but he lifted his palm and waved for her to continue.

She lifted her chin. "Does anyone enjoy Drury Lane?"

That was an easy one. I sat back, waiting to see how the men would ruin this one.

Rounds of *It's delightful.*

And variations of *The price is good, particularly in the seats by the orchestra pit* sounded.

Those were very cheap seats that didn't adequately protect women from insults, or even from being pelted by food being thrown from a rowdy crowd. I hoped Georgina realized these theater patrons were noes.

My musical student shifted in her seat. "Do we have drama lovers in here that admire Shakespeare?"

Another easy question. Georgie must be tired. Surely Torrance would put an end to this.

Yet what if she'd become so desperate to be married that she'd lower her opinions to find a potential candidate?

My stomach soured. What if I'd made her that desperate?

The scandal still stewed.

Though in the last days, there had been no new cartoons, I knew the ton had not forgotten. Gilroy might even have the audacity to come to the duke's ball.

A few men mentioned *Romeo and Juliet*. Another mentioned *The Taming of the Shrew*, which drew laughs, but not from the sisters or the duke.

"'She moves me not—or not removes, at least, affection's edge in me.'"

The voice, dark and passionate, came from the rear of the crowded room.

"'If she do bid me pack, I'll give her thanks, as though she bid me stay by her a week.'"

The booming voice grew louder, quoting lines from *The Taming of the Shrew*. Men moved out of the way as one person came forward.

"'If she deny to wed, I'll crave the day when I shall ask the banns, and when be married.' Oh, Miss Georgina Wilcox, Miss Scarlett Wilcox. 'Better once than never, for never too late.'"

Georgie stood and began to clap. "Mr. Carew, I did not know you liked Shakespeare. You always seem so reserved."

"Miss Wilcox, I visited under an official capacity to help your family when illness reared its ugly head. This is a social visit. Torrance, if I had known that you also hold meetings to discuss sonnets, I would find a way to fit them into my schedule."

Georgie's face lit. The sister's too.

The affable, handsome man responsible for the little girl's recovery was standing in the red study and making love to my Georgie with damned Shakespeare's help.

Was I wrong, wanting him to trip, to do something to look less assured, less elegant?

"Sir, I'm glad you could come," Torrance said. "Inviting you to this slipped my mind. That was an oversight. A very bad oversight."

The duke smirked at Georgina, then engaged Mr. Carew in a deeper conversation.

He dismissed everyone else to the dining room.

Resistant, I began to move.

"Let this all go, Sebastian. Let her go." Livingston's admonishment was right but didn't help.

I left as Georgie started smiling, those gorgeous goddess lips broadly curving and the sweet too-smart Miss Scarlett fanning, looking like she'd swoon.

A final glance at the duke showed Torrance slumping into his chair like a burden lifted. He should rest well. I believed he'd won his wager.

Chapter 35

GEORGINA—PRACTICING WITH A DISTANT CREATOR

Three days before the ball, Mark and I had our final practice. It had been a long practice, but I felt more confident.

Mark rested his hands on the keys.

"Georgie, you sound wonderful. Your exhibition will be phenomenal."

"Thank you."

That was one of the only pleasant things he said. My music teacher had been upset throughout our long session. He said nothing out of the ordinary, but his tense brow, his not glancing at me, spoke volumes.

Mark always looked for me. Even in a sea of men in the duke's study, I saw him turn my way. I liked that he was nervous for me. I like that he cared.

"I suppose this is coming to an end."

"Yes," he said. Then he began shuffling through his papers.

The ball was next week. Mark and I would no longer have these moments alone.

The duke would announce my new favorite, Mr. Carew, at the ball. The physician had sounded pleased, saying something about how his aunts loved knowing that a duke favored his expertise and that Carew would be taking time from his busy work to be social.

With the duke conversing with him about my prospects, the single, handsome gentleman would probably propose.

Mr. Carew had known my family for a long time. A man in his thirties who'd never been married was a good candidate. I would be respectably wed and the duke's bet would assure Scarlett and Lydia would be protected.

"How has your sister taken the news that she is going to lose the bet?" Mark's voice soared about the scales he played on the pianoforte. "You've told her you intend to let Torrance win?"

"Not exactly, but she's a smart woman, and the duke has more bark than bite. They'll figure things out. I suspect he'll release her from the bet."

Mark rested his hand on the keys. "You think a man in love will give up so easily?" He played a few more notes. "Well, he's in love . . . and will do what is best for the person he desires."

Mark wasn't talking about the duke and a lump appeared in my throat.

"Don't know if I can sing anymore."

"That's all right, Georgie." The music he now played was something new—lovely and ethereal.

"Is this more Pleyel? Something of his later works? It sounds different."

He peered up. "How so?"

"It's haunting and beautiful. Yet, it makes me feel grounded, like I can be confident. The world is ahead."

"Your world is, Georgie. And this is mine, my finished sonata. It's what I've prepared for the Harlbert's Prize. You are the first and only one to hear it."

It was done. I ran around the pianoforte. As though I were Lydia, I wrapped my arms about his neck. "Congratulations."

Mark embraced me, then kissed me quickly on my lips, then my forehead.

With my pulse racing, I released him.

His arms went away, and he began playing his song. "It's not perfect. I'm struggling in the final movement. With our practicing done, it will have my full attention. I will submit on time. I can't keep delaying my future. It's not the way to live."

In silence, I watched his tortured soul become a hymn. He poured his heart into each note.

To comfort him . . .

To stand by him . . .

It's what I wanted to do.

Yet, how could I? Our love would only draw me back to the place I'd run from—insecurity about our future, the harm his powerful family could do to mine.

I had to succeed where Katherine had failed. Mr. Carew made perfect sense.

"You sounded wonderful today. You will be brilliant at the ball. Bravo, Georgie. Bravo. Mr. Carew cannot help but love you as I do. And he will give you the best life. It's what you deserve."

My elation burst. Mark had said he loved me before, but this time it sounded like goodbye.

A woman in love should say nothing matters. She should run and catch her heart.

My feet were stone. I couldn't move, not now.

He ripped his hands from the keys. "I'm sorry, Georgina. I've made you feel bad. I didn't mean to. I understand about practical marriages."

"Practical? I suppose there are some that are impractical. What do you count as such?"

"I've missed your questions." He began packing up his papers. "Carew is well-off. Your backgrounds are similar. It must be a better match."

"Because he's a Blackamoor like me. Is that what you're trying to say?"

"No. Yes. Maybe." He shook his head. "His family will support and admire you. Mine will not. It will take years for them to come around, if ever."

I walked away to the painting of the cousins. "Do you think Dido had support from all her family?"

"Her uncle loved her very much. Her cousin, Lady Elizabeth Finch-Hatton, did too. Lady Elizabeth still lives, and her husband too. It was a love match."

"What of Dido?"

"I believe she married a Frenchman and bore him twin sons, three boys in total. I'd like to think they were happy. That she was happy in her short life."

Mark left the pianoforte. He stood behind me. I smelled ink, crisp and tart, and notes of sandalwood.

The sound of his breathing fell on my neck. If I turned now, like I readied to dance, I would be in his arms.

"She's beautiful, like you." His palm cupped my elbow. He started me turning. Eye to eye, he gazed at me. "Carew is the best man in the duke's parade. If you accept him, he will be the luckiest of men."

He said these words, yet his arms went about my waist. "Goodbye, Georgina Wilcox."

The pressure of his hands fell away. I wanted him to hold me tightly, but I watched him walk away.

Mark slung his satchel to his back and I listened to his boots clicking on the floorboards as he exited the music room.

The man I loved would be out of Anya House in minutes. I should move. I should run after him.

But I didn't. I let him go and surrendered to loss.

My frustration at Mark turned to respect. He was brave enough to say he loved me and strong enough to want me to have what I needed even if that was not the composer.

The sooner this scandal and ball and bet were over, the better off we'd all be.

Readying to leave, I saw a piece of paper on the floor.

Wedged between the pianoforte and the wall, I wiggled it free. It was music. I sat and played a few notes.

This was his sonata, maybe an earlier version but very close to what he'd played tonight. I folded up the paper and held it to my bosom.

Mr. Steele appeared at the door. "The duke's carriage is ready to take you to Ground Street."

"Thank you, sir."

About to put the paper on top of the musical instrument, I changed my mind. With careful creases, I folded it and put it into my pocket.

Upon retrieving my bonnet, I rushed through the hall toward the awaiting Berlin. The wide vehicle would take me across the river at sunset.

When I passed the hall mirror, I looked at myself. The proud woman looking back hadn't run from the parade of suitors or after a man who made her feel like music. Like the sheet of notes in my pocket, I was a work in progress. I was beautiful art, something to behold.

Outside, Mr. Steele helped me inside the carriage. "This house will be transformed when you see it next, Miss Wilcox. The duke throws a massive celebration. He embraces life like there is no tomorrow."

"I can't wait. I'll be ready to perform."

"Yes, you and Lord Mark sound exquisite. The performance, the two of you together, will be wonderful."

Yes. The two of us.

The music teacher and his student. No.

The composer and his muse. No.

The man and his fetish. No. No.

Partners, equally yoked. Yes.

"Good evening, sir."

Mr. Steele shut the door. The carriage started and I settled in. Yanking out the sheet music, I stared at Mark's careful handwriting and hummed.

This piece ran out of notes. No concluding bars, but Mark and I had them. We'd perform one last time. My heart had to accept that our song would end at the ball.

Chapter 36

GEORGINA—SISTERLY ADVICE

Bright and early the duke's dressmakers arrived at our house on Ground Street. It was chaos. The hullabaloo of designers and seamstresses pushing pins at us and draping silk about our arms and wrapping satin about our bosoms overwhelmed each of us.

Then the color choices. I didn't know that many existed.

Scarlett might've known about pompadour rose or stifled sigh pink, but I didn't. She did love to sew, the one appeasement she offered to Mama when she trained us in the domestic arts.

Just when I thought I could take no more pinning and spinning, the women announced they were done. Our new gowns, even one for Katherine, would arrive the morning of the ball.

They left and all the Wilcoxes remained in the parlor.

Scarlett and Lydia lay on a blanket on the floor. Bared toes warmed by the nice fire. Wilcox Coal heated everything just right.

Katherine stretched out on the sofa, while I sat at the pianoforte. I pulled out Mark's piece and began to play, trying to remember how he moved forward on the more complete version of the sonata.

All my sisters seemed to be listening.

"It's been a while since we've been here," Lydia said. "You know, in the parlor, just us."

Scarlett stroked her fingers in the little girl's curly braided chignon. "Mama used to gather us here when she was strong."

Katherine sat up. "Yes. And Papa would come through those doors after a coal run, smiling."

"I don't remember Papa much." Lydia's voice sounded sad.

My older sister scooped up our little girl. "He loved you a lot. Don't forget that."

She nodded. "Like the duke. He loves me."

Katherine snuggled the girl close. "I think so."

Then she bit her lips, clamping so tightly, nothing else could be uttered.

I began to play again. Mark's tune was infectious. I understood why it stayed in his mind.

Scarlett popped up. "I'm glad you are participating, Katherine."

"Yes," I said. "The ball will be lovely. It wouldn't be the same without you."

"I'll be there to watch you perform, then Lydia and I will retire for the evening."

Lydia sat up and glared at her. "No. No. We're supposed to have fun. The duke says fun all night."

The child took off, running out of the parlor and up the stairs.

Shaking her head, Scarlett went after her. "At least you are coming. That will have to be enough. You'll miss out on my triumph. Science picking Georgina's most compatible suitor."

When she left, Katherine folded her arms. "Is that true? Did the duke's crazy method work?"

Pulling my fingers away from the keys, I lifted my gaze to her. "His methods, enhanced with Scarlett's process and a bit of luck, picked Mr. Carew."

"Mr. Carew, Mama's physician, our family physician?"

"Yes. He's known us for a while. He's a good man and he's kept all our family's secrets."

Daring her to say it—to condemn the choice because of her

hatred of the duke, a selection that made sense—I stood and glared at her.

But she looked away. "The man is a good choice."

No fight.

No, Katherine knows what's best.

"You have nothing more to say?"

"Georgina, you're old enough and smart enough to make up your mind. And the duke is better at everything. Only a fool would keep resisting."

"Why do you hate him? It's obvious that he cares for you and us."

"And why are you forgetting what you feel about Lord Mark? It's obvious he's in love with you." Katherine came to me. Inches away, our gazes locked, she said, "You're afraid. You are masterful at playing the pianoforte but you won't play in public. Your voice is a gift but until the duke's ball you've kept it only for this house. And now you love someone, probably love him so much it frightens you."

"Is that what you are saying about your heart, Katherine?"

She backed up for a second. The smile lines faded to sadness. "Maybe the duke's a different man from the one I knew. Maybe he can be trusted. It doesn't change the past or the hurt—"

"That you've done to him."

Katherine started to go to the door.

"Don't run. It's you and me and Mama's piano. We assumed when you returned from your grand adventure pregnant that the babies' father had died."

"He was dead to me."

"Katherine, the duke?"

"I'm the blackguard. Everything is my fault. He couldn't tell his family in London about me. Too many were against him claiming his ducal peerage and to have a Black woman on the arm of a man who could pass as white was too much. What would Torrance's heir look like? Jahleel wanted time. I had no time. I tossed him away. Marrying Tavis was both redemption and punishment."

"Keep talking, Kitty."

She tugged on her shawl. "I was too frightened of his world and being rejected, so I rejected him first."

"And he never knew about the children in your womb."

"Never. Mama took care of hiding my pregnancy. Tavis wanted to marry me then, but I refused and came back here and drowned in everyone's scorn."

The pieces started to fall into place. "So when Tavis comes back into your life two years later, still wanting to marry you, you accepted."

"He was a viscount then. Mama loved that title. When he asked in front of her, she accepted for me."

"And the duke . . . You didn't marry Tavis until later. Were you waiting for the duke to come back?"

"I don't know, but he arrived at the chapel after the wedding had taken place. I told him I had a husband who wasn't ashamed of me. One who'd take me to London with pride. I never saw him again until I wrote the duke to come to Tavis's deathbed."

Katherine leaned on the doorframe. "You are me, Georgina. You're going to run from love because you are frightened. I'm telling you that it's fine to do so. If you think, for one moment, Sebastian will leave when things get tough or he'll run to his parents because he's afraid of failing, run. Run as quickly as you can. If Dr. Carew is a safe harbor, stay there."

I did run, straight to Katherine, and I held her. Pulling her into my arms, I let her be weak. Then I was weak. We clung to each other through our tears.

I should tell her to fix things with the duke, but there was much more at stake than those puzzle pieces fitting together. A powerful wronged man could do much harm.

He had the power to take away all that we loved.

With my hands to her face, I kissed her brow. "The duke's ball is a new beginning. You talk to him. Tell him what you can. Get him to release you from the bet."

Scarlett came back down. She glanced at us. "What did I miss?"

"Nothing." I went back to the pianoforte.

"Georgina talked me out of just staying for a little while at the ball. I have no choice, not with all three of you going. You'll need a chaperone all night. I'll do my best to keep all of you from scandal. That's my duty. As Mama always said, scandal is worse than death."

Scarlett came deeper into the room. "But remember what Papa said: You have to stare scandal in the face or the rumors will stab you in the back."

I glanced at her. She didn't know how accurate her violent words were.

I shrugged, but then we both went to Katherine.

Arms twisted and latched. We made a big woven hug, a rya of love.

"You, Katherine Wilcox Palmers, can do anything you set your mind to." I said this and meant it. "Even things that are difficult. Do the right thing."

Scarlett nodded. "We're Wilcox women. We can do anything."

Little arms wound about us, and I smelled Mama's lavender.

The little one had been in Mama's cologne water again. She'd come down to join in the Wilcox circle.

Katherine picked her up. "We'll stay at the ball until you are sleepy, but that is if you go to bed on time without fussing."

"Yes," she said. "I want to see who Georgina marries."

I ran my hand in her curly bangs. "How do you know about all that?"

Lydia leaned over and hugged my neck. "I know. The duke tells me everything. And he said he didn't know if it would be the music man or the medicine man."

It would be the medicine man. The duke had to win the bet and gain the family he'd been deprived.

Chapter 37

MARK—A VISITOR COMES KNOCKING

Standing in my Jermyn Street lodgings, I tied my cravat, a formal crisp white knot, in preparation for tonight's ball. The Duke of Torrance had the ton ablaze with talk of his first formal ball of the season.

Lent was done and hearty decadent celebrations were desired by all. There wasn't a doubt in my mind that the duke would offer a spectacle that would be the talk of London. I hoped the fanfare and grandeur were so overwhelming that the ton would no longer talk of my supposed secret faux alliance with Miss Wilcox.

The papers should have lost interest, but they reprinted Gilroy's cartoon of Georgina and me on the pianoforte. Someone from the *Globe* or the *Post* would be at the ball tonight looking for trouble.

Yet, I was spoiling for a fight. My family might not ever accept Georgie, but if we loved each other, it shouldn't matter. I could be my own man and stand up to the Sebastians. I had a finished sonata, a winning sonata. I had a future. Now I merely needed the woman.

A rare knock on my door made me pause my useless introspection. Livingston, I presumed. Didn't he know I intended to drive so that I could leave when Georgie rejected me a final time?

I charged to the door, flung it open and saw Chancey.

Grimacing, haggard-looking Chancey, my mother's butler.

"Sir, why have you come? Is all well?"

"Your mother. She's downstairs. She wishes to speak to you."

The longtime butler, who'd seen all manner of circumstances, even scandal in the Prahmn household, looked ashen, shaken.

"Chancey, what's the matter?"

"The marquess has returned. He's very unhappy with the circumstances of your rushed courtship."

Locking my arms behind my back to prevent myself from grabbing the butler's lapels and shaking out answers, I stayed still. "He should take his anger out on me."

"The marquess is a beast. Marchioness is leaving London for the country."

This indeed was a punishment for her. At the beginning of the season, unable to go to parties and dinners and gossip with the ton's mothers about their sons' and daughters' prospects was a horrendous torture.

"Tell her I'll be down, and I'll take her back to Grosvenor and reason with my father."

"No, my lord. She's been banished tonight. The Marchioness of Prahmn had to leave Grosvenor immediately. She barely packed two trunks."

"Two." Well, that was a way to flee. "I'll come now."

Dousing a candle, I grabbed my satchel, locked up the flat, and followed Chancey out to the street.

The sun had set. The sky was purple and indigo, hanging over a lone stately carriage.

"She's distraught. Be gentle," Chancey said, then opened the ebony door with our gold family crest.

I climbed inside.

A beautiful shadow clothed in a burgundy silk carriage gown sat opposite me. Silent in the low carriage light, I heard Mama sobbing.

Turning up the lantern, I witnessed the sad evidence of tears strewn across her face. My throat tightened. I couldn't get my tongue to ask what I always feared.

Did the man finally yell so much, say things with such venom, that he lost control and struck my mother? Did he hurt her?

I filled my frozen lungs. I worked my jaw. "Did he hit you?"

"What, Mark?"

As calmly as a son could, I asked, "Did my father strike you?"

"He took the house. He's sending me to the country."

"Mama, did he put his hands on you?"

"No. But taking my house hurts as much as Prahmn hurting me."

Feeling like a boulder had lifted off my chest, I took a long gasp. Sitting back, I let every muscle uncoil. My father was a boor, but he hadn't become a brute to her. Yet, he cut her where it hurt the most, her public name and partaking in London society.

"So Prahmn is back from his holiday. I guess he didn't offer an explanation as to where he's been or any sort of apology. The hypocrite is punishing you to punish me."

"He says the coal woman is my fault. That I've indulged you."

Indulged? Indignation coursed hotly through my veins. "You've allowed me to strive for music. You gave me a way to be free when the words couldn't come. I couldn't stand in church making sermons when I'd have to convict my father for how he lives."

"Mark, he says he saw you with that woman."

When? The park. The familiar shadows at a distance. That was Prahmn and his mistress. The adulterer disapproved of a wonderful friendship and a love he could only dream of, and had been lying about being out of Town.

"Mama, go to the country. Be away from Prahmn. I intend to get the goddess I love to marry me. Father will be very angry. Come back when you think he's done with current rages and needs consoling before he finds another holiday for his latest mistress."

"Wait. Mark. He's cutting off any money for you. He means to make you heel. I can't stand to think of what will become of you."

"Tell Prahmn I am no puppy. I'm the man my mother raised me to be."

"And who's that?"

"A gentleman in need of a good woman who cares for his well-being and sanity. And I know exactly where to find her."

She clutched my arm. "Come back with me. Tell him you are done with the Wilcox girl. Then he will rid his mistress from my house."

Her offer to let me be with the woman I loved disappeared when her world was threatened. My love, had she seen this?

"Miss Georgina Wilcox was done with me because she didn't believe I could be my own man. Prahmn is making sure I start being brave tonight. Good night, Mother, I have a ball to attend."

"No. He'll be there. He'll humiliate you."

"Groveling to my father and lying about my feelings or even trying to explain to his small mind who I love would be more humiliating. Write to me when you can."

My mother clutched my lapel. Wrenching the necklace from her throat, she handed me the sparkly diamond thing. "Take this. Sell it. When all this is over—"

I kissed her cheek. "It's time to stand on my own, Mama. I may foolishly wish that I'd kept this, but I need to make myself useful. I have to earn her."

As I tried to climb out, she grabbed my arm again. This time she slid off one of her rings. It was the small silver band her father had given her. "Take this. Let it see love again, Mark. Be blessed in your marriage. Godspeed."

I stepped back inside and held my mother. "You're the original goddess. Get away from Prahmn."

Holding her hand to my chest, I kissed her knuckles. After securing the ring, I took my satchel and left to retrieve my gig. There was a ball I needed to hurry to. Before midnight, I needed to have my true bride-to-be in my arms.

Chapter 38

GEORGINA—THE BALL

Mr. Thom drove us in the biggest Wilcox Coal carriage. He cleaned it, buffed it to a shine, and restored the rich leather seats to make everything immaculate.

Our wonderful satin and silk gowns wouldn't have a speck of coal dust. He handed my sisters and me inside. "Ladies, I get to escort you all to the Duke of Torrance's ball."

I sighed and lifted my gilded shoes. "I feel like Vasilisa, the princess. Scarlett, did she have glass slippers?"

My sister shook her head. "Highly doubt that. Shoes need to be flexible. Such a hard material would be like walking on windowpanes."

"No, that's not comfortable." Lydia shook her head and lifted her feet high on the seat. Folds of calamine-blue silk curled about her pearl-colored stockings and satin slippers. "No glass."

Scarlett's gown of aurora red had bursts of matching orange and red beads along the hem. I think she liked the sound it made when she walked, for she swished her skirt until she climbed into the carriage.

Katherine seemed almost shy coming out of the house. The color she'd picked, even the styling wasn't the design that arrived for her. Instead of a simple modest gray gown, she looked like a true Vasilisa. An off-white dress cut low in front, skimmed her beautiful bosom, showing off her long neck.

"If the duke didn't want me to be in half-mourning, he should've just said something."

"Kitty, he'd ordered this gown without asking, but he wanted you to shine." I couldn't believe she refused to see this as an act of a man who cared for her. This was the kind of man who'd forgive secrets. "You look lovely. I suppose the duke wants all eyes on you and not my exhibition."

"Heavy-handed, but Jahleel . . . he always had nice tastes."

Tugging on white kid gloves, she climbed inside. I followed in a bronze-green gown. Light and airy, it featured a ribbon belt with a gold buckle under my bosom.

I sat beside Scarlett and made sure my puffed sleeves, stiffened with a coarser muslin, stayed full.

"You can do this, Georgie," Scarlett said. "You will sing in public. Everyone will realize you were merely Lord Mark's student. No more troubles."

"You think it that simple." Nothing was ever that simple.

"Yes. I believe my analysis is correct. Science and logic can pick perfect pairings."

Scarlett was more talkative, and she'd even taken more time with her hair. Delicate curls looped about her ears. There was something in her eyes. Uncertainty? Was she trying to convince herself of Mr. Carew being my right partner, or me?

Mr. Thom stuck his head inside. "Ya pa. He'd be very proud. You were his gems."

The door closed.

The carriage began to move and I put my gloved hand to my heart, hoping it slowed enough to enjoy the sparkle of the Thames as it wished us well on the way to the ball.

The lights of Anya House burned brightly. Every window, every inch of James Street glowed as young pages wielding fiery torches waved carriages forward.

My breath caught. The duke's home had always been impressive, but it looked like a castle set in Mayfair.

"This ball will be phenomenal," Scarlett said. She tugged up her slipping satin gloves. "The dancing will go on and on."

Katherine's eyes were wide. Though she often tried to seem dispassionate, there was no hiding the pleasure that being in fashion and joining society brought.

Lydia offered a squeaky whistle. "Wow. Tavis never took us to a ball."

"Well, he was rather busy," Katherine said with surprising tact. But then she added, "I'm sure he would've if he could've."

Scarlett's lips parted.

She looked as if she was going to add a correcting remark, something that would sting and remind us again of all the ways our brother-in-law failed us.

Instead, she clamped her mouth shut and stared at the line of carriages ahead of us. "Well," she said, "this is a good way to re-introduce society to us."

A few minutes of waiting ended when Mr. Thom stopped right in front of Anya House.

Two grooms came to hand us down and our man-of-all-work announced us. "This is Lady Hampton and the Wilcox family. Make sure they have a good time."

"We sound like an acting troupe." I said this, then stopped at the first step. There were only a few to ascend before stepping into that other world.

My sisters stood behind me, but our Lydia took charge. "I want to find the duke."

"Wait." Katherine motioned us to the side.

Mr. Thom waved as he drove away, back to the other side of the Thames. In a few days, the duke would return us where we belonged when this fairy tale ended.

"Georgina," Katherine said, "you don't have to exhibit or do anything that you don't want to do."

She glanced at me and grabbed my hand. "If you don't feel comfortable exhibiting tonight, you don't have to. We won't think any less of you. I'll find the duke and apologize. Perhaps a ball can heal the past. We could all just be friends."

I knew what she was saying or trying to say, but it wasn't enough. It was my turn to sacrifice and fix things.

Capturing her gaze in mine, I said, "Make peace with the duke. It will only make things better. But tonight, I'm singing for our mother and father. This is what they always wanted, us shining in the lights. Then I will do what is best for me, for all of us."

Her eyes reflecting mine, black with golden flecks and tears, she tapped with a lacy handkerchief. "I'm not brave enough, Georgie."

"Yes, you are." I gripped her hand. She gave it a little squeeze, and we followed her into the duke's home.

It was crowded.

The music was loud.

People were talking and eating and carrying goblets of wine.

A juggler passed us in the grand hall. In a red-and-blue-striped costume, he juggled wooden balls. "Welcome!"

He shouted this at all the guests he passed, but the music was so loud it was like a whisper.

Before heading into the drawing room, Katherine stopped at a new framed portrait. "A new watercolor," she said.

Scarlett came to her side. "Do you recognize the place or the artist?"

"It's the place I recognized. It looks like Glasgow in the summer. She's such a great artist."

She? My sister knew who painted it. This was another of her secrets.

"I like colors." Lydia twirled, her dress floating above those perfect slippers. "Maybe the duke will let me paint."

All smiles, but we kept moving.

Then I saw Mark. He sat at a grand pianoforte, one bigger than the beauty in the music room.

He noticed me, smiled, then began a difficult piece by Mozart. Violinists accompanied him. Dancing filled the room.

Behind him, the grand portrait of Dido and Elizabeth hung.

Katherine led us to chairs at the rear near a large window that illuminated the garden. Torches lined the path to the maze.

A young blond woman came near the pianoforte and sang some lovely tune, something French.

Mark, as he did with me, followed her pitch and made the notes support and elongate her tone to the greatest effect.

Applause rang when the song ended.

He took her hand and they both bowed.

My stomach tightened, not from watching my music teacher escort this lady to dance but from the hardened gaze of an older man with graying dark hair. A taller, angrier version of Mark Sebastian glared at us, the Wilcoxes, like we didn't belong.

Chapter 39

GEORGINA—THE FIRST DANCE

The duke didn't make his appearance for several hours. He seemed to be one who suffered often from the spring sicknesses.

Yet when he did show, the man was immaculate—white breeches the color of snow, an ivory tailcoat resembling the freshest dairy cream and embellished with seed pearls that surely took weeks to stitch into place.

His white waistcoat glimmered with silver threads. I'd always thought the duke a handsome man, but this was breathtaking. I wasn't affected because of any sentiment of fancying him. It was how he carried himself. He seemed above everyone in this place. Much of the old money, the ton, was here to taste his wines and devour his foods, to find him lacking.

No one could. Not even the Prince Regent.

The shock and, now growing, awe could be seen on the older guards' wrinkled faces, their lowering snide noses. Why was it so hard to imagine a man of color with wealth and breeding could be anything less than amazing?

The faint tan in his light olive skin made him beautiful. With touches of art and even his beloved kartoshka piled on silver plates next to a beautiful white soup, he was as English as everyone here but also Russian and Blackamoor.

I felt very proud to know him. I was grateful the Duke of Torrance had championed the Wilcox family.

"Everyone," I said in a voice unable to hide my glee, "I think our host has found us and is coming our way."

"Yes, he is." Katherine sounded wistful. Then I noticed seed pearls on her train. The duke made their outfits match. She looked as if she were the hostess for his ball. Couldn't she see that if she confessed and told him everything about the pregnancy, the babies, he'd forgive her?

The duke passed the dancers and the performers who wove in and out of the crowd waving colorful flags of silver and gold.

"Welcome to my ball, ladies." He tapped his large nose as he seemed to examine us, chignon to slippers. "Lovely ladies. You honor my ball."

Scarlett raised her finger to him. "Sir, what is the significance of the flags?"

"Silver is redemption. Gold is for power. I think they are strong themes to suggest change." He looked us over again. "I wish to dance with the prettiest Wilcox."

His hand reached toward Katherine, but then he bent and asked Lydia, "Shall we, madam?"

For a moment, a tiny second, Katherine's blank expression formed a frown. Then she acquiesced and put the child's gloved hand in his.

"The duke has singled out our Lydia, Katherine." I waved them off. "That's good."

My sister turned toward the refreshments and disappeared.

Watching Lydia giggle, the duke whirled her around the dance floor.

"I think she's standing on his toes to waltz," Scarlett said. "That's adorable. He's so good to her."

It was a humorous, endearing sight, the big man and his biggest admirer swaying under the enormous crystal chandelier.

Mr. Carew entered the hall. Dressed in an ebony tailcoat and dark pantaloons, he looked formal and austere, not the relaxed, affable man we'd known for years.

His hands—they fumbled, rubbing together in white gloves. He seemed nervous. Then he saw us and smiled.

When he came toward us, he bowed. "You look lovely, Miss Wilcox. And Miss Scarlett Wilcox, you're breathtaking. I don't believe I've ever seen you in women's slippers, just your father's boots."

He laughed and extended his hand to my sister, and they began to dance.

Oh my. I realized that during the duke's parade of men, Mr. Carew didn't know of the competition. He was merely a man caught up in reciting Shakespeare.

Carew wasn't here for me or anyone.

The duke came to my side. "I didn't have a conversation with Mr. Carew yet. I thought you might want a little more time at this magical ball to discover your magic."

"Again, Duke." Lydia hugged him about his legs. "One more dance."

"But you can win the bet, Your Grace. Mr. Carew would not refuse to honor your request."

He stretched a hand to my cheek. "How can I win if you're the slightest bit unhappy? Don't fret. As Lady Hampton would say, the d'yavol will have his due."

The duke bent and picked up Lydia but held my gaze. "Be careful tonight, there are reporters here and darkness. Stay in the light, the brightness of your good heart. All will be well once you perform."

He turned me toward Mark, and then took Lydia for another spin about the ballroom. What could I do so that the duke and I were both victorious?

Mark came to me, directly from leaving the furious-looking man, the one I saw earlier sputtering. My music teacher, with garnet-colored cheeks and endearing dimples, bowed to me, then took my hand, kissing it gently before releasing it.

"Miss Wilcox," he said in a very formal, commanding tone, "good evening. I don't know how much longer I'll be able to stay, so I'd like to begin your exhibition of Pleyel. Are you ready to perform?"

Leave? Now?

We hadn't even danced.

He breathed hard. It wasn't passion. It was naked fury. "Prahmn is here."

The tension in his shoulders, the strain in his neck muscles above his fluffy starched cravat told me of his rage. Mark looked like my father on one of those bad coal days. Mama had us leave Papa alone, where he'd sit in her parlor and she'd play the pianoforte or quote him Psalms until he calmed.

Taking Mark's arm, I swayed him from heading deeper into the ballroom. Off to the side, under a sconce, I saw flames in his eyes.

"Ignore the noise, my lord. You know your worth and what's right. Nothing anyone says can change that."

"This said by the woman who refuses to marry me."

My gaze locked with his. "You know it's not that simple."

"It's a *yes, I can't live without you* or *no, I can*. No is very simple, Georgie."

If I knew how much I loved him and how much he needed me, I'd run, fancy gold slippers and all. "After the ball, we shall speak about everything."

Mark peered around my shoulder. "The woman's with him too. How disrespectful. His hypocrisy is astounding."

"Please calm down and make sense."

He bit his lip, and I could see fire and steam coming out my love's nostrils. "The Marquess of Prahmn told me how disappointed he was in me. I told him how disappointed I was in him. The exchange was unpleasant."

Mark closed his eyes for a moment. "Georgie, I ask you again to marry me, and I promise that you'll not regret a day of our union. I'll do anything to prove myself worthy. I seek your trust. I will build with you a future if you will accept me."

The word *yes* lifted from my tongue. But flames radiating in his father's red face, the scorn coming from his companion's painted countenance as they neared, chilled my spirit.

"I think we should discuss this tomorrow, away from the ball and prying eyes. They are behind us."

"Forget them. Georgie, let it be you and me against the world."

"Tomorrow, sir. There are too many people. The newspapers too. We should be alone and you can take your time convincing me."

His lips formed a tight line. Then he nodded. "Yes, I see you haven't had a chance to weigh all of your options. You don't need to tell me again that you want a man with an established profession—"

"You will be established. Your sonata is wonderful."

"Yes, my newly finished, non-award-winning piece that will be submitted to the Harlbert's Prize is wondrous."

He didn't believe in himself, not anymore. Prahmn had done that.

Then I saw my reflection on the silver finish of the sconce. I was guilty. I'd taken his confidence too.

He mopped at his brow. "Forgive me. I'm tired. I've lost everything tonight. Perhaps it was overdue." He sighed, letting out more heated breath. "Let's get your performance done. We'll stand before the crowd and finally kill the rumors that there was nothing between us other than a music teacher and his student or the fleeting respectability of true love."

He held out his hand, and I took it. I wanted to slow him, to give him more encouragement, but he'd already led us through the wild crowd and around the fire-breathing acrobats.

At the pianoforte, Mark adjusted his tailcoat and sat at the grand instrument. He began to dazzle the room with a wondrous introduction to Pleyel's hymn.

The packed drawing room began to hush. He took one palm

from the keys, grabbed my hand, and kissed my wrist. "Begin, Miss Wilcox. Show the ball that your voice belongs here."

I was ready.

We'd prepared. For the first time in public, I would offer my words in song. Opening my mouth, I struck the first note, but the angry gentleman, the Marquess of Prahmn, rushed at us and slammed his fist along the pianoforte's top.

Chapter 40

MARK—THE PERFORMANCE

When my father hit the pianoforte, I leapt up and drew Georgie behind me.

I sputtered but found a voice. "Back away."

"What?" Prahmn said, "I can't hear you, you abomination."

"Sir!" My throat opened fully, and I shook my fists. "Quiet down and back away."

I'd never taken to blows in public. In private, I'd broken up drunken brawls and evicted people from houses. I'd strike anyone who threatened any woman—father or peer or drunkard included.

"This is a disgrace. You openly make love to this creature like it's normal."

My emotions felt raw. I raged and could roar. "Leave now, Prahmn."

"I disown you, sir. You are—"

"Should he make his private concerns public like your distasteful whoring, Prahmn?" The duke's voice rang clear. He came through the stunned crowd. "Sir, I need you and your prostitute to leave my house. Never come back."

My father's eyes exploded. The fury he had at me turned toward Torrance. "You take that back, you half-bred twit."

"I'm sorry to annoy you with the truth. But to publicly bring a Saint Giles prostitute to my grand ball, clean her up, and then pretend this is an acceptable practice for a married man, I'm glad the Marchioness of Prahmn has left you."

"This is all a lie. You're twisting things."

The duke came within inches of Prahmn, towering over a man beginning to crumble. "You try to portray that you are the keeper of the morals of London, and you dare come to my Anya House with a common whore, a street prostitute. Will you cast off your poor by-blows in the mews of James Street or leave them on the curb?"

Prahmn grew redder. Sweat beaded his brow. He turned to the woman, who looked like the one with him in Hyde Park. "Is it true? You're not from Saint Giles parish, are you? You're a respectable widow."

The woman shrugged, then in an unmistakable Russian accent said, "*Da durak!* You old fool. *Svoloch!* Good one. Lord Prahmn, you pay my fees to show your horrible hide a good time."

The beautiful woman with dark sable hair had to be in her early thirties. Wearing a tight bodice of damson violet, she turned to the duke and dipped her chin before sauntering out of the room.

The laughter sounding all around made the tall, proud marquess look small.

"Sebastian, remove the trash. Take Prahmn out of here." The duke motioned to Livingston, who could barely contain his shock, glee, and amazement. "Help our friend. I hear you two are good at that."

The duke flung out his hand, like he'd done with the carriages, with other servants. The violinist noticed and began to play. Then he led a pale Georgie to the floor and started everyone to waltzing.

This was orchestrated.

I couldn't think on this. I had trash duty. Like a guard in the legion of the duke, I said to my father, "Don't make more of a scene. You've disgraced the Sebastian name. Your wife, your heir and spares are shamed. When everyone learns of your behavior, all will be mortified. Leave with Livingston and me with the little dignity you have left."

Shaken, clutching at his chest, my father walked out of the drawing room.

The earl and I followed, making sure his fevered head didn't burn down Anya House.

Chapter 41

MARK—THE TRUE BET

Like this was some odd farce being performed on Drury Lane, I trudged behind my father as we left the ballroom at Anya House.

As mad as I was at Prahmn, I could not help but feel used by Torrance. He'd erected the revenge Livingston had said that he wanted.

Unwittingly, I'd helped.

The three of us stepped outside.

Linkboys whirled torches.

Livingston stepped to the side. "I'll have your carriage brought round."

My friend still looked stunned, very pink-faced. He even wobbled. I wasn't sure how much champagne he'd drunk; it was more than enough.

I wondered if he knew this evening's events would lead to my father's disgrace.

"Your mother," Prahmn said, "she told me I was a fool to come tonight. She said there would be nothing to convince you to change course."

"She's right. The Marchioness of Prahmn would have prevented you from losing your temper in public. She'd keep your prejudice and foul dealings private. You don't deserve her."

He took an embroidered handkerchief from his pocket and

swiped at his face. "This will be in the papers. My humiliation will hit all the gossip sheets. You must savor that."

"Gossip is nothing to savor. The ton's tittle-tattle about whose alleged sins are exposed is of no interest to me."

Prahmn didn't look at me. "You're going to marry that one. You can expect no help from me. No recommendations—"

"Father, I hardly think anyone will want to be connected to your name anytime soon. No one likes to be exposed. And to see you be fooled by a prostitute . . . No, keep your sympathies."

He fisted his hand. "I'm still right. You . . . She's beneath you."

"You are wrong, and at least she can say her hardworking father built a company, while mine was exposed as a lowlife by a prostitute."

His carriage came around. I held the door as he slumped inside.

"Think long and hard, Prahmn. My mother deserves so much better. I hope she stays in the country for a long time. Go sit in her empty parlor, the one she consoles you in when your escapades end. Be alone with your prejudice and stupidity until even you are sick of yourself."

I slammed the door and sent his driver away.

Livingston was in the shadows of the housed portico. "You said all those words. Good ones. Good job. You all right, Sebastian?"

"Oddly, I feel numb. Prahmn has never been warm, but it's disturbing to see him brought low."

"I guess it was good for your mother to be gone."

I squinted at my friend, then realized this was the mothers' network in action. "I suppose the dowager countess had an earful this afternoon."

"Yes. It seems Prahmn's new friend encouraged him to get rid of the marchioness and send her to the country. The prostitute wanted to enjoy the season from the Grosvenor house."

That bit of foolishness saved my mother from sacrificing her peace and dignity to help my father recover.

The man responsible for this turn of events was in the hall showing Lydia Wilcox the new painting.

"Your Grace," I said, "might we have a word?"

His smile widened. He suspected that I'd figured things out. Bending down to the little girl, he snapped his fingers and the maid assigned to her appeared. "Take my princess to her room for bed, but stop by the map room when she's ready. The surprise is there."

Lydia looked as if she would fuss about being sent upstairs, but the mention of a surprise made her clasp the maid's hand and skip along to the stairs. "Love my duke."

"Love my dorogaya." The duke looked touched.

I had no such warm feelings. My dismay increased as I saw Georgie dancing with Mr. Carew.

Just because my father's life had spun out of control was no need for my own to follow suit. I knew what I wanted, I just had to figure out how to convince Georgie.

We walked toward the duke's study. With each step, I was further away from the future I wanted, but I needed to hear of Prahmn's downfall and to secure a promise from the duke, that he'd never again tamper with life to gain revenge.

Closing the door to the study so that onlookers wouldn't stumble inside, I waited for the duke and Livingston to pour glasses of brandy.

The sideboard was again cluttered with bottles. The duke filled a third glass and left it there. "You might need this, Sebastian."

"I might, but I think I'm owed the truth more."

Torrance took a sip, then sat on the edge of the desk. He lifted a green chess piece from a set I hadn't seen before; the marble chessboard set at his hip. "Free yourself. Say what's on your mind."

"My friend Livingston, he told me of the difficulties that my father caused in your life."

The duke put the pawn in front of the cornered king piece of the opposite color. "Checkmate. Talkative Livingston? I didn't think you spoke of anything but research and your stance against marriage."

The earl took a big swig from his glass. "Don't want to exactly be on your bad side, Your Grace, but when we met—"

"Met years ago in Brooks's. I'd had a miserable day at a hearing. My rights were again unnecessarily delayed. I was particularly angry because time can't be restored. I missed my sister's final days. The money for doctors that might've extended her life was denied. Lord Prahmn was the chief instigator. The heathen used everything—my faith, lineage, everything—to force narrow-minded men to delay seeing a marriage and birth records for what they were, accurate documents making me the sole heir to my father's estate."

Livingston finished his glass and poured another. His hands shook, clanking his goblet against the myriad of blue and green bottles. "So you plotted tonight?"

"Did I expect Prahmn to be taken in by a common prostitute? No. Did I expect that he'd like an enticing woman of loose morals with the appearance of being a widow wanting to be lavished by a man with no scruples or fidelity? Yes. Can a woman trying to advance in the world of fleshly pursuits take a bribe to ensure a fool's downfall? Yes. Will she fake an accent and learn a few choice Russian words so Prahmn would know this came from me? *Da*. Da. Da."

"And how did Miss Wilcox and I fit into this scheme?"

"You didn't, but I may have tested a reaction. Our drive in Hyde Park proved to me that Prahmn was still the biggest heathen and hypocrite. He'd be angry at his son's legitimate courtship of a Blackamoor woman while he took more and more risks to be with his new friend."

"Tell us about tonight." Livingston looked as if this was an experiment and not my life. "How did you know Prahmn would expose himself?"

The duke chuckled softly. "I didn't, but my mother has always told me that human nature always wins. So a fool will make himself a bigger one. Seeing you and Miss Wilcox actually in love, not in lust, would disturb a man who doesn't know the difference."

"Put enough kerosene or whale oil around matches and something will explode." I saw no flaws in his logic. I breathed easier, knowing that both I and Georgina weren't pawns. "Thank you for making sure my mother was away."

He nodded. "She's innocent of everything but trying to have peace in her home. I understand that. Mr. Steele advised Chancey to have her packed in case Prahmn's new mistress wanted her away. And the chance to flounce about Mayfair was a nice inducement for his new friend. The prostitute was handsomely bribed to ask, and the lustful fool drove the marchioness away."

I imagined that what Prahmn would require of my mother to achieve his public redemption would be incredibly shameful for her—to parade with him to church, to promenade in Hyde Park, to attend all the remaining balls of the season with him, helping to reclaim his dignity. Yet, I knew, as did she, he wouldn't change. He'd fall back to his indecent behavior as soon as he thought London had forgiven him. "I hope my mother stays away for years. I take comfort that she's not here feeling obligated to help Prahmn."

"I have a soft spot for mothers and for all women forced into uncomfortable situations."

"And apparently prostitutes who are willing to learn Russian." Livingston stood. "I suppose we should return to the ball. Three daring bachelors awaiting tonight's pleasures."

"I think I need to take a long moment before returning."

"No, Sebastian." The duke stood up. "You will have your head high. You must accompany Miss Wilcox on the pianoforte, perform, and then the two of you can determine what you do next."

It sounded as if I had the duke's blessings.

Not that I needed them. My heart had already determined that Georgie was the one.

"No, no, no. I know that look, Sebastian. Marriage is a mockery. You saw a prime example of that tonight."

"Livingston, he saw an example of a fool getting his comeuppance. Leave Sebastian alone."

"No," the earl said, drinking more of his third brandy. "You don't want to be married. You're too young. You'll ruin your whole life, marrying in your prime. Tell him, Your Grace."

"I'm alone, not by choice." The duke set his goblet down and folded his arms. "If he's found love, he needs to seize it."

"Oh, you daffy Russian man. We have to protect Sebastian from an institution that will eat his soul."

"Bitter much, Livingston? You silly man from Suffolk."

"I'm from Kent."

"Gentlemen." The two ignored me and began to fuss more. I went to the sideboard. As I picked up the filled glass, Livingston's animated motions knocked over jars. A blue one emptied its contents onto my fingers.

Then I couldn't feel them. Or anything.

I flexed my fingers, even flung them. "What is this? I'm numb."

The duke shot up and came to the sideboard. He took a pitcher of water and dunked my hands in it.

"That's for pain, bone-aching pain. You better sit down, Sebastian. You're going to feel—"

"Light-headed?"

"Could be. Could be more than that."

Livingston grabbed my wrist and felt for a pulse. "Torrance, what's in the witch's brew? What are all these things?"

"Tonics. Some help you sleep. Looks like Sebastian might want to take a nap."

As he said this, my chest began to feel like ice. It became hard to breathe. "Torrance, is this poison?"

"Just a little pain medicine. It'll wear off in four hours or more. You'll be fine. Perfectly fine tomorrow."

"But I have to play for Miss Wilcox tonight." My head began to spin, and I found a chair before I fell.

The duke, both of his heads, looked very concerned. "Mr. Carew is here. He may know what to do."

"No. He'll marry Georgie. If he hears my angel sing, he will marry her. Everyone will marry her. Remember, that was the plan."

I swung my arms like I swam in mud. "Send the earl away too. He might marry her."

Livingston stepped back. "I know exactly what to do."

My chest felt looser. My friend understood. "Bring her to me. My Georgie. I'll explain."

The earl was half out the door. "I'm going to tell her you're too embarrassed to show your face and that she needs to perform alone."

"Wait. No, Livingston. That's the opposite of what I want."

"Look. Your father is humiliated right now, but that doesn't change that you are virtually penniless. Prahmn will still make your life terrible. You can't afford a wife. Miss Georgina Wilcox deserves stability and love. I'm going to save you both."

My misguided friend was out the door.

I turned back to the duke, and both his mustaches. "Help me."

"Well, if Miss Georgina doesn't perform, she won't garner much more attention. Prahmn stole everyone's eyes. He will very much be the gossip of my ball. You still have another chance to tell her the truth, that you are ready to fight the wind for her." He went to the door. "Steele, stop Livingston. Get Carew, bring him here."

"Yes, Your Grace." A blurry image by the three doors disappeared.

Swatting my hands against my breeches like I was beating up a cyclone made no difference.

What if I could no longer play?

How would I support us? "Fix this."

"It will wear off by tomorrow. Pretty sure." He picked up the empty blue vial. "Rest, and then go tell the woman you love your heart. That even without music, you're determined to find a way to make things work. Not everyone is brave enough to make that promise."

Not knowing what to say, I staggered to my feet. "Let's stop Livingston. And then let her know I didn't do this on purpose."

Torrance dipped his fingers in a little bit of the spill and rubbed it across his palm. "Just joining you for moral support."

The duke grimaced, steadied me, then went to the door. "Let's go to the garden. Walk you around in the fresh air. Steele will stop Livingston. Then you and Miss Wilcox will talk."

I hoped Georgina would understand not performing. I'd never let her go up against the ton alone. I prayed she'd forgive me for everything and listen once more to my rambles of loving her.

Chapter 42

GEORGINA—THE PERFORMANCE OF A LIFETIME

A footman brought in lit candles, extra ones for the sconces behind the pianoforte, directed by the Earl of Livingston. I guess he didn't want anyone to miss the next performance.

He announced that a special song would be performed. Then signaled for me to be ready.

Oh. Mark and I would return to the pianoforte in front of this gossiping crowd.

"It will be fine." Katherine rubbed my arm. "Lively night, but you and Lord Mark will ease everyone's apprehension."

"Where is he? You don't think he went with his awful father."

A dutiful son might.

A fellow that felt obligated to his family and feared for the family name would definitely wish to help.

What we'd witnessed was horrible.

The Marquess of Prahmn and his repugnant life were exposed. Everyone saw, even the newspapermen in the crowd. Gossip would be everywhere.

Poor Mark. "I don't want Lord Mark tarnished too."

"Men fare better in scandal," Katherine said.

Scarlett gave her a sour-lemon look that said *Could you not be bitter this once?* "Just give a performance as beautiful as how you two have practiced. That will save you and him. And no one will believe the two of you would be together . . . not with a father like that."

Mark wasn't his father. I hoped he'd never be him.

The end of the next selection would soon come.

That was my notice to come to the pianoforte again.

My pulse raced in time with the music.

But my heart searched for Mark. He needed comfort.

I was ready to exhibit, ready for this ball to be done. It wasn't midnight, but this Vasilisa, Cinderella, needed to run away. Then she could leave with her gold slippers and not think of this night of scandals again.

A young lady sang and played the pianoforte, while my sisters and I held our positions in the rear.

"Miss Lydia Wilcox has gone to bed." The personal maid the duke assigned to our girl bowed and dipped away. She disappeared in a crowd that was sated with champagne, choice meats, and all kinds of baked puddings and kartoshkas. Those chocolate-dusted truffles enfolded with cream tasted so good. No wonder the duke loved them.

I wiped my gloves free of the powdery cocoa. "At least Lydia went to bed thinking me brave, a hero for surviving the bad man."

"Yes," Scarlett said, "Georgie the brave, not Georgie the runner."

"Where are you going, Georgina?" Katherine's voice made me still.

Unconsciously, I'd half turned toward the closest exit.

Each sister grabbed one of my arms. "We can all do this together," our eldest said. "We can be the singing Wilcoxes."

Kissing both their hands, I refused. "You two keep your heads up. Lord Mark will come."

The Earl of Livingston came to me. His countenance looked grim. "I think our friend had a little bit of an accident, so he may not show up to assist you. That's what he told me to say."

"So he told you to tell me something?"

"Yes, he did. You'll have to do your performance without him. I heard you sing. Do it a cappella. It will be even better. I think that's what Sebastian wants, for you to do everything without him."

That didn't sound like Mark, but the embarrassment he must be feeling was probably acute. If my brother-in-law had taught me anything, it was that you raise your head no matter how big the scandal. Tavis would go into rooms owing everyone, and still bet or borrow more.

My father had faced the stares with grace. I could too. I was his daughter. "I'm ready, Lord Livingston, but I can play the piece."

"Excellent." His gaze went about the room. "Mr. Carew is missing. Hopefully, he'll step back in, hear you sing, and see, like our scientific process said, you're his perfect match."

Following the earl, I again bobbed and turned and side-stepped dancers. At the head of the room, the grand pianoforte glistened in the bright light. Dido and Elizabeth looked over my shoulder.

"No one will miss seeing me, Lord Livingston."

"Did I have them add too many candles?"

"Yes, my lord, but it's better to see the music."

Now his head whipped. "No sheet music. Sebastian must have it, or he plays from memory. No matter, you can still just sing."

The fellow was extremely nervous. Then I looked out the window and saw the reason.

Mark, supported by the duke and Mr. Carew, was walking back and forth. In and out of the maze.

Was he injured or drunk?

Were they trying to sober him up?

Livingston gazed at me. "Found him. But now you need to stall. With all the gossip about his father, Sebastian will be stained too."

Seeing Mark in trouble, knowing that I could help by offering an attention-gathering performance, gave me courage. "I need no sheet music."

He clapped his hands. "Now, we will have a rendition of Pleyel's hymn by Miss Georgina Wilcox. She has been a student of Lord Mark Sebastian."

The crowd hushed. I was sure they recognized me from before, and now the earl had tied my name again with Mark's. I had to do well for him and my family.

Steadying myself to the hush of the crowd, I opened my mouth, but the words wouldn't come.

Hundreds of eyes stared.

My heart pounded.

My eyes wanted to turn and see if Mark was better.

My pulse raced.

Then my mother's voice sounded in my head. *Time for lessons, dear. Show Papa what you know. Make him proud.*

"Make him proud." I sang these words like a melody, like the song that wouldn't leave my head.

Sitting at the pianoforte, I began to play the notes I envisioned, that had imprinted before my eyes.

I added runs. My fingers sailed across the keys.

Shutting my lids, I added bits of me, of Mama and Papa, to this melody. Then I realized my thumbs touched the same ivory that Mark had.

In my soul, I played the tune that he struggled with. I found a new way to end it. I built a crescendo, and then banged out the last triumphant note.

Anya House seemed quiet. I thought I'd disgraced myself

until I heard the clapping. Thunderous applause filled the drawing room.

The earl came back, took my hand, and helped me stand.

The joyous reception to my performance continued.

Mark stood with the duke and Mr. Carew in the doorway.

They all smiled.

The duke came to me, clapping. "This is Miss Georgina Wilcox. She has been working with Lord Mark on a special piece of music to be debuted. It has been a secret. Their work has been shrouded in mystery and even intrigue. Yet this sonata is an example of unity. Please congratulate them again."

Mark didn't come to share the applause, though it continued for more than five minutes. He'd stepped away.

Then the duke had the musicians play and he waltzed me about the room. "All eyes are on you, my dear, as they should be."

"Your Grace is generous, but the man whose attention I want is not here."

"A man in love never takes his eyes from his heart for very long. He'll lose what he most desires. And there is Mr. Carew."

Over the duke's shoulder, I saw the handsome man now dancing with Katherine. "Ah, someone has finally danced with her."

The duke spun me and probably saw for himself the two enjoying the waltz.

"Why don't you go dance with Katherine, Your Grace? Fix the disagreement. You both will not win the bet tonight. Mr. Carew is nice. If I marry, it needs to be with someone more than nice. It should be to the man I love."

"Well, for me to dance with Lady Hampton, it might have to mean more than dancing. Miss Wilcox, I do intend to win the bet, but that was why I put in the caveat about our mutual friend as a draw. You found Lord Mark Sebastian in the garden. I suggest you go find him there once more before he leaves."

"Is he that hurt?"

"The feeling will return in his fingers."

"What?"

"Calm. Quiet. It was a little accident. But you played his sonata. Now that it's been performed in public, he can't enter it in the Harlbert's Prize."

I couldn't breathe. I'd stolen Mark's opportunity.

"Run, Georgina Wilcox. Go get the happiness you want."

That's what I did. As fast as I could, I charged into the garden, hoping to catch the perfect match to my soul.

Chapter 43

MARK—BY THE LIGHT OF THE STARS

On the bench, where my adventure began, I looked up into the stars. What a night. I'd lost my father, my song, and my girl. Searching the stars that I used to guide me through the maze, I hoped for a nightingale to sing to me, to lull my pathetic soul.

My hands were still too numb to grip the reins of my gig. Probably couldn't get a good hold on it, or the heart that had been ripped out of my chest.

Georgie ran around the corner. "You haven't left yet."

"This isn't the way to the mews."

"Right. I should remember that."

She seemed happy, a relieved expression on her face.

"Mark, are you all right?"

"Not quite." I wrung my hands. "Getting there."

Like my palms were baked bricks, I slapped the bench. "Sit, share the stars. The viewing is free."

"Should we? The house is full; someone could venture upon us. We'd be back in trouble."

"Well, this time I'd insist you marry me."

Her breath caught, and I saw what looked like hope burning on her olive-brown cheeks.

"You still want to marry me, even after I accidentally stole your sonata?"

"Oh, that little thing. I'll forgive you after a year or two of our blissful union."

I offered Georgie a smile and again pointed to the bench. But she didn't move. "Still, no. You won't take me up on my offer?"

"Be serious for a moment."

I was, but she refused to see it. Instead, I glanced at the vulnerable jet eyes of the woman who charmed and ruined me. "I still love you, Georgie."

"Mark, I-I didn't mean to. I didn't play it exactly like you wrote it. It could still be used, couldn't it? Or maybe you could change a few sections. I mean, I just played what I remembered in my head."

"You made it sound better than I created. And I have to be honest to win the prize. I have some integrity." Moving my fingers about made them tingle. Good, a new sensation. "Why didn't you tell me you could play?"

"I did. I think I did."

"No. Georgie, that's beyond anything I've heard. You're masterful at the keys. What you did was phenomenal. And you have taken the piece I've struggled with for a year, made it better, and played from memory."

"I couldn't sing in public, not without you." She took a step closer. "Mark, how do I make this right? I didn't mean to offend you. I didn't mean to steal your piece. I was out in front of everyone. I panicked. You've been in my head, even when I didn't want you there."

"Then you should definitely come sit beside me."

She didn't move. Instead, she clasped her elbows. "Please don't joke. All your dreams are destroyed. I should've run."

Rising from the bench, I went to her. With my numb fingers, I brushed away a tear. "No. No more sadness. There's been too much tonight."

"But you've been working for months on that sonata. Now you have nothing for the Harlbert's Prize. That was your future. I've taken it."

It was actually years, but I'd not found all the right notes, not until now. "All by accident, my dear."

"Doesn't make this better. I didn't want you to be embarrassed, not after what happened with Lord Prahmn. Your friend called your name as my tutor. I didn't want you shamed."

"Georgie, I'm a composer. I'll write again. That wasn't my only song. But you are my only love."

Before she escaped, or slipped away from my life or, heaven forbid, someone interrupted, I wrapped my arms about her. "I need you to know that I love you. I love you more than my family. I want you to become my family."

I kissed her wide, pert nose, then the hollows of her cheeks. When I got to her lips, I tasted and took my time. Then I fully claimed this heaven-sent mouth as mine.

Love was my best work. The composer in me found the right student, one who taught me to be a better man.

Sculpting this goddess to me, I drank in this kiss as far as I could. I needed it to be seared into my flesh, deep into my chest, down into my heart.

Then when she left me for the sensible, right thing to do, I'd still have a piece of her to guide me and write the music of the brokenhearted.

Chapter 44

GEORGINA—MY FUTURE

Tall Meg of a girl, kissing a man of similar height, objective forever— that should be what the gossips wrote if they saw me in the garden being swept away in Mark's embrace.

His passion, the way he held me to him was a little loose. I forgave his wandering hands, they were medicated.

But I felt his touch. I wanted it. I needed it everywhere.

I heard a noise and broke away from him.

"I love you, Georgie. Don't go. Don't run anywhere without me."

"Mark, what is our new plan? The Harlbert's Prize could be something you win next year. What do we do this year?"

He twiddled his fingers along my elbow like I were the keys of the pianoforte. "Our plan? Well, I accepted a commission for tonight's sonata. As a professional, I'm no longer eligible. The prize committee is committed to starving artists. *Hungry* is something my wife and I shall never be."

"How can you say that? You've no income. I don't have a dowry since neither the duke nor my sister will win the bet if I marry you. I come to you with nothing."

"I want you with nothing. You can wear nothing and love me."

I shook my head. "How do we live?"

He took a step toward me. "I'll work for your family."

"No. No one outside the Wilcoxes will ever run Wilcox Coal again."

He frowned. "I don't want to be outside. I want to be where love is. And Georgie, I don't want any part of operating your family's company. I meant work for the company. I can drive a coal dray just like Mr. Thom. I'm good with the reins. Just need to feel my hands."

"Being a mere driver won't hurt your ego?'

"Hey, I will work hard to be as good as Mr. Thom. And I can still gain commissions designing music rooms. I'll provide for you. I'll earn your trust every day."

He kissed my tears. His mouth grazed over my wet lids. "We're not false anymore. Georgie, the only responsibility I will demand is to be your husband. I'll drive coal wagons or sweep for you. You'll have to show me how to operate a broom better."

"Stop making me laugh."

"Georgie, it's music to me. I'll do anything to provide for my wife until I can earn enough from my music to lavish you in the manner I was formerly accustomed to. I'm pampered. I just left my mother's knee. I need a strong woman's influence to keep me on the straight and narrow. Order me about, woman."

He was saying all the right words. But didn't everyone until they got what they wanted? Yet, when I stared at Mark, I knew he spoke the truth.

"I'm scared. Marriage changes so much for a woman. And will you come to hate me when your family never visits or your father cuts us direct in public? Your brothers and their wives too?"

"My father's prostitute mistress just cut us all. I think I can handle anything. Anything as long as we do it together."

When he raised his arm, I took it.

"I felt that, Georgie. The feeling's back." He clasped my fingers and drew my wrist to his warm, hungry mouth. "Besides, half the commission is yours, and I'm terrible at division."

Scarlett would show him how to do calculations. "Then, yes, Mark. Yes, I'll marry you."

He lifted me about the waist and swung me around and around before enfolding me in a congratulatory kiss.

Then he tore himself away. "Go get a bag. Tell your sisters. I'll tell Torrance that we are eloping. No one will ever separate us, Georgie. No one."

"I will, but I need another kiss. That will seal our deal. And confirm that we've won the duke's bet by choosing us."

"Yes, ma'am. That's an order I can humbly follow."

Mark swept me into his arms again.

Warm, deep, searching, his kiss made me hear music.

Dizzy, I held on to him, and those talented, awakening hands began playing with my laces.

Then a cough and an "Oh my" made him stop.

Katherine and the duke had found us again, but not as innocently as before. With Mark's hands on my thighs, my arms wrapped tightly about him underneath his coat. I could say we were very far from innocent.

"Don't kill me, Torrance," he said. His palms came to the top of my skirt, anchored to my waist. "We are in love and eloping tonight. We'll be married in days."

The duke drew a hand to his chin, which I now thought of as his scheming pose. "Lady Hampton, are you familiar with a Cossack marriage?"

"No, Your Grace, I don't recall."

He cast my sister an odd, hurt look. "Well, two people in love say publicly that they are in love and want to be married. A prayer is then offered. The union is complete, save consummation. I believe these young people are starting their future in the wrong order, Lady Hampton."

"Yes, wrong order, Your Grace."

"And if we hadn't been taking a walk to settle our wager, I'm sure they'd have the order completely wrong. And start all that bad gossip up again."

"Don't care about blasted newspapers, Torrance. Nothing is ever wrong in loving Georgina Wilcox. Wait, there's a ball, with hundreds of guests, just beyond the maze. That's public enough."

He reached in his pocket and produced a tiny silver band. "Marry me now, Georgie."

My head nodded. My voice sang *yes* and my eyes teared as Mark slid the ring on my finger. "Now someone offer a prayer. Katherine, please."

She looked at the duke, then me and Mark. "May this union be blessed. May God keep you focused on how you feel right now. May you be unified in all things. Amen."

Katherine kissed my cheek, then Mark's.

The duke hugged me, then bowed to my . . . husband. "There's a suite upstairs at the end of the west hall. Go take care of your wife. You are married as Cossacks. But tomorrow, I'll have a special license here so the British will recognize this union too. You never know when such a thing might be challenged."

"Torrance," my husband said, "I don't know how to thank you."

"Easy thing, my friend. Never let her go."

Mark agreed and picked me up, his bluestocking bride, and carried me through the maze and back inside Anya House.

We passed Lord Livingston, who conversed with Scarlett as an annoyed-looking Mr. Carew looked on. The physician seemed to do a lot more examining of my sister since the phlebotomy and the duke's parade of candidates.

When the earl saw us, Mark spun my hand. I'm sure the gleam from the silver blinded him in the eyes. He wandered off looking sad and asking for more spirits.

Poor Scarlett looked scared, then delighted. I didn't have time to tell her I hadn't lost my mind but had found my heart.

Mr. Carew saluted, then whisked my sister back into the drawing room.

But Mark didn't go up the stairs, he went to the duke's kitchen. "Georgie, how long does it take to make your biscuits?"

"An hour?"

"I need everyone to leave, His Grace's orders. I need this room." He set me down, kicked the door closed when all fled. "An hour."

Laughing and happy, I stared at him as he wrapped an apron about my gown. "What are you doing?"

He put his arms about me. He kissed my neck, and then whispered into my ear, "I want your biscuits just for me."

My husband helped me make the dough between kisses.

By the time the room smelled of ginger, Mark's numbness had left and he finally sunk his teeth into my decadent treat.

With a basket full of Cornish Fairings, my husband and I ran up the stairs of Anya House to the grand suite at the end of the hall.

We entered a royal-looking room painted in brilliant white with gilded moldings. The bed Mark sat me on was decked with white linens and scented in honey.

The room had been prepared for someone . . . not us.

It was made for Katherine.

Mark's coat and shirt fell to the floor. He came to my side and took up my hand, placing it against his fast-beating chest.

The man was smooth and muscular. I could not stop touching him and letting him touch me.

"This room is beyond my imagination," he said. "It's magic."

He kissed me. "Now that I've tasted your biscuits, I think all my dreams can come true."

"The duke truly loves my sister. He's waiting for her to love him again. I could see him wanting to do this for her."

"Well, tonight, it is for us."

Music vibrated through the floor. The rhythm was soft, perfect.

Mark lifted his chin. "Torrance is a brilliant and dangerous man. My father deserved everything he got tonight, but the duke put everything in motion for Prahmn's downfall. I would hate to be on Torrance's bad side."

My husband began to kiss me and strip off my layers—the apron, the outer bronze-green gown, the inner of soft gold, down to my ivory corset and chemise. His fingers tugged at the satin ribbons holding me tightly. "Georgie, have I lost your interest, so soon? We haven't begun, and I feel you drifting."

I put my arms about him and held on to him to anchor me from my worrisome thoughts.

"You're shivering. Darling, you are cold." After stuffing a biscuit in his mouth and probably swallowing it whole, he pulled back the bedclothes and swaddled me in the sheets. "How is that, my Lady Mark Sebastian?"

"Perfect." For the first time in a long time, I wouldn't fret about the problems of the Wilcoxes. I had a husband who loved me, and we had the rest of our lives to help everyone out of their troubles.

"I love you, Mark. Please hold on to me."

"I love you, Georgie. I won't let you go."

In his arms, growing as close as our hearts would allow, I found a place to shelter, a place of safety and kindness. And I was sure my new husband would help me remember where to run when I was in want of love.

EPILOGUE

Jahleel walked deeper into the maze with Katherine. "It seems, Lady Hampton, that our bet is a draw. Lord Mark and Miss Wilcox have married. And will again in the morning."

"A Cossack wedding? At least I know it's not just some lie you toss to women in need."

"Yes, it's true. A Cossack divorce is just as simple. A groom stands in the middle of a public square and declares he no longer is loved. That his mate is dead to him. Remember?"

"The bride can too. Right?"

He refused to answer. Tonight was about Georgina and Mark. "Your sister looked very happy."

"Yes, she did. I hope they are happy forever. Young love is like that." Katherine stopped moving and turned her lovely countenance to the night sky.

Time had been kind to her olive face and figure. The gown Jahleel designed showed the delicate woman that mourning rags hid.

When she looked again at him, he could drown in her jet eyes. Could he truly blame Tavis for wanting Katherine? Her zeal and passion gave her power to break any man.

For a moment, Jahleel was ready to be broken again and reformed into a man she could love.

Yet, he wasn't so young anymore.

Time hadn't been kind. His body was weaker. He'd become slower and more deliberate. It wasn't a fair fight. He could be easily defeated by a determined Katherine Wilcox Palmers.

"Thank you for helping them, Jahleel."

He blinked twice and almost tugged his ear. "You're welcome. The two are genuinely honest souls. They deserve joy."

Chuckles. "Honest, Jahleel. That's not a word I thought you knew. That cartoon could've been us in the music room and you trying to make me kiss you."

"It looked nothing like us. But it proves that London is still a difficult place for our love."

She wrenched at her neck like there was strain. "Well, now that we're dressed alike, like the happy couple of a Cossack ball, the Duke of Torrance and his mistress, I wonder which couple Gilroy will draw."

"I suspect the svoloch Prahmn, the bastard of Grosvenor Street, will be in all the papers." Unable to watch her suffer, he asked, "Headache?"

"A little."

He lazily fingered her temples, making his thumbs smooth her skin and relieve her pain. Yet, Jahleel marveled at how a work of perfect cold marble could breathe.

She looked indifferent, but her eyes shut. Katherine didn't turn away. "I suppose their union was inevitable. The two chose each other. No one ran. They will be better than—"

"Than us?"

Startled, she put her hands to his waistcoat and pushed away. "Still too easy for you to charm me."

"Let me be charming. And I must say your fingers on my chest have always been a delight."

"Nyet," she said. "No delighting. I want a chance to repay the loans. I want to try and rebuild what my father created. I want out of our silly wager."

"Oh, Katherine, I had so much hope in winning. I want to see how cavalier you are catering to my needs."

She huffed but kept her beautiful countenance smooth. "It's silly to bet. We were arguing. We lost—"

"I've never lost but once. I don't intend to lose again." He walked deeper into the maze.

And she followed, like a bee searching for a place to sting. "Jahleel, let this be over. I don't want to fight anymore."

He didn't stop until he was deeper into the maze. The high walls added privacy and an intimacy that the two hadn't shared in forever.

"Jahleel, please."

"You don't need to be concerned. We are even. Georgina chose Sebastian. From the onset of our wager, we said that would mean a tie. Whoever chooses the husband for Scarlett will be crowned a winner."

"Why? Why can't you be generous and let us stay tied?"

He spun back to her and glanced at her hurting eyes, gaping at Jahleel like all of this was his fault. "Our bet was for the two sisters. We have one left. And I like this bet. We've been civil, and I adore every moment the Wilcoxes come to Anya House. With no bet, there would be no reason for you to visit. Unless you had a reason to keep coming to see me?"

Her chest rose and fell, but she did not answer.

Why was she so afraid of feeling anything for him? "I'm attached to the Wilcoxes. I want Scarlett and Lydia to have all the things they should've had if your heart had stayed true to me."

"You're bitter? Remember, you left me."

"It was to be a moment. Katherine, you shouted out at me that you didn't love me. You took back our Cossack vows. How is that my fault?"

"I yelled it, and I'm not free. You're still in my life."

"Then leave me Scarlett and Lydia. And go live your life alone. Take Wilcox Coal and make it a success or run it into the ground. Do all the things you wanted to do if you hadn't the responsibility of younger siblings or a foolish lover. I remember your complaints, how you feared the responsibilities thrust on you too soon."

"That's not fair." She balled her fists, looking gloriously mad. "I'll not shirk my responsibilities."

"No one, least of all me, will ever hold you back from what you want." He waved his hand at her, pointing her toward the way out the maze.

"You're dismissing me like I'm a servant?" She came very close to him, breathing hard, smelling of roses, letting him count the gold flecks in her dark eyes. "Why are we fighting for custody of people you have no claim upon?"

"Open your eyes, Katherine. I've staked a claim. I made a promise to Tavis to take care of all of you. Now I've made promises to each of the girls. I'll never abandon them, which means I can never abandon you."

He'd blame the roses or the way she stood up to him for drawing him closer, like a fly to a spider's web.

How could she still drive him wild and not know the torment he endured not kissing her, not hearing her say she still loved him as he loved her?

Knowing Tavis lied about Jahleel, that he confused her, kept Jahleel going and hoping for the day she wouldn't keep slicing his heart with her frowns.

Yet, here he was clinging to her thorns hoping for nectar.

Stiffness set in, his limbs ached. He flexed his hands for relief. He'd need to sit, to rest before she saw how weak he was.

"I guess it's my fault, as always. Or maybe it's no one's that we're here and you hate me. Does the past consume you so much that you aren't willing to let me help your sisters?"

"Jahleel—"

"You forced a man who gave up betting into this gamble. Finish the wager, Katherine."

Her breath came in spurts as fury lit her face.

He held up his hands. "You have a whole year to try to repay me. See, I'm generous. But you and Scarlett and Lydia will continue to visit. I'll get Scarlett prepared for society. Perhaps she'll be presented at court. Our wager is still on. Or forfeit and just marry me."

She balled her fists and hissed, "You're impossible."

"Marry me now. I'll have two licenses in the morning. And we can walk back into the ball and declare in public that we are man and wife again."

He touched her warm apple cheek. "You can decide when you wish to visit my suite. The one I had prepared for you is presently occupied."

"You're still plotting. You think I will surrender."

"Yes, sweet dorogaya. My lovely sweetheart."

Katherine didn't pull away, but she did take his cold hand and shake it. "Good. I have a year to repay you. Then, one way or another, I'll be free. I will leave you this time, and it will be forever."

She picked up her skirts and withdrew, walking back toward the house.

"Good night, Lady Hampton. When you check on Lydia, kiss her brow for me. I love her so."

The fiery woman stumbled. Then she straightened. "Good night, Your Grace."

Jahleel let her go. Katherine Wilcox Palmers had her own secrets, and he was more determined than ever to discover them. A year was enough time to find them all.

With his hand feeling more numb, Jahleel went to his study. He passed Mr. Steele, who'd begun to have his team of servants pick up the glasses and litter his party, with the guests numbering three hundred, give or take a prostitute, had created.

"Will Anya House live, Mr. Steele?"

"Yes, sir. This was a good one. Feel proud. Be proud of your Wilcox family."

Jahleel liked the sound of that, his Wilcox family. "Good man, do not stay up too late. You can have everyone clean in the morning."

"You run your business. I'll see about this house." Mr. Steele laughed, and then returned to the drawing room.

A light was on in Jahleel's study.

Guests?

Or a special one. Had Katherine changed her mind?

His heart skipped five beats, and he hit at his chest to make it work.

Opening the door, he didn't find Lady Hampton. A rush of disappointment hit.

"Miss Scarlett Wilcox, shouldn't you have retired upstairs? The party is over. The maid assigned to your care is waiting to assist you."

One of the walrus-tooth carved rook pieces of his new chest set sent from Kholmogory dangled in her fingers. "I had to speak with you."

"You could do so without rummaging through my desk."

She dropped the piece, this one shaped like a ship. It fell on his blotter but didn't break the mast. "Sorry. But you have a lot of these games."

"I like chess, not games." Jahleel slipped inside. "Perhaps I'll need more if you continue to be clumsy."

Scarlett lowered her eyes for a moment. "I'll be leaving Anya House early. I shall be dressed in men's clothing. I don't want anyone to say a word about this."

Stretching his hand, wriggling his fingers, he closed the door. "Why is your choice of attire my concern? I'd probably only object if you possessed a hideous cravat knot or something."

"Mr. Thom helps me get away to do my research. This is Anya House. Your rules. Your servants. Mr. Steele is everywhere. He will tell if I don't have your permission."

"This visit, Scarlett, will it get you killed?"

She stood up fast from his chair. The beads of her aurora-red gown jiggled. "No. I'm not signing up for war."

"Will it get you compromised? We just had a devil of a time clearing your sister's name."

"If I'm caught, it will probably ruin my reputation, but the Royal Society won't let women enter."

"But they'll let a woman of color dressed as a man in? Is that it, Scarlett?"

"Men of color have been men of science. Benjamin Banneker studied the mating cycles of locusts in 1789, twenty-eight years ago."

He shook his head. "Bugs, Scarlett? That's why you wish to risk your reputation?"

"No, there are others like Onesimus, the enslaved man who remembered inoculations performed in his African tribe, which led to the prevention of smallpox in Boston in the early seventeen hundreds. Almost eighty years before a vaccination. There are probably more. There needs to be more. I'll do my part to push open doors."

Tapping his chin, he came to the desk and sat as he'd done with Sebastian and Livingston. It was easier listening to men's struggles. They were always simpler. "Tell me who you fancy. Tell me why you must run off to see him."

She circled and stopped in front of him. "No one. I'd not risk my reputation for a man. Don't be ridiculous."

"Fine. Then why are you doing this?"

"Science. They will be discussing blood research. I'm very curious. You should be too."

Trying to seem uninterested, he flexed his fingers. "I don't see why. But as your impromptu guardian, I'm concerned about you sneaking out."

Scarlett tossed him a saucy look, then went to the vials on the sideboard. She opened a drawer of more medicines. "I'm a would-be botanist. I dabble with herbs. I've tried to create things for my mother and Lydia. If I could, I'd be an apothecary."

"Those are nice aspirations. You should go to sleep and not think of sneaking away."

"Your Grace, even a blind person can see this amount of pain medication and cure-alls to eliminate symptoms you've been hiding is a lot. Tell me what's going on."

Did she know or was the young woman bluffing? "Now, Scarlett, I dabble in medicines too."

"This is more than dabbling. This is to help a sick man who wants to get better or enjoy the time he has."

The skill in this one was strong.

Jahleel didn't know if he should push. Better to make a deal. "You want to go to science lectures? Mr. Steele will take you. He'll see you there and back. No one has to know, but I will be comforted knowing you're safe. Now run along."

Scooting her toward the door didn't work. The vixen wasn't done. "You want to win this bet with Katherine?"

"What has she told you, Scarlett?"

She smiled wide, then pouted and shook her fingers at him. "Enough to know she broke your trust. And you hers."

Great, more half-truths. He leaned on the bookcase. "Well, my friend, I heard no specifics. I guess with all the books you've read, you haven't had time for mind reading. Probably wouldn't be scientific."

"I'm serious. I'll let you win the bet. I'll choose someone to marry. You make it happen. You win."

"Scarlett, you're a beautiful young woman. I have to arrange for you to be presented and do a proper season. How would you know who to marry?"

"Marriage at best is a partnership. I need my research to count. But as a woman, I'm running into obstacles. I need someone respectable who I can give my research to and they can get it published."

"That doesn't get you credit for your work."

Her head dipped. "I think having the knowledge put into the world is much more important than whose name is credited."

Noble. Very admirable. And shortsighted. "No. This is a recipe for disaster. Everyone wants credit for their personal accomplishments. And I don't want you unhappy. A bad marriage will be horrible."

"I've thought of that. That's why I need a pretend husband. Someone who will be the conduit for publishing my research. I need somebody who has a scientific mind and who is able to answer questions if needed. I want the work to be legitimized."

"So you're looking for a fake husband to publish some true academic papers? You women of the 1810s truly need to have bigger goals."

"I need this person to be extremely convincing. And I think that someone like you will be able to apply the proper pressure to make it happen. And you get to win the bet. You'll have my sister in your bed. I've watched you. Your eyes rarely stray from Katherine for anything more than a few minutes. You're in love with her."

"So this research is so important that you will willingly betray your sister?"

"Yes. Because I think we're looking at the same cure. These drugs, these symptoms that you have, the weakness, jaundice. It's the same sickness that Lydia has. It's the illness that killed our mother. And it's killing you. The blood sickness needs to be solved."

Scarlett Wilcox was the most dangerous woman in London. She knew Jahleel's secret, and in her tiny conniving hands, she might have the potential cure. The only question was, could such a volatile creature be trusted to be cautious and not destroy Jahleel's carefully constructed world?

AUTHOR'S NOTES

I hope you enjoyed *A Gamble at Sunset*, the first book in a new series, The Duke's Gambit. Ever since I learned of the Black prince of Russia, I had to know his story. Then one can trace his lineage to many peerages in England, so I had to write a story to reflect this.

These stories are meant to be heartfelt and funny while touching upon the need for a cure for an ancient disease that began in Africa. Sickle cell anemia has affected my family and friends. I have cousins who were ravaged by this horrible, unfair disorder. Discovering how the disease is passed through the generations, I felt compelled to weave it into this story.

I do play with elements of discovery and of what was possible to make the characterizations more interesting and to focus upon the crippling aspects of the disease and treatment.

This series entwines the Wilcox sisters and the duke in a story of hope, politics, and undying love. I hope you'll follow along and enjoy the twisty ride.

As always, enjoy the diversity of the Regency and the inclusion of differently abled people. The time period had it all.

It is my hope that in Georgina and Mark's journey you find your voice and path and run the race until completion. *Let your light shine in the darkness, for darkness cannot overcome it* (John 1:5, paraphrased).

Visit my website, VanessaRiley.com, to gain more insight.

For more information on sickle cell anemia, contact:

The American Sickle Cell Anemia Association: https://ascaa.org/

The Sickle Cell Disease Association of America: https://www.sicklecelldisease.org/

St. Jude Children's Research Hospital—Sickle Cell program:

https://www.stjude.org/treatment/disease/sickle-cell-disease.html

Mulattoes and Blackamoors During the Regency

Mulattoes and Blackamoors numbered between 10,000 and 20,000 in London and throughout England during the time of Jane Austen. Wealthy British with children born to native West Indies women brought them to London for schooling. Jane Austen, a contemporary writer of her times, in her novel *Sanditon*, writes of Miss Lambe, a mulatto, the wealthiest woman in the book. Her wealth made her desirable to the ton.

Mulatto and Blackamoor children were often told to "pass" to achieve elevated positions within society. Wealthy plantation owners with mixed-race children, or wealthy mulattoes like Dorothea Thomas from the colony of Demerara, often sent their children abroad for education and for them to marry in England.

Dido Elizabeth Bell and the Kenwood Painting

The famous portrait commissioned by Lord Mansfield from the artist David Martin painted two cousins: a Black woman, Dido Elizabeth Belle, and her White cousin, Lady Elizabeth Murray (later Lady Elizabeth Finch-Hatton). It was unusual for the times because the cousins are painted as equals. Martin captures a moment: Elizabeth seated, reading a book, reaches out to stop Dido from passing by. Dido is painted with movement and expensive clothes and jewelry. The painting was housed at Kenwood, which had its music room renovated close to the timing of this story.

Blood Research

Examining blood under a microscope can be traced back to 1656, when Pierre Borel, physician-in-ordinary who worked for

King Louis XIV, looked at a sample under the microscope. In 1657, Athanasius Kircher, a Jesuit priest and man of science, looked at blood from plague victims and saw disease and described it as "worms" of the plague. In 1678, red blood corpuscles were described by Dutch naturalist and physician Jan Swammerdam.

Bloodletting or phlebotomy is the extraction of blood from a patient to prevent or cure illness and can be traced back as far as 400s BC. Physicians have used leeches and incisions of the flesh to perform the bloodletting to balance the humors, the bodily fluids, which can maintain health or eliminate disease.

Sickle cell treatments have investigated reducing viscosity to make blood flow better. Bloodletting can do this. This could've been an accidental cure that may have alleviated symptoms. In the story, it's presented as a possible treatment, but this would more likely be an accidental treatment. Bloodletting was a normal treatment to all manner of conditions.

1816—The Year Without a Summer

In April 1815, volcanic disruption caused worldwide effects, when Mount Tambora exploded, killing thousands of people on the Indonesian island of Sumbawa. The plume of ash went up and for the following year, 1816, the residual ash caused unusually wet and cold conditions across Europe and North America. The Thames froze several times. There was lots of snow and cold even in the summer months.

Black Russian Princes and Princesses

The Black Russian princes and princesses can be traced back to Gannibal.

Sold into slavery as a child, Abram Petrovich Gannibal was bought to be a servant to Tzar Peter I, also known as Peter the Great. As one of the tzar's favorites, he was elevated to a generalin-chief. He became the tzar's godson and one of the most educated men in Russia. Though not technically princes or princesses, his descendants were referred to by the press and lay people as Black princes and princesses.

Author and poet Alexander Pushkin is a direct descendant. Many British aristocrats descend from Gannibal, including Natalia Grosvenor, Duchess of Westminster, and her sister, Alexandra Hamilton, Duchess of Abercorn. A more recent royal, George Mountbatten, 4th Marquess of Milford Haven, a cousin of Queen Elizabeth II, is also a direct descendant.

Cesar Picton, Black Coal Millionaire

The Wilcox family is my homage to Cesar Picton (1755–1836), a very wealthy coal businessman. Originally enslaved from Senegal, he became a protégé of the wealthy Sir John Philipps, and by the end of his life was a successful coal merchant, having lived in Kingston, Thames Ditton, and elsewhere in Britain. Picton is often described as a "gentleman," which suggests his rise up the social ranks.

Benjamin Banneker

One of the first documented African American scientists is Benjamin Banneker (1731–1806). In addition to his research on the mating habits of locusts (cicadas), he is known for building a precision time clock entirely out of wood. In 1789, he made astronomical calculations that enabled him to successfully forecast a solar eclipse. He was a wizard in mathematics and astronomy and kept detailed journals.

Onesimus

An enslaved man given the name Onesimus offered detailed descriptions of an inoculation process that he undertook in Africa that exposed him to smallpox, which made him immune. Local Boston doctors listened to his enslaver and put Onesimus's procedure in place, saving hundreds of lives in Boston. This was decades before Edward Jenner discovered the smallpox vaccine in 1796.

Cossack and Early Russian Culture

There are several references to cultural touchstones from eighteenth- and nineteenth-century Russian culture. My approach is to try and define the word or phrase in context.

Gilroy the Cartoonist

Gilroy is a made-up cartoonist I've created from the careers of James Gillray and George Cruikshank, two of London's most famous satirists and illustrators. Their styles of artistry are different but their crass drawings of the most scandalous versions of events were very similar. I have a few of their sexist, misogynistic, and racist cartoons in the research section of my website.

Normalization of Foreign Words

In the past, writers would italicize all non-English words within a text. This was meant to ensure a reader not stumble over the words. However, a reader knows if a word is unfamiliar to them whether it is called out in formatting or not. For me, I'm considering the point of view of the speaker as well as the point of view of the person the scene is written dictates whether a word should be italicized or not. For example, Jahleel naturally speaks English and Russian. In his point of view, neither set of words are foreign. However, if he's been speaking English and switches to use a Russian phrase, it might be italicized to show emphasis on the words. Moreover, Georgina, having heard "dorogaya" before, will not be shocked or puzzled if it is used again.

ACKNOWLEDGMENTS

Thank you to my Heavenly Father, I'm inspired by Your grace.

Felicia M, you make each story better.

To my sister agent, Sarah Younger, I'm grateful for your guidance and support.

To the Kensington team, for all you do to make this series shine.

To those who inspire my pen: Beverly, Brenda, Farrah, Sarah, Julia, Kristan, Alyssa, Maya, Lenora, Sophia, Joanna, Grace, Laurie Alice, Julie, Cathy, Katharine, Carrie, Christina, Georgette, Jane, Linda, Margie, Liz, Lasheera, Alexis, and Ann—thank you.

To those who inspire my soul: Bishop Dale and Dr. Nina, Reverend Courtney, Piper, Eileen, Rhonda, Angela, and Pat—thank you.

And to my family—Frank, Ellen, Sandra, David, Rhonda—love you all so much.

Hey, Mama. I miss the biscuits.

Love you always.

Georgina's Ginger Biscuits or Cornish Fairings

You should love these crisp, tender biscuits (cookies).

Ingredients

1 egg
½ cup butter (use very high-quality butter)
1 cup castor sugar (or 1 cup and 1 tablespoon granulated
   sugar)
2½ cups sifted self-rising flour (sift, then measure; you
   need the flour aerated)
1 tsp. baking soda (also called bicarbonate of soda)
2 tsp. ground ginger (or 1 tsp. ground ginger and 1 tsp.
   fresh finely grated ginger)
2 tbsp. Lyle's Golden Syrup (or 2 tbsp. honey)

Line a cookie sheet with parchment paper.

Melt syrup and butter in a pan over low heat. Stir, then set aside.

Add the flour and ginger into a large bowl, and then stir in the sugar. Once everything is incorporated, add in the syrup and butter mixture. Stir well and set aside.

Whisk the egg with the soda. When they are well incorporated, add to the flour butter mixture.

Stir everything together until you have a nice dough. Wrap the dough and put it into the refrigerator for 10 minutes.

Flour a board to roll out the biscuits. Take the unwrapped dough and roll it until it's less than ⅓ to ½ of an inch thick. Cut biscuits out. I like 3-inch circles.

Place biscuits on the parchment paper and bake for 8 to 10 minutes at 350°F.

Like Mark, keep an eye on the biscuits, so they don't burn or overcook.

Take out the biscuits and cool them on parchment paper over a wire rack.

Visit our website at
KensingtonBooks.com
to sign up for our newsletters, read
more from your favorite authors, see
books by series, view reading group
guides, and more!

BOOK | CLUB
BETWEEN the CHAPTERS

Become a Part of Our
Between the Chapters Book Club
Community and Join the Conversation

Betweenthechapters.net

Submit your book review for a chance to win exclusive
Between the Chapters swag you can't get anywhere else!
https://www.kensingtonbooks.com/pages/review/